THE
SECRETS
YOU
KEEP

ALSO BY KATE WHITE

FICTION

The Wrong Man

Eyes on You

So Pretty It Hurts

The Sixes

Hush

Lethally Blond

Over Her Dead Body

'Til Death Do Us Part

A Body to Die For

If Looks Could Kill

NONFICTION

*I Shouldn't Be Telling You This:
How to Ask for the Money, Snag
the Promotion, and Create the
Career You Deserve*

You on Top

*9 Secrets of Women Who Get
Everything They Want*

*Why Good Girls Don't Get
Ahead but Gutsy Girls Do*

THE
SECRETS
YOU
KEEP

A NOVEL

Kate White

HARPER

NEW YORK • LONDON • TORONTO • SYDNEY

This is a work of fiction. Names, characters, places, and incidents are products of the author's imagination or are used fictitiously and are not to be construed as real. Any resemblance to actual events, locales, organizations, or persons, living or dead, is entirely coincidental.

HarperCollins books may be purchased for educational, business, or sales promotional use. For information, please email the Special Markets Department at SPsales@harpercollins.com.

FIRST EDITION

Designed by Jamie Lynn Kerner

Title page illustration © Shutterstock/Arsgera

Library of Congress Cataloging-in-Publication Data has been applied for.

ISBN 978-0-06-244885-9 (pbk.)

22 23 24 25 26 LBC 17 16 15 14 13

To Cheryl Brown Lohse, adored friend for
soooo many years

Chapter 1

IWAKE TO THE SMELL OF SMOKE.

It's faint but enough to rouse me, and I jerk up in bed, eyes wide open. For a few seconds I freeze there, propped on an elbow and trying to make sense of it. What's *burning*?

I start to shove my legs out of bed, but the top sheet fights me. I have to wrench it loose from the mattress so I can force my feet to the ground.

As my eyes adjust to the dark, I realize that I'm not at home. I'm in a hotel room. I've been traveling on business . . . yet I can't remember where. The burning smell intensifies, boring into my nostrils and propelling my head back. Panic surges through me. Fire, I think. *Fire.*

Using my hands for help, I edge around the second double bed in the room, fast as I can. Warning phrases I've read bombard my brain: *Fill the bathtub with water. Wet a towel and cover your mouth with it.* But I don't have time for that. I need to get *out.*

Then there's a noise, a tapping sound, and I realize someone's knocking at the door. Maybe hotel staff, warning people.

"I'm in here," I yell. "Don't go, I'm coming."

Now I can actually *see* the smoke wafting toward me. I stub my toe hard on the outside wall of the bathroom, but I keep going, practically hurling myself forward.

Suddenly I hear a man's voice—from behind me in the hotel room.

"Bryn, are you okay?" he calls out.

"Yes," I respond. "But we've gotta go."

"Wait," he says. "There's something—"

"I can't. We have to run. Hurry."

Reaching the end of the hallway, I frantically pat the wall until I locate the light switch, but nothing happens when I tap it. The power's off. Even without any lights, I see smoke boiling from the crack at the bottom of the door. I moan in anguish.

More fumbling until my fingers find the security latch on the door and flip it over. To my relief it's not hot to the touch, just warm. I take a second, trying to picture the exit sign in the corridor. Was it to the left or the right? I have no freaking clue. I still can't recall the hotel, or the city, or even checking in at the front desk. I grasp the handle and press down, my fingers trembling.

Horrified, I feel the handle begin to dissolve. It sears the skin of my palm, and I snatch my hand away in pain. My lungs start to scald, and I cough again and again, unable to stop.

Somehow, though, the door swings open. *Yes, yes,* I think. Then I see it. A mass of smoke and pulsing red light fill the hallway. I stare at flames devouring the carpet, licking up the walls.

There's no way to get out.

Chapter 2

AMOMENT LATER I'M SURFACING, STRUGGLING through webs of sleep. It's only a dream, I realize. Another one of those nightmares. Though I'm fully awake now, my heart's still thrumming. My skin is hot, like I've sat too long in the sun, and the T-shirt I'm wearing is damp with sweat.

I glance around, not sure at first where I am. It's daylight, maybe late afternoon, and then I know. I'm on the screened porch in the house we've rented in Saratoga Springs, New York. From outside I hear the distant, buzzy drone of a lawn mower and one short bark from a dog.

I hoist myself up and take long deep breaths, in through my nostrils and out through my mouth, a technique Dr. G taught me when I started having sessions with her.

Finally my pulse slows. I reach for a pencil and pad lying on the coffee table, and jot down fragments from the dream: hotel room, smoke, dissolving doorknob, the wall of flames. It's the fourth dream like this I've had in the past few weeks. Dr. G suggested I keep track of them because they seem to be about the car accident, the one I was in three months ago.

She thinks writing them down will help calm me—and if I'm lucky, ultimately fill in some blanks.

I close my eyes again, trying to recall more details, but the dream begins to unravel in my memory, like a pile of dried leaves lifting apart in the wind. If it was trying to tell me something, I have no clue what it is.

I force myself off the daybed and traipse into the main part of the house. It's Victorian in style, built a hundred-plus years ago. Though there aren't a ton of rooms, they're spacious and elegant, with high ceilings and dark, intricate moldings and paneling. Not the kind of house I would have picked for myself—it's so prim and proper—but I'm okay with being here for the summer.

I wander back to the kitchen, with its white subway tiles gleaming in the June sun, and pour a glass of iced tea. I drain it in four gulps. Though the tea quenches my thirst, it does nothing to quell my unease. I glance at my watch. Four thirty. Guy will be home by six, and I'm already looking forward to seeing him. Maybe we should eat on the patio, since it's bound to be a beautiful night.

I will myself up from the chair and clear the soup bowl and utensils I used for lunch. Next I take two chicken cutlets out of the freezer and begin snipping the green beans I bought earlier.

Finished, I head upstairs and straighten the duvet in the master bedroom. For the first time I'm struck by the sheer ridiculousness—and irony, too—of me snapping the fabric into place. Until now my life has been, at least literally speaking, a litany of *un*made beds, beds I've always been far too busy to fuss with and happy to just stumble into at the end of crazy days. I know why I've given myself this little task each day. It's a way to avoid what I'm really *supposed* to be doing.

Coming to Saratoga for the summer and renting a nice house here was meant as a chance for me to get my mojo back now that my broken bones have mostly healed. I was also going to conceive and pound out a proposal for my new book, the one that had been delayed by the car accident and recovery. But it's just not happening. I alternate between bouts of panic and feeling totally jet-lagged, like a traveler who's stumbled off an airplane after crossing a dozen time zones.

And then there's the writer's block. I knew it might take a while to get back in a groove, but I've spent days now staring at a blank computer screen. It seems at times as if my brain's been sucked dry by aliens. At my most panic-stricken I worry that I'll never squeeze out another word, never again share what I've learned, never again command a room of appreciative readers.

As I give the duvet a final shake, I catch a glimpse of my reflection in the mirror above the dresser. Because, until recently, I needed to negotiate shampooing and blow-drying with a cast on my arm, I chopped my light brown hair fairly short. The cut is cute enough, I guess, but because of the weight loss, my overall appearance leans toward beleaguered. I look like I'm ready to board an orphan train.

My cell phone rings, startling me from my thoughts. I tug it from the pocket of my sweater. I smile to myself when I see Guy's name.

"Hey, babe," he says. "I didn't disturb a siesta, did I?"

Is that the impression I've been giving him? That I indulge in a postlunch nap every day? Well, I do, don't I?

"No, just taking care of a few things. How about you?"

"I've got a donor crisis on my hands but hopefully nothing I can't handle."

Guy runs the development office for Saratoga's small but well-regarded opera company, Springs Opera, and his job calls for reeling in contributors and then keeping them on board.

"Oh, that's a shame. Which donor?"

"The guy who pledged a hundred grand last week. Unfortunately I'm going to have to grab drinks with him and see if I can fix this."

"*Tonight?*"

"Yeah, sorry. If I don't put this fire out now, it's only gonna get worse."

I sense him catching himself too late about the phrase he's used, probably wondering if he should excuse the comment and then deciding it would be worse to draw attention.

"I'm sure you can fix this, honey," I say.

"Hope so. I'm going to try to find one of the artists and ask him or her to join us. Maybe Mario."

"Mario. He's brilliant with people, right?"

He chuckles, and I can picture the grin on his handsome face. Guy's a fixer, a solver, a person undaunted by problems that can frazzle many of us, like canceled flights, lost luggage, and credit card snafus.

"Absolutely. And he's savvy enough to know how to talk to a skittish donor."

He asks about my day, and without having intended to,

I find myself padding the details, Hamburger Helper-style. I say, "I went shopping this morning," instead of *I bought a bag of green beans at that little market.* I say, "I took a walk," instead of *I stood in the backyard and watched the ferns shiver in the breeze.*

"How's the writing coming?" he asks next. "You starting to feel in the swing again?"

"Yup, a bit. I made some notes for the next book." That's not exactly true either. All I did was write the word *reinvention* with a question mark and stare at it for twenty-seven minutes. "Shall I wait and have dinner with you when you get home? I don't mind eating later."

"No, don't wait. I'm honestly not sure how long I'm going to be. Just stick a plate in the fridge for me, okay?"

"Will do," I say, disguising my disappointment.

"You feeling all right about tomorrow night?"

"Yes, definitely. It should be fun." Tomorrow I'll be playing hostess for the first time in this house, at a dinner party we're hosting for two opera company donors and their wives. It's a chance for Guy to take advantage of the house, and yet I know he's hoping I'll find it enjoyable, a way to engage again and meet a few people from the town. It's being catered through his work, so I won't have to lift a finger, just spend the night chatting with the guests, the kind of activity that until March of this year I've *relished*, both in my personal life and my work. But I find myself dreading the mental effort it will demand.

"That reminds me," I add. "I should poke around the dining room and see what's in there in terms of napkins and stuff. Both donors are bringing their spouses, right?"

"Yes, though there'll actually be five besides us," he says. "I decided to invite that journalism professor from Ballston College, Derek Collins. The one I met when he brought his class to the performance hall for a discussion. He's a big fan of yours."

"He's not bringing anyone?"

"No, he's single and said he'd prefer to come alone."

"All right, I'll see you later then."

"Looking forward to it. I love this new luxury of being able to see you every night now."

Up until three weeks ago, Guy and I have had a commuter relationship for the entire two years we've been together. He understood that I wasn't up for relocating to a small town, and he's been more than happy to travel to Manhattan on weekends until the time comes for him to pursue a job in the city. And though we've made the commuter thing work, seven days a week in each other's company instead of two and a half has been a great change for us.

Except when Guy's work hijacks one of our evenings.

"Ditto."

After I hang up, I feel a little swell of guilt from having deceived Guy about what I've accomplished today. I don't like telling him little white lies. At a time when we've never been closer, it only adds distance.

But in the last month or so I've begun to sense a small tear in his patience, a silent chafing at my inertia and failure to rebound. Isn't that so often the case, that sympathy for someone ends up weirdly entangled with irritation, or maybe even spawns it? People feel sorry, they truly do, but they also want to stop worrying about you at some point, however much they love you. They want you to reassure them that their concerns are exaggerated, that the crisis is past, and that you will soon be more yourself again. So they check if you're still fatigued and taking afternoon siestas. They invite journalism professors to dinner in order to goad you into thinking about your own work again.

The key is for me to get my energy back. And then there won't be a need for little white lies.

I wander back downstairs, to the small room near the kitchen that I'm using as an office. When Guy found the house for us, he reported that there was a perfect spot for me to write in. What he had in mind was the room in the turret reached by stairs from the second floor. It would be like a writer's garret, he said, but I found it both dusty and claustrophobic, and I preferred the idea of being on the ground floor. So I commandeered the tiny room across from the kitchen, once a mudroom, I assume, and moved a desk in there. Hardly ideal—there's a lingering scent of wet wool and rubber boots emanating from the wainscoting—though I doubt the words would be flowing wherever I was.

I check email, diverting most of them to my assistant in New York to contend with, though I send off quick replies myself to friends inquiring how I'm doing, and one in response to my brother, Will, in his third year of working for a bank in Jakarta, promising more later. There are several requests for interviews and podcasts, which I politely decline, and two from my speaker's bureau about well-paying gigs. These get nixed as well. Speaking to groups about the subjects of my books has always been a thrill for me, but I can't fathom pulling that off right now.

My gaze falls to the icon for the proposal folder on my computer desktop. Maybe I should make another go at it before I fix dinner. But the mere thought makes my stomach tense. My phone rings, sparing me. It's Casey, my agent, returning a call I made to her earlier.

"How's it going up there?" she asks. "Have you seen what's-his-name race yet? Seabiscuit?"

I laugh at her little joke. "Seabiscuit died in the nineteen *forties*. But they've got a big statue of him on the main street in town and I've petted it a couple of times."

"It sounds like you're getting out and about."

"Yup, starting to." After working on three books together, I consider Casey a friend as well as a colleague. At forty-two, she's only three years older than me and she's always got my back, but I've been cautious about divulging too much to her about my situation. I've confessed that I'm in a bit of a slump. What I've never uttered to her is the phrase Dr. G used: *acute stress reaction*. Or maybe worse for Casey to hear: *hopeless writer's block*.

"Well, I bet a summer away will be great for you. The publisher asked for a meeting to discuss the paperback launch, but I told them they'll have to do everything by phone for a while. You're not planning to be back in the city, are you?"

"No, not until September . . . By the way, do you know if they finally hired a replacement for Paul yet?"

There's a beat before she answers.

"Uh, I heard they promoted the guy who's been filling in," she says.

"Oh, good to know. He seems strong. . . . Here's the reason I called actually. I've been thinking of contacting Paul's widow, Stephanie, and just wanted a second opinion on the idea. I've always felt so bad that I wasn't able to attend the funeral."

Maybe because of the dreams, Stephanie—who I've never met—has been on my mind even more these days. I keep thinking that a conversation could be beneficial for both of us, possibly help me from feeling so stuck.

"You mean write her a letter? I thought you did that three months ago, after the accident."

"Yes, but I was thinking of having a talk with her."

There is total silence on the other end. I glance at the screen to make sure the call hasn't failed.

"I don't know," Casey says at last. "I heard she's still reeling. Maybe now's not the right time."

"Okay." Her answer actually surprises me, but I trust Casey's instincts.

"Before I let you go," she says, "do you mind if I nudge a little?"

Oh God, I should have realized this would happen if I answered her call.

"Sure."

"They're getting restless about the proposal. I've put them off a few times, and they've been understanding so far, but you're under contract for another book and their patience is going to start to wear thin. You've made them a ton of money and they're hungry for even more."

"Casey, there's no way I can turn in a proposal any time soon. I . . . I haven't even really started."

"Do you have an idea at least? A working title?"

"How's 'Self-Help Author Fails to Help Self Write?'"

"You really don't have anything?"

She's surely wondering why the woman who wrote the bestseller about choices can't make a decision herself.

"I have a germ, maybe."

"Okay, that's really all you need to bide your time with. I know you like your proposals to be fairly fleshed out, but they'd be more than happy with five pages. It would reassure them. And it might even help kick things in gear for you."

"Um, that seems doable." In truth the idea makes my heart start to race so fast I can hear the blood pumping in my ears. "Can you give me two weeks?"

"Sounds like a plan."

After we've said our good-byes, I rest my head on the desk, one cheek against the cool surface. How will I ever summon the energy for five pages? I don't even know if I can stand the idea I've drummed up.

Finally I force myself out of my office and prepare dinner, just a simple sauté for the chicken, along with the green beans. I put one plate in the fridge for Guy and take mine out onto the screened-in porch, along with a glass of wine.

The porch is my favorite room of the house, with its antique iron daybed and the black wicker couch and armchairs, their cushions done in faded floral. Living in Manhattan, I almost forgot that places as serene as this still existed.

As the daylight finally fades, I don't bother to switch on a lamp right away. I just sit in the darkness, listening to the voices of children calling to each other in a nearby yard. Do kids still play capture the flag? I wonder.

It was a game that I was bewitched by from the moment a neighborhood kid returned from a weekend at a cousin's house and taught a bunch of us how to play it. While other twelve-year-old girls I knew were already boy crazy, this was my personal obsession. I loved the rush that came from darting through the darkness, eluding capture again and again, setting people free from jail, and, best of all, grabbing the other team's flag and racing to home base.

In a certain respect it was the model for how I came to approach every challenge in life: assess, plunge ahead fearlessly, and savor every second.

I wasn't naïve enough to think that this strategy would work after the accident. There was no flag to capture this time. But I told myself that if I refused to hole up in Pity City and just put one foot ahead of the other, it would all get better in time.

The crash happened just about an hour southwest of Boston on a cold, crisp March day. I'd gone there to deliver a speech based on my most recent book, *Twenty Choices*. The audience, as usual, was made up mostly of women, many of them hoping that they still had time to make a choice that would put their lives or careers on a course closer to the ones they'd always fantasized about. I loved connecting with people at talks like this, loved the comments they offered as they had their books signed later. And it thrilled me that something I said might inspire them.

To my surprise, Paul Dunham, the paperback director for

my publishing house, had sidled up to the table just as I was signing books for the last few people in line. Tall and broad-shouldered, Paul was a guy who'd played college football and looked like he had, though his face, topped by his short blond hair, had a Waspy patrician look.

He was in town on business, too, he said, staying at another hotel, and had decided on the spur of the moment to drop by. It was a chance to hear me speak, he said, plus an opportunity to check out my fan base, which would prove useful as he geared up for the paperback launch. When he invited me to dinner, I explained I had other plans that night, but I accepted his offer for a lift back to the city the next day. I thought it would be easier than taking the train.

But it hadn't been easier at all. On a perfectly dry stretch of the Mass Turnpike, Paul had run the car off the road, smashing into a guardrail at close to seventy miles an hour. Somehow I'd managed to free myself from the air bag, stagger out of the car, and tumble hard down a ravine. Or at least that's what I learned later. I remember nothing from the minutes before the accident and little from the time immediately after. Just hazy memories of heat and flames and dark smoke billowing from above the ravine. Sirens. Then waking later in the hospital, with a broken arm and pelvis. And finding out that Paul hadn't survived.

I didn't need a shrink to tell me that I was suffering from more than grief afterwards. There was guilt, too, tons of it. I had lived and Paul had died. And I still had no idea how he'd lost control of the car.

As unmoored as I felt, I saw it as part of a process. It would take time, but I'd get better, physically and mentally. Throwing myself into my work would surely aid in that. However, a month later, shortly after my life seemed to normalize again, my grief began to shape-shift into something else. The bouts of panic started, followed by stretches of numbness and lethargy. When I finally tried to write again, nothing materialized. Making words come was like trying to generate warmth on a late autumn hike when your clothes are soaked through with rain.

Finally I get up and switch on a table lamp. As I do, my eyes fall to the pad on which I scribbled notes from my dream. I pick it up and stare at the words again: "hotel room, smoke, dissolving doorknob, wall of flames."

My recent nightmares all have the same terrifying elements, but slightly reconfigured each time, as if my brain prefers to torture me with a fresh twist each time: There's always a hotel room I'm surprised to find myself in, the smoke and the flames, and the fact that I'm never able to escape, though the reason changes. Once it was because the door was too heavy to open. Another time because there was no door at all, just a thick, impenetrable wall.

And then I remember. There's a detail about my dream today that I've neglected to write down: the unseen man calling out my name.

It's brand-new. Until now, I've always been alone in the room.

I don't think the man was Guy. The voice belonged to

someone else, not a voice I can place, but not a stranger's either, because there was nothing about the man's presence that frightened me.

So who was he? I wonder, my heart skipping. And why was he insisting that I wait?

Chapter 3

I'M IN BED ASLEEP BY THE TIME GUY ARRIVES HOME, and I stir when I feel him slipping under the covers. He spoons me and rakes his fingers lightly through my hair. I relax into the curve of his body, soothed by his touch.

When I wake in the morning, the other side of the bed is empty. From the bedside clock I see with a start that it's nearly eight. Guy will have to split soon, and I want time with him before he goes. I close my eyes again, trying to recall if there's been another dream, but no, nothing. Simply fuzzy, meaningless fragments in my mind.

I toss the covers back, struggle up, and slip on jeans and a cotton jersey. A few minutes later, walking into the kitchen, I find Guy reading the news on his iPad, coffee mug in hand. He's dressed in a perfectly cut suit, one of his navy-blue ones, and a blue-and-white-checked shirt. No tie today.

For the first time I notice that his face is already a little tanned this season, mainly from grabbing an hour here and there on the tennis court. As he looks up at me, with his slightly hooded, slate-blue eyes, I feel a moment of déjà vu. It was two years ago this July, as I stood on my friends' deck in Rhode Island, that I saw him slide open the glass door and step outside. Tall and well-built, he was deeply tanned then, and his full, gorgeous lips were chapped from both wind and sun. He caught my eye and smiled. I knew in a split second that something was destined between us. And he did as well.

Yes, I could tell he was older than me—seven years, I soon discovered—which was just fine. It was time for a guy mature enough to be truly comfortable in his own skin and who wouldn't flinch at my success, the way Marc, my previous boyfriend, had. I wanted a guy eager for a full partnership.

"Morning," he says, and flashes a smile. "I was afraid I might have to go more than twenty-four hours without seeing those baby blue eyes of yours."

I cross to the table, lean down, and kiss him hello. He smells fresh from his shower, with a hint of citrusy-scented cologne.

"I didn't even hear you getting dressed," I say.

"I was trying to do my best quiet-as-a-mouse routine."

"From now on, wake me in the morning when you get up, will you? Even if I curse loudly in protest."

"You sure? You looked pretty zonked out this morning."

"Yes, please." My gaze drifts across the table to the place where I usually drink my coffee in the morning. On a small plate sits a huge, scrumptious-looking scone. "Oh my God, what's this? Manna from heaven?"

Guy laughs. "Manna from Mrs. London's bakery. I dropped by yesterday at lunch and picked you up a few blueberry scones."

"Oh, honey, that's so sweet. You know how much I adore

these." Guy and I spent our honeymoon in London and then the Scottish Highlands, and I devoured scones and clotted cream almost every day I was there.

I pour a cup of coffee and open the fridge for butter. "So tell me about last night. Did you make any progress?"

"Seems like it. I convinced Mario to join us and he even sang a little at the table. People applauded. I'll know tomorrow if the donor's fully back on board, but my bet is yes."

"That's fantastic."

I planned to mention the dream to him, to see if maybe he could offer an objective view on what the new detail means, but he gulps the last of his coffee and I sense he's ready to fly.

"About tonight," I say instead. "How fancy are people likely to dress?"

"Not too fancy, at least compared to New York. The guys will wear jackets and the women will be kind of dressy but probably conservative. Not Derek, though. The few times I've seen the guy he's been in old cords and a sweater—and usually the same ones."

I laugh. "Okay, conservative then. I'll leave the slutty tops in the drawer."

"Just until the weekend, okay?" He smiles and then checks his watch. "I'd better split. I've got an eight-thirty."

He taps off his iPad, rises, and kisses me good-bye. Once he's gone, I shower and dress. Back downstairs again I glance distractedly at the news online, and then putter stupidly around the kitchen, wondering if we have everything the caterers will need tonight. Finally I force myself into my desk chair and open the proposal file on my computer. I stare at the word I typed yesterday: *reinvention*. It's a topic that's been written about plenty but deep down I sense I could bring a fresh perspective. And yet all the word does is stare back at me. Once, I could write for hours on end, even on planes, or in airports or crowded cafés. Right now, though, I feel like someone trying to write a sentence in a language she's never learned.

I close the file and jump up from my desk.

After an early lunch I slip into a lightweight anorak and pull on the messenger bag I've been using as my arm has healed. I drive downtown in the small car I've rented for the summer, stopping first at the ATM for cash, just to have it on hand, and then the florist. There are endless bunches of tulips at the front of the shop, and on a whim I buy more than I planned to: four dozen in white for the dining room and two dozen in pink for the living room.

Back home I set the table with flatware, glasses, and the perfectly starched embroidered white napkins that I found late yesterday in a drawer. Then I arrange the vases I've filled. The result of so many splashes of white—napkins, tulips, and candlesticks—on the dark table is dazzling. It makes me think of a comment my mom used to make when she was alive: *Sometimes* more *is more.* Though she's been dead twelve years, I still hear her lovely voice in my head, offering the little aphorisms she loved to share.

Gazing at the table, I realize I'm experiencing a kind of adrenaline surge I haven't felt since late winter, since before the accident. Maybe it's all a matter of motion begetting motion, I decide. I need to give myself a couple of projects each day, along with some physical activity. I've been banned for the time being from running—something I sorely miss—but I could at least force my ass onto the sidewalk each day for a walk.

But as soon as I've positioned the other tulips in the living room, I feel the energy being sucked away, so fast it almost leaves me breathless. I stagger out to the screened porch and collapse on the daybed.

For a while I just lie there, listening to the jeering call of a blue jay in the yard. And then, above the bird sounds, I hear knocking. It's someone at the front door, I finally realize. I glance at my watch. Too early for the caterer.

After forcing myself up, I make my way to the entrance hall. When I swing open the wooden door, I find a woman standing on the other side of the screened one. She's tall and statuesque, early forties, I'd guess, her black hair cut in an attractive shaggy style. Even through the screen I noticed that one of her hands holds a small shopping bag with a tuft of lavender tissue paper poking out from the top.

"I'm so sorry," she says. "I hope I'm not disturbing you."

I suspect she's wondering if she's busted a closet afternoon napper. I should never have answered the door.

"How can I help you?"

"I'm Sandra Dowd. Are you Bryn? Bryn Harper?"

"Yes."

"I'm on a committee for the Saratoga Arts Council, and I wanted to drop off a package for you—on behalf of all of us."

"Oh, that's so thoughtful of you," I say. Though all I want to do right now is slink back to the daybed, it would be rude to do anything but swing open the screened door. Which I do, and Sandra Dowd steps into the entrance hall. She's smartly dressed: a dark red blouse, the shade of a pomegranate—and which she more than fills out—cream-colored pants, and nude pumps with at least three-inch heels. The only slightly off thing about her appearance is her nose. It's nearly vertical, straight up and down, as if she had a bump taken off years ago.

"I know that the last thing you need is some Welcome Wagon–type person dropping by in the middle of your day," she says, her tone light and breezy, "but one of the members heard you'd moved to town and were renting the Jessup house. We thought you'd appreciate a bit of material about the area." She hands the bag over to me. "There's a calendar of events for the summer, that sort of thing. And I dropped my card in there."

A thought rustles in my brain, but I can't get hold of it. "Thank you. I've spent a few weekends here over the past two years, but I'm still not very familiar with the area."

"Full disclosure," Sandra says, looking as if she's about to spill a naughty revelation. "We'd love the chance to pick your brain at some point, though no rush on that. Maybe after you're settled."

With my energy at sloth level these days, I can hardly imagine helping out in any way, but I don't want to obviously blow her off.

"Let me see how the summer unfolds, okay?"

"Are you here just for the season then?"

I nod. "My husband's job is in Saratoga, and he usually commutes to the city on weekends. We decided it would be fun for me to spend the summer here. I just moved up three weeks ago."

"He must be thrilled to have you in town."

"It's been really nice, yes."

"I was in a commuter relationship myself, so I know the challenges." Her gaze wanders around the large center hall with its gold-and-cream-striped wallpaper and mahogany staircase. "What an amazing house. I've driven by it plenty of times, but I've never been inside."

"We were really lucky to find it. Guy has an apartment in town, of course, but it's tiny and there's no room for me to write. I was able to set up a little office off the kitchen here. Would . . . would you like to come in and have a glass of iced tea?" It seems discourteous not to ask.

"That's lovely of you, but unfortunately I've got to scoot. I'm headed out of town on a business trip."

"Are you with one of the colleges?"

"No, I run my own small firm. Public relations."

It's not a surprise that she's an entrepreneur. She seems confident, full of energy.

"I'd love to take a rain check, though," she adds, "or maybe we could have lunch in town." She lifts her chin toward the living room, which is just off the center hallway. "This must be the perfect place for entertaining."

"We're actually giving our first dinner party tonight."

"Oh dear, I shouldn't be keeping you. Are you doing the cooking yourself?"

"Thank God, no. It's for several of my husband's clients, so he's having it catered."

"That's the secret, isn't it?" She gives me that fun, slightly conspiratorial look again. "I hope you found a company you like. We finally seem to have a few caterers in town who serve something other than baked ziti and glutinous chicken Marsala."

"It's a firm my husband uses a lot for work and he swears that they're good." At last I realize what's been gnawing at me. "By the way, how did this person on the arts council even know I moved here?"

"Through the grapevine, I assume. She loves your books, especially the new one about choices. I'm sorry to say I haven't read it yet, but I just ordered a copy online."

"Please don't feel any obligation."

"Oh, I'm dying to. I'm shocked I wasn't aware of it already, since it's been such a huge success."

"Actually, why don't I grab a copy for you. You can try to cancel the one you ordered or give it to a friend."

"You really wouldn't mind?"

"It's my pleasure. I have a box in one of the spare bedrooms."

I do as promise, winded by the time I finally return from upstairs. I have to catch my breath as I sign the book for her.

A minute later, watching her hurry down the sidewalk, I decide that it may be nice to have her come by again or have lunch in town with her. Someone new, someone with an energy level that may be contagious.

The thought, however, is quickly trampled by another: Could *Guy* have given the arts council my info and suggested they try to recruit me as a volunteer? He'd have contacts with the organization, of course. Is this a secret tactic of his for propelling me off my butt? Maybe he meant well, but I don't like it at all. I return to the screened porch feeling oddly wired now, unable to sleep.

At five o'clock two waiters arrive at the kitchen door, both dressed in black pants, white shirts, and skinny black ties. One is probably in his early thirties, dark-haired, with a mustache and close-cropped beard and a tattoo that darts like a lizard from inside his shirt collar whenever he moves. His name, he says, is Conrad. The other guy is blond and gangly and probably only in his early twenties. Hopefully he's more experienced than he looks.

They make a couple of trips back and forth to a van, carrying aluminum roasting pans and also a cooler on wheels. Immediately they start peeling back the tops of the pans and unloading items into the fridge. I pick up the scent of almonds.

"I don't even know what we're having tonight," I tell them. Guy's running the show since it's a work dinner.

"It's probably best if we let Eve explain," Conrad says.

"Eve?"

"Eve Blazer. She's the owner and the chef. She'll be here at six."

When I reenter the kitchen an hour later, she's there, swirling olive oil in a pan. She's pretty and lusciously curvy, a woman who's obviously unabashed about sampling—and relishing—the dishes she creates. Her hair, fittingly enough, is the color of fresh butter, and most of it is tucked beneath a small white chef's cap.

To my surprise, she greets me coolly. Her eyes slide off mine as if I've introduced myself as the person who'll be taking coats.

"Do you need me to show you where anything is?" I ask.

"I think we can manage," she says. "Are you still planning on an eight o'clock sit-down?"

"Yes, that sounds right." The guests, Guy's informed me, are arriving at seven fifteen. "What are you serving tonight?"

"No one's told you?" she says, as if I'm the nerdy girl who's clueless about what all the popular kids are up to. I don't understand why she's taking this tone. Maybe she's just truly surprised that I've been left in the dark, so I give her the benefit of the doubt.

"No, my husband's secretary made the arrangements."

"Chicken tagine. And a crème brûlée for dessert."

"Sounds good. Why don't I let you get to work?"

I head upstairs and dress for dinner—black leggings, heels, and a breezy white silk blouse. For a few minutes I sit on the edge of my bed, trying to siphon energy from some secret reserve in the universe, but to no avail. I lift my hand from my lap and touch the linen duvet cover. I'd love nothing more than to flop on the bed and let my eyes fall closed for the night.

Finally, pressured by the insistent clicking of the digital clock on the bedside table, I rise, descend to the ground floor, and do a last sweep through the house, making sure lights are on and the rooms are tidy. On the screened porch, I notice the pad on which I've scribbled down the dream. As I'm scooping it up, a shadow crosses the room and I turn. Guy is standing in the doorway.

"There you are," he says. "Sorry to be running late. Is everything under control with the caterer?"

"Seems to be. I offered to show the chef where stuff was, but she didn't want my help."

"I'm sure she's a pro at finding her way around unfamiliar kitchens."

"She's not very friendly—though if the food is good, I won't hold it against her."

"Probably just preoccupied." He looks tired, I realize.

"How was your day?"

"Good, good." He crosses the room and gives me a quick kiss. "How about yours? Have you been writing?"

"Not really today." It feels good to be honest. Then I realize he's talking about the notepad in my hand. "Oh, this. It's just a dream from yesterday. That kind I keep having."

"The fire dream? In the hotel?"

"Yes. But this one had an odd new detail. There was a man in the room with me and he told me to wait."

Guy smiles ruefully. "Should I be worried?"

"Honey, don't be silly. Dreams aren't literal. But there was something about this man that seemed significant. I'm not sure why, though."

He takes a deep breath, and I sense him measuring his words before he speaks them.

"Dr. Greene really thinks this is a good idea?"

"Definitely. She says that though most of our dreams contain just garbage from the day, recurring ones are worth paying attention to. It can be the unconscious trying to send a message."

"I just worry this is stirring everything up for you."

"Actually I don't mind that happening. It may help me remember."

"But couldn't it be a blessing *not* to remember? Maybe this is your brain's way of sparing you the horrible details."

"I want those details. The car crashed, a man burned to death, and I still don't completely understand why."

He touches my shoulder with his hand.

"You've made such progress, Bryn. I want you to keep moving forward, not getting dragged back."

Could the dream journaling—or whatever it's called—be dragging me back? Is this the reason I've felt even more lethargic since moving here?

"I'll check in with Dr. G about it when we talk next week, okay?"

But even as I say it, I know I want to continue with my notes. I sense the man in the room has something worth hearing.

"That sounds smart," Guy says. "I'd better go change."

I stuff the pad into the drawer of a wicker side table, sit for a few minutes to summon my strength, and then wander back to the main part of the house. In the dining room I find the blond chef standing arms akimbo, surveying the table. I follow her gaze. With a start, I notice that she's refolded all the napkins—turning them from simple rectangles into stiff bishop caps in the center of each place setting. And then I see the vases. They're not on the table anymore. Instead, they've been herded off onto the side table, like children not allowed to mingle with the adults at a party.

"What are you doing?" I ask.

She half turns toward me, as if I don't deserve her full attention. "Doing? I'm getting the table ready."

"But I've already set it."

"We usually set the table, or at least dress it up a little."

"But why did you move the flowers?"

Now she makes a full turn toward me. Her lips are pursed in an almost defiant pout, and her gray eyes assess me coolly.

"We don't set our tables with flowers. The scent overpowers the smell of the food."

I'm almost speechless that she's moved things around without checking with me. And her dumbass rule about the flowers.

"Please put them back," I tell her. "There's absolutely nothing wrong with flowers on a table."

"Of course." Her tone is like a shrug. As she moves the flowers back to the table, she appears both unfazed and unapologetic. Guy enters the room a moment later, and she doesn't acknowledge him, just slips quietly back into the kitchen through the swinging door at the rear of the room.

He waits until she's gone before he speaks.

"Is something the matter?"

"That woman, Eve," I say, my voice lowered. "I don't know what her problem is."

"What do you mean?" His brow furrows.

"She redid the table after I'd spent so much time on it. And she acted impertinent when I asked her about it."

He's taken aback, I can tell. A second later, though, I realize his reaction seems centered on me.

"Bryn, the caterer is supposed to set the table. She's probably annoyed you usurped her job."

I can't believe he's taking her side and not mine.

"It's not always the caterer's job," I say. "And once she'd seen I'd done it, she should have asked me before changing anything."

He throws up his hands.

"I can't seem to win with you, Bryn," he snaps. "One minute you need bed rest, and the next minute you're annoyed if someone's helping. What the hell am I supposed to do?"

I can feel my jaw drop in shock. I lift my eyes, trying to form a response. As I do, I see the swinging door to the kitchen shudder. As if a hand has touched it.

As if someone has been standing next to it, listening.

Chapter 4

I GLANCE BACK AT GUY AND THEN TURN AWAY, MY anger flaring.

"Bryn, hold on a minute," he says.

"Maybe I should just bow out tonight. It's your party after all."

With that I hurry into the hall, through the living room, and out to the screened porch.

I'm both pissed and stunned. In the two years we've been together, we've disagreed at times, of course, but we've never resorted to snapping at each other.

And Guy's words disturb me even more than his tone. With one brusque comment he's confirmed my suspicion, that he's totally frustrated with the glacial pace of my recovery.

In the beginning he was so *there* for me. Once I was sent home from the hospital in Massachusetts, I urged him to return to Saratoga during the week—it was a critical time for him at work—but he refused. He used vacation time to stay with me in the city, and for a month after that, he took the train to New York on Thursday nights instead of Friday, working remotely the next day.

It was my idea, not his, for me to decamp to Saratoga for the summer, but he lit up when I suggested it. Does he feel he's been forced into the role of nursemaid?

"Bryn." Guy has come onto the porch.

"I can't believe you spoke to me that way."

"I know, it was horrible of me. I'm so sorry."

"Is that how you really feel? Totally frustrated?"

"No, I swear. Not with you anyway. Just with my inability to help. I hate seeing you struggle and wish I knew what to do."

"There's nothing you *can* do. Except be patient for a little longer, okay? It's taking more time than I'd like, but I sense things getting better. I really do."

Pants on fire, I think. There's that need again on my part to fudge.

He steps closer, pulls me to him, and folds his arm around me.

"I have all the patience in the world for you, Bryn. I just think we need to—I don't know—talk a bit more about this, so I know how you're doing and what you need from me."

My little white lies are definitely not helping. I've got to be honest going forward. In fact, we both do.

"Did you send someone from the Saratoga Arts Council here to encourage me to volunteer?"

"What? Of course not."

"A woman named Sandra dropped by today, bearing brochures. She said they'd heard I'd moved to town."

"They definitely didn't hear it from me." He flashes a grin. "I can't help it if women all over the area are in desperate need of your wisdom."

I smile back, relieved. I've needed Guy to cut me a break and maybe I need to cut him one, too. I know that part of what attracted him to me was my drive, and it's got to be tough for him to see that missing in action. It will come back, though. It has to.

"Can you accept my apology, honey?" Guy asks.

"Yes. Of course."

"This dinner isn't too much for you?"

"No. Let's have fun tonight."

The words are barely out of my mouth when the doorbell rings.

The two couples, it turns out, have arrived simultaneously, though the Donaldsons live in town and the Emerlings are from a suburb of Albany, about thirty minutes south. Guy introduces me to everyone—the couples seem to know each other—and we usher them through the entrance hall into the living room.

I take a deep breath as I settle into an armchair. *Engage*, I command myself. *Be fully present.* When the waiter Conrad takes our drink orders, I ask for a glass of sparkling water, fearful that any wine will leave me feeling wiped.

Guy does most of the talking at first, which I'm grateful for. After all these years in fund-raising, he's a master at this kind of evening, and he fills the guests in on the upcoming opera season, as well as details about the artists who'll be performing.

All four guests appear to be in their early to mid-forties. Jerry Donaldson, Guy has told me, is a successful local attorney, so I'm surprised to discover how soft-spoken he is, almost a whisperer. His wife, Barb, is one of those bighearted blond talkers who don't like to see any grass grow between comments. She answers questions directed at her as well as any meant for Jerry, but he seems to have no problem with this.

As for the Emerlings, they present as a little sharper around the edges. Nick has made his money in commercial real estate and he's obviously shrewd, the kind of guy who could sell you a rainbow, and he's quick to voice his opinion. His wife, Kim, is more stylish than Barb—she's a blonde too, but her hair is in a short, razored cut that makes her dark brown eyes seem even larger—and she doesn't say a word when we first sit down. I sense her calculating something, though what I'm not sure what.

"I grew up in Saratoga, and I used to fantasize about this house," Barb says as the two waiters pass trays of hors d'oeuvres. "I wanted to live here so I could have the turret as my bedroom."

"It's romantic-looking, isn't it?" I say, relieved I finally have something to contribute. "But it's too small for a bedroom or even a little sitting room. I considered putting my desk there, but it's awfully claustrophobic, so I'm working in a room off the kitchen."

"So what's the turret been used for?" Barb asks.

I laugh. "Perhaps just for keeping an eye on the neighbors. It's empty, and I get the idea that it's always been that way."

"Maybe it's haunted." It's Kim talking. For a moment I assume she's being playful, but from across the room I see there's no amusement in her eyes. What was that about? I wonder.

Derek Collins finally arrives, fifteen minutes late but apologetic. He's attractive in a way that I can't put my finger on and younger than I expected—probably no more than forty. Contrary to Guy's prediction, he's not in cords and a sweater, but rather jeans and a blue blazer, his longish brown hair brushed back and just skimming the rear of his shirt collar. He's carrying a bouquet of yellow tulips.

"Oh dear," he says, spotting the pink ones. "Is there such a thing as too many tulips—outside of Holland that is?"

"Not at all," I tell him.

"I second that," Barb says. "And I own a flower shop."

I hand over the tulips to Conrad, requesting that he locate a vase. Guy introduces Derek to the other guests, and I see Kim take him in from head to toe.

As I sit back down again, I can practically feel the energy seeping out of me, as if I'm a pool float with a leak. I take two big gulps of water, hoping it will revitalize me. Guy catches my eye and smiles. Though I still feel slightly unsettled by our tiff, I realize it was probably good for us to force the issue out in the open. Now we can move on.

Just before eight Guy disappears briefly and returns to announce that dinner is ready. We make our way to the dining room. The lights have been lowered and the room is aglow with candlelight.

"How lovely," Barb exclaims.

"My wife not only has a way with words," Guy says, "but a way with a table."

I return his smile, appreciative that he'd doing his best to make amends.

I'm at the opposite end of the table from Guy. Derek is

to my left, which is a relief because he'll be easy to talk to. He held his own during cocktails—even through the opera chat—and he has a natural warmth. Kim is to my right. Despite her earlier reticence, she turns out to be a talker but a different type than Barb. Her chatter, I soon realize, is more like sonar, used to suss out a person's hot spots.

"Have you moved up here full-time now?" she asks as we start on our soup. It's cream of asparagus and luscious.

"No, just for the summer actually."

"What a shame. The fall is amazing here."

"Oh, I know. But I have a couple of projects happening in New York in September. Plus, I'll miss the city if I'm gone too long."

"Really? New York just seems so *gritty* to me. I honestly don't get why people love it."

I let it go, and before I can work in a question for her, she's on to the next one.

"What made you decide to write a book about choices?"

"There's been some interesting research in recent years about how tough it is for us to make choices these days because of all the options we have. I thought it would be intriguing to come at it from a different angle. To find the common denominators among ten people who'd made life choices they were happy with. And the same thing with ten people who regretted the paths they took."

She stares at me, her face expressionless, as if I've answered in Flemish and she hasn't understood a word.

"Do you write every day?" she says at last.

"Um, I try to. Not the whole day. I'm usually just good for

four or five hours and then my brain gives out." I'm speaking about the past of course, in a galaxy far, far away.

"It must feel very isolating, being cooped up in a room like that. How do you manage?"

Is she always like this, I wonder, or has she just taken a look at my face and decided she doesn't like me? Under other circumstances, I might have tossed a zinger her way, but I don't have the mental energy. More importantly, she's the wife of a donor, and I have to behave for Guy's sake.

"It *can* be isolating, but I play music. Take breaks. Enough about me, though. Tell me about your kids. Guy says your son is an incredible hockey player."

She riffs about her children for a moment, then zeros in on Derek with a series of questions about teaching millennials. She's still the agent provocateur but a flirtier version for him. He's gracious enough to engage with her, but he's not spellbound in the way she was probably hoping for. Finally, sensing defeat, she shifts her focus to the other end of the table. Good. Guy will know exactly how to diffuse her verbal provocations, and I won't have to deal with her anymore tonight.

My energy is flagging even more, and as I turn my full attention to Derek, I pray he'll do most of the talking.

"What a fantastic meal," he says. "This leaves the Ballston College cafeteria food in the dust."

"I'm so glad you like it."

He smiles warmly at me, as if sensing I need a boost. I still can't get a handle on why his features end up working so well together. He's got soft hazel eyes, but his eyebrows droop at the ends, and his nose is, well, huge—flat at the top and center, kind of bulbous at the tip and dented on one side. But the end result is attractive, a whole-being-greater-than-the-sum-of-its-parts effect.

"Did you make this tagine yourself?" he asks.

"Gosh no, there's a chef in the kitchen. She runs a place called Pure Kitchen Catering. Have you ever heard of her?"

His expression turns pensive.

"Yes, actually I have," he says after a beat. "I've never had any reason to use her but a friend of mine has."

"And?" I sense there's something he's not saying.

"As far as I know he was pleased with the results."

"I'm not impressed with the chef personally," I say, my voice lowered, "but I have to admit this chicken is incredible. It's one of those dishes that could make a reluctant boyfriend propose marriage if you served it one night."

"You don't condone that, do you?" he says, one eyebrow lifted mischievously.

"Using food to entice a proposal? It seems pretty harmless—unless, of course, you never make the dish again."

He smiles. "That's not exactly what happened to me, but close."

"What do you mean?"

"I proposed to my now ex-wife not long after she served me this incredible roast chicken. She later admitted it was a rotisserie bird from the supermarket, that kind you see in the deli section, turning on spits in those big furnaces."

I laugh. "Well, did she say she'd made it herself?"

"Not *outright*, but she presented it in a big pan, sprinkled with rosemary and surrounded by roasted vegetables."

"That's not why you broke up, is it? When you discovered the fowl play, so to speak?"

"No, no. She's a great woman, but we got married far too young to really know each other."

"Does she live here, in Saratoga?"

"She's still in California. I was a reporter out there for a number of years. First in San Diego and later in LA."

"How long have you been here, teaching at Ballston?"

"Three years. I'd always had a secret yearning to teach and happened to know the head of the journalism department, who fast-tracked me to the job. I've really loved it. The school doesn't hold a candle to Skidmore, but it's got a great mission. Many of the kids come from underprivileged backgrounds and they're hungry to learn."

"Do you see yourself in Saratoga indefinitely?"

"Actually, I'd love to live in New York City at some point. Teaching and writing there." He pauses, as if deciding whether to elaborate. "If I get there, I'll actually have your book to thank."

"Really?" I say, stirred by his words. "How so?"

"I know women are more your target audience, but I picked up your book because I felt stalled on a few decisions that needed to be made. It inspired me to finally finish my novel.

"Fantastic. Have you submitted it anyplace yet?"

"Yes. And it's coming out this winter." He laughs. "I wasn't even forced to go the self-publishing route."

"Congratulations, Derek. I can't wait to read it."

And I mean it. I'm touched by his words, the fact that

my book impelled him to move forward in life. Plus, it's been weeks and weeks since I sat at a dinner with someone new, enjoying his or her company.

"By the way, I'm sure you could spot this request coming from a mile away," he says, "but I'd be incredibly honored if you could speak to one of my summer classes. I've got one called Writing for Fun and Profit, and there's so much they could learn from you. Unfortunately there's no honorarium. The most I could offer is an umbrella with the college logo. Still, it's one of those huge golf umbrellas that fit at least fifteen people underneath. Do you travel in packs?"

"Not unless hunting for prey," I say, smiling. "But let me think about it, okay?" I'd like to help him, I would, but right now it's hard to imagine summoning the strength to find my way to the campus, let alone plan a class and teach it. Just the thought of it makes my head start pulsing with a dull pain.

"Okay, but I warn you, I can be like a dog with a pork chop." He scribbles his email address on a scrap of paper from his jacket pocket, and I give him mine in exchange.

After a couple of awkward moments between Derek and me, Guy thankfully directs attention his way with a question to the table. I use the diversion to sneak upstairs to the master bathroom and pop two ibuprofen. I sit for a few minutes on the edge of the bathtub, trying to recharge.

Returning downstairs, I cross paths with Nick Emerling in the front hallway, coming, I assume, from the powder room by the kitchen. Was he aware of Kim's little game-playing tonight? I think she managed to do most of it out of his earshot, but surely he must have her number by now.

"Terrific evening," he says. He looks, I realize, like he could be a local TV news anchor, with his thick brown hair shellacked into place. "I'm sorry I didn't have the chance to chat with you more."

"Same here," I say. "So we'll just have to do it again."

"Next time, our treat, okay?"

Dessert is served moments after Nick and I return to our seats. It's crème brûlée, with a hint of mango. After the meal tonight, it's easy to understand why Pure Kitchen is successful. That doesn't mean I'm going to be eager to ever use them again.

Over coffee, there's brief talk of the upcoming racing season. Saratoga is home of the legendary thoroughbred race course.

"Speaking of large beasts," Barb says, "we have a black Lab who needs to be walked. I'm afraid we have to say good night."

This acts as a cue for the other guests to take their leave. People rise from the table and then cluster for a few moments in the entrance hall, saying good-bye and complimenting Guy and me on the evening. From the dining room comes the sound of dessert dishes being cleared from the table.

Once all the guests have departed, Guy embraces me in a hug.

"I thought that went brilliantly. And you were fantastic, Bryn. Thank you so much for this."

"I felt it went well, too. And I enjoyed talking to Derek. He's an interesting guy."

"I thought it would be nice for you to have someone to chat with besides the donors. Though the wives seemed nice enough. Maybe they'd even be fun to get together with one-on-one at some point?

"Sure." I don't say that connecting with Kim again would be about as much fun as bone surgery without anesthesia. Why spoil the mood?

A clanging sound echoes from the kitchen.

"We should tip them," Guy says.

"All three of them?" I ask. He can't be serious if he's talking about a bonus for Eve.

"No, no, just the waiters. The chef has left already anyway. Let me run upstairs and see what's in my wallet."

"I've got twenties down here in my office. Why don't I just grab a few of those?"

Guy nods, and leaving him in the front hall, I hurry back to my office. I'd stuffed the cash in my desk drawer after stopping by the ATM earlier.

But when I slide the drawer open, I see to my shock that the money's gone. I open the drawer a little wider just to be sure, but the eight twenties are definitely missing. And there's an object in their place, something I wouldn't have ever stuck in this drawer—a box of kitchen matches. Goose bumps shoot up on the back of my neck.

I lift the box from the drawer. The front is red and blue and gold, with a brazen banner across the front that reads "Strike Anywhere." It's not a familiar box, not one I've noticed in the house before. What in the world is it doing here?

On instinct, I give the box a shake. Things jiggle inside,

but oddly they feel lighter than matches. Taking a breath, I slide open the drawer of the box.

Inside are at least a hundred kitchen matches, but they've all been burned down so that each tip, as well as the stick, is black and crispy. They look like rows and rows of tiny, charred bodies.

And wafting from the box is the awful, bitter scent of smoke.

Chapter 5

I DROP THE BOX ON THE DESK, SCATTERING MANY OF THE matches. Suddenly my body feels hot and my face is flushed. The smell intensifies until my nostrils are overwhelmed with the acrid smell of burning rubber. Something's on *fire*.

I spin around and search the room with my eyes. There's no smoke and no sign of fire. It's just in my mind, I realize. I grab the edge of the desk for support and take two deep breaths. And then two more.

From my position I have a view across the hall into the kitchen. The older of the two waiters, Conrad, is zipping up his black hoodie, and the younger guy's perusing a message on his phone, his lips pursed in confusion. One of them, I realize, has taken the cash and left the burnt matches in its place. To mess with my head.

Or maybe Eve herself has done it.

I grab another breath, cross the hall, and step into the kitchen. The younger guy keeps reading, but Conrad glances up. I want to respond to the theft and the matches, but I don't see how I can make an accusation without knowing who the guilty party is. But maybe he'll give himself away.

"Good night," I say coolly, though my pulse is still racing.

"Good night," Conrad replies as the younger waiter finally takes his eyes off his phone. "Hope you enjoyed it."

I try to assess their body language. If they're guilty, they don't betray it, nor do they seem disgruntled over not being rewarded with a tip. Within seconds they are schlepping the trolley and cooler out the side door to the van.

I return to the living room, where Guy can tell from my face that something's wrong.

"Bryn? What is it?"

"One of them took it," I say in a rush. "Or maybe they did it together."

"Took the *money*?"

"Yes. All the twenties I had in the drawer are gone." At that moment we hear the van pulling out of the driveway. Reflexively, Guy looks in that direction.

"I can't imagine they'd risk their jobs by stealing," he says. "I'm sure the money will turn up."

"It's more than the money, though. Come, I have to show you."

I start back for the kitchen with Guy trailing me. As fatigued as I am from the long evening, I feel electrified with anxiety.

"Did they break something?" he asks from behind me.

"No, worse than that."

When we reach the office, barely big enough for both of us, I point to the box that I've dropped on the desk and the burnt matches scattered around it. "They left this for me."

"They probably didn't know where the matches belonged,"

Guy says. "I'm sure one of the waiters used them to light the candles in the dining room."

He's clearly not getting it, that there's a sinister intent here.

"But all the matches are *burnt*."

"It was probably the younger guy, the one who looked as smart as a shoe." He shakes his head in displeasure. "The matches should have been doused with water after they were used."

"Guy, I don't care what the fire marshals might think. These aren't even the kind of matches we have in the house. Whoever took the money clearly wanted to rattle me. They must know about the accident, about the car catching on fire."

Guy's mouth parts as he finally comprehends. He reaches out with one arm and pulls me toward him in an embrace.

"Honey, I know this must have thrown you," he says, "but there has got to be a reasonable explanation. Even if one of the waiters pinched the money, what reason would he have to try to rattle you? How would he even know about the accident?"

I look off, considering his comment. *Is* there another explanation, one I'm just too wigged out to see?

"Well, the *chef* had a motive," I say after a pause. "She seemed miffed that I spoke to her about the table."

He cocks his head, doubtful.

"Look, I know there was an issue with her tonight, but I can't see her jeopardizing a client relationship with a prank like that. Maybe one of the waiters always carries matches with him when he's working and stupidly likes to stick any used ones back in the box. But tonight, during cleanup, the other guy spotted them, thought they belonged here in the house, and dropped them in the desk drawer."

"And, seeing the money, just snatched it?"

"Possibly. Though, like I said, I think the money will materialize. There's a decent chance you put it someplace else and just don't remember right now."

"Um, maybe," I say, wondering now if I've blown this whole thing out of proportion. Perhaps my instant dislike for the chef has made me project, jump to a ridiculous conclusion.

"Why don't we head up?" Guy says, putting an arm around my shoulders. "We can try to sort this out tomorrow."

While Guy's in the bathroom brushing his teeth, I dig out my wallet from my bag and check it. The twenties aren't there.

Later, in bed, I can actually hear Guy descend into sleep: the soft sigh as he lets his body settle into the mattress, the deeper and deeper breathing, and finally the sound of light snoring.

For once, I'm not felled by exhaustion. I'm perfectly wide-eyed, caffeinated from agitation. I can't chase the burnt matches and missing money from my mind. On the one hand, Guy's right: the idea that one of the kitchen crew would leave the matches behind as a kind of mindfuck doesn't make sense on any rational level. But something keeps gnawing at my gut, telling me my first assumption wasn't wrong.

Even if Eve didn't know about the accident before tonight, she could have overheard Guy's comment to me about bed rest and then Googled me from her phone. I have to figure out who did this, but I have no idea how.

When I wake in the morning, with my head still pounding, I discover Guy tying his tie with quick, jerky movements. He's overslept, he says, has a big meeting, and doesn't even have time for breakfast. I climb out of bed and we kiss goodbye. We've talked about possibly going out for dinner tonight, and he says he shouldn't be any later than seven. Everything seems okay between us, back to normal after the little blowup last night. But the incident with the matches is still weighing on me, as if it never left my mind as I slept.

Before I even make coffee, I grab my bag and search the pockets, just to be sure I didn't stuff the twenties in one of them. Nope. I also check the pockets of the jeans I wore yesterday into town. Nothing, just the receipt from the ATM.

There's one more place I need to investigate. I head to my office, where the matchbox is still sitting on my desk, a dozen burnt sticks scattered around it. Cringing, I scoot the matchsticks back into the box and set it aside. Then I tug the desk drawer all the way out, making certain the cash hasn't gotten bunched at the back along with the unused note cards, paper clips, and pens I've stored in there.

I'm inclined now to trust my initial instincts. Certainly about the money. One of them took it. As for the burnt matches, there's a message there. Maybe none of them knew about the car accident, but there's an inherent threat: *Don't play with fire or you might get burned.*

So the next step is deciding what to do about the situation. It seems I have only two choices: Move on and try not to dwell. Or confront Eve about what happened. I go with the latter, because I know I'll dwell endlessly if I don't.

While I'm downing a second cup of coffee, I look up the

address for her company. It's not far from the center of town, on a street I'm familiar with. I won't have any trouble finding my way there.

It's breezy today, and as I button a light jacket, I consider what tactic to take. I know I can't box her into a corner—she looks like the type who might bite if you tried that—so I'm going to have to execute a subtler approach. I stuff the matches in my bag and go.

As anticipated, I find the place easily enough. It's in a small blue clapboard house, a single-family home, but as soon as I step onto the porch, I can see through the windows that the entire first floor has been gutted and much of it turned into a large kitchen.

Just as I'm reaching for the handle, the main door swings open, and a guy steps out. It's Conrad, I realize, the older of the two waiters from last night. I tense at the sight of him. There's not even a flicker of recognition in his eyes, and I realize that out of the context of my house, he hasn't registered it's me.

And then in a split second I see him make the connection.

"Hello," he says, locking eyes with me. Confident, sure of himself. "Can I help you?"

"I'm looking for Eve actually."

"She's inside."

"Thanks."

As I reach for the door, I hear the sound of his footfall on the porch steps, and yet I can almost feel him turning and looking back at me.

The kitchen is impressive. Not state-of-the-art, but quality appliances, including a couple of restaurant stoves, a large work island, and three steel racks on wheels, with trays for food. Despite all the metal in the room, there's a bit of a kitschy country feel to the space—a raffia wreath on a wall, and a red-and-yellow rooster clock.

Two young women are at work in the space, both in jeans and white aprons, one chopping carrots using a large butcher knife as a fulcrum, the other tugging a piece of Saran wrap from a mounted metal holder. They look up in unison as I step inside.

I'm about to ask for Eve when she strides into the kitchen from a back room. I see her body straighten when she recognizes me. She's in an apron herself, the upper half folded over and tied around her waist. On top she's wearing a tight pink scooped-neck sweater that reveals more than a little of her ample cleavage. Channeling her inner Giada, I guess.

"Yes?" she says, walking toward me and not bothering with even a smile. She knows something's up, that I haven't stopped by to ask her if she'll share the recipe for the mango-flavored crème brûlée she served last night.

"Do you have a minute?" I say. "There's a matter I need to discuss with you."

"Is it about the dinner last night?"

"Yes, sort of."

"All right. Why don't you come this way?"

I have to hand it to her. She doesn't read the least bit flustered.

I follow her, watching her long butter-blond braid bounce against her back. The two women return to their work, but I sense them on alert, maybe even exchanging a look. Trouble's brewing, they can tell.

Eve enters a decent-sized office with me right behind her. There's just one desk in the room—hers, I assume—and there's a small table with a desktop computer, used perhaps by whoever keeps the books. The rest of the space is taken up with filing cabinets, a couple of folding chairs, and plastic storage boxes. Eve rests one cheek of her butt on the front of the desk, not bothering to offer me a seat.

"Is there a problem?" she asks.

"Actually yes."

"If there was something about the food or the service that you didn't like, I wish you'd raised it last night. That way I could have addressed it."

"It's not about the meal or the service." I reach into my bag and pull out the matches. "These were left in my desk drawer last night."

She doesn't accept the matches, just glances down at them. I watch her face and her body for a reaction, but she gives nothing away.

"I'm sorry," she says after a moment, though there's not a sorry-sounding note in her tone. "I'm just not following."

"I'm wondering who on your team put them there."

"On my *team*? We use lighters, not matches." I see a tiny smile form at the corners of her mouth, as if she's amused. "So you're more than welcome to them."

"They've all been used. And it's actually more complicated than that. A hundred and sixty dollars is missing from the same desk drawer."

The smile vanishes, as if it were never there.

"Are you suggesting that one of my waiters stole the money?"

"Yes, it's a definite possibility. The cash was there before dinner, but when I opened the drawer again at ten thirty, it was gone."

"I've never had a single problem with either of the guys I used last night. They're incredibly trustworthy."

"Then where do you suppose the money went? And who left the matches?"

She crosses her arms over her chest and looks off for a split second before bringing her eyes right back to mine.

"I'd suggest you try asking your husband."

Chapter 6

"WHAT'S *that* SUPPOSED TO MEAN?" I SAY. I CAN'T BElieve this. Is she crazily accusing *Guy*?

She tightens her gaze, saying nothing for several beats. Then her lips part.

"It means you should ask him about the people he invited—one of *them* could have taken it."

I shake my head in disbelief, but her comment reverberates in my mind. Should I have actually considered that?

"I saw one of the women use the bathroom," she adds. "And I heard someone else go in there later."

I was upstairs for about ten minutes toward the end of the dinner, so I don't know what female guest she means. But I did run into Nick in the hallway. The powder room is across from the kitchen, just before my office. And I'd mentioned over cocktails that my office was downstairs. But it makes no sense to think one of the guests would be responsible.

"None of them would have had a reason to steal a hundred and sixty dollars. Frankly, I'm surprised at your response. I thought you'd want to know that someone who works for you might be a thief—and not a very nice one."

Her back is up, I can tell, but I see something begin to shift in her demeanor. She doesn't want a problem, not with the wife of an executive who hires her regularly.

"Why don't I look into it," she says. "I'll speak to the waiters and get back to you." She's all business now.

"I'd appreciate that. And if the person admits it, I'd like to know the reason the matches were left in the drawer."

Of course, if it was Eve herself who did the deed, I'll never find out.

I turn and leave, striding quickly back through the large open kitchen. The two helpers keep their eyes lowered, but I hear their movements slacken as I pass, the chopping and the whipping losing speed. They're wondering what's just happened in the back office.

They've seen this *before*, I think as I tug the door closed behind me. Not necessarily someone complaining about stolen money or rogue kitchen matches, but the occasional disgruntled client, offended by Eve's less-than-ingratiating attitude. Probably mostly women, because it's hard to conjure up Eve playing the bitch card with a male client.

I don't go straight home. Instead, I drive downtown to Broadway, the main street through town. It's lined with well-preserved, four-story brick buildings from the early 1800s, with shops on the ground floors selling everything from honey to olive oil to guitars, as well as a seemingly endless number of cafés. Unlike many old northeastern towns, Saratoga has enhanced its historic charm over the years—its fortunes bolstered in part because of the racetrack and Skidmore College. Some of the buildings are unpainted, but others have been given a coat of moss green or beige, and most have an awning on the lower level—in blue or green or garnet.

I park on Broadway, right by one of the cafés. Though the morning is on the cool side, tables have been set out on the sidewalk, and I take a seat at one of them and order a latte.

My conversation with Eve gnaws at the edges of my mind, and not just because of her smug dismissal of me. It's because of the comment she made about the dinner guests. *Could* one of them be the thief?

I weigh the possibility. There's little chance any of them is desperate for money, so the motive would have to be spite. I can't imagine what either Guy or I could have done to provoke that. Yet there's Kim, isn't there? And the odd hostility I sensed from her minutes after she arrived. It's hard to believe, however, that instant distaste for me would have compelled her to sneak into my office, steal the cash, and leave a menacing message behind. And surely she didn't just happen to arrive with a box of burnt kitchen matches tucked into her evening bag.

No, it can't be her or any of the other guests. It's got to be one of the waiters—or Eve herself. And what frustrates the hell out of me is the fact that I may never know.

Wind gusts down the street, snapping the awning above me and sending paper napkins airborne from the tables. A cluster of young women dash by, laughing over something one is showing the others on her phone. I can't remember the last time I *dashed* anywhere—or looked that happy. Am I really going to spend my summer in Saratoga napping the days away and fretting over issues I can't solve?

I rest my elbows on the table and press my head into my hands, hurrying my thoughts along. What I need to do, I realize, is put myself in motion. Buying the flowers yesterday and arranging the table reinforced that for me. Motion begets motion. And if I can get enough motion going, maybe the energy will help me finally generate words on a page.

Derek's class. That's one idea. Maybe I *should* say yes, even if I have to hitch myself across the classroom floor like a seal. I can at least meet with him in the next week to discuss the possibility.

And then there was the woman who dropped by yesterday. Sandra Something. I'm not wild about the idea of sitting down for lunch with a stranger at this point, but she seemed eager, and it would be an *activity*, at least.

Once I return home, I expect my energy to flag, but surprisingly it doesn't yet. I immediately shoot an email to Derek, or rather two. He's already written to both Guy and me this morning, thanking us for the dinner. I reply to that one with a cc to Guy, and then compose a separate note saying he's piqued my interest about the class and I'd love to discuss it with him when he has the chance.

It occurs to me that, down the road, Derek may even be someone I could interview for a book on reinvention. If I could just get the damn proposal off the ground.

I open the Word document I've been using, and, thinking of Derek and his novel, I tap out a few sentences about how reinvention isn't always about something brand-new. It can be about taking an old dream and wrestling it from the darkness.

Not much but better than yesterday. At least it's not "All

work and no play makes Jack a dull boy," like that terrifying scene from *The Shining*.

Next, I retrieve Sandra Dowd's goodie bag from where I've stashed it in the hall closet. I don't find a business card, but there's a note card with her name and number scrawled on it. She answers on the fourth ring with just a hello.

"Sandra?"

There's a pause and I sense her trying to place my voice.

"Yes?"

"It's Bryn Harper.

"Oh, hello. How nice to hear from you."

"I was just following up on the idea of us having lunch."

"I'd love that. The only hitch is that I'm still in Syracuse, on business. I was only supposed to stay for a day, but I may be here through Sunday. Can I call you once I know my schedule?"

"Of course."

"By the way, how was the dinner party? Were you happy with the caterer in the end?"

"There were a few issues, unfortunately."

"Oh dear. Was the food bad?"

"No, but I think one of the staff stole some cash." I regret the remark as soon as it's escaped my lips. I shouldn't be gossiping up here.

"That's terrible."

"The owner is looking into it, so hopefully it will be resolved. Give me a call when you get back, okay?"

"Definitely."

I provide my number and hang up. Setting the phone down, I spot a response from Derek, and an invitation to lunch on Monday to discuss next steps. I email him back saying that works perfectly for me.

I feel almost giddy from this burst of productivity—too giddy, it turns out, for my own good. At around three, I'm ambushed by what seems like a tsunami-sized wave of fatigue. I stagger out onto the screened porch and collapse on the daybed. In seconds I'm out cold.

When I finally wake it's almost four thirty and my phone is ringing. I see Guy's name on the screen.

"I hope you don't mind," he says, "but Nick Emerling wants to hijack me tonight for a cocktail party at the dance museum. I know we'd talked about going out to dinner since it's Friday night, but it's probably best not to turn him down."

"Of course, you go," I say, though I'm not thrilled. It's the second dinner in a week to be hijacked by Guy's job. "There's chicken tagine left from last night, and it's crazy to waste it. I can just reheat that for us when you get in."

"Sounds good."

There's an odd flatness in his tone.

"Is something wrong?"

"Not wrong, but frankly I'm a little mystified. I just heard that you went to the caterer's office and accused them of stealing the money."

"That woman Eve called you?" Why am I surprised? I should have predicted she'd pull a move like that.

"Not me directly, but she talked to Miranda," he says, referring to his executive assistant.

"I didn't out-and-out accuse her. But I told her that the money was there when her team arrived and missing after they left. I searched everyplace this morning, by the way." As I'm talking, I realize I probably should have given Guy a heads-up.

"I just wish you'd told me before you decided to take this on. It's related to my business. If the catering firm ends up in a snit, we may not be able to use them again."

"Well, if one of them *did* take the money, you'd hardly want to use the company again anyway. But you're right, I should have let you know. By the way, that woman actually had the gall to say I ought to ask *you* about it."

"What?"

"She said I should ask you about your guests. That one of them could have stolen the money."

"That's ridiculous."

"You sure?"

"Of course. I hardly think there was a kleptomaniac in the mix last night."

"Why did she call? To complain about my coming down there?"

"According to Miranda, she was upset. She's probably worried about losing the business. How'd you leave it with her?"

"She claimed that she'd look into it, talk to the waiters."

"Well, regardless of what she says, please let it go after this. It's a hundred and sixty bucks, not the end of the world."

"It's not the money that's really bothering me. It's the matches. They were meant as a threat of some kind. I just feel it."

"I still think that's just a weird coincidence. Look, I'd better get back to work. I'll see you around eight, okay?"

I spend the early evening answering new emails from my assistant. Finally finished, I settle back to respond more fully to my brother's email from yesterday. Because of the crazy time difference between here and Jakarta, phone conversations are tricky for us, so we do a lot of our communicating online these days.

I adore my brother, and though we've always been close—he's two years younger than me—our mother's death twelve years ago, followed one brutal year later by our father's, made our bond even tighter. I hate being so far apart, and I know he does, too. He's hoping to relocate back to the States within the next few years.

As connected as we were in our grief, we handled things totally differently. For Will, the dual loss was a hole that desperately needed to be filled. Within six months of my father's death he was engaged to his girlfriend, someone I never pictured him marrying, though for now it seems to be working out, and they already have two small children.

I yearned for the complete opposite—nothing to tie me down anymore. I ditched the guy I'd been seeing for six months and quit my job as a newspaper reporter in order to tackle my first book. When the research part was finished, I took off for Europe for almost a year, doing the actual writing there. The constant motion—moving from one city to the next, writing in endless cafés, and jogging at dusk each night through whatever park was nearby—helped to keep the crushing grief at bay. That's what makes my current lethargy so frustrating. I know it's not helping in any way.

I ask Will about his job and family and toss out a few details about Saratoga. Since the accident, he's been worried about me—he was on a flight to New York as soon as he learned the news—and it would be great to confide in him how stuck I feel, but I don't want him fretting about me when there's nothing he can do while continents away.

When Guy arrives home, closer to nine than eight, he seems preoccupied, and I wonder if he's still irritated that I contacted Eve Blazer without warning him. Immediately he heads upstairs to change. From the kitchen, I hear the shower run for the next five minutes. When he returns, he's in slim khakis and a blue crewneck cotton sweater, smelling of the grapefruit wash he uses. He smiles as I pass him his dinner plate, not looking at all annoyed.

Gazing at him, with his wet hair slicked back and his skin still dewy from the shower, I realize with a start that it's been over a week since we've had sex. Because of my broken pelvis, our sex life had been on hold for two months after the accident, but with my doctor's blessing, we gingerly began again about a month ago. I can't kid myself. Since the accident, my libido has felt at times like a glow stick left in the grass all night long, and I've said yes to sex not because I've exactly craved it but for Guy's sake. I wonder if he's held back because he's sensed reluctance on my part.

We eat the leftover tagine off the coffee table in the den behind the living room and watch a documentary Guy says he's been dying to see. I'm actually pleased we haven't gone to a restaurant in town. This is nicer, no fuss. Guy drapes an arm over my thigh and gives it an affectionate squeeze.

I steal a glance at him. There's something undeniably magnetic about Guy. And I'm talking not just about his looks but rather his whole personality. Some of it, I know, has come from his training as a fund-raiser—you have to learn how to charm the pants off donors—but in Guy's case, most of it is just who he is. I want to make love tonight, I realize. I want to succumb to the full force of that magnetic pull and relish its power.

"Ready to go up?" I ask as soon as the show ends.

"Yes, but I think I need to jump on my computer for a bit."

Again tonight I feel a swell of disappointment, an even bigger one this time. As we rise from the couch and my eyes meet his, I'm surprised by the worry in them.

"Is everything all right?"

"Yes. No, not totally. I'm afraid I might have miscalculated some numbers at work and it's been gnawing at me all night. I want to review a few Excel sheets before Brent sets eyes on them."

Brent Hess is Guy's sixty-year-old boss. He's run the company for years and seems to know what he's doing, but he's unpredictable and easily aggravated. And a bear when he is.

"Is there any way I can help, honey?"

"Just keep the sheets warm, okay?"

I manage to read for a few minutes in bed but fall asleep mid-page, hearing the book clunk on the floor as I drift off. Once during the night I wake to the sound of rain drumming against the window, and I sense Guy next to me, his body totally still. But when I wake in the morning, the bed is empty. Descending the stairs, still in a camisole and pajama bottoms, I realize that the house is silent except for the slow drip of water from the gutters outside.

Where *is* he? I wonder. I feel a flutter of anxiety, like a moth trapped inside a light fixture. In the kitchen, there's a note tucked under the saltshaker on the table: "Ran to the office. Think I figured out what the problem is and I want to deal with it before Monday. Call you in a bit. xo."

And he does, thirty minutes later, as I'm toweling off after a shower.

"Any luck?" I ask.

"Yeah, I figured it out. Looks like a few numbers were accidentally transposed, making it seem as if we were behind from last year in donations. That would have made Brent go batshit crazy."

"Want to meet downtown for an early lunch?"

"As long as I'm here, I'm going to catch up on a little paperwork. I'll be back by midafternoon. And let's definitely go out tonight. You can wear one of those slutty tops of yours."

I say good-bye, relieved that he's sorted out the problem. This job is important to Guy, the last step before applying—or being courted—to run something himself. He needs to nail it. And I like the slutty-top request. It's time to get our sex life back up to speed.

I've barely set the phone down when it rings again. Not a number in my log.

"Mrs. Carrington?" a female voice asks.

"Yes?" I never use Guy's last name, so I realize it's someone who doesn't really know me.

"I work with Eve at Pure Kitchen Catering." The voice is wispy, baby-doll-like.

"Yes?" I say again, curious. I wonder if it's one of the women who I encountered working in the kitchen yesterday.

"Eve has something for you. Can you come down here today?"

So this must be her assistant calling. Eve clearly has gotten to the bottom of what happened Thursday night. Maybe I underestimated her.

"Is it the money?"

"She didn't tell me. But it's important that she see you this morning."

"You're open today? On Saturday?"

"Yes."

I haven't even had my coffee yet, but that can wait. I'm eager to know what's up.

"Fine, I'll be down shortly."

So I was right after all. One of the waiters has obviously copped to the theft, and if I'm lucky, he's admitted the motive for leaving the matches. I can't help but indulge in a few moments of satisfaction. I *wasn't* imagining the whole thing. I'm tempted to call Guy but decide to wait until I have all the details.

It's stopped raining by now, but it's misty out, a light fog sitting all cottony in the trees. When I reach the blue clapboard house, I find an empty space on the street in front and park. It's only nine o'clock, and it's hard to imagine many people will be working inside already, unless of course they're catering a luncheon today. I notice a bicycle leaning against the porch. Maybe it belongs to Eve—or the woman who called me.

As I climb the steps, I'm surprised to see that there aren't any lights on inside. Was the girl calling from another location and assumed Eve Blazer would be here today? But there's the bike, so someone must be in. I try the handle and the door opens. Setting a foot inside, I find the kitchen empty.

But then I hear a sound, a rustling, and I turn quickly to my left. Through the dimness I make out the shape of a young woman at the far end of the kitchen, standing just in front of the doorway to Eve's office. Her back is to me, but I can see she's wearing a billowy top and a pair of yoga pants. At her feet there's a dark cloth bag, with the tips of seven or eight baguettes poking out from the open end.

She's heard me, too, and jerks around, her long, curly brown hair swinging with her like a twirl skirt. Her hands are at her face, fisted, and she's bug-eyed at the sight of me. I've clearly startled her.

"I'm sorry," I say. "I was looking for Eve." I assume this is the girl who called me earlier, perhaps the person whose bike is leaning against the porch. But she doesn't say anything. Instead she makes a gurgling sound in her throat.

"Are you okay?" I ask, moving toward her. I see now that's she's trembling.

I reach out an arm to comfort her, and my eyes are drawn to open doorway of Eve's office.

The overhead light is on and right away I notice that the room looks different than it did yesterday. The desk is a mess, with papers scattered as if someone has swept an arm hard and fast across the surface. There's been a spill, too—food or maybe wine. There's a spattering of endless spots on all the papers, like liquid sprayed from a canister.

I step closer to the threshold, and my eyes are forced to the floor. Off to the right, Eve is lying faceup on the linoleum. I gasp in horror.

There's an ax protruding from her face, stuck there as if her head were a piece of wood. Blood has oozed from around it and caked along the edges. On the side of her face is a yawning vertical gash, extending through her eye socket and her cheek. It's crusted with dark red blood.

Someone has driven an ax into her face, stepped back, and done it again. And then left her lying there dead.

Chapter 7

FOR A FEW SECONDS I JUST STAND ON THE THRESHOLD staring, waiting for the scene to reconfigure to normal. But it doesn't. A wave of panic swamps me, like water crashing over the side of a boat too small for the sea.

No, I think. This can't be. My stomach starts to uproot itself, propelling its way toward my throat. I dry heave.

I cover my mouth, trying to force the sensation down. At the same time, I step backward and spin around, remembering the curly-haired girl. She's still standing there, rocking in place, and I see that there's something in her left hand. For a split second I wonder if she's the one who's done this to Eve, but then I notice she's only holding a phone.

Is the killer still *here*? We need to get out, get out of the house. Fear seems to have bolted me to the floor, but I tear free, grabbing the girl by the arm and nearly dragging her through the kitchen. I swivel my head back and forth, frantically checking the room as I run.

We reach the front door and I grab for the handle. But it won't turn. It's like the dream, the door refusing to open. I let out a cry and rattle the handle furiously. Finally it shifts and the door flies open.

"We have to call the police," I tell her as we spill out onto the porch.

"I . . . I did," she says between chattering teeth.

"9–1–1?"

She looks at me bewildered, as if she doesn't even grasp the question. I've thrust my hand into my purse, searching desperately for my own phone, when she finally nods. "Yes, 9–1–1." She starts to rock back and forth again.

"And they said they're coming? Right away?"

"Yes. Omigod, someone *did* that to her. Someone killed her."

I search the street with my eyes. There's not a person in sight, not even forms moving behind the windows of the houses.

"Let's go to my car, okay?" I say, noting how much distress she's in.

I lead her to the street, fling open the back door of the car, and encourage her into a sitting position, with her body facing out and her feet skimming the curb. Warm, I think. You're supposed to make sure that people in shock stay warm. I tear off my jacket and wrap it around her shoulders, then grab a bottle of water from the seat pocket. I notice for the first time that my own hands are trembling.

I look back to the house, making certain no one's there. Part of me is terrified, overwhelmed by what I just witnessed, but another part seems detached and eerily calm.

"Did you see anyone?" I ask, glancing back at the girl. I

twist the cap off the water bottle and hand it to her. "In the house or running away?"

She shakes her head hard, like a dog with a toy in its mouth.

"The house was empty," she says. She takes a sip of water clumsily, as if she's forgotten how to do it. "Except for her—for Eve."

"You just got here? Right before I came?"

"Yes. I . . . I called out, but no one answered. Then I saw the light in the office. Omigod, I can't get it out of my head."

"Are you the one who called and asked me to come down here?

"*What?*"

"You work here, right? Did you call me this morning? I'm Bryn. Uh, Mrs. Carrington."

"No, I don't work here. I sell them bread."

As she says that, I recall the baguettes nosing out from the bag on the ground. And besides, it couldn't be her. The woman on the phone had a baby-doll voice, not like this girl's.

So where had the person been phoning from? And where is she now?

I glance up and down the street, wondering what's taking the police so long.

"What's your name?" I finally think to ask.

"Sara. Sara Cummings. Who *did* that to her?" She's almost wailing now. "Who?"

"I don't know." In my mind's eye I see it again. Eve's butchered face, the frantic spatter of rust-colored blood.

A memory comes, unbidden, of me in a Massachusetts

hospital three months ago. I'd woken at dusk, dressed in a blue-and-white-print hospital gown and throbbing in pain. I'd been sponge-bathed by then, but when I turned over my arm, I discovered smears of blood leftover from the accident. It was brown, just like the blood in Eve's office. I realize now that she must have been murdered hours ago.

"Sara, was Eve married, do you know?" I ask. "Or involved with someone?" There was a provocative, challenging air to her. What if she spurned a man who was obsessed with her? Or cheated on him? He could have become infuriated, murderous even.

"I don't know. I don't think so."

I glance back toward the house, to the second story. "Did she live here?"

"Yes, upstairs, above the kitchen."

So maybe a break-in instead. She could have come downstairs last night and stumbled upon a burglar who'd figured there might be cash in the catering office.

But all that blood. The savagery. It's not a burglary, I tell myself. It's *personal*. I start to dry heave again and fight it back.

I grab a water for myself, and as I unscrew the cap, another thought pushes through. I accused the waiters of stealing my money, and based on the phone call I received this morning, it's likely that Eve confronted them and even induced one of them to return the cash. Could he have returned later in a rage?

If that's the case, I've set this all in motion, caused her death. No, please, it can't be true . . . Paul's death and now this.

I need to call Guy. But right when I reach for my phone, I hear the sound of a car approaching. I look to the right. A black-and-white police cruiser is barreling in our direction. It lurches to a stop, and moments later two cops emerge, both with hands resting lightly on their guns. One's a female, super tall and a brunette, the other a dark-haired guy with pock-marked skin.

"Did one of you call 9–1–1?" the female asks. Her badge reads "Robichaud."

"I did," Sara says between teeth that have resumed their chattering. She thrusts her chin toward the house. "They killed her with an ax."

"You *saw* it?" the male cop says. "Are they still in there?"

"I don't know. I just came with the bread."

Before I can attempt to translate, both cops turn simultaneously in my direction, as if sensing they'll have more luck with me. That's hysterical, I think. I, the walking basket case, am about to be the most coherent one at the scene.

"She was making a delivery," I explain, "and I came in right afterwards. We found Eve Blazer's body in the office, at the back of the first floor. No one else seemed to be around."

Robichaud asks for our names, and after she scribbles them down, she orders us to stay right where we are until she and her partner have searched the house.

"And don't talk to anyone," she adds. "That means no phone calls, too."

The two cops exchange a look and then hurry up the short cement sidewalk to the house.

Sara moans and collapses onto the backseat again. I let my

body sag against the car. The cops are inside the house now, and through the big front window I can see their dark shapes receding toward the rear. They're about to find her, see what we saw. Once again the awful image muscles its way into my mind.

A few houses down, a woman steps onto her porch and cranes her head in our direction, super curious. I feel desperate to reach Guy, to let him know what's going on, and yet Robichaud's warning echoes in my head.

And then I think of the girl again, the one who phoned me this morning. I distinctly remember she said Eve wanted me to come "down here," which implied *here*. If she was calling from this location, wouldn't she have seen the body?

It's ten minutes before the cops reemerge from inside, but instead of coming back to the car, they begin to cordon off the house and yard with yellow tape stamped "Police Line Do Not Cross." A van approaches and empties out three people who I assume, from their clothes, are crime scene personnel, and I watch them trudge into the house.

By now a crowd has gathered on the street, adults lit up with curiosity, and kids, too, a few on bikes, zipping back and forth, sometimes doing wheelies on the still-damp pavement. God, I think, it's starting to look like a street fair; the next thing you know someone's going to start selling funnel cake and lemonade.

Finished securing the perimeter, the patrol cops hustle back over to Sara and me and take down our addresses and phone numbers. Sara begs to know when we can leave, and they inform us that we must wait to be interviewed by detectives, who are due to arrive shortly.

It actually turns out to be just one detective, a forty-something woman with olive skin, thick brows, and short dark brown hair with a band of white running along the roots. She immediately separates us, escorting Sara to stand by one of the cop cars. I sense from the consternation on the detective's face that the patrol cops will get a tongue-lashing for not having done this earlier. When she returns to me, she introduces herself as Detective Corcoran and explains that she will interview both of us once she's surveyed the scene inside.

Another fifteen minutes of waiting before she reappears. She starts with Sara, I assume because she was the first on the scene, and finally, after ten interminable minutes, she returns to me.

"You doing okay?" she asks. "This has got to be tough."

"I'm hanging in there," I say, appreciating the sympathy. I take her through what happened, starting with my visit yesterday to inform Eve about the missing money and, of course, the call from the assistant this morning. What I don't include is any reference to the burnt kitchen matches. I can't imagine what that could have to do with the murder, and it seems smarter not to divulge anything too personal.

"And you saw no one else in the area, either before you went into the house or afterwards?" Corcoran asks.

"Not a soul."

"This assistant who spoke to you. Did she give her name?"

"No, not that I recall."

"And there was no sign of her whatsoever when you arrived?"

"None." For the first time I wonder if she's okay. What if the killer has done something to her, too?

Corcoran furrows her brow, clearly as confused as I am by this odd disconnect.

"Okay," she says at last. "Thank you for your assistance. It's important that you not share details of the crime scene with anyone. And please be aware that we may need to talk to you again."

"Of course." Though the patrol cops have already requested my full name and number, Corcoran asks me to write the info in her notebook. As I do, I notice that my hand is still doing a little jig.

Corcoran returns to the house, and I sigh in relief, finally free to go. Though I'm desperate to meet up with Guy, I realize I should offer Sara a ride home, but when I turn around, I see she's gone, as is the bike. At least now I can drive straight to Guy's office. I want to tell him the story in person rather than on the phone. As I pull away, a van from an Albany TV station jerks to a stop in the spot my car had occupied.

Halfway to the opera house, I realize that I'm going to have to call Guy after all since he works on the ground floor and the building will be locked today. I pull the car over to the curb. To my surprise he doesn't answer his cell. In my hyped-up state, it irritates me. Why wouldn't he have his phone on him? I try his office phone next.

Another surprise. Guy's assistant answers, or at least I think it's her. She says "Hello" rather than the standard weekday "Guy Carrington's office." I have no clue why she's working on the weekend

"Miranda?" I say.

"Oh, Bryn, yes, it's me. There are a few of us in today. Did you want me to find Guy for you?"

"He's not in his office?"

"He just dashed upstairs. There's a short rehearsal today and he wanted to speak to one of the performers about a fundraiser he's singing at."

"Can you just let Guy know I'm driving over to see him? Something urgent's come up."

"Oh dear, anything I can help you with?"

"I might need you to let me into the building."

"The side door is actually open—because of the rehearsal. I'll find Guy and let him know you're on your way."

When I pull into the parking lot a few minutes later, I spot Guy standing in the side entrance, dressed in jeans and a blue-and-white-striped dress shirt, his face pinched in worry. He's looking in the opposite direction from which I've come, expecting me to be driving from home, and I'm out of the car and nearly at the entrance by the time he notices me.

"What's wrong?" he asks in a rush.

"Something horrible happened. Not to me, to someone else."

I step quickly inside. Before I can blurt out the news, two crew members trudge by, rolling a piece of stage scenery on a trolley. In the far distance, I hear the muted refrains of an aria.

"Let's go to your office, okay?" I say.

Guy ushers me down the long cinder block hallway to the suite where his office is located. Miranda's in the anteroom, thumbing through a stack of papers on her desk. She's dressed in jeans—because it's Saturday, I guess—and her ginger-colored hair is tied uncharacteristically in a ponytail. Though she's in her forties and the mother of two college-aged kids, she's got a youthful air and, according to Guy, is eager to meet a new man. She says a polite hello but then returns to her work, shrewd enough to know this is not the time for chitchat.

"What *is* it?" Guy asks after shutting the door to the inner office.

"The chef, Eve? She's been murdered. Someone killed her at that kitchen of hers."

He stares at me blankly, as if his mind is struggling to decode my words, the same way I couldn't grasp the horror show I'd stumbled on this morning.

"Good God," he says finally. "How did you hear this?"

I shake my head, and for the first time all morning tears spring to my eyes.

"I *saw* it," I say, my voice choking. I tell him—about the phone call, the shell-shocked baguette girl standing in the kitchen, and the grisly scene inside the office.

Guy grips the side of his desk, steadying himself. "Jesus . . . You called 9–1–1, I take it?"

"The girl, Sara, already had. I wanted to call you, but we couldn't talk to anyone until the cops quizzed us. The police are still there. And there's press now, too."

"This is crazy, totally crazy," he says, looking off. Finally he glances back and seems to finally take me in. "What about you? Are you okay?"

"I don't know. It was just so awful to see. I guess I'm still reeling from it."

"Had it just happened? God, Bryn, you might have been in danger."

"No, the blood was dried. It looked as if she'd been killed hours before. Maybe last night . . . Guy, there's something we need to consider." My voice starts to choke again. "Her death might be related to the stolen money."

"What do you mean?"

"If Eve was planning to reimburse us—and it sounded that way—she probably busted one of the waiters. Even if she didn't extract a confession and decided to pay us back out of her own pocket, the gig was up. What if the thief confronted her last night and ended up killing her?"

"For a hundred and sixty dollars? That seems hard to fathom. I mean—"

"But let's say he was an addict and stole the money for drugs. It could mean he's unhinged. And violent."

He pinches his lips together so tightly, the edges turn white.

"This isn't good," he says. "If it comes out that her death is related to the opera company, that's going bite me in the ass big-time."

"But it's not as if we're responsible. Reporting the theft to Eve was the right thing to do."

"Donors hate anything controversial, whether you're at fault or not. I suggest we wait and see how this plays out. If the cops catch the killer immediately and the situation is clearly unrelated to us, there's no reason to loop them in about the money. But if no one's apprehended, we'll have to raise the issue, and then I'm gonna have to initiate major damage control."

"But, Guy, I already mentioned the theft." I can't believe he's suggested I keep a key detail under wraps from the cops. "I didn't bring up the box of matches, but I told them about the missing cash, that it was the reason I'd gone to Pure Kitchen this morning."

"But why in the world open that can of worms?"

"Why *wouldn't* I? It might be connected to her death. And I had to explain why I'd shown up twice in two days."

There's a flash of exasperation on his face—just like in the dining room the other night—but quickly his expressions softens and he lets out a ragged breath.

"Of course, of course," he says. "That was the right thing to do. I've just been totally thrown by this."

"At the very least, they needed to know about the person who called me. It was so strange. On the phone she made it sound as if she was on the premises, but when I arrived ten minutes later, only this girl Sara was around."

He's only half listening now and glances at his watch. "Brent made a surprise appearance in the office today and he wants to see me at noon. I better get down there. Do you want to wait here for me and then we can head home afterwards?"

Fatigue has finally reared its head, and my body feels as if it's been filled with wet sand. All I want at this moment is to collapse on the daybed and melt into the cushions.

"I think I need to get back to the house sooner than that. Why don't I meet you there."

"You sure you're okay?"

"Yes, I'm fine. Just shaken."

"Give me a half hour to meet with Brent and then I'll take off." He hugs me good-bye.

But the hug does nothing to comfort me. As I exit into the parking lot a few minutes later, I'm still bothered by what Guy initially lobbied for, that we keep the police in the dark for the time being. He's hardly a goody two-shoes, but he's always come across as someone with an overall respect for authority, the kind of person who might at times let the speedometer in the car sneak up near eighty on the highway but would never act belligerent if pulled over by a trooper.

Deceiving the police today would have been stupid, no matter how much damage control seems necessary for his job.

His job. For the first time I ask myself if Guy's feeling more under the gun than he's confided to me. I think of his concerns about the transposed numbers, the whole reason he's spending Saturday ensconced at the office. It certainly can't be pleasant dealing with a man as mercurial as Brent.

I wonder, too, if playing nursemaid to me these past months has distracted Guy from what matters most in his work.

Crap, I think. I'm just raining death and destruction down on everyone.

Halfway to my car I realize to my dismay that I've left my messenger bag in Guy's office. I trudge back to the building and retrace my steps down the wide dark hall. Guy has already left for the meeting with Brent, but Miranda is still there, standing behind her desk and staring into space. My presence startles her.

"Sorry, I forgot my bag." I scoot into Guy's office to retrieve it.

When I reemerge, Miranda, her brow furrowed, steps from behind her desk, reaches out, and touches my arm. I'm closer than I've ever been to her, and I can see the freckles on her lovely, creamy skin.

"Guy told me the news," she says. "That the caterer we use was murdered."

I wonder if this is part of Guy's damage control, to sprint out ahead of the situation by announcing the news around the office himself. I doubt, however, that he's divulged that I was actually at the crime scene.

"Yes, it's awful."

"You met her, right? When she did those parties at your house?"

I stop, snagged by the question. Eve was only at our house the one time.

"Parties?"

"The dinner party the other night. And the cocktail party a few weeks ago? The one for the new director in residence."

What? I think, but quickly try to hide any sign that I'm taken aback.

If Eve Blazer catered another party at our house, it had to have happened before I arrived.

And Guy never said a word about it.

Chapter 8

DON'T LIKE WHAT I'VE JUST HEARD. WHY WOULDN'T Guy have mentioned the party to me?

"Yes, I met her," is all I say. The last thing I'm going to do is probe Miranda on the subject and arouse her curiosity. After offering a quick good-bye, I hurry out of the office and back to my car. I'm winded and panting by the time I slip behind the wheel.

As I drive home, I try to replay my initial encounter with Eve on Thursday night. I'm positive that when I asked if I could show her around the kitchen, her blunt reply had been something like, *I think I can manage*. No hint from her that she already knew the lay of the land.

And then later, when I informed Guy that Eve had re-buffed my offer for a tour, he'd made a comment about caterers being able to find their way around unfamiliar kitchens. Not *Well, she won't have a problem because she's been here once before*.

It's not a glaring, horrific omission, not on the same plane as forgetting to mention you have another wife and kids stashed away in Buffalo, but it's *weird*. And it bothers me.

The second I step into the house, my unease spreads without warning. I realize that if one of the waiters killed Eve over
the money, he'd be in a rage against Guy and me. I bolt the
kitchen door behind me and check that the other two doors to
the house are secure as well.

I crave the comfort of the daybed on the porch, but I know
I won't feel safe there now—there's only a hook-and-eye latch
on the screen door to the yard. I stagger to the den and collapse onto the sofa. I try to make my mind go blank, but soon
enough, an image begins to bleed in from the edges. It's Eve
standing in her office looking smug and self-satisfied, and then
an ax splicing into her face with a horrible thwack.

Am I *responsible*? Did I set the whole horrible thing in
motion by raising a stink about the money and matches? I
imagine how it might have played out. Eve summoning both
waiters to her office—probably separately so there'd be no
safety in numbers. She might have rested her butt on the desk
like she had with me, her body close enough to each guy to be
intimidating.

And she wouldn't have been coy. She would have demanded the truth point-blank. A confession might have been
offered by one of them, followed quickly by his being fired.
Even if the thief failed to come clean, he might have worried
that Eve could see through his lie, and that it was only a matter
of time before he was out of a job. Maybe he hadn't killed her
then, but instead came back later with the ax. Or found the ax
on the premises.

I wish I could reach out to the woman who called this
morning. It's seeming to me now that she must have been at

another location. She didn't sound fully in the loop, but she might know *something* that could prove useful. Regardless, I decide it doesn't seem smart to call. I'd surely sustain a tongue-lashing from Corcoran if she found out.

Of course, the murder might have no connection to either of the waiters who worked at our house. It could just have easily been committed by someone else, a boyfriend perhaps. A gruesome crime of passion.

I take deep breaths, the way Dr. G suggested, and count back slowly from ten. Eventually my heart quiets, and from pure exhaustion I feel myself drifting asleep.

When I wake with a start, I find Guy's hand on my shoulder and realize that he's been gently jostling it. I struggle up to a sitting position, my now damp T-shirt sucking at my skin. It takes only a split second for the horror of the morning to come rushing back. I moan at the memory.

"Sorry to wake you," Guy says, lowering himself onto the sofa, "but I wanted to be sure you were okay."

"Thanks, honey. Is there any news?"

I sense there's another question around the edges of my mind, an insistent one, but it ducks from my grasp.

He sighs. "Not a thing. They mentioned the murder on the radio, but no word about any suspects."

"Do you think the cops up here have the resources to track down a murderer?

"Let's hope so . . . Can I get you anything? An iced tea maybe?"

"That would be nice." The caffeine may help me out of my stupor.

As Guy rises from the sofa, the elusive question strays within reach.

"Did Eve do another party for you?" I ask. "Before the dinner Thursday night?"

"Well, more than one. As I told you, she catered a bunch of events for the opera company."

"I mean here in the house, before I moved to Saratoga. Miranda said there was a cocktail party."

He squints his eyes, as if the answer requires a mental search and rescue, and finally nods.

"Yes, that's right. She catered a very small cocktail party a couple of weeks before you arrived. I decided on the spur of the moment to toast the new director in residence."

The disquiet I felt in the car creeps back.

"But why not tell me about that?"

"Didn't I? I guess it just never came up on the phone."

"But the other night, when I told you that Eve didn't want me to show her around, you said she was probably good at finding her way around unfamiliar kitchens."

"Well, she'd never cooked an actual meal here. At the party they served hors d'oeuvres, which I'm sure were prepared in advance."

"But after the money was taken? You didn't think it was worth pointing out that she and her team had been here previously?"

"It honestly slipped my mind, sweetheart. Come to think of it, she had a different crew with her that night anyway. Two women."

Maybe I'm being silly. There's so much more to worry

about right now, and I need to move this to the inconsequential list.

"Okay." I shove aside the chenille throw that I'd pulled over me. "By the way, how did the meeting with Brent go?"

"It was fine. He just wanted to show me the new ads we're going to be running, get a second opinion. The problem is you never know with him. One day he's all smiles and compliments, and the next day he's a human blowtorch."

That can't be fun, I think again, and I'm finally recognizing how much of a pain in the ass Guy's boss has become for him.

"It won't be forever. Are you still planning to start looking for a new job at the end of the year? In New York?"

"Maybe sooner. This fall even."

"Ah, I like that idea. Us living under the same roof for good."

"I like that idea, too. I'll get you the iced tea."

"Guy," I say as he starts to exit the room. "Let's keep the doors locked even during the day, okay? We don't want to take any chances."

It takes him a moment to register what I mean, and then he nods, understanding.

"I hear you."

For the rest of the afternoon I hang in the den, answering emails and reading a few articles online about reinvention, hoping they'll kick start my brain. I try to keep thoughts of the murder at bay, but it's impossible, and at moments they trample over me. I check out the police blotter on the website of the *Saratogian*, the local newspaper, to see if there's any development. "Local Chef Found Slain in Office" is the first item. It doesn't mention the ax, only that Eve Blazer was brutally killed. No suspects at this time. No mention of either me or Sara. Or any other woman who might have been at the scene.

Leaning back against the couch cushions, I hear Sara's words echo in my head: *Who did that to her? Who?*

Though Guy and I had originally planned to go out for dinner, neither one of us is up for it now. He makes a run to the butcher and picks up a steak, which he panfries for us. I nuke a couple of baked potatoes and toss a salad with vinaigrette.

Later in bed, Guy spoons me and I wonder if he's going to initiate sex. But within a minute or two I hear his long, slow breaths, the sound of him surrendering to sleep. As much as I want our sex life back in sync, I don't think I could have faced it tonight.

The next day is rainy and raw. Guy and I spend most of it in the den, reading and watching movies. He's dressed in jeans and a heather-colored Henley shirt, with his feet bare, a casual look I love on him.

Halfway through the third movie, I glance over to see if he's getting bored like I am. I catch him staring off into space.

"Where'd you go?" I ask.

"Hmm?"

"You seem lost in thought."

"Oh, just ruminating about some work issues. A Sunday night habit."

"You figured out that problem with the numbers, right?"

"Yes, that's all resolved, thankfully."

"Is it the murder? Are you still worried it might impact your job somehow?"

"That's a possibility, but I'm trying not to borrow trouble. Let's just see what happens."

In the morning, after Guy's left for the office, I notice an email from Derek Collins, suggesting we meet at a restaurant on the ground floor of an old hotel on Broadway. Damn, I think. Having lunch with him totally slipped my mind. My first instinct, in light of everything that's happened, is to cancel, but I talk myself into going. I need to stick with the decision I've made to *do* more, to get out, to recapture my life.

It's sunny today and pleasant, in the high seventies, so I skip the jeans and opt for a cotton dress and sandals. As I'm heading out the door, there's a call on my cell phone from a local number and I wonder if it might be Derek.

It's not.

"Ms. Harper? Good morning, this is Detective Corcoran. We spoke on Saturday."

She'd mentioned the possibility of a follow-up call, but still, it unsettles me to hear her voice.

"Oh, good morning."

"We appreciate your help the other day, but I had a few additional questions."

I wonder if it's about the money stolen from my office. I cringe, realizing that the murder might indeed blow back on Guy and me. We could really be in danger.

"Of course. What would you like to know?"

"It would be best if we could do this in person. We may ask that you look at some photos."

My chest tightens. "Photos? You mean of the waiters?"

"Why don't I explain when you arrive."

"All right. I have an appointment in a few minutes; I could stop by afterwards. Around two thirty. Does that work?"

She agrees and gives me the address on Lake Avenue, which is right off Broadway and not far from the restaurant. When the call is over, I warn myself not to jump to conclusions. Maybe they've zeroed in on a suspect who isn't one of the waiters and she just wants to know if I saw the person in the vicinity.

I try Guy on his cell, planning to alert him, but the call goes straight to voicemail. I leave a message asking him to return my call. I also leave a message on his office phone.

I lock up the house and manage to sprint to the car, searching the area with my eyes as I move. Derek is already at the restaurant when I arrive, sitting on the veranda of the legendary hotel. He smiles warmly when he sees me, and by the time I've mounted the steps, he's stood and pulled out one of the rattan chairs for me. Still no sighting of the infamous cords. He's dressed in jeans, with a V-neck sweater over a T-shirt.

"I've been dying to eat here," I say after I'm settled.

"Don't tell me that word of their chop salad has reached Manhattan."

"Ha, not that I know of. I just wanted to sit on this veranda. When I drive by, I picture people from a hundred years ago hanging out here during the summertime."

"Even longer ago than that. This building is pre-Civil War."

"Do you know a lot about the area?"

"A fair amount—and it's fascinating. Are you aware that

the Battle of Saratoga was a turning point in the Revolutionary War?"

"Gosh, I think I *do* recall that, though I'm rusty on details."

"It was 1777 and the colonists were demoralized. When they won at Saratoga, it revitalized the whole war for them. And, of course, it forever changed the world."

The waitress interrupts and we place our orders.

"I haven't been to the battleground yet," I say after she departs. "And I don't think Guy has either. He's been so crushed with work since he moved here."

"He's not from this area originally?"

"No, California, though he worked in Chicago, both before and after business school, and then Miami. He ran a business there that handled fund-raising for small organizations who couldn't afford their own teams."

"He did a great job taming that woman Kim the other night. Personally I had to resist the urge to fling a spoonful of crème brûlée in her direction."

"I *so* wish you hadn't resisted."

He smiles, and in the sunlight I see that his eyes are actually green, not hazel, lined faintly with crow's-feet.

"Regardless of her, I still had a terrific time."

I'd wondered if there was a way to get through the lunch without summoning up the murder, but now it seems weird to skirt the issue, especially since Derek and I chatted briefly about Eve at the table.

"I assume you heard about the murder," I say.

His expression darkens. "Yes, I was going to mention that. I'm sure this must be weird for you. She was just in your home."

"Weird, yes. And scary, too."

"The college is concerned, needless to say. They're putting on extra security at the dorms in case there's some crazy person out there. Are you anxious being in the house alone during the day?"

"Yes, a bit. And it doesn't help that I was actually at the murder scene. I saw the body."

"*What?*"

"I dropped by the catering office Saturday morning—to follow up on something about the dinner—and I arrived right when another woman had come across the body. It was awful."

"Oh, Bryn, that's terrible." He picks up his fork and lightly jostles it in his hand. "Did you get a read on what happened? I mean, was it the result of a break-in?"

"I . . . I couldn't tell. The police warned us not to share any details, but trust me, it was brutal, and it's hard to believe a burglar was responsible."

"Did they hint whether they had any leads?"

"No, they didn't," I say, deciding not to bring up my appointment with the cops. "You mentioned that an acquaintance had hired her. Do you know anything about her?"

"Not really, no. He only used her once, I believe."

As might be expected, the topic casts a momentary pall over the conversation. Fortuitously our food arrives and Derek switches subjects.

"Okay, so this is when I turn particularly obnoxious. How do I talk you into teaching one of my summer classes and turning me into a hero to my students?"

"You don't have to talk me into it. I'd be happy to do it."

"Fantastic. You just made my day."

"You said the name of the course is Writing for Fun and Profit. Do you want me to concentrate on the fun or the profit part?"

He laughs.

"Both! A lot of these kids are very earnest about their writing, and though that's fine in one sense, it can also be limiting. Not many people can count on having the success you've had, but I want them to see that there's potential to make money if they work hard and watch where the whole business is going."

"You mean that print journalism is dying?"

"Exactly. Believe it or not, some of them are still enamored with the idea of working in print. I'm trying to make them see that they need to think of themselves as content creators and be willing to pivot. It would be great if you could talk about your own path and whatever strategies you used."

I shrug. "I wish I could say there's been a ton of strategy, but some of my success has been due purely to luck and circumstance."

"You're being way too modest."

"Look, I admit I've always been ambitious, and I worked my butt off during the years I was a journalist. I also didn't kid myself about how the newspaper business was changing. When a book editor saw a piece I wrote and offered me a contract, I jumped at the chance because I knew I needed a plan B. But in some ways I have fate to thank for how my first book sold, which, of course, led to the *next* book and so on."

He cocks his head, his eyes intense with curiosity. "How so?"

"My mom died when I was in my twenties, and then twelve

months later, my dad did, too. I had planned to write the book while I was still working, but after my father's death, I bagged my job and threw myself into the research. My perspective changed, and writing the book became my passion and priority. I loved interviewing people and writing up their stories. I think having the time to do that made all the difference for me personally—and also for the book."

"Is this something you'd feel comfortable talking to the kids about it? Because life really *does* come down to playing the cards you've been dealt."

"Sure, I'd be willing to share whatever you think would be of help to them. But if possible, I'd appreciate doing it in a couple of weeks. I've been a little under the weather lately, and I want to be sure I can give it a hundred percent."

Derek goes quiet for a moment, his eyes lingering on mine.

"I read about the accident," he says. "I wasn't being nosy, but when you agreed to lunch, I did my research. What you went through this year must have been harrowing."

"I'm trying to finally put it behind me. I mean, it happened three months ago." To my surprise, my voice falters.

"That's not very long in the scheme of things. I'm sure there are plenty of days when it still troubles you."

His comment catches me off guard. "Yes. Yes, it does."

"Do you want to talk about it?"

"No, but I appreciate your asking." And I do. It's as if he's granted me permission to feel as lousy as I still do. "Enough about me. Tell me about your novel—if you feel comfortable, that is."

He smiles. "This will probably come as a big shock, but

it's about a guy in his late thirties, licking his wounds near the town of Saratoga Springs."

"Has he been hoodwinked by a rotisserie chicken?" I ask, grinning.

"Ha, no. It's 1777 in the book, and the main character has just survived the Battle of Saratoga."

"Oh, fabulous. It's historical then."

"Yup. I really related to what you said a minute ago about research. It's what I loved as a journalist, and it's not only a great stress reliever for me but a total turn-on."

"How nice to have someone besides me confess that. I always feel a little nerdy admitting that."

I ask more about his novel-writing process, and Derek shares some of the research he undertook. Listening to him is not only engaging but also relaxing, and it's only over coffee that I think to check my watch. To my shock I see that it's twenty minutes after two.

Once Derek learns I need to be somewhere else shortly, he flags down the waitress for the bill. I try to split the check with him, but he insists that the college will pick it up. Our parting is more hurried than I would like, but we agree to be in touch by email about the class.

I set out on foot for the police station. It's at the back end of city hall, a redbrick building that runs the length of a short block. I swing open a glass door and step into a nondescript foyer. Behind a glass partition there's a bunch of crammed-together desks occupied by uniformed cops, all male. It takes about a minute for one of them to acknowledge me and saunter over to the partition.

I explain my presence, and he asks that I wait. I park myself on the wooden bench in the foyer. Hopefully this will be a chance for me not only to assist the cops but also to secure information myself and assess how vulnerable Guy and I might be. What if one of the waiters really did commit the murder? And what if he's still at large? That would explain the need for me to look at photos. I realize that I never heard back from Guy, which only adds to the tension I'm experiencing.

At least ten minutes pass before Detective Corcoran emerges from behind the cheap plywood door and leads me through a labyrinth of desks to the one that belongs to her. There's a silo-sized plastic container of what looks like iced coffee in front of her, and she takes a sip through the straw as I settle into a seat.

"How are you doing today?" she asks, setting down the cup. "You feeling any better?"

"A little, yes. Thank you."

Corcoran picks up a notepad, thumbs back through a couple of pages, and, pursing her lips, peers intently at what she's written.

"As I mentioned on the phone," she says, "I want to review a few of the details you provided. Just to recap, you visited Ms. Blazer on Friday and told her that a hundred and sixty dollars was stolen from your home on Thursday night?"

So this *is* about the money.

"That's right."

"You thought one or both of the waiters might have taken it?"

"Yes, but I didn't know for sure." Of course, I suspected Eve, too, but I let that lie. "Did you want me to look at photos?"

"Photos?"

"On the phone you said you might want me to look at photos."

"That won't be necessary after all. And then, let me see, you received a call the next morning from a woman. What did you say her name was?"

"As I told you, I don't think she mentioned it."

"But she said she worked for Ms. Blazer?"

It seems so odd to hear her called that. She didn't seem like a Ms. Blazer. She seemed like an *Eve*.

"Correct."

Corcoran purses her lips again, confused. I feel my breath quicken a little. There's something about the pad and the pen and her creased brow that's so evocative, thrusting me momentarily back to my hospital room in Massachusetts, where a state trooper pumped me for details about the accident as my head felt ready to explode.

"And you're sure about that?" she asks.

"Sure of it?" I don't really understand what she's getting at.

"Sure she claimed to work for Ms. Blazer."

"Well, she didn't out-and-out say, *I work for Eve Blazer*, but she implied that. She said Eve wanted me to come down."

"I see."

"Are you having trouble finding her?"

"You could say that. We've spoken to every woman who works for Pure Kitchen Catering, and not one of them says she called you."

Chapter 9

START TO BLURT OUT MY SURPRISE AT THIS NEWS AND catch myself. An internal pinging warns me to wait a beat, to answer carefully. I root through my memory, searching for any relevant detail from the phone conversation that will clarify matters, but come up empty.

"I got the impression that she was an assistant or helper," I say, "or even one of the women I saw working in the kitchen when I went down there. But maybe it's something else."

"Like what, do you think?"

"Maybe . . . maybe she's a freelancer, not a full-time employee. I don't know. Or a friend. I suppose the chef could have asked a friend to make the call."

Corcoran entwines her fingers, with the two pointers straight up, steeple-style, and then taps them to her lips as she considers my comment.

"A friend," she says, letting the word just hang there for a moment. "Kind of odd to have a friend make the call."

This whole situation is making no sense. Could one of the women in the kitchen be lying? And then I remember.

"Oh, wait, I have a record of the phone call, of course. She called my cell."

I dig in my purse for my phone and scroll through the log. It occurs to me that the catering company may have a landline, and the caller could have used that to reach me, but at least there'll be a record of it.

I find the number easily enough because I've barely used my phone since then. The call came in at 9:17 Saturday morning.

"Here it is," I say, flipping the screen toward Corcoran. "Do you want me to jot it down?"

"No, thanks, I've got it." She picks a pen from a ceramic mug that reads "Caffè Lena, Good Folk Since 1960" and copies the number.

"And when she called, she didn't give a name, not even a first one?"

I've answered this question twice already, both today and on Saturday.

"Like I said, I don't believe she mentioned it, and if she did, I wasn't paying attention. I do remember she sounded young, with kind of a baby-doll voice. I asked her if it was about the money and she said she didn't know, but I assumed that it had to be."

I'm blathering. But her tone is unnerving. It hints that I've created an annoying wrinkle in the investigation or I'm not being completely transparent. I think again of the state trooper in my hospital room, the annoying cock of his head that suggested I was holding back information.

"Let's jump back to that for moment. The money. It went

missing on Thursday night, right? At a party Ms. Blazer catered."

Okay, I shared this with Corcoran on Saturday, too, and she's got it all scribbled down in that little notebook of hers. But maybe the case *is* pointing toward one of the waiters and she's being careful to dot all her i's.

"Yes, that's right."

"What kind of party was it? Big, small?"

"A dinner party. For seven people."

"Did you give the party yourself?"

"Well, with my husband. He works for the opera company here."

"And during the party, did Ms. Blazer interact with any of the guests?"

She holds my gaze, her eyes almost hooded by the weight of her thick dark brows. Oh please, I pray to myself, don't let her ask for the names of the guests.

"No. She was in the kitchen the entire time." I hold my breath, as if that could freeze her need to keep barreling down this road.

Corcoran slides her gaze back to her notes without moving her head and momentarily purses her lips. "I believe you said that when you noticed the money was missing, the waiters were still there, but you didn't speak to them about it."

So I've dodged the dinner-guest bullet, it seems—at least for now. I exhale slowly, hoping my relief isn't obvious.

"No. I wanted to go through the house later and make sure that I hadn't actually put the cash someplace else. Though I was nearly positive I hadn't."

"And when the money didn't turn up, you decided to contact Eve Blazer directly. According to the two women who assisted her in the kitchen, you arrived at about ten. Did you call first?"

"No, I figured it was better to explain the situation in person."

"And how did that go? What was her reaction?"

Where is this *going*?

"She didn't take it particularly well. She said she had used the waiters before and never had a problem." What I don't say is that Eve implied one of our dinner guests might have taken the cash. Besides the fact that such a revelation would lead her back to the donors, it doesn't seem relevant now.

"So she got her back up about it?"

"Yes, a bit." I realize that the women in the kitchen may have overheard the conversation and confirmed this. "But in the end she said she'd look into it."

"And then the call the next day."

I nod. "I'm sure when you reach this woman she can tell you more."

Corcoran nods her head lightly, and I can't decide if she's agreeing with me or simply considering what I've said.

"Do you think one of the waiters did it?" I ask. This is all I really want to know right now. If that's a possibility, Guy and I need to up our security.

"Ms. Harper, you must realize I can't discuss possible suspects with you."

"But if one of them is the killer, and it relates to the money, my husband and I could be in danger."

"I can only offer you the same advice I'd offer anyone in Saratoga right now. Be cautious. Lock your doors. There's a killer at large."

Oh, that's helpful, I think. Next, she's going to tell me to leave a porch light on at night.

She purses her lips again and flicks through a few more pages of her notebook.

"I believe that's it for now," she says. "You mentioned the other day that you're up here for the summer. So if we need to ask you additional questions, you'll be available?"

"Yes, I'm around for the next few months."

I pray it won't take that long for them to solve this. I hate the idea of the murder hanging over our heads all summer.

I start to rise, and Corcoran raises an eyebrow.

"One of my colleagues mentioned that you're an author."

"Yes, that's right." I force a smile.

"Working on another book while you're here?"

"I am, yes," I say, grateful I'm not hooked up to a polygraph machine.

She thanks me and walks me out through the labyrinth of desks. Though most of the other cops keep their eyes focused on their work, a couple glance up quickly, checking out my presence. In the foyer, Corcoran nods good-bye.

"We appreciate your cooperation. Have a good day."

I exit, wondering how good of a day I can possibly have now. I thought I'd be leaving with a hint of whether the police are seriously eyeing one of the waiters, if they even have him in custody, but she gave nothing away.

Plus, there was that whole weird business about the mystery woman who called me Saturday morning. Does Corcoran think the caller knows something about the murder—or could even *be* the killer? Instinctively I touch my hand to my bag, where my phone is, wondering whether I should try to call the woman back. But the cops would hardly appreciate that.

At least Corcoran didn't demand the names of our dinner guests, though that could change in a heartbeat. If one of the waiters *is* the murderer, the cops will surely want to speak to everyone at the party that night.

As I make my way back up Lake Avenue, fatigue plows into me from behind, nearly knocking the wind out of me. I've overdone it, with both the lunch date and the trip to the police station. Where have I parked my car? I don't even remember.

By the time I reach Broadway, I'm swaying. I look to the left, squinting toward the row of cars parked along the curb, trying to spot my own. I raise a hand to my brow, trying to steady myself.

"*Bryn?*"

I swivel to my right. It's Sandra, the woman from the arts council. She's juggling a soft leather briefcase and a large purple shopping bag bulging at the sides. I do my best to smile in greeting.

"Oh, hello," is all I manage to get out.

"What a nice surprise . . . Wait, are you okay?"

I obviously look as pathetic as I feel.

"Yes, thanks, I'm just awfully tired suddenly."

"But you're white as a ghost. Has something happened?"

She glances over my shoulder in the direction I've come, as if that'll provide an explanation.

"I had to give a report—at the police station. It . . . it turned out to be very draining."

"Why don't we find a place to sit down? There's a café right up the block."

She pushes the strap of her briefcase farther onto her shoulder, relocates the shopping bag to that arm, and uses the other arm to guide me the short distance along Broadway. Though there's outdoor seating at the café, she suggests we venture inside toward the rear, where it'll be quieter. Just sitting down makes a difference.

Sandra flags the waitress and orders us each a cup of tea and an ice water for me. As my brain begins to defog, I notice she's dressed today as chicly as she was the first time I saw her—a navy pencil skirt and a white lace blouse with a piping of navy around the collar. Her rescue of me has surely interrupted her workday.

"There, that's better," I tell her after I take a few sips of the ice water. The swaying sensation has subsided.

"Did something happen to you? Is that why you went to the police?"

"No, no." I lift the glass of water and hold it against my cheek, relishing the cold on my skin. "I mean not to me personally. But . . . well, do you remember me saying I was using a caterer for the dinner party last week? The chef, the woman who runs the company, was murdered."

"My goodness, Eve Blazer, of course." Sandra's deep brown eyes cloud with worry. "I saw it on the news, and the whole thing has me scared out of my mind. I didn't realize that's who you'd hired."

"Yes," I say, keeping my voice low. "And you know how I told you some cash was missing that night? I went to her office to follow up on it and discovered the body."

"That's dreadful. And the police, they're just getting around to interviewing you about it now?"

"No, they talked to me at the scene, but they had follow-up questions. I had to dredge it all up again."

"That couldn't have been a picnic."

I smile grimly. "It was like one of those moments at airport security when the TSA agent asks you to step aside and you start wondering if you've inadvertently packed a Glock handgun in your roller bag."

"Oh boy, I can relate to that. The one and only time I was stopped for speeding, I was overwhelmed with this ridiculous fear that the cop was about to open my trunk and find twenty bags of heroine piled inside."

We laugh together, and I take a small amount of comfort in the fact that I'm not the only person whose free-floating anxiety balloons around law enforcement.

Our teas arrive in white ceramic pots.

"Here, why don't I do this," Sandra suggests, and fills my cup first. Her nails are beautifully manicured with the palest pink polish and French tips, reminding me that it's been ages since I've bothered with mine. I take a long, slow sip of tea and feel the blood start to flow back to my face. "But you survived? You got through it okay?"

"Yes, I guess so."

She eyes me quizzically, perhaps trying to read between the lines. I don't want to send a signal that there's a problem. "I mean, it was fine. It's just tough to revisit it all again."

"Poor girl," Sandra says. Startled, I think she means me and then realize she's talking about Eve Blazer. "It seems trouble followed her around."

"What kind of trouble?" Goose bumps shoot up along my arms.

"I've just heard rumors over time. A former colleague of mine booked her for a party once and then swore she'd never do it again. She was pretty upset."

"What was the issue?"

She cocks her head, thinking, and then slowly shakes it.

"From what I recall it wasn't about the food or the service. Something weird happened, but at the time she didn't say what it was."

Money or valuables missing from the premises? I wonder. Eve had stated adamantly that she'd never had an issue with her staff, but that could have been a lie. I've let my eyes fall to the table, and when I glance back up, Sandra is studying me.

"Do you want me to try to find out?" she asks.

I do, but I don't want to say so. Plus, I suddenly feel desperate to be home.

"That's not necessary," I say. "I was just curious, in light of everything that's happened."

"I don't blame you. This must be upsetting for both of you."

"Both of us?

"You and your husband. I assume he met her at your house, too."

"Yes, it was especially troubling for him because they've worked together in the past." I regret my words the second they're out of my mouth. The goal for Guy and me has been to distance ourselves from Eve, and I'm doing the exact opposite.

"I'm sure you're a wonderful comfort to each other."

"I like to think so, yes." I need to drop the subject pronto. I spot the waitress and raise my hand for the bill. "I should let you get back to whatever you were doing, Sandra."

"This is my treat, though. Please."

"Absolutely not. I can't tell you how much I appreciate you rescuing me."

She snaps up the bill as the waitress sets it down and laughs again in that conspiratorial way she has.

"Well, you rescued *me*, too. I'm supposed to be assembling swag bags for a client event and I was dying for an excuse to put it off. Everyone wants swag bags these days. Free food and booze are no longer enough."

"Is that what you were shopping for today?" I ask, nodding toward the bag on the chair beside her.

"Yes, this is the last batch of scented candles I ordered."

Once she's paid for the tea, she escorts me to my car, which I've thankfully recalled the location of.

"I'm so glad I ran into you," she says. "I only got back in town last night and was planning on reaching out. Why don't I phone you in a day or two and we can arrange a lunch if you like."

"I'd love that."

She starts to move but then turns back to me and taps one of her French-tipped nails against her mouth.

"I hope it isn't out of line for me to say this, but just be careful if you have any more contact with the police here."

That pinging sound goes off in my brain again, like it had in the police station.

"Oh? Why do you say that?"

"I can see I've alarmed you and I'm sorry. It's only that I've had to interact with them a few times in relation to clients, and they can be indiscreet. And you don't need that at this point in your career."

"Thanks, I'll keep that in mind."

As I drive away, her comment lingers in my mind, worrying me. I didn't want to press her, and now I'm left trying to translate what she meant by "indiscreet." If one of the waiters is arrested for murder, Guy and I will both end up in the local news—there's no way to avoid that—but what additional information could the police possibly leak?

Thinking of the cops reminds me that I haven't yet told Guy about my trip to the station today. It's a little after four when I reach the house and Guy will be home in two hours. Rather than interrupt him at work, I decide to share the experience once he's back.

By the time I've unlocked the door and entered the kitchen, the crushing fatigue from moments earlier has dissipated and I feel oddly wired instead. My mind keeps replaying the interview with Corcoran, pondering why she still can't find the woman who phoned me on Eve's behalf. I wonder if the caller really might have something to do with the murder or is even a victim herself. Plus, there's still a risk of the situation unspooling, threatening to drag Guy and me with it, but I don't know how to protect us.

Wandering into my office, I realize there's one little thing I *can* do. After the dinner guests departed Thursday night, Guy mentioned that it might be nice for me to reach out to the two wives, to get to know them better. Though it's something I initially had zero interest in, particularly when it came to Kim, being on friendly terms with the wives would help if there's any fallout from the murder. I don't have the stomach to meet with Kim, at least this week, but I email Barb, asking if we could meet for lunch or drinks.

I'm still in my office when, much later, I hear Guy come in through the kitchen door. Before I have the chance to rise, he enters the room, places his two hands of my shoulders, and kisses the back of my head.

"Hard at work, babe?" he asks.

"Just dealing with a few loose ends. I called your cell earlier. Did you get the message?"

"Oh, yeah, sorry. I only noticed it when I was heading out the door."

"I called the office, too. Miranda didn't tell you?"

"No, but her head was in the clouds today. Was it important?"

"Yes. But let's discuss it over a glass of wine, okay?"

I sense him on high alert as he trails me into the kitchen, stripping off his suit jacket as we go.

"Tell me," he says before I've even uncorked the wine.

I explain about the call from the police and going down there, how they wanted me to review details about the dinner party.

"Jesus," he says, tossing up his hands. "Are they going to talk to the donors?"

"So far it doesn't look that way. I mean they didn't press for their names and I certainly didn't volunteer them. But if it turns out one of the waiters killed Eve Blazer, that may change."

"Beautiful. That's all I need."

I pour his wine, hoping a glass will ease his nerves. But though I take a swig from my own glass, he ignores his.

"Would it make sense to give Brent a heads-up now?" I ask. "Then, if one of the waiters is arrested, it won't be such a rude surprise."

"It's going to be a rude surprise no matter *when* he hears it. The guy loathes any kind of bombshell."

The jarring sound of the front doorbell pierces the air, startling both of us. I glance at the clock on the microwave: it's 7:20. Who would be showing up here at *this* hour?

"Are you expecting anyone?" Guy asks.

I shake my head and follow him to the front door. In unison, we peer through one of the antique, lightly pocked windows on the side.

A man and woman are standing on the wide front porch. I don't recognize the man. But the woman is Detective Corcoran.

Chapter 10

THIS CAN'T BE GOOD. I WAS AT THE STATION MERE HOURS ago, so why would Corcoran show up here unless there was a serious development? I assume the man is her partner.

"It's the police," I whisper to Guy, realizing he has no clue who these two people are.

"What are they doing *here*?"

"Maybe they've made an arrest." That would be a relief, but if it's one of the waiters, it would put the murder right at our feet.

"Let me handle this, okay?" He steps around me and swings open the heavy wooden door.

"Good evening," Corcoran says. She nods at me and then directs her attention to Guy. "You must be Mr. Harper."

"I'm Guy Carrington. But I'm Bryn Harper's husband if that's what you're asking."

There's a slight curtness to Guy's tone, not his usual MO with strangers. He's anxious, I think. Just like I am.

Corcoran introduces herself to Guy and her partner, Detective Mazzola, to both of us. He's younger than she is, maybe midthirties, with short spiky hair. He's dressed in khaki pants, a blue button-down shirt, and a scuffed brown belt that, based on the imprints in the leather, has been used on about three different notches over the years.

"Is it all right if we come in?" she asks. "We'd like to speak to the two of you."

"May I ask what this is about?" Guy says. Again, his tone catches me off guard. "I thought my wife already provided you with all the details she could."

"Ms. Harper has been very helpful, but we have an update we'd like to share."

An update. My stomach clenches. It has to be about one of the waiters.

"All right, come in then," Guy says. He shuts the door behind them and leads us all into the living room. Neither cop comments on the house, but I notice Mazzola letting his gaze roam over the space, making a judgment I cannot read.

Guy gestures for them to be seated, and they take the two armchairs by the fireplace; we lower ourselves onto the couch directly across from them. My heart is racing now, simply in anticipation. I don't want this to create trouble for Guy at work. But it's more than that. I dread that I've been the unwitting catalyst for Eve Blazer's murder.

"Have you lived here long?" Corcoran asks. I can't believe she's starting with chitchat. That was her approach this morning, too: the faux-friendly question about how I was doing. Is that some kind of technique she uses?

"About a month," Guy says. "We're renting the house for the summer."

"You work in Saratoga, your wife said."

"Yes, I do. I'm head of development for the opera company."

"But this isn't where you usually live?"

Guy quickly sums up our situation. A commuter relationship, him with a small apartment in town, me coming up for the summer, prompting the need for a roomier place. The side of Corcoran's mouth is tugged upward, as if she's thinking, *Must be nice.*

Please, I beg silently, *just get on with it and tell us why you're here.*

"You said you had an update," Guy says.

"Yes, that's right." Corcoran's tone is polite enough, but the pace of her words suggest she's not about to be hurried or bossed. "We know there's been concern on your wife's part that the murder could be related to the theft of money from your home last Thursday."

"There's been concern on *both* our parts," Guy says. He reaches out a hand and lays it over mine. "We feel terrible about what's happened."

"As you'd expect, we're not in the business of keeping witnesses up to speed on developments in our investigations. But because of your fears for your safety, we're making an exception in this case."

Guy doesn't comment, but I feel a mild tremor in the sofa cushion as his body shifts almost imperceptibly.

"Well, you can breathe a little easier," she continues. "As it turns out, each waiter has a confirmed alibi for the time of the homicide. Neither one is a suspect."

I can't help it; I let out a gasp of relief. I haven't set this gruesome chain of events into motion after all.

"So the murder had nothing to do with the stolen money?" I say.

"It doesn't appear that way."

I turn to Guy, expecting him to respond as well, but he's silent, his face expressionless. Finally he nods as if it's taken him a few moments to grasp the news.

"Thank you for telling us," I say. "It doesn't change what's happened, of course, but it's a relief to know."

What I'm still in the dark about is whether one of the waiters actually did take the money, and I'm probably going to remain there, and also never learn whether the matches were a taunt or just a bizarre coincidence.

"Let me echo my wife's feelings." It's Guy, finally speaking up. "We appreciate the information."

And now they can go, I think, and we'll finally be done with all this. But Corcoran appears as unwilling to budge as Jabba the Hutt.

"Of course, that leaves us still looking for her killer," she says. "So any insight on your part would be helpful."

"Insight?" I ask. This morning Corcoran didn't want to divulge an iota about the investigation, and now she's asking me to play junior deputy.

"I assume you interacted with Ms. Blazer when she catered your dinner. How did she seem to you?"

"How did she *seem*? I'm not sure what you mean." Does she want a read on Eve's mood that night?

"Was she on edge in any way?" It's Mazzola piping up for the first time as he simultaneously pulls out a pen and notebook. "Acting nervous."

I find the question ridiculous. Do they really think I could have surmised in one night's interaction whether Eve Blazer was in fear for her life?

"I spoke to her only briefly, but from what I could see, she wasn't on edge."

"What about the next day, down at her place of business? Anything odd about her behavior?"

"Not that I recognized."

"But didn't you say her back was up on Friday?" It's Corcoran. Am I just imagining it, or is there a "gotcha" trace to her tone?

"Yes, but that was concerning the money. I don't believe she was pleased with the idea that one of her staff might have taken it."

Corcoran does that pursed-lips thing of hers. Perhaps it's a tell, a window into her thoughts and intentions, but if that's the case, I'm clueless about what it means. She shifts her gaze to Guy, and I can feel his utter stillness through the cushion. Is he finding this as absurd as I am?

"And what about you, Mr. Carrington? You'd worked with Ms. Blazer a number of times."

"Well, my organization had. We used her catering company fairly regularly."

"Did you have a chance to speak to her when she was here?"

"I said hello as I came in through the kitchen after work—and oh, I gave her the heads-up when we were ready for the dinner to be served."

"Did you notice anything out of the ordinary?"

"Not during those thirty-second encounters, no. And even if we'd spoken more, I doubt I would have been able to gauge whether she was worried about her safety. Isn't this a question that would be better put to her employees? If she'd had concerns, she might have raised them with a colleague."

"Our job is to speak to as many people as possible," Corcoran says.

The comment just hangs there, like a leaf caught on a current in midair. Please, I think, just don't ask about the dinner guests.

"Of course," Guy says. "Unfortunately we really have nothing to contribute about her state of mind. Is there anything else we can help you with?"

Again, his tone surprises me. It's vaguely patronizing. Corcoran shoots her partner a look and then turns her attention back to me.

"There *is* one thing," she says. "It's about the phone call you received on Saturday."

"Yes?" I assume by now she's finally reached the caller.

"You see, we still can't locate the woman. It's all a bit of a mystery."

I feel a prick of anxiety. What's going on? I wonder.

"Did you try the number I gave you?"

"We did. But it's for a disposable phone that's no longer in operation."

Could I have given Corcoran the wrong number from my log? But no, that's not possible. That call was the only one I received Saturday morning besides the one Guy made to me from his office. Guy, I notice, has gone quiet again, and I assume he's trying to interpret what Corcoran is saying. I never had the chance to catch him up to speed on this.

"Maybe . . . maybe the woman who called me had lost her phone," I venture. "And she was using a disposable one for a couple of days."

Corcoran says nothing in response but levels her gaze at me. Like at the station, her manner suggests that I'm making trouble, creating roadblocks in the investigation.

"If the waiters aren't suspects, why does it even matter anymore?" I say, trying to regain my footing.

"In a murder investigation, *everything* matters," she says coolly.

Of course it does, I think, recognizing how dumb my comment was. The caller had more or less indicated she was in the blue house, making her a person of interest to the police.

I wonder what's coming next, but Corcoran rises slowly, with Mazzola following suit.

"All right," she says, though nothing actually feels all right. "Thank you for your time."

I let Guy see them to the door, and I head back to the kitchen, where I grab my glass from the table and take a large gulp of wine. I should be *less* stressed now that they're gone, now that they've revealed that neither waiter is an ax murderer, but the discomfort I felt upon their arrival has swollen like a fresh bruise.

Everything about Corcoran's visit feels so weird to me. The way they pressed Guy and me for our impressions of Eve Blazer's mood that night. How could we be expected to have read her thoughts? Plus, this whole crazy thing about the woman who called me and now can't be located. I'm struck, too, by the fact that the entire time Corcoran and her sidekick were here, there seemed to be two conversations going on: the one they were conducting with Guy and me, and the unspoken one between just the two of them.

A frightening question forms in my mind: Am I a target in the investigation? I was the one who found the body, after all—or at least one of the ones—and aren't the police always suspicious of the first person on the scene? But Corcoran *can't* suspect me. What could my motive have been?

Guy comes up behind me and I jerk in surprise.

"Oh, I didn't hear you. Do you want some wine?" I ask.

"Not now, thanks. Maybe later."

"You must be relieved, right? Since the waiters aren't suspects, it doesn't look like the police will need to talk to the dinner guests."

"Well, at least for now it doesn't seem that way."

I scoff. "Unless they want to ask *them* whether the chef seemed on edge that night. I can't believe they thought we'd have any insight."

"What's this business about the phone call?"

"It came up this morning—at the station—so I never had the chance to tell you. They claimed they spoke to all the women employed by the catering company and no one admitted to having called me."

He frowns, as if he doesn't understand.

"Why would the person who called you hold out on the cops that way?"

"I don't know, but it's troubling. When I spoke to that woman, I had the impression she was at the house. So maybe she went into Eve's office after the call—to tell her she'd reached me—and found the body. She might have panicked so much that she fled the scene and doesn't want to admit to the cops she was there. *Or* she may know something about the murder and wants to distance herself as much as possible."

"Well, that's for the police to figure out."

"I just hate the way that Corcoran makes it seem as if I'm holding out on her about the call. She pressed me the same way at the station. You don't think she believes I had something to do with the murder, do you?"

"Don't be silly. Though it's smart you didn't bring up that verbal exchange you had with Eve Blazer that night. You don't want to give the cops anything to sink their teeth into. I have serious concerns about their competence."

"Of course I wouldn't have said anything about that," I say, wondering why he'd feel the need to dredge that up. "It's not even relevant . . . What about dinner? I could throw together a salad."

"I think I'm going to head upstairs and tackle a bit of work for a while. I'll fix a sandwich for myself later."

"Are you okay?" I ask.

"Yes, I need something to take my mind off this whole ugly mess."

After he leaves the room, I carry my glass of wine to the

screened porch and curl into one of the wicker armchairs. Now that I know one of the waiters isn't the killer, I can relax a little about being out here, especially with Guy in the house.

I haven't bothered switching on any lamps, so after a few moments dusk begins to fill the room like fog. I take another sip of wine and set the glass on the floor, realizing that I don't want any more, that it's doing nothing to ease my stress. Something feels off center, as if I'm trying to sleep on the opposite side of the bed than I usually do.

What's unsettling me, I realize, isn't simply the way the cops talked on two planes. It's Guy and his behavior tonight, details that seem out of character for him. Like the curt tone when the cops first introduced themselves. And his inattention toward me since they left. He must know I'm rattled by this whole experience. Why not sit with me for a while as we both decompress?

There's something else, too. His sudden stillness on the sofa midway through the conversation, like someone trying to decipher an odd sound coming from another room.

I wonder if he's experiencing what I went through earlier at the station, that discomfort that arises simply from sitting across from a detective and being quizzed. I recall what Sandra said today about the unnatural guilt she experienced being stopped for speeding.

The room darkens. There's a hint of honeysuckle in the air.

And then fatigue sneaks up behind me, like it had earlier in the day. I start to rise, ready for bed, but my arms and legs feel too heavy to move. I flop onto the daybed and close my eyes. It'll be just be for a minute, I think, until I summon my energy back.

And then I'm dreaming, half knowing it's a dream. I'm in the hotel room again. There's the smell of smoke. And the man behind me. He calls for me to wait, and I tell him I can't. This time I feel him reach for me and touch my arm.

"Listen," he says. "You have to listen."

Chapter 11

WHEN I WAKE THE NEXT MORNING, A LITTLE AFTER eight, I'm in the master bedroom, not on the screened porch. I'm alone. It takes a moment to recall being led here by Guy after he heard me cry out during the nightmare.

"It's just a dream," he kept saying. After I was tucked into bed, I lay awake, achy from fatigue but unable to fall back to sleep. Finally, close to three, I drifted off. I'm sure that Guy has left for work by now and I'll find a note from him in the kitchen.

And I do. "Have a good day, sweetheart," it reads. "I'll be home by 7. Call me when you have a chance."

Normal-sounding Guy, nothing distant or detached-seeming. And yet I still feel unsettled by Corcoran's visit. My weekly Skype appointment with Dr. G is just an hour away, and I'm hoping that talking with her will help burn off my unease.

I fire up my laptop a few minutes early, just to be sure there's no glitch with Skype. Dr. G signs in right on time, and it's good to see her warm, friendly face. She's about sixty, with expressive dark eyes and long black hair that she usually wears in a French twist, and she has an elegance that I wasn't expecting when I first went to her. I'd only been to a therapist once before, a grief counselor who helped me after my parents died, and she was more of the classic therapist stereotype, right down to the flowy knit tops and makeup-less face.

"Good morning, Bryn," Dr. G says. "How are things?"

Usually I start kind of slow with her, groping for words to explain my state of mind at the time, even though I've always tried in advance to gather my thoughts. But today I start by blurting out details—first about the murder, then back to the dinner party and the burnt matches in my drawer, and then to the delightful pop-up interview with the police last night. Dr. G doesn't try to disguise her concern as she listens.

"Bryn, this must be so troubling for you," she says.

"I have this awful sense of dread these days. Maybe from knowing the murderer's still out there."

"Is this stirring up feelings about your accident?"

"A little. When I first thought that one of the waiters might be the murderer, I felt so guilty, like I may have set the whole thing into motion by going to see the chef. It's like the guilt I still have about the accident at times."

I mention the dream last night, how it seems significant that I would have it in the thick of this, and how there's now this mysterious man calling out to me.

"The first time you had this new version of the dream, the one with the man, was it before or after the murder?" she asks.

"Um, before."

"All right. Though your anxiety about the murder may have triggered the dream again last night, it still seems related to your car accident. Are there any clues to who the man might be?"

"No, I never see him. And I don't recognize the voice. But there's this sense that I know him, that he's familiar to me."

"It sounds like, regardless of his identity or what he may represent, he has something important to say to you. I suspect you'll eventually discover who he is because the dream becomes more revealing each time you have it. Keep jotting down notes, okay?"

"Okay. But if the dream is really about the accident, why does it take place in a hotel room?

"Dreams patch weird elements together. You *were* in a hotel room the night before."

When I look at the clock on my computer screen, I realize we've been speaking for almost thirty minutes. I have only fifteen left.

"Let's go back to what happened the night of the dinner party," Dr. G says. "The box of burnt matches. You think someone was trying to rattle you?"

"That's what it seemed like. One of the waiters or even this woman Eve herself. Or perhaps one of the dinner guests."

"Could there be another explanation for the box being there?"

"I was thinking lately that the person who took the money might have placed it there as a diversion, so that I'd be confused about whether I'd actually left cash in the drawer. But why burn all the matches down first? It seems like a message."

"So that must be adding to your dread—wondering why someone would try to send a message like that."

"Yes, though I haven't thought as much about it in the past day or so. Now I'm more preoccupied with the murder, and all these crazy interviews with the cops. It feels so oppressive."

"Why oppressive, do you think?"

I relate some of the questions they asked, as well as the fact that Corcoran hasn't been able to locate the woman who called me.

Dr. Greene straightens in her chair, and from her eyes I can see she's trying to make sense of Corcoran's approach.

"It's hardly your fault that they can't find the woman."

"I know, but the way she pressed me made it seem like I'd done something wrong. That I wasn't being totally forthcoming."

"Could it be that she's just frustrated with the investigation? She may think this woman has valuable information or may even be a suspect."

She has a point.

"True."

"I'd try not to worry about the police right now. You've done nothing wrong. It sounds like you may be transferring the anxiety you've been feeling onto your encounters with them."

"All right." Her advice gives me something I can actually latch on to, a life raft in dark, turbulent waters.

"How about your writing?"

"I was making a little progress, but the murder's derailed me again."

"Consider giving yourself a goal of writing just ten minutes a day at first. And remember to practice your breathing, Bryn. Do it whenever you feel the least bit stressed."

I glance at the clock. Only three minutes left. I haven't even had a chance to tell her about Guy.

"How are things with Guy?" she asks. She has a way of reading my mind. "Has he been helpful during this time?"

I let out a long sigh and rake my hands through my hair.

"Things have been . . . off."

"In what way?"

"I can't quite explain it. He was upset initially that the murder might create an issue with the donors who were at the dinner. And now he seems distant. I think the police interview wigged him out, too."

"Why don't we really focus on this next week. In the meantime, could you try asking Guy about it?"

"You mean why he seems distant?"

"Yes, but don't put him on the spot. Ask him about his impressions of the police interview now that the dust has settled. See if you can get him to open up about it."

Something else to latch on to. A plan.

Before signing off, she asks whether I'm still okay with the mild antidepressant I'm taking, and though I'm about as much fun as a fever blister these days, I say I want to stick with the same dose for now.

After the call, I'm better, less agitated. Maybe she's right about the police. And I do need to talk to Guy. I've been tip-toeing around him, worried he's annoyed with me for traipsing down to Eve's office in the first place.

I notice, as I start to close my laptop, that I've accumulated a slew of emails in the past few days. I forward many of them to my assistant, asking her to handle as best she can, declining interview requests and assignments for guest blogs. It makes me feel as if life is hurtling by, leaving me behind. I want to engage again, I want to be the girl who captures the flag, but I still can't summon the necessary energy.

There's also an email from Barb responding to the one I sent her. Rather than meeting for lunch, she wants to know if I'd like to come by her florist shop today and have a glass of wine with her there. Four o'clock. Now that it seems likely that the police won't be bothering the dinner guests, I feel less of an urgency to connect with her, but I decide to accept anyway. Sharing a drink with her not only will help take my mind off the murder, it will be *doing* something.

The ping from an arriving text startles me. I look down at my phone and see that it's from Guy. I've forgotten to call him like he'd asked.

"In meeting but wanted to be sure you're ok. Let me know. xo."

I write back that I'm definitely better and look forward to seeing him tonight. Dr. G was right. I need to be more direct with Guy, the way I always used to be in our relationship. No more tiptoeing. It's time to leave the murder behind and get back to our lives. And from there I can hopefully make strides to put the accident behind me, too.

Later, I take off for Barb's florist shop. It's not in the center of town but rather on the outskirts. I lose my way, despite the GPS instructions, and end up being ten minutes late.

"Don't worry about it," Barb says, greeting me at the door.

"I'm just so glad you could drop by." She's dressed in a pink-and-yellow sleeveless Lilly Pulitzer dress, and her bright blond hair is pulled back with a pink velvet headband. She leads me into the store.

I'd been expecting a typical florist shop, stuffed with potted philodendrons and spider plants, and a glass-fronted refrigerator showcasing roses, daisies, and mums. But it's more of a garden store, and absolutely charming. There are huge, lush bouquets of blue and purple hydrangeas and captivating jungle-like blooms I don't even recognize. Lots of garden accessories, too, and off-beat items to put both outdoors and in: weathered urns, lanterns, bleached elk horns, mounted sea coral, and plaster copies of centuries-old Greek and Roman busts.

And the smell is intoxicating, both rich and exotic.

"This is absolutely gorgeous, Barb," I tell her. "What inspired you to open this?" My guess is that her husband, the soft-spoken Jerry, footed the bill so she'd have something to occupy her time once the kids were in school.

"Come, I'll tell you." She turns to the girl behind the counter. "Stacy, honey, I'm going to be in my office. Only interrupt if one of the plants starts screaming, *Feed me.*" She glances back at me. "Ever see *Little Shop of Horrors*? Sometimes when I'm alone here at night, I can't help but get freaked."

Her office is cozy, more like a den, with a pink love seat and an embroidered slipper chair. On a coffee table, which is actually an old Louis Vuitton trunk topped with glass, she's set out a plate of crackers, Brie so ripe it's dripping, and an ice bucket with a bottle of chardonnay. She pours us each a glass of the wine.

"Cheers!" she says. "And welcome to the area."

"Thanks so much. Did you grow up around here?"

She nods as she sips and then sets the glass down. "And except for college, I've been here ever since."

"So tell me about the shop. How long have you had it?"

"Just five years. I admit it was a risk because we're not exactly the typical florist shop. I won't even let a carnation in the door. But we're doing really well, especially during the racing season. I mean, no one's going to buy me out one day for a ton of dough, but I love it. And it got me out of investment banking."

"Investment banking?" I've guessed entirely wrong about her.

"I was with First Albany for years. But I woke up one day and realized I hated it. You work your fanny off in that kind of job and you never get to see your kids. I also realized I wanted something *prettier*. There's nothing pretty about banking."

A reinvention story, I think. She's someone else I might consider interviewing for my book. If I could just finish the damn proposal.

"Well, this is as pretty as it gets," I say. "I wish I'd known about your place before I bought the flowers for the other night."

As soon as the words are out of my mouth, I mentally kick myself. The last thing I want is her mind inching toward a certain question: *Eve Blazer wasn't your caterer, was she?*

"Oh, your table was lovely," Barb exclaims. "But if you're ever doing a big event and want assistance, we'd be glad to work with you."

"What kind of flowers are people most interested in these days?"

She toggles her head back and forth.

"It depends," she says. "If it's for an event at Skidmore College, they want elegant but understated. But the people who rent during racing season can be pretty extravagant. To them, a roomful of calla lilies is just another form of cock-blocking."

I laugh at the comment, unexpected but maybe it shouldn't be. Barb has a go-big style about her. I take a small sip of wine. The buttery taste is pure heaven, but because I'm driving, I won't allow myself more than half a glass.

"Tell me about *you*," she says. "I was sorry I wasn't at your end of the table the other night. Are you working on another book now?"

"Sort of. Getting started at least."

"I've ready *Twenty Choices*, of course—my whole book club has. Don't kill me for asking, but is there any chance you could make a guest appearance at one of our meetings this summer? That would blow people's minds."

"Sure, I'd be happy to." That's overstating it, but it'll be something else to focus on, like Derek's class.

"Great. I was a little afraid that Kim might have beaten me to the punch."

"What do you mean?" I ask, taken aback.

"I think she'd kill to have you at *her* book club. She's read all your books, you know."

I can't be hearing straight. There is no way she can mean the same Kim who seemed intent on pushing my buttons between bites of chicken tagine.

"Are you and Kim friends?"

"Not BFFs, by any means, but our social circles intersect at times, and I ran into her right before the party. She hadn't known until a few days ahead of time that you were Guy's wife, and then she was all in a tizzy. She was trying to find out everything she could about you."

Everything she could. That suggests a Google search, where surely she'd stumbled upon information about the accident, and the car exploding into flames.

"And did she? Find out everything she could?"

"Probably. That would be Kim for you."

And what about dirty tricks? Would that be Kim for you, too?

"Funny, she never said a word about being interested in my book."

"Maybe she felt intimidated once she finally met you."

I let the subject drop, figuring I'm hardly going to get the answers I really need from Barb. She tops off her wineglass and offers to do the same with mine; I raise a hand, declining.

For the next thirty minutes or so, we hang in her office, chatting. Or rather she chats, and I listen. Barb seems to run partly on the energy of her own voice, but I don't mind. I ask more about her decision to leave banking, how the dream for the shop evolved, as well as how she developed her terrific aesthetic.

At close to five thirty, I announce that, as much as I've enjoyed our visit, I need to be heading home. I want to allow enough time to fix a nice dinner tonight, which will give Guy and me a chance to really talk, as Dr. G suggested.

Barb walks me to the car and plants a kiss on my cheek, promising to email me time slots for my appearance at her book club.

On the drive home, the revelation about Kim weighs on me. If she left the burnt matches, I can't fathom her motive, though over the past few years I've discovered that certain fans can be simultaneously admiring and resentful. A few years ago, an author friend of mine learned that a woman slamming her on the Internet had once met her in person and claimed to love her books, even reciting whole passages to her.

Of course, it's going to be next to impossible to determine if Kim really *is* the culprit. I certainly can't confront her, not with her husband providing big bucks to the opera company, and even if I could, she's probably too slick to give anything away.

There's something that doesn't add up, I realize. If Kim's the one who took the money and left the matches, what was Eve planning to give me Saturday morning? I want to put the murder behind me, but how can I when there are still so many unanswered questions?

As I drive through downtown, a gourmet market beckons. Why not cook something special tonight, I tell myself, and decide on a pasta dish that Guy and I love, one we first tasted together at a little restaurant in Rhode Island where we had lunch the day after we met. I pick up a baguette, fresh fettuccine noodles, cream, and Gorgonzola cheese.

Back home, I put a pot of water on to boil, prepare the dreamy sauce, and make sure that there's a bottle of white wine chilling in the fridge.

Based on the note he left this morning, I expect Guy by seven, but fifteen minutes after the hour, there's no sign of him. I text to double-check his arrival time. No reply. I try his cell and his office phone, and both calls go straight to voicemail.

At a quarter to eight, I'm still alone in the kitchen. I feel a prick of annoyance. I wonder if he's made plans and forgotten to tell me. I take the lid off the pot and see that half the water has boiled off. I've been counting on dinner as a chance for us to have a normal conversation, maybe even as prelude to sex, and I don't want to end up irritated, with the mood spoiled.

At eight I try him again on both phones and still nothing. For the first time I feel a ripple of concern. It isn't like Guy to be incommunicado, and I can't help but wonder if there's a problem.

And then, at eight thirty, I hear the car pull into the driveway. I jump from the table.

"There you are," I exclaim, relieved, as Guy swings open the door.

He hasn't noticed me in the kitchen at first and jerks in surprise. He offers a wan smile that seems incongruous for the moment.

"Is everything okay? I was really starting to worry."

He lets out a long sigh. My heart jumps, though I don't know why.

"Bryn, there's something I need to discuss. I should have told you this weekend, but I just didn't know how."

Somewhere in the back of my head I hear a line spoken by a wife in an old movie, as he's about to confess to something that will uproot their marriage: *You're scaring me.*

"What is it? Is it something about work?"

"No, not work. It's about Eve Blazer."

Chapter 12

I STAND STOCK-STILL, AS IF FROZEN IN PLACE BY A WIZARD or sorcerer.

"You mean about the murder?" I ask.

"No. Something else."

My heart picks up speed. Guy's grim tone has unnerved me. "What is it?"

He's slipped out of his suit jacket by now and has draped it on the back of a kitchen chair. He places both hands on his hips, letting his arms sag, like someone momentarily at a loss.

"I had a drink with her. A few weeks ago."

"A *drink*? What do you mean?" I know that Guy occasionally discusses business over lunch or drinks with female colleagues and donors, but Eve would hardly have fallen into that category.

"At a restaurant. We had drinks at the bar."

Blood rushes to my face, as if I've been shamed. I can't believe what I'm hearing. "You mean like a *date*?"

"Lord, no. She called one day to say she wanted to show me a venue that might work for an event I was planning, one that allows you to use outside caterers. Once we'd looked over the space, she suggested having a drink there."

"Why didn't you mention this before?" Anger has started to merge with alarm now. Am I supposed to believe, yet again, that another relevant detail about Eve just slipped his mind?

"To be honest, I wasn't sure how to raise it. As soon as I sat down with her, I got the sense she might be coming on to me. I felt incredibly awkward about it."

"You don't *do* awkward, Guy," I snap.

He pulls his head back a little, caught off guard by my tone. He's not used to that from me.

"I mean awkward about bringing it up with *you*, in light of all you'd been going through. I didn't want to share something that might upset you for no good reason."

"What exactly did she do? This so-called come-on."

He shrugs, as if bewildered. "She ordered a martini for starters. It just seemed, I don't know, a little over the top for the occasion. When she said a drink, I assumed she meant a glass of wine. And then she let her hand sort of graze over mine. The first time I thought it might be an accident, but when it happened again, I could see she was up to something. I asked for the check right afterwards and said I had to head home."

I stare at him. Guy and I became exclusive shortly after we met, and he has never given me any reason not to trust him. I've fretted at times, of course—I'd be a fool not to with us living apart half the week. He's a charismatic, good-looking guy, and I know women check him out because I've witnessed it with my own eyes. But I've never seen him return a woman's gaze, never noticed anything the least bit fishy about his behavior, never caught him being secretive.

Except he's kept a secret about Eve, hasn't he? I think of my early impression of her, that she came across as manipulative and contemptuous of other women, meaning she was probably perfectly capable of making a play for someone's husband, including mine.

"You said a few weeks ago. You mean before I came up here?"

"Yes."

"Where? Where did it happen?"

"At the Sorrel Horse Inn—just so you know, it's only a restaurant, not an actual inn. It's on the road to Schuylerville."

"*Schuylerville?*" That's easily twenty minutes out of town. "Why would you go that far away?"

"She said it would be a nice change of pace for the reception I was arranging and really worth checking out."

A little voice inside me whispers: *People meet out of town when they don't want to be seen.*

"And so why are you telling me this now?" But as soon as the question spills from my lips, I know what answer is coming.

"When those two detectives admitted they didn't have a suspect, I knew they'd be looking into Eve Blazer's life," he says. "I thought they might get wind of the fact that I'd been at the bar with her that night and would raise it in front of you. I didn't want you to feel blindsided."

He shifts position finally, turning and stepping toward the sink. He pulls a glass from the cupboard and fills it with tap water, then takes a long swig. His dress shirt is usually still crisp at the end of the day, but not tonight. It's limp from sweat, I notice.

I don't know what to say or do. There's a weird discordance to his words, like a song sung off-key. Is there more than he's letting on? The question I'm about to ask sickens me.

"Did you have an affair with her, Guy?"

He spins around so fast the water jostles in his glass. His expression reads stunned.

"Bryn, honey, for God's sake, no. It was one drink, which I assumed at the start was totally innocent. And when I could see that it wasn't innocent in *her* mind, I took off."

"You're saying you haven't been unfaithful."

He looks off for a moment and then back to me, shaking his head.

"Absolutely not. You know me better than that."

"But if you were so aghast at her behavior, why invite her into our home?" I say, my anger spiking again as this question forms in my mind. "And you took her side over those fucking flowers."

"I'd already invited Nick and Jerry, and I couldn't cancel on them. I asked Miranda to find another caterer, but no one else was available on such late notice. So I told myself to simply act as if it was business as usual. That's why I barely said two words to the woman. And that stuff with the flowers—that wasn't about her in any way. As I told you at the time, it was about my frustration over not being able to help you."

For a few moments I stand there bewildered, my emotions in a hopeless tangle. The room is utterly silent except for a drip from the faucet into the deep apron sink.

"So what are you going to do about the police?" I ask finally. "Are you going to tell them this before they find out about it?"

He swipes a hand along the side of his head. "I already did. That's where I've been, why I'm late."

"You went to the *police*?"

"Yes, it seemed best to do it that way. To come forward and explain the situation for what it was in case someone from the bar saw us and reported it."

His answer makes me catch my breath.

"But, Guy, shouldn't you have consulted a lawyer before you talked to the cops? What if they think you *were* having an affair? What if they think you *killed* her?"

My whole body goes cold as I utter the last line. Guy could very well end up as a suspect.

"I considered calling an attorney, but I was afraid it would look suspicious to go in there all lawyered up. And besides, I have an alibi for the night of her murder. I was with Nick, remember? We went to that event at the dance museum, where thankfully about sixty people saw me."

Was that the night of Eve's murder? Yes, I remember now. Guy had been hijacked by Nick, and later, after he arrived home, we ate leftover chicken tagine in the den.

"The cops must have been pretty curious about why you hadn't brought up the drink when they were here last night." A snideness has crept into my tone, but I don't care.

"I said it hadn't occurred to me at the time. They were so focused on the crazy phone call you told them about and what that might mean."

I stand there trying to process everything. My glance wanders to the steam still shooting from the pot of boiling water. Guy follows my gaze.

"You were putting dinner together. Gosh, I'm so sorry, Bryn."

"I'm not actually in the mood to eat anymore." And I'm not. I've totally lost my appetite. "You'll have to help yourself to whatever's in the fridge."

"Let's sit at the table at least and keep talking."

"No. I just want to be alone."

I turn off the flame below the pot of simmering water. Guy reaches out, grasping me gently by my arm.

"Bryn, please," he says. His touch, both smooth and strong, seems suddenly foreign. I pull my arm away. "Don't run off. We need to talk this through."

"What more is there left to say? Unless you haven't told me everything."

"I know you're angry, and you have every reason to be. I've totally sandbagged you with this. But please step back and see this for what it is—a dumb little mistake. I had what I thought was a business drink with a woman who turned out to have something else on her mind. I did nothing to encourage her. Yes, in hindsight, I wish I'd told you, but you've been in a bad place, and I was afraid of making it worse."

His voice is calm and reassuring, the Guy I'm so familiar with, and there's a temptation to let that voice soothe me now. Yet part of me resists, and I'm not sure why.

"I don't know what to say, Guy, I really don't. I have to think about this. And right now, at least, I really want to be by myself."

I walk through the house, out to the screened porch. Outside, the trees make a swishing sound as the leaves stir from a breeze.

My stomach is roiling. I ask myself for the first time if I'm overreacting, perhaps due to the vulnerability I've felt since the car accident and my anxieties over the nursemaid role Guy's been relegated to. Since my husband has never given me a reason to distrust him, shouldn't I simply accept his story as true? But here's the problem: I don't *like* his story.

Maybe he did hightail it from the bar the moment Eve came on to him, but I don't get why he allowed himself to be bamboozled into a date to begin with. He's too savvy for that.

I stare into the night, but what I'm really doing is looking inside my head, zoning in on a moment from my *own* life. There was a time, pre-Guy, when I said yes to a drink with a male colleague, assuming it was a friendly thing, and then realized, a beer and a half into the evening, that it *wasn't* just a drink after all. Through both his tone and his body language, this guy had begun to launch heat-seeking missiles in my direction, attempting to discover how receptive I'd be if he came on to me full bore. *Dumb* of me, I remember thinking. Dumb for not having seen it coming.

On one level it seems unfair to fault Guy for the same kind of poor read on a situation that I've been guilty of myself.

And how can I blame him for not wanting to divulge the experience to me? Because of my never-ending funk, he's been on eggshells with me, and it's no wonder he'd want to avoid triggering any turmoil—like the kind we're in right now.

And yet Guy's confession gnaws at me. I'm bugged by

the way he looked off when I asked if he'd cheated, a micro-expression of evasion nearly too fast for the eye to detect.

There's something else, too, now shoving itself in my face. I'm remembering the words Eve spoke when I challenged her about the money: *Why don't you ask your husband?* Was there more to that comment than I ever imagined?

A sound pierces my thoughts. It's Guy's footfall on the stairs in the hallway. He's either wolfed down a sandwich or skipped dinner entirely. I'm conscious suddenly of how ex-posed I am on the porch all by myself, with Guy on the second floor and only a hook lock on the screened door. Eve may not have been killed by one of the waiters, but there's still a vicious murderer at large.

I back up from the screen, spin around, and hurry from the room. Once I'm in the living room, I shut the door and shove the bolt into place.

As spent as I feel, I'm not ready to lie beside Guy in bed. I sit in the den instead, reading a book without really absorbing the words. Finally, at close to midnight, I head upstairs. The master bedroom is dark, and through the half-open door I can see the shape of Guy's body lying facedown in bed, his arms stretched above his head.

I crawl silently into bed, staying closer to the edge than the middle. The time I spent alone tonight hasn't helped me sort out my feelings. I've been trying to weigh Guy's words and judge their veracity, but I realize I have nothing to use in my calculation other than my two-year-long sense of him as an honest and faithful man. That may not be enough.

In the morning I wake to the soft thud of the closet door

closing. I start to open my eyes but don't, and my stomach quickly cramps as memories from last night piece together in my mind. Guy's footsteps recede from the room, and I hear him descend the stairs. Only a few minutes later I pick up the muffled sound of his car pulling out of the driveway on the other side of the house. He clearly didn't bother with breakfast today.

I dress and go downstairs. Not surprisingly there's a note from him on the kitchen table: "Please let's talk tonight, Bryn. I'll be in Albany until after lunch, home early. I love you."

We'll *have* to talk, I realize, as I make coffee. I can't go on indefinitely parking myself rooms away from Guy and clinging to the edge of the bed. I'm going to have to either accept his explanation as completely true and let him off the hook for being naïve, or believe that there's more to the story than he's let on, that he's confessed to the drink rendezvous only because that information could leak out now that Eve's former life is under scrutiny.

And if I choose the latter, *then* what?

To distract myself, I wander into my office, open the reinvention file on my laptop, and start to type. It's not proposal-worthy bur rather simple stream of consciousness, ideas I've been noodling over in the last day or so, as well as a few observations based on what Barb shared yesterday about her decision to leave banking and open her shop. At least there are words on the page.

My cell phone rings right as I'm closing the laptop. It's Sandra. I'm grateful for yet another diversion.

"I'm so sorry I never called yesterday," she says. "I should have made sure you were okay; I ended up in swag-bag hell for most of the afternoon."

"Don't worry about it. I actually should have called *you* and said thanks for the tea . . . How did the bags turn out?"

"They're not exactly red-carpet caliber, but they'll do. I'm sure you've been given your share of swag at events, and it's never quite as good as you hope, is it? Gift certificates for places you won't ever set foot in. Cheap pens. At least these each have a nice candle."

"A girl can never have enough candles."

"Very true. So tell me, are you feeling better today?"

"Yes, much. I appreciate you checking up on me."

"My pleasure . . . There's something else I wanted to mention. It's about the chef, Eve Blazer."

My heart skips. Am I ever going to be *done* with this?

"Yes?"

"I decided to do a little snooping after all."

"About the murder?"

"No, about Eve. Remember I mentioned that an acquaintance of mine who used Eve was unhappy with her, and you asked what the problem was. I thought I'd try to find out."

"Oh, no, that's not necessary," I say hurriedly. "It was just a momentary curiosity."

The last thing I need at this point is for the cops to find out I've enlisted a pal to go trolling for details about Eve.

"I already tracked down the information. And frankly, I was curious, too. It turns out this woman walked in on Eve being extremely flirtatious with her husband. That's why she decided never to hire her again."

I take a deep breath, processing the revelation.

"What exactly was she doing, did your friend say?"

"Eve was giving the husband a taste of one of the dishes, and she was not only leaning extremely close to him but talking provocatively—and the husband was lapping it all up like a pathetic puppy dog. The wife's words, not mine. I thought it was interesting in light of what happened. You can't help but wonder if something like that caught up with her. That she set off a jealous wife. Or a jealous lover."

I warn myself to dump the topic, but I can't.

"Did your friend suspect that something more than flirting was going on?" I've tried to say it casually, though I worry that my tone betrays me, hints at my neediness for hard data on just how far Eve liked to take it.

"She didn't say, only that she gave them both a withering look that she hoped scorched their eyelashes off, and later that night she read her husband the riot act. Want me to see if I can find out anything else?"

God, no.

"Oh, that's not necessary. I appreciate you sharing the information, but I'd like to put the whole matter out of my mind at this point."

"I know what you mean. I've just been hoping it was a crime of passion so I wouldn't feel so freaked out. I actually had new locks put on both my doors.

"Do you live alone, Sandra?"

"Yes, which has never given me a moment's concern until now. But enough about that. Are you still up for lunch?"

"I'd love that. And my treat this time."

"Can you give me a couple of days, until I've made a bit more progress on this event?"

"Of course."

After we hang up I rise from my desk and wander through the house, mulling over what Sandra's divulged. It's hardly a surprise to learn that Eve came on to this woman's husband. Beyond what Guy has told me, I saw her in action myself—the sexy aura she exuded, the low-cut top she was sporting that day in her office. What astonishes me is that Eve would take such a chance in a client's home. That's not simply flirtatiousness; it's downright reckless behavior.

And that, I have to admit, adds a bit of credence to Guy's version of events—that Eve made a play for him. Was that the end of it? I have only my husband's word that he paid the check and ran.

I find myself at last in the kitchen, staring out at the yard behind the house. I'm back to the bottom-line question: What am I supposed to *do*? Accept Guy's story as the truth and move on? Or not? I watch the cluster of ferns at the back of the yard quiver gently in the light breeze. Guy will be home in a few hours, maybe even earlier, since I know he wants to sort this out. I have to *decide*.

A memory surfaces. It's a comment made by woman I interviewed a couple of years ago as a background source for *Twenty Choices*. She ran a large research organization, helping business leaders make decisions about where to take their companies. "In certain instances," she told me, "the right choice isn't obvious despite all the information you've gathered. So what you must do is gather even *more* information."

That's what I need, I realize. More information. I have to find a way to confirm whether all I have to blame Guy for is a flash of naïveté. As I watch the ferns wave, an idea takes shape.

I back away from the window and grab my messenger bag and car keys. The trip takes only ten minutes. As I pull to a stop in front of a row of brick and beige-painted clapboard town houses, I notice I've left a film of sweat on the steering wheel. I feel nervous, like I've decided to shoplift a piece of clothing from a department store and escape with it stuffed down my pants.

Fortunately there's no one around, only a middle-aged man perched on a power lawn mower in a nearby yard, lost in whatever music is coming from his earphones. Most of the neighbors are probably at work at this hour.

I head up the path to the closest town house and pause at the entrance of the apartment on the lower level. *Guy's apartment.* The one he'd rented a few months before I met him, after he'd taken the job at the opera company. I've been here around a dozen times since I met Guy but only once this year, a few weeks before the accident. If Guy *was* having an affair with Eve, he may have used the apartment, and it's possible there's evidence inside.

I take a long, ragged breath, find the key on my ring, and shove it in the lock. I'm about to do something I've never done before: spy on my husband.

Chapter 13

DESPITE THE BRIGHTNESS OF THE DAY, IT'S PITCH-black inside the apartment. I fumble until my fingers finally locate the light switch on the wall. Once I flip it on, the small foyer springs into view, like someone jumping out from the dark.

I step from the foyer into the living room, locating the wall switch for the overhead pin lights. As soon as they pop on, I understand why the place is so dark. Before moving into the house, Guy lowered all the blinds on the windows and pulled the drapes closed over them.

I shake out my hands. I feel even more jittery now that I'm inside. Technically speaking, this is my apartment, too, so I have every right to be here, but it's sneaky and sly of me to have come without informing Guy.

Get it over with, I tell myself. I swing my gaze over the small, L-shaped room. The place appears no different than when I was here last—the dark brown couch against the wall, two small armchairs in beige faux suede, the nondescript coffee table and end tables. After he accepted the job at the opera company, Guy had only two weeks to move from

Miami, locate a place to live, and prepare to hit the ground running at work, so he'd rented this apartment with the idea of upgrading once he was fully settled. The two of us met not long afterwards, and within a short time, he was spending almost every weekend with me in Manhattan. It suddenly seemed pointless for him to switch apartments, especially in light of his determination to relocate to the city in the not-so-distant future.

I take a few steps forward, glancing toward the short end of the L. It's empty, like a dark hole, and then I recall that Guy's desk once sat in that space. It's now in the house, in one of the bedrooms he's using as his home office this summer.

So far that's the only thing that seems different. And yet . . . I sense something oddly awry, a detail I can't put my finger on. And then it comes to me. The room feels unlived in. The books on the coffee table are perfectly stacked, the throw pillows neatly arranged and dented just so in the middle, like fedoras. Guy is neat but not *this* neat. It's like the photo of a room on a vacation rental website.

He's had it cleaned since he left, I realize. Which makes sense, I suppose.

I wander into the galley kitchen. The countertop is totally clear, everything put away, not that there was ever much in the way of tchotchkes. Glancing at the sink, I see that there's an empty glass sitting all by its lonesome in the basin. I pick it up and peer inside. Droplets of water at the bottom. Guy, I know, has come by the apartment once or twice to pick up extra clothes, and he must have had a glass of water while he was here.

I tug open the refrigerator door. Just a few condiments like mustard and mayo, bottled water, and a shriveled lime.

There's only the bedroom left. My pulse picks up in anticipation. Please, I think, don't let me find anything. The door is closed, and it creaks as I push it open. Once again it takes a few seconds for me to locate the wall switch before I can flood the room with light.

The blinds have been lowered in here, too, and the bed has been stripped of its sheets, with the duvet folded neatly at the base. Nothing's out of order.

I check the bathroom next. It's as clean and clutter-free as the kitchen, with no sign that anyone has used it in weeks. I exhale deeply in relief. There's nothing to suggest that Guy has brought a woman here, though I remind myself that he could have done so without leaving any evidence. Or he could have gone to *her* place.

I pass back through the bedroom, and as I'm about to turn off the light, I notice the picture on the bedside table, the photo from our wedding in a silver frame. It's a shot of me, Guy, my brother, and Guy's mother, who sadly died of a heart attack a few months after the wedding.

We held both the ceremony and reception at an inn on the coast of Rhode Island, near the town where we'd met, and kept it small, about thirty people in attendance. It wasn't marriage per se that mattered to me but rather a life with Guy, and therefore I wasn't in need of a big production to kick it off. And with my parents deceased, doing anything elaborate seemed inappropriate to me. It would have made their absence even more painful.

I step closer, lift the picture, and study it momentarily. Guy is wearing a gauzy white shirt and white pants, a wide smile on his face, and his arm is wrapped around me. I'm beaming. I'd just married a man with whom I felt in perfect harmony, someone who respected both my accomplishments and my independence and yet could also be a rock when life grew turbulent.

I set the photo back down and start to turn, eager now to leave. For the first time, I notice a faint scent in the room. It's unfamiliar, not something I associate with Guy.

Thank God there's nothing perfume-like or feminine about the smell. Rather, it's woodsy and almost incense-like, hinting at exotic places far away from here. I freeze in place and breathe deeply, trying to interpret what I'm smelling, but the scent soon evaporates. Maybe I imagined it, like a ghost silhouette in a corridor.

Two minutes later I'm back in my car and headed home. *Okay*, I tell myself, *you checked out the apartment, found no evidence of an affair, and now you have to decide how to respond to Guy.* But as I pull into the driveway, there's still a jittery buzz in my body, and I realize what it means: I'm not done snooping.

As soon as I'm in the house, I ascend the stairs to the second floor and push open the door to Guy's home office.

It's incredibly spacious, almost as big as the master bed-room, and, thanks to east-facing windows, bursting with sunshine today, a far cry from the gloomy apartment I've just come from. The windows are covered with elegant cream-colored drapes, tied back to let the light in, and the walls are decorated with a Victorian-style paper, featuring endless pale green palm fronds.

Guy has made a few adjustments to create more of a study/office feel. He's turned the bed so that it runs horizontally against the wall and doesn't hog so much room, set his desk between two of the windows, and pulled the armchair and ottoman out from the corner. Unlike in the apartment, I can actually feel Guy's presence here. He's left a blue crewneck sweater tossed on the ottoman along with a book he's reading, and there are two empty espresso cups perched on the fireplace mantel. Guy may not be messy, but he likes to own the space around him.

The desk bears signs of him, too. No laptop—he takes that to work each day—but there are several stacks of papers on each side of the blotter. I step closer.

There's no kidding myself now about the appropriateness of what I'm about to do. The apartment was one thing; Guy's office is a whole other story, a space he considers fairly sacred. Though he'd never fault me for popping in to grab a paper clip or an envelope when he wasn't around, that's not my plan today.

I also can't miss the irony of my morning activities. After weeks and weeks of being a slug, I'm now Miss Energizer Bunny, totally invigorated by my task.

I cross over to the desk and search the surface with my eyes. The papers, I see, are all work-related—promotional brochures for the opera, schedules, spreadsheets of numbers, and a draft of a solicitation letter. The only semipersonal item is an orange Post-it on which he's scribbled down the name and number of a restaurant we'd talked about going to this past weekend, before the murder upended our lives.

I'm not a hundred percent sure what I'm looking for. Maybe a receipt from a bar or restaurant he's never mentioned. Or a note that suggests he and Eve were more than professional colleagues. But there's absolutely nothing of that nature in view.

The desk has a narrow center drawer and two deeper drawers on either side. I start with the middle one. Neatly organized inside are basic office supplies—pens and pencils, a few note cards, and a box of staples. I search the other drawers next, but there's nothing of significance in either of them. I've started to feel vaguely nauseated. I'm rifling through my husband's desk, and I don't like that fact at all.

Something creaks behind me, and I spin around, my heart in my throat. For a second I wonder if Guy has come home midday, hoping to talk things out, but I realize it's just the house shifting, a sound I'm still growing accustomed to. I shove the last drawer closed and hurry from the room.

Descending the stairs, I realize I'm even more agitated than I was when I started on this sorry mission. Not only do I have squat to show for my efforts, I feel sullied by my spy mission.

In the kitchen, I spot a text from Guy on my phone: "Headed back from Albany. Home by 6. Please let's talk."

I still have no idea how I should respond. Part of the problem, I suddenly recognize, is that in my attempt to verify Guy's trustworthiness, I've gone about things ass-backward. My search has entailed looking for clues that Guy might have deceived me, all the while hoping I'd never find anything. Even if Guy *has* been unfaithful, the chances of finding evidence are slim. It would probably be smarter to try to confirm the specific story he told me: that he sat down for a drink innocently enough, that he left the bar as soon as Eve came on to him, and that he wanted to find another caterer for our dinner but had no luck. And yet I can hardly show up at the Sorrel Horse Inn and ask the bartender if he remembers a disconcerted-looking forty-something-year-old man hightailing it from the premises one night as a haughty blonde sat stewing alone at the bar.

And then I think of a way to verify at least one aspect of the story. It won't be hard, but I'm going to have to proceed carefully. I dial Guy's office number.

"Hi, Bryn," Miranda says, obviously having seen my name pop up on the screen. "Guy's not here at the moment, but he'll be back around two. Or you can try him on his cell."

"I was actually calling to speak to you—if you've got a minute."

"Of course." Her tone is pleasant enough, though she hesitated ever so slightly—wary, I'm sure, of whatever I'm bound to say next. She's Guy's person, after all, and I'm always reminded in subtle ways that her loyalty is banked exclusively with him.

"I feel kind of morbid bringing this up, but I have to find a new caterer. I need someone for a dinner party I'm putting together myself."

"Oh dear, yes, we're going to have to turn up someone new ourselves."

"I was hoping you'd have a couple of suggestions."

There's a pause, and I pray that she's reaching for a folder, one that lists the names she mustered when Guy supposedly requested she find another caterer.

"Gosh, I don't know," she says. "We used Pure Kitchen so consistently. But I'm glad you brought it up. I need to hustle and figure out who we can count on in the future."

Out of pure desperation, I give it one more shot.

"Um, I thought Guy had looked into backups at one point."

Another pause. I hold my breath.

"Actually, that's right," she says. I can almost taste my relief. "He'd been thinking of making a switch for the dinner party at your home, but no one was free. I can give you the names of the places I tried, but I can't really vouch for any of them. They're just suggestions I found here and there."

"That's okay, it'll be a start at least. Can you email them to me?"

"Of course."

And now is when I really need to tiptoe.

"But don't mention it to Guy, okay? I'm going to keep the dinner a secret until that night."

"Of course. I'm not forgetting about his birthday, am I? That's in September, I thought."

"Right. This is for something else—a party for old friends of his who are coming to town to surprise him."

I've put her in the kind of double bind I hope will guarantee she'll keep quiet. She's the type of executive assistant who doesn't want to withhold anything from her boss, and yet she also wouldn't chance blowing a special treat for him.

"I should let you go," I add. "Have a nice day, Miranda."

"You, too, Bryn. I'll shoot you the email this afternoon."

I thank her, and as soon as I disconnect, I exhale. So Guy's told me the truth, at least about that one key detail. He was definitely trying to bail on Eve for the dinner party, which supports the idea that her behavior had made him uncomfortable about the idea of being in the same room with her.

My choice is obvious now: accept Guy's story and move on. After all, I have no good reason to suspect my husband of anything really inappropriate. Of course, we're still burdened with issues that must be faced and dealt with. Our marriage is currently off-kilter, out of rhythm, and we need to find our way back to that easy connection we had before—forged by love and support and sexual heat. I'm going to work like hell to get us there.

I text Guy back: "Yes, let's talk. I love you, too."

Strangely my energy has not yet started to flag, and I feel the urge to *do* something. Though I'm still banned by my doctor from running, walking is not off-limits. I locate my sneakers and stuff my feet into them.

After locking up the house, I saunter through the neighborhood, along cracked cement sidewalks twinkling with shiny fragments of stone. Most of the houses in this area are on the posh side, and their yards are lush with flowers—azaleas, petunias, and impatiens.

As I walk, breathing in the intoxicating summer air, I fight off thoughts about Eve Blazer's murder, as well as the lingering guilt I feel about rifling through Guy's belongings. I just want to relish the sensation of my legs moving, of being outdoors on this sunny afternoon and not splayed like an old dog on the daybed. With any luck, I'll be jogging again by midsummer and savoring the rush that will bring.

As good as my body feels, I don't want to push it, so I keep the walk short, promising myself I'll repeat the experience tomorrow—and go even farther that time. I let myself into the house and climb to the second floor. At the top of the stairs I turn left. Before I can take another step, I hear what seems to be a rustling sound sneaking from the open doorway of the master bedroom.

I freeze in alarm. It sounded for a moment as if someone was in there, moving around. But it can't be, I tell myself. I made sure all the doors were locked when I went out for my walk. I've surely just heard the house settling.

I wait for a moment, to be sure, and then take a few steps toward the bedroom, eager to kick off my running shoes. The rustling sound comes again and this time I haven't any doubt. *Someone's in there.*

With my heart in my throat, I start to spin around, ready to flee. Before I turn fully round, I see Guy pass in front of the doorway. He jerks in surprise at the sight of me.

"Bryn—I wondered where you were."

"What are you doing here?" I blurt out. I'm relieved that it's Guy, but at the same time concerned. Maybe there's been another issue with the cops.

"I'm sorry I startled you," he says. "When I didn't see you downstairs, I came up here."

"But why are you home so early?" I cross the threshold into the bedroom and notice he's still in his work suit.

"I got your text on my way back from Albany. I . . . I was

so happy to see it. I thought I'd stop home for a minute to say hi."

"That's nice." And I mean it. The anger I felt last night has finally dissipated. "Though it may take my heart a few minutes to recover from the shock."

"I should have warned you." He glances down at my shoes. "Were you out for a walk?"

"Yes. I came in through the front and didn't see your car in the driveway."

He closes the gap between us and grasps my arms by the elbows.

"Bryn, please let me make this up to you."

Looking into his eyes, I feel an intense longing—part emotional, part physical—stir deeply inside of me.

"You don't have to make anything up, Guy," I say. "You just have to promise to be honest with me. There can't be any more 'I forgot to mention it' stuff or 'I didn't feel *comfortable* mentioning it.'"

"Agree. Totally. I realize that during these past weeks and months, I've been treating you like a china doll, afraid of making the situation worse for you. But things are so much better when we *do* communicate."

I smile. I've made my point and he *gets* it. Guy smiles back, taking me in with his slate-blue eyes. He leans down and kisses me on the lips.

My body melts a little into his as his soft, full mouth presses against mine. For the first time I realize that part of my worry has been from our lack of *physical* connection lately.

Unexpectedly, my body flushes with desire. I kiss Guy more deeply and let my hand run up the inside of his legs.

"I want you, Guy. Right now."

He questions me with his eyes, as if asking, *You sure?* and I kiss him again, more urgently. He nearly tears off his suit as I tug off my own clothes, and we fall onto the bed. We make love slowly at first, gently, but then with a mounting urgency that leaves me breathless. By the time we've both climaxed, my cheeks and chest are burning red. We roll onto our backs, and Guy rests a hand tenderly on my thigh.

"What a brilliant idea of yours, Ms. Harper," he says. In the dimness of the room I can barely see him, but I sense his grin.

"Not exactly a nooner. More what you'd call a three o'clocker."

"I wish I didn't have to head back to work, but I've got a four-thirty with Brent. The guy just loves to call a meeting that kicks off at the end of the day."

"Don't worry about it," I say. "I'll hang out and enjoy the afterglow."

"I should be back reasonably early, unless there's some issue with Brent." He hoists himself out of bed and grabs his clothes from the chair where he's tossed them. "Nick emailed and asked if we wanted to join him and Kim for a last-minute dinner at the Saratoga Golf Club, but I said we were tied up. I couldn't imagine you wanting to go."

Ever since Barb described Kim's fascination with me, I've wondered if she was the one who left the matches. A dinner with her and Nick would offer the opportunity for a better read on her. I have another motive as well, one that I hate to admit even to myself.

"I wouldn't mind actually," I say, propping myself up on an elbow. "Can you call him back and accept?"

"Really? To tell you the truth, it would be good for me to make the time for him. I can see now that he requires more hand-holding than I first expected."

"Let's do it."

Guy grins. "I owe you big-time for this. Let's figure around seven, and I'll let you know for sure."

As he flies out of the bedroom, I lean my head back on the pillow, luxuriating in the moment. There are still a few hours left to the afternoon, and I decide that once I'm up and dressed again, I'll take another stab at my book proposal. But suddenly my eyelids grow heavy. I feel a gentle wave of drowsiness wash over me, the intoxicating postcoital variety. It seems so refreshingly normal, so different than the body-slamming fatigue that generally ambushes me at this time of day, and I can't help but give into it. Soon I feel myself slipping into sleep.

And then the nightmare's back. I've woken in a hotel room, smelling smoke. I wrench the blanket off my body and thrust my legs out of bed. *Please*, I pray, *let me get out of here.* My feet hit the floor, and I propel myself forward, but the smoke thickens, making me gasp for breath. Each step toward the door is like trying to force myself through water.

"Bryn, wait," a voice calls from behind me.

"I can't," I say. "We need to get out."

"Please, just wait," he calls.

For some reason I turn around this time. By now the room is choked with smoke, and suffused as well with an eerie red glow. I squint, desperately trying to see. At first there's no one in sight, and then a man emerges out of the gloom. He's tall and broad shouldered, and his expression is fraught with worry.

"Bryn, *listen* to me," he whispers.

I wake with a start. I know who the man is, the one calling out to me.

It's Paul. Paul Dunham. The colleague who died in the car crash that day.

Chapter 14

SHOOT STRAIGHT UP IN BED. MY FISTS ARE CLENCHED and my heart is beating hard.

"*Paul*," I say out loud, into the utter stillness of the room.

The reveal is a shock, and yet it probably shouldn't be. I've suspected all along, because of the fire, that the dreams are connected to the accident. But I never considered that the man calling out to me was Paul.

Maybe . . . maybe the nightmare is nothing more than a crystallization of my crazy need to know the truth about that morning, the reason Paul drove the car off the road. And in the dream he's asking me to wait so that he can tell me what I don't know or can't remember.

Bryn, I'm so sorry, but I didn't sleep well the night before, and I dozed off at the wheel . . .

I saw a hawk overhead and let my gaze wander from the road . . .

It just came to me at that moment—a desire to die. Forgive me . . .

But I don't get why my unconscious chose to place him in a hotel room with me. It suggests sex, an illicit rendezvous.

The idea unsettles me. Paul was handsome in his own way, but I never experienced even a flutter of attraction toward him. And even if I had, he was married, and so was I, and I would have squelched any feelings immediately.

Positioning my upper body against the headboard of the bed, I dispatch my memory back to that night before the accident in Boston, to me sitting outside the hotel ballroom as a line of plucky, hopeful women, eager to have their books signed, snaked toward the table. Paul showed up out of nowhere—and also out of context. We'd brainstormed several times in meetings at the publishing house in Manhattan, and we'd even been to lunch twice, once in a group and once alone, but his appearance at the event surprised me. The explanation he offered had made sense—that this was an opportunity for him to sneak a look at my fan base as he generated marketing ideas for the paperback release of *Twenty Choices*—and there was nothing the least bit flirtatious about his manner, no suggestion of a come-on. And yet I realize now that on another level I'd found the whole thing slightly *odd* that night. Odd that he should arrive out of the blue; odd that he should ask me to dinner. I'd agreed to the ride home in part because he was a colleague and it would have been rude to say no.

Had there been an underlying motive that I missed, sexual or otherwise?

Maybe the location in the dream is simply because my encounter with Paul that night was at my hotel.

I slip out of bed and dress quickly. I'm now remembering a moment in my recent conversation with Casey that had seemed slightly odd as well, something I hadn't been able to put my finger on.

Downstairs, I grab my phone and call her. Her assistant informs me that Casey is on another line, but she asks me to hold, saying she knows Casey will want her to interrupt the other call so she can take mine. That's what bestseller status will do for you. As I wait, I pace my kitchen.

"Everything okay?" Casey asks when she picks up thirty seconds later.

"I'm not sure. I have a question and I need you to be completely honest, okay?"

"Of course. About the proposal?"

"No, something else. When we spoke the other day, I mentioned I was considering contacting Paul's widow, and I asked what you thought. You said you didn't think it was a good idea. Tell me why."

An awkward silence ensues, exactly like the one that occurred when we were discussing Paul earlier.

"Uh, it's just what I told you before," she says. "I hear she's still in a terrible state. I didn't think it would be beneficial for either one of you to talk right now."

"You hesitated, as if there's something more going on. Is there, Casey? Please, I really need to know."

I hear the deep intake of her breath.

"There *is* something, and I had every intention of sharing it. But I wanted to wait until you were feeling better. You've been dealing with enough as it is."

"Does his wife think I was having an affair with him?" I say. It finally hits me that if Paul surfacing at my talk in

Boston had seemed strange to me, it might have to her as well. "Is that it?"

Another pause.

"Apparently she's had concerns, yes," Casey finally says. "And unfortunately there's been buzz around the publishing house, too. People thinking that you and Paul were having a fling."

The news sickens me—not only do people assume I've behaved inappropriately, but also Stephanie has had these ugly rumors piled onto her grief.

"But why would they assume that? What are they basing it on?"

"Apparently Paul never told anyone, even his assistant, that he was planning to give you a lift back to the city."

"He wouldn't have mentioned it because it was decided only that night, when he came to my talk."

"But he hadn't mentioned his plan to do *that* either. It all seemed kind of secretive and clandestine to people."

My chest tightens, as if someone has gripped me from behind with both arms and is squeezing hard.

"This is dreadful," I say. "I can't imagine what his poor wife is going through."

"Now that you know, we should probably discuss how to handle it. You don't even have to tell me if the rumor's true or not. Just whether you think we should leave it alone, figuring the gossip will burn off, or institute any kind of damage control."

Damage control. That obnoxious phrase again.

"It's *not* true, Casey. There was absolutely nothing going

on between Paul and me. I admit—and this is just between the two of us—I was a bit surprised when he dropped by that night, but his explanation sounded legit. He was in the area, and he was starting to drum up marketing ideas for the paperback."

I'm trying to rationalize with her the same way I did with myself earlier.

"He didn't get flirty in any way?"

"*No.* He did ask if I wanted to grab a bite to eat, to which I said no, but there was nothing flirtatious about his behavior. In fact, if anything . . ."

And for the first time since that evening, a thought returns to me, like a muscle memory.

"What?"

"If anything, he seemed preoccupied, like there was something on his mind."

"Maybe he was trying to find the nerve to tell you."

"Tell me *what*?" I ask. It's as if she's had a glimpse of the final scene in my nightmare.

"I mean, let you know of his attraction. Make a move."

Despite the fact that Casey and I aren't face-to-face, I find myself shaking my head vigorously.

"I doubt it. And it's really beside the point because nothing happened between us. I can't bear that Stephanie thinks we might have been sleeping together."

"Okay, as we're talking, I'm deciding we should probably take action. It used to be that the best approach with a rumor was to let it run out of oxygen. But things are different now because of crap like social media, and we don't want this one gathering steam, especially since there's not a shred of truth to it. Let me come up with a strategy, okay?"

"Yup. Can you let me know as soon as you do?"

"Absolutely, and don't worry. We'll take care of this."

I hang up, shaken. And I can't miss the ugly irony of what Casey has divulged. I'm not the only one who's been agonizing about her husband's fidelity quotient. Not wanting any more time to pass before I jot down the dream, I retrieve my notebook from the screened porch and quickly make a note of this new detail.

It's not merely the dream that has my insides churning. It's that vague feeling I've recalled from the night of my speech, my sense that it *was* strange for Paul to drop by unannounced. Plus, my memory of him seeming distracted. Casey's remark replays in my mind, the one suggesting that Paul might have been summoning the nerve to come on to me. But that doesn't gel with what I knew about the guy. If anything, he seemed like a straight arrow, a man with a strong moral compass. When I'd asked him about his family at the lunch we had alone, he practically beamed as he described Stephanie and their two young boys.

Maybe there'd been a professional concern on his mind. Or even a personal one. Since *Twenty Choices* was published, more than a few friends and colleagues have taken me aside and asked for guidance on a confusing or daunting choice presenting itself in their life.

Regardless of what Paul's true intentions were, I need Casey to kill the rumor. For Stephanie's sake as well as my own.

I close the notebook and carry it with me back upstairs,

where I tuck it into the drawer of my bedside table. I probably should tell Guy about this development, but I have to find the right time.

It's after five. I shower for the second time today, still feeling sweaty from the sex. The night is warm, so I pick a sleeveless black dress for the evening, along with a pair of strappy sandals, the kind of dressy look I haven't worn since before the accident.

As I'm dabbing on makeup in front of the bathroom mirror, I'm struck by the fact that I look less weary today, less like an orphan-train girl. And I *feel* less weary, too. I'm glad we're going out. I have my ulterior motives for wanting to be with Nick and Kim, but it's more than that. This will give me a chance to be supportive of Guy and to bolster his efforts at work.

Guy texts me to say he doesn't need to change for dinner and will swing by and pick me up at seven, as planned. When I hop into his BMW an hour later, he's taken off his tie and jacket and laid them across the backseat.

"I figured I'd kill the jacket since Nick mentioned he'll be dressed casually," he says by way of explanation. "He was playing golf at the club this afternoon."

"I thought he had a really demanding job."

"He's got a big job in a business inherited from his father, with a lot of people reporting to him, though I'm not sure how *demanding* it is." He smiles wryly. "I have the feeling he hands off a lot and stays way above the fray."

"Should I have worn a Banlon golf shirt instead?"

He's pulled out of the driveway by now and glances over, taking me in fully.

"You look *perfect*, Bryn. Besides, I can't imagine Kim dressing casually. I get the sense from Nick that she's pretty high-maintenance."

"Does that work his nerves?"

"Not sure. He let it slip recently that she's wife number two, and maybe he wanted high-maintenance this time around. Some guys secretly dig that."

From the moment I met Guy, I'd sensed that high-maintenance was the last thing *he* found appealing. He's often said that, considering the craziness of his work, he appreciates how easygoing I am. What I'm unaware of is whether his appreciation is based on bad experiences with the opposite type of woman.

We don't actually know a ton about each other's romantic histories. He's heard about Marc, of course, and how things grew tense between us after my first book took off. And Guy has shared a little about Meg, the woman he was engaged to in Chicago before she broke it off—leaving him gun-shy about marriage for years—and about Julie, the doctor he dated for a while in Miami. Due to the whirlwind nature of our relationship, and the commuter aspect of it as well, we haven't had many long, leisurely talks about the past.

As I stare out the window, I realize I also don't have much insight into Guy's history fidelity-wise. I've always counted on him to be faithful to me—we've discussed the importance of trust—but I never out-and-out asked, *Did you ever cheat on your fiancée or any of your girlfriends?* I've been focused on *us*, on the present. Plus, my overriding sense of Guy from the start has been that he's open, honorable, and forthcoming, and I haven't required a lot of personal data to back that up. Maybe, though, I should have asked more questions. I'm not going to kick myself for not having done so, but now may finally be the time, as a way of helping me understand Guy better.

The place we're eating tonight, the Saratoga National Golf Club, is just outside of town. As we turn into the driveway, I ask Guy how I should respond if either Kim or Nick brings up the murder.

"Why don't you let me handle it," he says as a valet attendant opens the car door for me. "I'll figure out a way to redirect the topic."

Stepping out of the car, I take in the imposing stone-and-wood building in front of us. According to Guy, the golf club is open to the public, but it's clearly been designed to have the look and feel of a private club.

Once we're inside the clubhouse restaurant, we're led by the maître d' through the dining room to a covered flagstone terrace, where we find Kim and Nick waiting at a table right at the edge. Behind them is the lush green fairway with a pond that sparkles from the late-day sun.

Nick rises to greet us, and Kim, to my surprise, does so as well, kissing both Guy and me on the cheek and offering us a warm smile. Go figure, I think.

Guy's predicted correctly about Kim. She's not doing the casual thing. In fact, she's dressed in a stretchy red crop top, with the shoulders dropped down and big disc-shaped gold earrings, a striking contrast to Nick's Ralph Lauren polo shirt and khaki pants, and far sexier than her outfit the other night.

"Glad you could join us on such short notice," Nick declares.

"How do you turn *this* down?" Guy says, sweeping his hand toward the fairway. "Great company, gorgeous view."

We take our seats, and Nick wastes no time summoning the waitress. Guy, to my surprise, requests a martini, a drink I've never seen him indulge in during the week. As I request a glass of white wine, I sense Kim studying me, but when I look up, she simply smiles again, nicely. Maybe her behavior the other night was a total fluke or she morphs into an agent provocateur only when Nick is out of earshot.

"So have you been writing up a storm since we saw you?" Nick asks me. "I hear that when an author is hot, it's important to get a book out every year."

"That's true with certain types of fiction—like thrillers," I say. "But if you write nonfiction, you can let more time go between books."

"I'm sure your fans are already eager for the next one," Kim says. Again, sweet as pie, but no mention of whether *she's* a fan, as she supposedly admitted to Barb. "Have you already started on it?"

"I've been toying with a concept. But hey, if you have any ideas, I'm definitely open."

"Writing takes such discipline," Guy interjects. "I really admire Bryn for parking herself in that chair and doing it."

Is he covering for me, I wonder, or does he really believe I've been balls to the wall each day?

"Well, it's an honor for us to have you in our neck of the woods," Nick says. "Is this your first time here in the club dining room?"

"Yes, actually it is. I've been to a few spots in town, but generally when I came for up for weekends, we stayed in and cooked."

"Oh, that's right, you're still practically honeymooners," Nick declares, with a slightly lascivious overlay to his words. "Well, you'll love this place. And you should definitely give one of the steaks a try."

We take a minute to peruse the dinner menus, and by the time the waitress returns with our drinks, we're ready to order. Nick mentions he's not bothering with an appetizer, that we should go ahead if we want, though of course we follow his lead, and I'm relieved. It will mean a relatively early night. I just need to use it my advantage. I want to gain a better sense of Kim, and whether she has it out for me.

And something else. I want to learn for sure that Guy's told me the truth about attending the dance museum fundraiser with Nick. It will be one more way to bolster my trust in him.

During cocktails, Nick launches into the history of the club—where the land came from, how it was developed, new plans for expansion, his possible involvement in that expansion. The guy either loves the sound of his own voice or is simply enthralled with any aspect of real estate—or most likely a combo of both. Guy listens enthusiastically, because that's what his job demands, and I force myself to look attentive.

From time to time, I steal a glance at Kim. She seems to be eating up everything Nick says, as if she's his biggest fan—or she's faking it brilliantly.

Guy shoots a bunch of questions Nick's way, which he

gladly answers. It's not until the food arrives that Nick finally quiets down. He picks up his fork and steak knife and directs his full attention to the shoebox-sized piece of beef on his plate.

"How are the kids, Kim?" I ask. "Will you be taking a family vacation this summer?"

She twitches a little in her seat, clearly eager for the chance to finally sneak a word in. "We've got a cabin on Lake George, and spend weekends there, as well as most of August."

"Guy and I took a drive up to the lake once last year. It's gorgeous."

"Isn't it? The kids are now total rock stars on their water skis, and they can't wait for Fridays. Do you water ski?"

"Not since I was a girl." As I say the words, an idea forms, a way to possibly flush her out and determine if she left the burnt matches. "And unfortunately it's out of the question these days. I was in a car accident a few months ago, and I'm still on the mend."

I read the surprise in Guy's eyes. The accident is a subject I never bring up in public, so I'm sure he's wondering why I've raised it now.

"I'm so sorry to hear that," she says. "It didn't happen up here, did it?"

She either knows nothing about the accident or she's doing a good job pretending not to.

"No, when I was traveling on business."

Nick raises his head, like a jungle cat whose attention on a bloody carcass has been diverted by a sound from the brush.

"That's dreadful," Nick says. "I assume that living in New

York means you have access to top-notch docs, but Albany Medical has some terrific people, too. If you need any referrals, just let me know."

"Thank you, that's good to have in my back pocket." I say, keeping one eye on Kim, who looks all sympathetic.

"You're on the board there, aren't you, Nick?" Guy asks. From there Nick launches into a lengthy discussion of the center and his disdain for Obamacare. Guy indulges him, lobbing thoughtful questions. Kim beams. Plates are cleared and coffee is ordered. There's still another piece of information I crave, but I can't imagine how I'm going to tease it out.

As we sip our coffee, I hear the faint buzz of Guy's phone in his pants pocket. I assume that for courtesy's sake he'll let the call go to voicemail, but he excuses himself and disappears into the restaurant.

"Well, this has been fun," Nick announces.

"I'm so pleased you asked us." I grab a second to compose my next comment so that it won't seem obvious that I'm fishing. "I know Guy has really enjoyed the time the two of you have spent together."

"It's mutual. And I appreciate you letting me steal him last week for that dance museum event, and then keeping him so late."

Reeling in the truth turns out to be far easier than I'd imagined. I experience a flash of guilt from having checked up on Guy but instantly give myself a pass. I had to know that he was where he said he was. And he was.

"No problem whatsoever," I say. "Guy had a terrific time."

"Yeah, he said he enjoyed the dance performances, though I never got much of a look at them. I was there mainly to schmooze."

Guy returns to the table and says that if everyone's set, he'll signal for the check. Nick informs him that he made arrangements to have the bill paid before we even sat down. We both offer thank-yous, though Guy's mind seems to be elsewhere. He gnaws briefly on the edge of his thumb.

"Shall we?" Nick says, rising.

We cross the terrace and exit through the wood-paneled dining room, still half full with customers. Nick quizzes Guy about the opera schedule, and I end up walking alongside Kim.

"How's your friend Derek?" she asks, her voice as low as a purr. "He seems very charming."

"He's not actually my friend. He's someone Guy met through work and thought would be fun in the mix."

"Oh, really? You seemed so nice and cozy together, I assumed that you'd known each other for ages."

So here she goes again, now that Nick can't hear. In light of the rumors about Paul and me, her comment annoys me even more than it should. But I bite my tongue for the sake of Guy's job.

"Thanks again for tonight," is all I say. "It was lovely."

We're at the front of the restaurant now, close by the maître d's stand. Guy is reaching out to shake Nick's hand. I think Kim is about to do the same with me, but instead she dunks her hand quickly into a huge ceramic bowl on a table next to the stand.

"Here you go," she says, thrusting her arm forward and dropping an object into my hand. "You never know when you'll need them."

I look down, startled by the gesture, and squint at what's there.

It's a tiny box of souvenir matches.

Chapter 15

For a few seconds I stare at the matches, stunned by the brazenness of her gesture. When I raise my eyes, Kim is flashing a guileless smile, acting like the charming hostess who simply wants to make sure I've scored my cute little take-away. I glance quickly toward Guy, hoping he witnessed what just transpired, but he's caught in a last-minute exchange with Nick.

"No, thanks," I say, tossing the matchbox back into the bowl. "I've got all I need."

I hold her gaze and watch her eyes widen. My bluntness has caught her off guard, but I don't care. If she did take the cash and leave the kitchen matches, I need to completely rebuff her, regardless of Guy's position. And even if this is all a weird coincidence, she's a nasty woman. Her dig about me and Derek proved that.

As soon as Guy and I are seated in the car, I start to share what happened but catch myself. Guy is biting on his thumb again as he drives one-handed, his mind clearly still miles away.

"Is everything okay?" I ask.

"Yeah. I don't know, I guess I wish we hadn't come tonight

in the end. I like my job, but there are times when sucking up to a blowhard really gets under my skin."

"Wait, don't tell me you're not actually fascinated by the subject of commercial real estate and the ins and outs of site selection."

He smiles wryly. "Bingo."

"I thought you handled Nick perfectly. But it's clear he likes having you in his orbit and is going to do his best to keep you there. Could you figure out a way to distance yourself?"

"I don't think so. At least not right now. Maybe down the road."

Even in the dark, I see how hard his right hand grips the wheel, and I sense that his entire body's wound tight.

"Is there something else?"

"Just work stuff that's come up. I hate to lay it all on you, especially with everything else you're dealing with."

"Don't be silly, tell me. Does it have anything to do with the call you got tonight?"

"The call? Uh, yeah, exactly. It's another donor with cold feet."

"How badly do you need him?"

"A lot, if I want to beat last year's numbers."

"You'll figure it out, Guy. If this donor bails, you still have half the year to court new people."

"I'm going in early tomorrow to see if I can come up with an alternative plan for him, so he's not as jumpy. Still aim for the same pledge in dollars but maybe let him pay in installments."

As much as I want to bring up Kim's move, I decide not to go there tonight, not when Guy is both stressed and distracted.

Though it's not even ten when we arrive home, we both head straight to bed. My body aches with exhaustion, though my mind is totally wired. As I lie in the dark, I replay those crazy last moments with Kim in the restaurant.

If the matches weren't a bizarre coincidence and she really *is* the thief, I can't imagine what's behind her behavior. Is it a weird form of envy? Out of nowhere, I recall an incident in middle school. A teacher had read an essay of mine to the class, gushing about how good it was, and later, as I was hurrying into the cafeteria, a girl from class bumped into me and spilled an entire orange drink on my brand-new top and skirt. "Oh, I'm so sorry," she said, looking stricken, but I knew it hadn't been an accident.

As I scrunch the pillow, trying fruitlessly to find a comfortable position, I hear the shallowness of Guy's breathing and sense that he's still awake as well. Perhaps fretting about the cold-footed donor. I wonder for the first time whether his job might be in jeopardy. If he doesn't beat the fund-raising numbers from last year, it will put him in a tough position. One down year shouldn't be reason enough for him to be canned, but there's no way to predict how a hothead like Brent will respond.

I feel a pang of worry for Guy. Losing his job wouldn't be the end of the world—and it would nicely accelerate our plan for him to move to the city. Still, he's always believed that if he wants to take his career to the next level, he needs to have a three-year stint with the opera company under his belt.

Finally, endless minutes later, I feel myself drifting off. When I wake a little before eight the next morning, I discover that Guy is already gone, his side of the bed barely disturbed. Once I'm in the kitchen, I notice that he hasn't bothered with breakfast; he made an espresso and set the empty cup in the sink. Tonight, I tell myself, I have to encourage him to talk more about the situation at work and see if I can offer an objective perspective.

I drop a bagel into the toaster, wander into my office, and pop open my laptop. I'm determined to get back to my proposal, picking up from the stream of consciousness I started the day before yesterday. I first check email, wondering if there's any word from Casey.

No, nothing.

Without being fully conscious of what I'm up to, I drag the computer mouse so that the cursor lands on my address book, as if my hand is being tugged across an Ouija board. I click on the icon, and once inside, I type in Paul Dunham's name. The page opens. When I wrote to Stephanie after the accident, I recorded their home address. It's in Hastings, New York, a suburban town just north of the city. I wonder if she's moved, having found the house painful to live in after Paul's death. But no, she can't have. She would have surely decided that relocating would be too disruptive for the kids.

I lean back in my chair, pondering the dream once again, wondering why Paul is standing in my hotel room, calling out to me. What is it that he needed from me—or wanted to say?

I return to the kitchen for my bagel, and as I pluck it from the toaster, I see the red message light flashing on the base of the landline that's nestled by the canisters at the back of the counter. We'd originally planned to use only our cell phones in the house, but since Guy already had a portable phone at his apartment, we ended up lugging it here as a backup—only to ignore it most of the time. As far as I know, the red light has been blinking futilely for days.

I press the play button. A man begins to speak, someone with a voice I don't recognize.

"Guy, good evening, it's Chip Maycock. We need to talk, pronto. I tried your cell without any luck, but I'll give it another shot in thirty minutes. Call me no matter when you get in. They're insisting we come in tomorrow, and you and I should meet beforehand."

The call, I realize, must relate to a situation at the opera company, a serious one based on the urgency in the man's words and tone. I need to alert Guy right away, in case Chip Maycock never reached him. First, though, I play back the message so I can hear the time it was left and relate that detail to Guy as well. Wednesday, 8:17 p.m. *Last night.* About a half hour before the call Guy responded to at the restaurant. Maycock must be the donor with cold feet.

As the message continues to replay, my mind snags on the last line spoken. *They're insisting we come in tomorrow . . .* What's *that* supposed to mean?

Out of curiosity, I pick up the landline receiver and push redial.

"Good morning," a woman says cheerily after the third ring. "Maycock, Villa, and O'Hare."

Sounds like a law firm, and the thought unsettles me. I confirm my hunch with a question to the woman at the other end and then hang up. The muscles in my stomach have tightened like a fist.

Guy led me to believe that the call he jumped on last night was from a donor. It could be that Maycock *is* a donor, but based on the language he used—as well as the shit storm swirling around us—the more likely possibility is that Guy's gone ahead and retained an attorney, someone to help him navigate the situation with the cops.

That would mean he's done it again. Deceived me. After swearing to be totally straight with me going forward.

I can't believe this. I don't know how I can trust anything he tells me in the future—or *has* told me in the past. Maybe my earlier instincts were right and he *was* involved with Eve. I can't help myself. To my disgust, I imagine him touching Eve, kissing her, having sex with her.

Moments later my fury is heaved aside by dread. People are insisting that Guy and Maycock, "come in." That could very well refer to Corcoran and her sidekick, which would mean that they want to dig deeper about Eve.

I grab my bag and lock up the house. It's cooler out today, and the sky is overcast and swollen, but I don't bother returning for an umbrella. I want to hightail it to Guy's office and hear straight from his mouth what the hell is going on.

As I drive, I force myself to stay focused on the streets and be alert to the endless stop signs, but my mind keeps snaking back to the urgency in Maycock's voice. I fear that on the other side of the morning, there's a story waiting for me, and once I hear it, my life won't be the same.

After pulling into the parking lot of the opera company, I

take a few minutes to compose myself. The last thing I want to do is give Miranda a hint that there's anything wrong, so I can't tear in there like a she-wolf. And maybe nothing really *is* wrong. I have to wait to hear Guy's explanation.

The building is open today, so I don't have to worry about gaining access. I enter through the side door and make my way along the nearly empty corridor to Guy's office. I take a deep breath before tapping the door frame and stepping into the anteroom.

Miranda is standing by the file cabinets, a folder in hand and her mouth pinched in concentration. She's wearing a brown-and-white wrap dress that shows off a hint of cleavage and accentuates her curvy hips. Her red hair is tucked back behind her ears as if she's been at her work full bore today.

After catching a glimpse of me, her lips part in surprise. This is my second unannounced appearance in about a week, which she's got to find curious.

"Morning, Miranda," I say. "Is Guy here?"

"Oh, Bryn, hi . . . No, he's actually gone out."

"Do you know where? I need to reach him and he's not picking up his cell." That's a lie, of course, but I don't want to call Guy first and have him surmise from my tone that something's up. I want to confront him, face-to-face, and read his body language.

Miranda's back straightens, and I sense that protective vibe from her, the same one I detected on the phone the other day. She's Guy's person, and in her view there's certain information I may not be privy to, including his whereabouts this morning. For the first time I find myself wondering if Guy has had his eye on *her*.

"Unfortunately he didn't say. Is there anything I can help with?"

Her response seems genuine, suggesting that the Maycock appointment definitely isn't related to opera company business.

"Did he mention when he'd be back?"

She drops the file into the drawer and slides it shut. "He didn't, no. But it shouldn't be too long. He has appointments here late in the morning."

"No problem. I'll figure it out."

"You sure I can't help?" My attempt at a breezy "No problem" probably hasn't fooled her, but I can't worry about that now. I offer a rushed good-bye and take off.

Back in the car, I spend several minutes thinking through my next move. Guy might already be at the police station, and it would be foolish of me to turn up there. If I'm lucky, he's at the law firm. I Google directions and take off.

The law offices turn out to be in a large white clapboard house less than a mile away, and as I approach, I instantly spot Guy's BMW. My pulse starts to race from both trepidation and red-hot anger. Guy must have driven home from the restaurant last night fretting over this meeting and lain in bed losing sleep over it. And yet he never breathed a freaking word about it to me.

I pull in two spaces behind the BMW. My first urge is to storm in there, but I squelch it, praying there's still a chance I'm reading the whole thing wrong. Instead, I twist in my seat, giving me a view of the building, and wait for Guy to emerge.

Five minutes past, then ten. I turn on the radio, hoping the music will soothe me, but it's like nails on a blackboard and I finally shut it off.

It's a good forty-five minutes before Guy swings open the door of the building and steps onto the stoop, raking his hair with his free hand. Before descending the steps he glances in both directions on the street, perhaps making sure no one he knows has spotted him. His face is wrinkled in worry, not a familiar look on him.

I wait until he's reached the main sidewalk before climbing across the seat and pushing open the passenger door. The movement startles him, and it takes a couple of seconds before he registers that it's me emerging from the car.

"Bryn," he exclaims. Watching him, it's almost as if I can see how his mind processes my presence. There's clearly an initial thought that we've simply ended up on a particular Saratoga street at the exact same moment, an event destined to happen sooner or later in this small town. And then, like a key in a tumbler lock pushing up the next pin, he realizes this isn't a coincidence.

"I want to know what's going on, Guy," I say. "Why are you here?"

I sense him assessing, as if he's trying to calculate how much I know before he tosses out an explanation.

"You were right about me needing a lawyer, so I've hired one."

"You made a promise the other night to be honest with me, to keep me in the loop, and then one day later, you're sneaking off to see an attorney behind my back."

He glances back toward the law offices, checking, I assume, to see if anyone might be observing us, and then turns back to me.

"Did you *follow* me here?" he asks. There's an edge to his voice.

"No, I didn't *follow* you. Your attorney left a message on the answering machine. He said someone was insisting you come in again. Is that the police?"

"Yes, they want another meeting," he says, his tone softening. "Later today. I know I promised to keep you in the loop, but at the same time I didn't want to alarm you for no reason."

"For *no* reason? This affects me, too. Why do the cops want to see you?"

His shoulders sag as if in resignation, and my body tingles with fear. Something is coming. Something is coming that will change everything.

"The cops—they've been looking at Eve Blazer's phone record. You know, her calls and texts. From what the lawyer's gathered, they're curious about times we contacted each other."

"Wh—"

"It's all easily explained. The woman did a lot of events for the opera company, and that meant phone calls between the two of us."

"But wouldn't that be *Miranda's* job—to talk to the caterer?"

"She *was* in contact with her generally. But Miranda, as you know, leaves at six each day, so when there was a dinner, I might have to call Eve myself—if I was running late, for instance."

My mind almost hurts from exertion, and I realize that it's the result of trying to listen to him on two different channels.

I'm focusing not just on his words but also on what might lie beneath or between them, whether there's an odd choice of phrase that could suggest an alternate meaning to what he's saying. It seems utterly absurd, like I'm attempting to decipher a letter from my husband written in code.

"So you want me to believe these were all business calls?"

"Yes, absolutely. And even if for some reason the cops want to misconstrue them, I was with Nick the night of the murder. There's no way they could consider me a suspect. "

A word darts across my mind. One Guy said a couple of moments ago.

"What about texts? You said they looked at texts."

He glances down at the sidewalk, and then back up with brows raised. My breath freezes in my chest.

"Unfortunately, from what I can remember, there's one text they might take the wrong way." He grimaces. "It was perfectly harmless, but you've seen how Corcoran is."

"Tell me," I demand.

"I don't recall the exact words. Eve was confirming a menu with me, and she asked if I wanted a dish she'd fixed once before or had I found it too saucy, and I said something back to be cute. It was stupid of me."

"*What?*"

"Just something dumb. Like . . . like *You know I'm a fan of saucy.*"

The words feel like a slap across my face.

"That's not dumb or cute, Guy. That's *sexual.*"

"Bryn, please, it was just a silly thing I wrote off the cuff. You've bantered with male colleagues, haven't you?"

The truth begins to hammer at me, insisting I acknowledge it.

"You cheated on me, Guy, didn't you? I need to know."

Instinctively, he glances off and then, at light speed, looks back. My heart sinks.

"Admit it," I say. "You slept with her."

"Bryn, *no*. I already told you. There was nothing between me and Eve. You've got to believe me."

But I don't. His story is like a liar's tale, unraveling a little each day, rendering disturbing new details every time he's forced to discuss it. There's the way he looks off, too, afraid to meet my eye. And the text to Eve. It disgusts me to think of my husband sending a message like that to another woman.

"I want you to move back to the apartment, Guy. At least for now." The words come out of my mouth without me even having consciously thought them. I don't regret what I've said for a second. "I need time by myself, to think."

"Bryn, you—"

"I'll be back to the house in an hour. You can use the time to grab what you need and go."

I yank open the passenger door, hitch myself across the seat, and start the engine. As I pull out, I see him in the rearview mirror, his eyes riveted to the car as I drive off.

Without any plan at all in mind, I drive downtown and then keep going on Broadway. A McDonald's appears, and I turn into the lot, find a spot, and park. Within seconds the overwhelming smell of greasy french fries and cooked beef permeates the inside of the car, intensifying the queasiness I feel. I quickly roll up the window.

Is this the beginning of the end of my marriage? I wonder. I don't *want* it to be. I love my husband and it's hard to fathom he would cheat on me. But then I lay it all out in my mind: Guy regularly employed a sexy, provocative caterer; he used her at our house once without telling me; he had a drink with her and confessed only after it became clear I might find out because of the police investigation; he called her frequently and sent her a sexually suggestive text.

Despite Guy's protestations to the contrary, it all feels horribly fishy. And the text can only mean one of two things: that my husband is the type of guy who thinks nothing of sending a professional contact a message like that, or he sent it to a woman he hoped to sleep with or had already. I don't know either of those men.

That could be the real reason he tried to find another caterer for the night of our dinner. Once he'd begun a relationship—or a flirtation—he didn't want her under the same roof with me. No wonder he was annoyed when I went charging down to Eve's office the day after the dinner party. If they were screwing each other, the last thing he needed was for me to confront her. That comment she made comes to mind again. *Why don't you ask your husband?* Was she toying with me, daring me to discover the truth?

And maybe, I realize with a start, it was Eve, after all, who took the cash and left the matches. She'd have known about the car crash from Guy. If she saw me as competition, she might have taken special pleasure in fucking with my head.

Outside the car, the breeze sends a McDonald's bag skidding across the windshield, startling me. My eyes prick with tears. Tears of both anger and despair. A month ago I moved here to be closer to Guy, to de-stress, and to help myself heal both physically and mentally from the accident. Instead, I've got cops hounding me for answers I don't have, and I've just sent my husband packing.

What if I pulled out of the parking lot and kept driving all the way to New York? I could be back in my lovely apartment, close to all my old friends. But if I flee town, that's only going to ratchet up the police's interest in Guy and, in turn, me. To protect my possibly unfaithful husband, I'm going to have to park my butt in town.

What I need, I realize, is guidance from Dr. G, and I need it before our next session. I send her an email, asking for an emergency appointment.

Finally, when enough time has passed for Guy to have collected what he needs from the house, I return home. I hurry up the stairs to the second floor and tentatively open the door of the closet in the master bedroom. Part of me prays that Guy's clothes—the crisp dress shirts and beautiful dark suits—will still be hanging there, that I've imagined this whole horrible thing, but many of them are gone. So is everything from the top of his desk in the spare room.

Back downstairs, I try to distract myself in my office. I check email. There's a slew of messages, many from my assistant, eager for yeses and noes, and I send off a few responses. To my annoyance, I see there's still nothing from Casey spelling out a strategy for how to deal with Stephanie Dunham. Despite how preoccupied I am with both Guy and the murder,

I'm intent on quelling Stephanie's concerns, and I shoot an email to Casey urging her to get back to me.

I turn to the book proposal next. To my surprise, I dash off four more pages, working at an almost manic pace. After weeks and weeks of lethargy this sudden burst of energy seems bizarre, but right now I'm totally grateful for it.

Without warning, the room dims. I realize that the sun has finally sunk from the sky. I rise from my desk and cross the hall to the kitchen. It's dark in there, too, and I quickly snap on the overhead lights. As I glance toward the stove, an image comes to me, unbidden. Eve swirling oil in a saucepan. And then Eve on the floor of her office, an ax protruding from her face. I squeeze my eyes tight, trying to force it away.

I slosh wine into a glass and, taking it with me, move through the house, flicking on lights as I go. With so many empty rooms, the place seems desolate. When I first saw the house, I wondered why Guy had rented something this large for the two of us but quickly told myself that his goal had been to make the summer special. But the house feels overwhelming now.

I unlock the door to the screened porch and step out there, switching on one of the table lamps. My nostrils fill with the now familiar scent of honeysuckle, and from just off in the distance, I hear the neighbor's dog bark angrily and then abruptly stop. I glance at the daybed where I've spent so many hours.

Did Guy even *want* me here? Perhaps my suggestion that I move to Saratoga for the summer inadvertently foiled his plan to spend more time in bed with the buttery-blond chef.

She was killed in a rage, I think, and not, as it turns out, by one of the waiters. Probably by someone who'd been seething with jealousy or unrequited lust. Involuntarily, I press my hand to my lips as an idea registers. If Guy was sleeping with Eve, that puts the two of us in the orbit of her killer. It's possible that the murderer was a former lover of Eve's—or even a current one—who found out about Guy or even saw them together. Eve might have been killed *because* of Guy. The killer might want Guy next. Or even me.

I don't want to be out here, not with just a hook-and-eye lock on the door to the outside. I turn to go.

And then I see it.

The shape of a man. He's standing in the dark, on the other side of the screen, staring in at me.

Chapter 16

I JERK BACKWARD, AS IF FEAR HAS SNATCHED ME BY THE nape of my neck. The form doesn't move. It's frozen, like a statue. I wonder if it might be a shadow, one cast by the moonlight.

But then I see it shift, almost imperceptibly.

I glance toward the door to the yard, trying to calculate the seconds it would take the man to reach there and tear it open. I have to get out of the room, back into the house.

With my heart pounding, I step backward. My butt knocks against the edge of the couch and I stumble. The wineglass slips from my hand and shatters on the brick floor, wine splashing everywhere. I right myself and start to turn, desperate to flee.

"*Bryn?*" It's the man in the yard. For a split second, I think it might be Guy, but then realize it isn't.

"Who's there?" I call out.

"Bryn, I'm so sorry I startled you. It's Derek. Derek Collins."

I can't imagine what he's doing standing outside my house in the dark.

"You scared the hell out of me," I say. I still see only his form.

"I know, I feel terrible. I wanted to drop something off for you, and it was stupid of me to come around this way."

I exhale, relishing the relief that's pouring through me.

"Why don't I let you in? But be careful. I just broke a glass."

I cross the room, lift the metal hook from the eye, and push open the screened door. As Derek steps into the light, a folder in hand, I can tell by his expression that he's embarrassed. He immediately offers to help me clean up the mess on the floor.

"Thanks, but let me get a broom first."

I return a minute later with a broom, dustpan, paper towels, and a wet sponge. Together we cautiously dab at the spilled wine and sweep up the shards of glass. Despite the mess, I'm glad he's here. It's good not to be alone in this big empty house tonight.

"Fortunately white wine blends in beautifully on a brick floor," I say, smiling.

"You're nice to let me off the hook."

"Don't be silly. Would you like a glass of wine? I'm going to pour another for myself."

"I'd love that if you don't mind."

I lead him from the porch, bolting the inner door behind me, and then into the kitchen, where I take two stemmed glasses down from the cabinet. I motion for Derek to take a seat at the table. He's wearing jeans and a navy T-shirt, and he's had his hair trimmed since I saw him the other day, perhaps preferring a shorter cut for the summer. It highlights those crazy features of his that, improbably, end up coming together in such a compelling way.

"Again, so sorry for nearly sending you into cardiac arrest," he says. "I've been hauling around this folder that I wanted to drop off for you, and by chance I ended up on your street tonight. When I saw all the lights on, I figured you might not mind if I popped in. I started up the path but then noticed movement on the porch, so I circled around to the side."

"What's in there?" I ask, nodding toward the folder. Derek slides it in my direction, and as I reach out to accept it, there's an awkward moment when our fingers accidently brush.

"A little bit about my students, plus a description of what we've focused on during each class. I thought it might be useful to have background when you prep for your talk."

"Perfect, I'll take a look." I wonder if I'll even *be* in Saratoga in a few weeks time, but I can't alert Derek to that.

"I told the kids this week that a very successful nonfiction author is coming in as a guest lecturer. They seem really amped about it."

"I hope they're not expecting Lena Dunham or someone incredibly fun and cutting-edge like that."

"Doubtful. I get the feeling they find me horribly square—they're probably expecting the woman who wrote the book on the Japanese art of tidying."

I smile again. To me there's nothing square about Derek. Rather, he seems grounded, someone who's given careful consideration to what matters most to him—teaching, for instance, finishing his novel—and acted accordingly. He takes a drink of wine and sets his glass down on the table with a clink. "Where's Guy tonight?" he asks.

"He's out with a potential donor," I say, probably too

quickly. I like Derek and I feel comfortable with him, but I'm certainly not going to drop even a hint that there's a problem in my marriage.

"I bet he must have to do a lot of that in his line of work."

I nod in agreement. His gaze sweeps across the room, and I wonder if he's thinking about the dinner the other night and how Eve was in this very room.

"I hear they still don't have a suspect in Eve Blazer's murder," he says.

"Is that on good authority, or only local buzz?" I don't want to appear overeager, but I need to learn as much as I can.

"Pretty good authority. I heard it from a local reporter who's a buddy of mine."

"The cops must have *some* clues, though, right?"

"I don't know. What he *did* say was that they're interviewing guys she used to go out with. Apparently she had a pretty active social life."

"Dating a lot of guys at once, you mean?"

"Well, *dating* would be the polite way to put it."

My stomach twists. It's exactly what I feared, that the killer might be a former lover of Eve's. This, I suddenly realize, may be why the cops have an interest in Guy despite the fact that he has an alibi. If he slept with Eve, they'll want to uncover what he knows about any other men in her life.

Derek takes another slug of wine. "What have you heard from your end?"

"*My* end?" Why does he assume I know anything?

"I thought the cops might have been in touch with you because she'd worked at your house."

"No, I haven't heard a thing. I doubt they like to share."

He studies me quietly for a few moments. Does he sense how frayed my nerves are? Has he guessed I know more about the police investigation than I'm letting on? I try to think of a breezy comment to throw out, but my brain goes blank.

"Sorry to have gotten off on such a grim topic," he says. "How are things going otherwise? Are you enjoying being here?"

"It's had its ups and downs," I admit, because I'm not up for telling yet another lie. "The murder's weighed on me. Plus, I haven't really had a chance to experience the town yet."

"Well, we have to fix that. Why don't you let me show you around the battlefield? Guy, too, if he can make it."

"I'd like that. Perhaps in a few days, okay? I want to finish a proposal I'm working on."

"Deal."

Derek takes a final swig of his wine and rises from the table.

"I should let you get back to your evening. Let me know if you have any questions once you've read over the material."

I see him to the front of the house. He smiles, says good-bye, and starts to turn. Then he looks back.

"Bryn, what you said about the murder weighing on you. You've had a lot to deal with this year. If you ever need anything, don't hesitate to reach out to me."

"Thank you, Derek." His comment touches me but also adds to the slight awkwardness I'm feeling. "I appreciate that."

I shut the door behind him, slip the bolt into place, and stand for a moment in the large hallway. I hear the sound of Derek's car starting up and receding down the street. My dread balloons again at the thought of being alone tonight in the house.

I make another sweep around the downstairs rooms, checking doors and windows. I leave every light blazing. To anyone driving by, the house probably looks like a cruise ship steaming across the ocean at night.

As expected, I can't fall asleep to save my life. The house, which seemed so silent before Derek's arrival, now begins to creak and groan. *It's shifting*, I tell myself, but the sounds are like footsteps and doors being stealthily opened and closed. What if the murderer is watching the house, wondering where Guy is? What if he knows I'm all alone here?

When the noises aren't torturing me, my thoughts do the job. I don't know what to believe about Guy and Eve, or how I'll ever figure out the truth. Even if I *do* learn the facts and discover that Guy's biggest sins are a flirty text to Eve and consenting to a drink with her, I'm not sure how I'd respond. For some women that would hardly be grounds for divorce. Maybe he was simply hungry for a little female attention this spring because I've been as tantalizing as a rag doll.

What seems like hours later, I finally nod off and wake a little after seven, bleary-eyed. When I see the empty side of the bed, my first thought is that Guy is already up for the day, and then reality slams into me. My husband isn't here. My marriage is in trouble.

Downstairs I make an espresso and chug it down. I half expect there to be a message from Guy on my phone, urging me once again to believe him. But there's nothing, just a text from Derek, thanking me for the wine.

Despite how sleep-deprived I am, I feel a sudden urge to *do* something, to take control of my life. I stand for a few moments, cup in hand, waiting for my gut to tell me what it should be.

And then I know. It comes to me as hard and undeniable as a shove from behind. I'm going to drive to Hastings and talk to Stephanie Dunham. I'll let Casey do what she can to fight the rumor that's spread at the publishing house. Stephanie is a separate matter, and I need to handle that myself.

For a reason I can't explain, this decision takes priority in my mind, even with all the other drama going on in my life. If I can put Stephanie's fears to rest, perhaps I'll be better able to focus on everything else. There's more to it than that actually. A part of me hopes that a conversation with Paul's widow may provide insight into the message my nightmares are trying to convey.

I could call Stephanie, of course, instead of showing up at her door. I worry, though, that she'd hang up before I could get more than my name out. Besides, this is a discussion that needs to happen face-to-face so that Stephanie can read me and see I'm telling the truth, that Paul and I were never involved. There's a chance, of course, that she won't be there. But she's a stay-at-home mom, and if I hang by the house long enough, she'll hopefully appear.

I'm in the car by nine, with a small cooler from the pantry that I've packed with a sandwich and a couple of bottles of iced tea. Based on what I've found online, the trip should take just under three hours. One thing becomes crystal clear the moment I shove the key into the ignition. In my determination to make the trip, I've neglected to factor in what it might be like for me to be behind the wheel on a major highway. This will be the first time I've driven on anything other than a city street or rural road since the accident.

Panic starts to roll through me as I back out of the driveway, and I do my best to squash it. There's a greater task at hand that I need to attend to, and I can't have my pants scared off at the sheer thought of the drive. I pop in a CD of soothing classical music and control my breathing like Dr. G taught me.

Periodically I sip on iced tea, and halfway there, I devour half the sandwich. I keep waiting for that now-familiar wallop of fatigue that loves to arrive midmorning, but oddly it never rears its head. And miraculously, I manage to keep my mind focused on the journey and not the awful mess I've left back in town.

Here and there along the way, road signs announce the distance to New York City: 170 miles, 150 miles, 120 miles. How easy it would be, after visiting Stephanie, to jump back on the highway and drive south rather than north. As I cross the Tappan Zee Bridge and spot the silver skyline of Manhattan, in miniature from this distance, I find the idea hard to let go of. While it's tempting, I also know it won't help matters in the long run.

Once I'm in Hastings, I locate the Dunham residence easily enough. It's a pretty stone-and-clapboard house, probably four bedrooms and set on a plot that slopes downward into a kind of hollow, thick along the sides with firs and maples. There's a soccer net in the front yard and a lolling golden retriever, prevented from absconding, I assume, by an invisible electric fence. The dog suggests that someone is indeed home.

Of course, that's only the first hurdle crossed. This conversation is going to be clunky as hell, and there's a chance Stephanie won't buy what I have to say.

There's no path to the house, just the driveway, so I choose that over crossing the yard. The dog has raised its head by now and is wagging its tail in an enthusiastic welcome. Well, at least someone is glad I'm here.

As I step onto the small porch, I pick up the sound of kids playing in the front of the house. I ring the doorbell. A boy's voice yells, "I'll get it," but I hear a woman tell him no, to let her. I take a long, deep breath.

A moment later a woman swings open the main wooden door. I'm still standing behind a glass storm door, one so smudged with fingerprints that it's hard to make out the features of the person on the other side, but I have no doubt it's Stephanie. She's in mom jeans and a short-sleeved blouse, and her hair is raven black. That's the one thing I remember from the picture Paul tugged from his wallet at lunch.

"Can I help you?" she asks, opening the glass door a few inches.

"You must be Stephanie," I say. "I'm Bryn Harper, and I was hoping we could talk." But before I even get my name out, I see that she recognizes me, and her body stiffens. I feel like a witch who's come bearing poison apples.

"What about?" Just two little words, but they easily betray her bitterness.

"There's something urgent I need to tell you. May I please come in?"

For a moment I think she's going to send me packing, but she lets out a ragged sigh, nods, and opens the storm door wider. As I step over the threshold, the dog muscles in along-side of me.

"We can talk in the kitchen," she says.

I follow her in, with the dog trooping behind us. As I'm led down the hall, I spot a gaggle of young boys in the living room. Improbably, they are neither watching TV nor playing video games and instead are using a huge packing box as a fort or castle, scrambling inside and out of it. I assume I've come on a day that falls between the end of the school year and the start of any kind of summer camp.

The kitchen is large and painted a welcoming shade of yellow, with a sofa and chairs at the far end. It couldn't be more cluttered, though, with counters and tabletops strewn with an endless array of random items—six-packs of soft drinks, bags of peanuts still in the shell, shoe boxes, books, a faux gold trophy, Kadima paddles, a toolbox, jumbo bottles of shampoo and conditioner, and a multicolored papier-mâché piñata, per-haps reserved for an upcoming birthday party. The disorder seems to be a testament to how overwhelmed Stephanie must be by grief and single parenthood—and, of course, the awful doubts she has about Paul.

"Do you want to sit down?" she asks, nodding toward the denim-covered sofa. I suspect she would prefer the answer to be no, but my gut tells me this will go better if we sit rather than try to talk while standing in the middle of the chaotic kitchen.

"Sure," I say, and take a spot on the couch. The dog walks over and lies not by my feet but directly *on* them. After a mo-ment's hesitation, Stephanie lowers herself into an armchair across from me.

She's not a classically pretty woman—her eyes are plain, and her mouth is unusually small, like the bud of a flower—and yet she's attractive in her own way. There's that great raven-colored hair, practically gleaming, and she's got a nice figure. But what's most startling about her are the deep gray-blue circles under her eyes, almost like bruises. I can only imagine how much pain Paul's death has caused her.

"Butch," she says to the dog. "Go play with the boys."

"No, really, he's fine . . . I want to get right to the point. My agent told me on the phone this week that there's been talk at the publishing house that Paul and I were involved—and that you've heard this gossip, too. I want you to know that there was absolutely nothing going on between the two of us. I feel terrible that you've been subjected to this."

She presses her lips together tightly, and I can practically see her tossing my words around in her head.

"The two of you just happened to be in Boston on the same night and then decided to drive back in the car together?"

"Yes, that's exactly the way it happened."

Her eyes register nothing but skepticism.

"I'm not sure what business Paul had in town, but he dropped by the event totally on the spur of the moment," I add. "He said it might give him a few ideas for marketing the paperback of *Twenty Choices*. When I was in the hospital, I explained everything to my editor, and also the state police, and I assumed it was shared with you."

She lowers her head and wipes what I guess to be a tear from her eye.

"They told me what you said, but it doesn't add up. Why

wouldn't Paul mention to me that he was planning to drive you back to the city?"

I realize in this moment that I'm in the exact same boat as she is. Forced to examine and reexamine little clues that hint maddeningly at infidelity but don't provide any real answers.

"That was a spur-of-the-moment thing, too. He asked if I needed a lift home, and I decided it would be less of a hassle than taking the train. The bottom line is that Paul and I were *just* colleagues. There was never anything inappropriate about his behavior."

She stares at me, clearly still skeptical. I worry that I've begun to sound like I'm protesting too much. But I don't know where to go from here. I have no proof I can present her.

"There's something else," she says finally.

She rises from the chair, crosses the room, and disappears down the hallway. I can't imagine what's coming next. A few minutes later, she reenters the room with a piece of paper in her hand. She approaches the couch again and thrusts what she's carrying toward me.

It's an envelope.

"Go ahead," Stephanie says. "Open it."

I raise the flap with my thumb. Is there a note inside? I wonder. Words Paul wrote about me? I don't find a note however. Instead, there's a photograph.

For a few moments I study the image. My heart's beating a little faster, though there's nothing obviously alarming about the photo. It's a posed shot of Paul, me, and one other person, Jason Klein, the well-regarded president of the publishing house. Jason's attention has been momentarily diverted, and he's looking off to the left, but Paul and I are staring straight into the camera, smiling, and Paul has placed an arm around my shoulder in that convivial way people do for group shots. At first I think it must be a photograph from the launch party for *Twenty Choices*, but then I notice my long-sleeved dress and knee-high boots and realize it's actually been taken at a smaller party last November, one the publisher organized spontaneously to celebrate my book sales blowing through the roof. My editor is at the very edge of the frame of the picture, chatting with Guy, who'd driven down that night from Saratoga for the party.

"But, Stephanie," I say, "we were just posing for a picture at a party for my book."

"I found it hidden under the blotter in his home office. As if he didn't want me to see it."

"You have to believe me. Nothing was going on between us."

One of the boys has popped his head into the kitchen from the hallway.

"Can Aiden stay for lunch?" he asks.

"Yes, but he needs to let his mother know."

"Can we have grilled cheese?"

"Maybe. But right now I'm busy. Please go back and play."

He shrugs and retreats. Stephanie returns her attention to me.

"Look at the other side of the envelope," she says.

Slowly I turn it over. On the front there's something scribbled in pencil. It looks like a man's handwriting, so I assume it must be Paul's. Just five words.

"This is all I have."

Chapter 17

HAVE NO WAY OF KNOWING WHAT THE WORDS ACTU-
ally refer to, but they unsettle me. They suggest forlornness,
perhaps a man feeling desperately alone in the world. Regardless, though, it seems improbable that these words could have
anything to do with me.

"Stephanie, it makes no sense," I say, looking up. "Is this
definitely Paul's handwriting?"

"Yes."

"Was Paul— Was he depressed recently?" I've considered
more than once that Paul drove the car off the road intentionally, and I was collateral damage from his suicide.

This time Stephanie's eyes swell with tears.

"Not that I could tell. But he suffered from depression in
the past—when his father died right before we were married.
He was on medication for a while."

"Maybe he stuck the photo in an envelope with these
words already written on them, and they have nothing to do
with the picture whatsoever."

She rolls her eyes dismissively. "So you're giving him an
A-plus for recycling then?"

"I'm simply trying to figure out a possible explanation. Because it's hard to believe that the words relate to me. We'd met only a handful of times."

Stephanie shakes her head, not so much as a no, but in frustration that she probably will never know the real story behind the photo and the mysterious phrase jotted on the envelope. Over my shoulder, her son calls out again.

"Mom, we're starving, *please*."

"I should go," I say. I rise from the couch.

"In a minute," she tells her son. "Have Aiden call his mother and let her know he's staying."

"Maybe," I say, as her son ducks from the room again, "it's the only photo Paul had of the event that night, and he was making note of it." But even as I offer that explanation, I realize it's stupid. Paul would have access through the company to all the photos taken that night, and besides, why would they have mattered to him? He would be focused on consumer rather than trade marketing, and he would have had little use for the party photos.

Stephanie rises, too, and sighs heavily.

"There's one more thing," she tells me. She twists her head, making sure, I assume, that her son isn't hovering. "A few weeks before the Boston trip, I walked in on Paul when he was speaking to a friend of his in the den, and I overheard him mention your name. He quieted down the minute I came in the room. I tried to tell myself I was imagining it, but after the accident, I realized I hadn't been. It *meant* something."

"Was this a friend from work? Maybe they were talking shop. Talking about my book."

"No, it was one of his best friends from college, Gavin Bloom. He lives in Texas and doesn't have anything to do with publishing. It seemed like he was confiding in Gavin about you."

I pause for a moment, organizing my thoughts. My hope today had been to ease Stephanie's mind, but it doesn't seem like I've made a dent with that. I give it one last shot.

"Stephanie, I have no idea what the conversation was about, or why Paul saved that photo. All I can tell you is that nothing inappropriate ever happened between him and me. Not even a flirty exchange. These things must be weird coincidences."

"Perhaps he was infatuated without you knowing it," she says, her voice betraying her anguish.

"No, I would have sensed that and I didn't."

Finally her expression softens. The anger seems to have dissipated, and there's just sadness in her eyes now. She reaches out a hand and touches my arm.

"Thank you," she says. "Thank you for coming."

I'm momentarily tempted to raise the subject of my nightmares—after all, one of my goals today was to see if she might be of help in deciphering them—but it doesn't seem fair to prolong the painful conversation.

Back in the car, I sit for a couple of minutes, decompressing. I don't regret the trip, and yet I'm not sure how much I accomplished. I'm pretty certain I've convinced Stephanie that Paul and I were never lovers, but my guess is that she still believes Paul was smitten with me.

Was he? Despite my reassurance to his widow, it's possible that Paul fancied me without my being aware of it. There are all those weird clues to consider: his unannounced arrival at my talk, the tucked-away photo, my name overheard in a conversation. *Still*, he never came across as a man in the throes of infatuation. Perhaps Gavin Bloom could shed light on the situation, but I wouldn't have been comfortable asking Stephanie for his contact info.

Making my way out of Hastings, I reconsider a theory I posed to myself the other day, that Paul might have wanted my insight on a personal or professional dilemma. Perhaps he'd confessed his intentions to Gavin Bloom. If that was the case, however, he could have simply taken me out for coffee in New York.

Unless this was someone who hadn't been thinking or acting rationally at the time. There's still the possibility that Paul was suffering from depression. Taken one way, the words he scrawled on the envelope hint at a deep sense of isolation. It tears at my gut to think that Paul might have driven the car off the road in despair. Perhaps he'd seen me as a beacon of hope, someone who—because of my book—could provide guidance on a matter that was really troubling him, and then decided, in our short time in the car, that I actually had absolutely nothing to offer.

If only those last minutes would come back to me. We'd been on the road a half hour when the accident happened, and I remember only random snippets from the first portion of the trip. Paul lifting my roller bag into the trunk of the car, chunks of ice on the Charles River, passing through the toll booth on the Mass Turnpike, noting how surprisingly light the traffic was. After that it's all blank.

I toy with the idea of grabbing a coffee for the road, but don't want to take the time, and then quickly regret my decision once I'm back on the highway. I've started to feel dense with fatigue. It doesn't help to know that I'm going home to an empty house.

Halfway to Saratoga, I pull off the road for gas and a silo-sized container of coffee. While fueling up, I see that there's an email from Dr. G, replying to yesterday's plea for an emergency appointment. She explains that she's at a conference but could speak for about twenty minutes at five today—by phone, not Skype.

There's also an email from Sandra saying that she could use a break from her event planning and is hoping we can have lunch tomorrow. I respond with a yes. With the way things are going, it may be smart to have allies like her in Saratoga. Sandra must be online because, before I can drop the phone in my purse, she suggests noon at a place called Dock Brown's on Saratoga Lake, a few miles from town.

Lastly, I shoot an email to Casey, apprising her of the fact that I've jumped the gun and spoken to Stephanie. How it seemed like the right thing to do.

It's close to four when I pull into the driveway. I make a sweep through the first floor, making sure that nothing's amiss, and then mount the stairs. I check both the master bedroom and Guy's makeshift office, wondering if he returned briefly for something. There's no sign that he's been back.

An almost crushing sadness descends on me. Is this the *end* for us? I picture myself returning to the city and announcing to friends, one by one, that my marriage is over. And I can imagine what at least a few of them will say to one another. Comments like *I'm not completely surprised. How well do you really get to know a person in that short amount of time?*

After descending from the second floor, I head straight to my office and open my laptop. I bring up the LinkedIn site, drag the cursor to the search bar, and type in "Gavin Bloom." It's essential I talk to this guy, I realize. I need to know if he and Paul were really discussing me and, if so, in what context.

Though the name seems unusual, there are actually several Gavin Blooms listed with the site, but only one in Texas. I read through his profile. He's a lawyer with what sounds like a big firm in Dallas. I notice, too, that he attended Tufts. I recall from Paul's obituary that he graduated from there, too. Yes, this must be the guy I'm looking for.

If I send a message to Bloom through LinkedIn, he might not see it right away. Instead, I jot down the work number he's listed and call. It's going to be tricky to get through his assistant, but I'm willing to use Paul's name if I have to.

To my surprise, Bloom picks up the phone himself, announcing his name as salutation.

"Mr. Bloom, this is Bryn Harper," I say. "I was given your name by Stephanie Dunham, though she has no idea I'm calling. Do you have a minute?"

"Okay," he says, drawing out the word. I can practically feel his wariness through the phone.

I don't beat around the bush. I confess that I'm still struggling to figure out what happened the day of the accident, and I'm hoping he might be able to offer insight. Plus, I tell him, there are disturbing rumors flying around about Paul and me, rumors that Stephanie has found credible in part because of the conversation she overheard between Paul and him. I need his help in reassuring Stephanie.

There's an agonizingly long silence after I finish. I sense Bloom deciding something. To hang up or keep talking?

"I'm very sorry for all you've been through, Ms. Harper," he says at last. "But I'm afraid I can't be of any help to you."

"Do you feel uncomfortable discussing the situation with me?"

"No, it's not that. I simply don't have any information to offer. I hadn't spoken to Paul for a couple of weeks before the accident. I didn't even know he was headed to Boston that week."

"What about the conversation you had with Paul at his house this winter?"

"I believe Stephanie did come into the den when we were talking. But . . . you weren't the subject of our discussion."

I hear it: the tiniest of pauses between the *but* and the *you*, a hesitation that feels like a dodge. He's lying.

"Did Paul ever mention me at any other time?"

"No. No, he didn't."

I consider begging for the truth, but instinct tells me that won't work. If he knows something, he has no intention of spilling.

"Stephanie really thinks you had an affair with Paul?" he says into the silence.

"Hopefully I convinced her otherwise. I think she still believes he may have been infatuated with me. When she was going through his home office, she found a photo of the two of us in an envelope. The words 'This is all I have' were written on the back. Can you talk to Stephanie and reassure her? I don't mind if you tell her I called you."

"Yes, I'll speak to her. Now, I'm afraid I have to go."

"Please, just one more question. When you saw Paul at his home, did he seem at all depressed to you?"

"Why do you ask that?"

"I'm thinking of the words on the envelope, trying to figure out their significance."

"Are you wondering if Paul committed *suicide*?"

"It's hard for me to get my arms around that idea, but yes, that *is* what I'm wondering. There's never been an explanation for the crash."

"Paul wouldn't have done something like that, especially if it put another person's life in jeopardy. And besides, he was in great spirits when I saw him."

I thank him for his time and end the call.

He lied, I think again, when he said that my name hadn't come up that day in the den.

With elbows on the table, I rest my head wearily in my hands. I haven't the faintest clue what to do now. There's a secret at the heart of this, a gnawing secret that won't let me put the accident behind me, and there's no one left to ask what it might be.

And there are secrets about my marriage, too, I think, secrets I have no idea how to uncover. I glance at my watch. My phone appointment with Dr. G is in ten minutes and I want to be sure to be on time. I fix an espresso and drink it while I pace the kitchen, waiting to make the call.

Because our time is limited, I've tried to mentally plot out the most important information to share, but in the first ten minutes I find myself blurting out what's happened willy-nilly, ricocheting back and forth between the trouble in my marriage and what I've learned—and haven't learned—about Paul.

"Bryn, I know how angry you must be with Guy, but it's important to keep the dialogue going," Dr. G says when I finally shut up. "Would you be open to reaching out and trying to have a conversation with him this weekend?"

"To talk about what specifically?"

"To just talk. And try to get a better read on the situation. It's going to be hard to determine what's really going on with him if you're at a distance."

"Yes, I can do that," I say.

As pissed as I feel, I know Guy and I have to be in contact sooner or later.

"What if the situation is nothing more than what Guy has described?" she asks. "That the drink was him reading the situation poorly and the text was a momentary bout of stupid guy behavior. Could you forgive those?"

"I guess I would have to try." I'm not sure I believe that, though. On paper, Guy's actions don't seem to qualify as divorce-worthy, but they won't stop eating at me.

"What is your gut telling you about Guy right now?"

"That . . . that something more is going on. That he really might have been having an affair with Eve."

It stings to say those words out loud for the first time. Voicing them seems to quell any chance that the truth might be otherwise.

"Because?"

"He seems evasive when he's talking to me. His body language. The way tidbits keep emerging, as if he coughs them up only when he's feeling cornered."

"Before you moved to Saratoga, did you have any inkling that Guy might be cheating?"

"None. Oh, there were nights when he was out on business up here, and I couldn't get him on the phone until later, and I'd feel a sliver of worry. It didn't seem based on anything rational. He never gave me a reason not to trust him." I sigh, frustrated as the next thought emerges. "Besides, we've been married less than a year, together less than two. What kind of man cheats just months after his honeymoon?"

Now Dr. G sighs. Not a comforting sound.

"There's a certain type of man who, despite how he comes across, has a difficult time with intimacy."

"That's not Guy," I say. Even to me, my tone sounds defensive. "He's always been loving and supportive."

"In the beginning this kind of man *is* loving and supportive. But as the relationship intensifies, he begins to pull away. And he has affairs, even early in the marriage. I'm not saying that's Guy, but it's something to be aware of."

I recoil at the thought.

"I've never sensed Guy pulling away," I say. "He's seemed a little frustrated lately, as if he didn't expect my recovery to take so long."

There are a few moments of silence, and I sense the doctor thinking.

"What?"

"You've had a commuter relationship with Guy from the beginning. If he does have a problem with intimacy, he's always been given a temporary reprieve by returning to Saratoga on Monday mornings. Once you moved up there, it may have thrown him off-kilter, made him feel boxed in. But let's not get ahead of things. There may be nothing more to this than poor judgment on Guy's part. Try to arrange a time to talk this weekend and assess the situation close up."

"Okay," I say. It feels as if there's a brush fire racing across my nerves, and I try to pull my thoughts together. "What about this whole matter with Paul?"

"I know it's important to get to the bottom of that, too, but for the next few days it's probably best to focus on your marriage. Talk to Guy. Is your overall sense of him still the same? Do these mistakes seem like minor blips, or do they hint at something more? I'm afraid I have to get off now, but we'll catch up more by Skype next week."

I hang up, feeling worse than when I began the call, a sensation I'm not used to experiencing following appointments with Dr. G. If Guy has difficulty with intimacy, that's not one of those problems you just MacGyver with a sexy weekend getaway and a bottle of Dom Perignon.

She's right, though. I have to call Guy and reconnect with him in person. I thought that I'd have more clarity if we were apart, but I see now that the only way to possibly resolve our issues is to be in Guy's presence. That way I can take measure of his words and behavior, and examine how I respond.

As I rise from the desk, my glance falls onto the scrap of paper on which I've scribbled Gavin Bloom's phone number. Despite Dr. G's urging to put the Paul stuff to the side now, I don't want to. In a strange way, Paul and his showing up at my hotel in Boston seem to matter right now. And yet I'm at a dead end in terms of understanding why.

I pick up my phone, ready to call Guy. It seems so strange that the prospect makes me nervous, as if I'm reaching out to a man I've recently met.

But before I can tap the digits, the phone rings in my hand. It's a local number, though not one I recognize immediately. I say hello, on guard.

No one responds. There's only the sound of a person breathing, and I'm transported back to the morning I found Eve's body, the call from the mystery woman with the breathy voice.

"Ms. Harper?" a woman says finally. With a start I realize I recognize the voice.

"Yes."

"This is Detective Corcoran. We'd like you to come down to the station."

Chapter 18

Tonight?" I ASK.

"Tomorrow morning will be fine," Corcoran says. "We have some additional questions for you."

I want to scream in frustration. This ugly business about the murder stubbornly refuses to go away—though, based on what Guy confessed yesterday, I should have guessed the cops would be circling back to me.

"What's it in regards to?" I ask, trying not to sound flustered. Maybe she wants to verify a response Guy gave her, or probe to see if *I've* had any suspicions about Guy and Eve Blazer. Though I can't see what difference my answer would make in either case because Guy has an alibi for the time of the murder. Of course, she may simply want to resume torturing me about the mystery caller. That's clearly become a favorite pastime of hers.

"Why don't I explain when I see you," she says. "Let's say nine thirty tomorrow morning."

My mind scrambles. I can't show up alone this time, that's for sure. I need a lawyer with me, but it may be impossible to line one up on such short notice, particularly on a Saturday.

Guy's lawyer, I think. The best strategy is probably to recruit him into accompanying me.

"I think that should work," I say. "If there's a problem, I'll let you know." This way I've secured myself wiggle room if I can't cough up a lawyer before then.

As soon as I disconnect, I call Guy and he picks up right away.

"It's good to hear from you, Bryn," he says.

"Guy, the police want to see me again. Do you have any idea why?"

"Wow, I don't know. Maybe . . . maybe they want to ask more questions about the missing money. That's one of the points they kept harping on yesterday. They wondered why you thought Eve had taken it."

"I never accused *Eve* of taking the money. I asked her if one of the waiters might have done it."

"Well, you can clarify that with them. But you shouldn't go alone. Do you want me to call the lawyer I'm using?"

"Yes, I was going to ask you that." I pause a moment, gathering my words. "I don't want to be caught off guard during the interview, Guy. So I need to know. Are there any ugly surprises waiting for me?"

He knows exactly what I mean by "surprises": other sexy texts to Eve or meet-ups with her that he hasn't disclosed to me.

"No, there won't be any surprises, Bryn. As I told you, I did *not* have an affair with Eve Blazer."

I can't help but detect the hint of frustration in his tone. It's almost a snippiness. He's close to his limit, I guess, with being questioned and doubted and sent packing. But I'm not ready to say, *Come home.* First I want a face-to-face conversation with him, as Dr. G suggested, one in which I can take full stock of him.

We end the call with him promising to call Maycock pronto. Ten minutes later Guy phones back, announcing that the lawyer will accompany me to the station but wants to meet with me first at his office to prep.

"Good." I hesitate briefly, making sure I'm okay with what I'm about to say. "Do you want to meet sometime later tomorrow and talk?"

"Yes, I'd like that. Why don't we have an early dinner in town?"

After we've signed off, I sit for a minute, aware of the relief I'm experiencing over the plan to see him. He's sworn there won't be surprises, so maybe all I'm looking at *are* two small episodes of poor judgment on his part. I don't know if I can let go of those moments—not because of the actions per se, but because of what they betray about Guy—and yet I think I'm willing to try.

I crash in bed at ten that night, the house once again lit up like an ocean liner. Despite how tired I am, sleep completely rebuffs me. There are the noises again, the house creaking and groaning.

And then there are the noises in my head, as my mind chews over the call with Guy, the trip to Stephanie's, the awkward conversation with Bloom, and of course the looming meeting with Corcoran.

What more can I possibly tell the woman? If, as Guy suggested, she wants to probe about the missing money, it doesn't make any sense because the waiters aren't suspects. Unless the cops have managed to puncture one of their alibis.

I open my eyes and stare into the darkness. The murderer is still out there somewhere. Perhaps nursing a rage toward me. It's three o'clock before I drift into a fitful sleep.

I'm at the law firm precisely at eight, having done my best to camouflage the dark circles under my eyes with concealer. Maycock himself opens the door to the house-turned-office building. He's in his fifties, I guess, heavyset, with a square-jawed face, deep blue eyes, and brown hair heavily tinged with silver. He's dressed in a crisp cotton dress shirt and gray pin-striped suit pants. The only thing undermining the distinguished aura is a florid complexion. His face is the pinky red of a sunrise.

"Come in, Ms. Harper," he says. Pleasant but professional. "We don't have much time, so let's get started right away."

He leads me from the small entranceway toward the back of the house, which has been gutted and turned into offices and conference rooms. Most are dark today, and the place smells as if it's been sprayed with one of those air fresheners named "Linen" or "Sky."

Once we're seated in Maycock's office, he grabs a legal pad and asks me to take him through everything from beginning to end. He jots down notes as I speak, with hands as pink as his face.

When I'm done racing through the details, Maycock taps the pen against the pad several times, making a light thwacking sound.

"Did Detective Corcoran give you any indication why she wants to see you?"

"No, she was totally cagey. And I've told her everything I possibly can."

"Then you'll just have to repeat what you've said. Do your best not to sound irritated, and don't elaborate. That never does any good."

"Okay . . . Do you think she'll ask about Guy? About his dealings with Eve Blazer?" To my embarrassment, my voice catches as I speak.

"Yes, most likely. Again, keep your answers short and to the point."

And now the question I hate having to ask. "What if she springs something on me about Guy and Eve that I'm not aware of?"

Maycock relaxes his professional demeanor and extends a sympathetic look.

"I know you're concerned there might be land mines—Guy mentioned that to me—but your husband's given me his word that there aren't any."

I take comfort from this assurance. It would be stupid for Guy to deceive his lawyer.

Maycock announces that it's time to go and slips into the pin-striped jacket that's been draped on the back of his chair. He suggests we travel in his car so we'll have to secure only one parking space.

This time there's no desk-side conversation. Detective Mazzola ushers us to an interview room painted soggy-dishrag gray, with nothing but a metal table and several folding chairs. Corcoran, dressed in an un-summery burgundy blazer, is waiting there, already seated at the table. After she checks out

Maycock, I catch her shooting her partner a mocking look, one that seems to translate as, *So Miss Smarty Pants lawyered up, too. Why am I not surprised?*

"We've probably interrupted your Saturday plans, haven't we?" Corcoran says as soon as we're seated.

The comment seems weird. Because she clearly doesn't mind interrupting my plans.

"Not a problem," I say.

"It must be nice to be up here this summer, spending more time with your husband."

"Yes, it is."

"Up until now, you two have had a commuter relationship, right?"

I'm confused about where she's going with this. Is it the small talk thing she always does in the beginning of an interview?

"Yes. It's not a perfect situation, but we've made it work for us."

She cocks her head. "I don't know if I could do it myself. That's got to be tough on a couple."

Not good, I think. It sounds like this interview is going to revolve around Guy and me, not the money, as Guy suggested.

"Ms. Harper has already commented on this," Maycock announces. "Can we move on?"

Corcoran pauses briefly but never takes her eyes off me. "Are you aware that before you moved up here, your husband had a drink at a bar with Eve Blazer?"

Okay, so here it comes. *Stay cool,* I warn myself.

"He mentioned that, yes."

"At the time?"

"Pardon me?"

"Did he mention it the night it happened? Before he went out?"

"It came up after the fact," I say carefully.

"Did that concern you? That he'd had drinks with another woman?"

"Because of his work, he often has drinks with people. There wasn't any reason for me to be concerned."

Can she spot I'm lying? Can Maycock? I'm certainly not going to admit to the contrary because it could end up fanning any suspicion that Guy was screwing Eve.

"And are you aware that, according to your husband at least, Ms. Blazer came on to him the night they had drinks?"

"He mentioned that. He said he wanted me to be in the loop about what had happened."

I realize I'm elaborating, exactly what Maycock cautioned against, and I prompt myself to be more careful.

Corcoran purses her lips. "Didn't it bother you that another woman was preying on your husband?"

It's starting to get personal, and I'm not sure how to respond. I wish I could glance at Maycock and read advice in his eyes, but I worry that will make it look like I'm being calculating.

"Well, I certainly don't admire women who behave that way," I say.

"Speaking of women, we never did find the one who called you and told you to come down to the catering kitchen."

So we're finally back to *that*.

"I wish I could help. But I've told you everything I remember about the call."

Corcoran drums the table lightly with her fingers and then locks eyes with me so intensely, it throws me off balance. Something's wrong, I think, but I don't know what. She lets her hand go still.

"And you're sure there really *was* a call?" she says. "That you didn't buy a phone and call yourself?"

I can't believe what I'm hearing. She's suggesting that I fabricated the call. Does she think my Saturday morning visit to Pure Kitchen was totally on my own initiative, an attempt on my part to exert more pressure on Eve about the missing money?

"What possible reason would Ms. Harper have for doing that?" Maycock interjects before I can respond.

I hold my breath, waiting for the answer.

"You tell me," Corcoran says.

"There *was* a call," I blurt out. "Yes, I was upset about the money, but it wasn't like I needed to rush down there again and check on it."

"I don't think the money was your main concern," Corcoran says. "What *really* worried you was the fact that Eve Blazer might be having an affair with her husband."

Fear explodes in me, like a firecracker. Now I see what this is all about. She thinks *I* might be the killer, that I took an ax to Eve out of raging jealousy.

"This is ludicrous," Maycock says. "Are you saying that Ms. Harper is a suspect in your investigation?"

Corcoran doesn't even look at Maycock, just holds my gaze.

"Where were you a week ago Friday night?" she asks.

I do my best to tamp down my fear. They can't have a shred of real evidence pointing to me.

"I was at home."

"Did—?"

But before she can get another word out, Maycock interrupts.

"I'm ending this interview," Maycock says, starting to rise. "And unless my client is under arrest, we are both leaving. Any future correspondence with my client regarding this investigation must only occur in my presence." He taps his fingers against my elbow, motioning for me to stand as well.

"If you have any plans to leave Saratoga Springs, I suggest you cancel them," Corcoran calls out as we reach the door.

As we head through the labyrinth of desks on our way out, I feel every set of eyes boring into me, as if we're on a walk of shame. Maycock doesn't even let me catch my breath on the sidewalk, and instead guides me quickly to his parking spot. I can hear the sound of blood pounding in my ears.

"They can't really think I did it, can they?" I say as soon as we're in the car.

"Unfortunately, it does seem like they're considering it," Maycock says, firing up the engine. "That you killed her and then faked the call so you could show up the next morning and look shocked—or simply to check out the situation."

It's the clichéd story line of a cop show: the killer returning to the scene of the crime. Corcoran had seemed sympathetic toward me the morning of the murder, but she was probably already eyeing me suspiciously. And this explains why the previous interviews with her always felt loaded.

"What am I going to *do*?" I say, nearly pleading.

Maycock noses the car out of the parking space. "Let me ask you. Is there any possibility the cops could trace the disposable phone back to you?"

"Of course not." Maycock is clearly toying with the idea that I *could* be guilty.

"Tell me about the night of the murder. Were you alone?"

"Yes—but only until nine or so, when Guy came home."

"Did you make a phone call, chat with a friend?"

"No," I say without even having to think. I've done so little chatting with friends since I've been up here.

"Were you online? That can serve as proof that you weren't out killing someone."

My mind is addled with panic, but I force my memory back to last Friday. Before Guy arrived home—and we ate the leftover tagine—I'd sat for a while in the den alone. With my laptop.

"I sent a bunch of emails that night," I say, simultaneously stuffing a hand into my bag. "Here, let me find them for you."

He holds up a hand. "Unfortunately I have a family obligation right now. After I drop you off, why don't you go home and search for anything you sent out that night? Forward all those emails to me. And whatever you do, don't delete *anything*, even if it's something private you don't want the cops to see."

I nod in agreement. At the next stop sign he fishes for his wallet and hands me a business card with his email address.

Two minutes later, I'm sitting in my car, my heart still racing. *I'm a person of interest in a murder investigation.*

I upend my messenger bag, dumping the contents into the passenger seat, and paw through it until I locate my phone. I scroll through sent emails until I reach the night of the murder. There are more emails between seven and nine o'clock than I recall sending—a batch to my assistant, and then a long one to Will in Jakarta. I nearly cry with relief. Hopefully this will be enough to get Corcoran to back off.

Noting the time on my phone, I remember my lunch with Sandra. I hardly have the stomach or the psychic energy for chick chat now, and yet, as I've already considered, it could be good to have an ally in town. I opt not to cancel.

There's over an hour to kill before lunch with Sandra, but I've no intention of going home and brooding in that big, empty house. I head for downtown with the idea that maybe I'll find a spot to have a coffee. As I drive along Broadway, though, the idea of pulling over someplace holds little appeal. The town that I once found so charming seems oppressive today, with all its dark brick buildings.

Instead, I just keep driving, and before long, I realize I'm headed in the direction of the Saratoga Race Course. Part of the plan this summer was for Guy and me to spend time at the track during thoroughbred season in August, but that's not going to be. I pull over by a weathered green-and-white building that must have once been a horse stable and park beneath an oak tree at the side of the road. As I turn off the engine, I realize that my hands are wet with perspiration.

You can't let it get to you, I tell myself. The cops are clearly flailing around in their investigation and are targeting me for lack of anything better. The worst thing I could do is to allow my nervousness to make me *look* guilty. I have to stay calm, keep a cool head, and get the best legal advice possible. At some point, too, I'm going to have to loop Casey in on this development. If Maycock can't make this go away immediately, it could have ramifications for my reputation as an author.

At eleven thirty, I tap in the address for Dock Brown's and drive out there, first along Route 9 and then on a rural road that rings Saratoga Lake. The landscape is flat except for low, muted blue mountains in the distance.

The restaurant emerges at the far side of a village. It's in a gray clapboard building in front of a small tan blanket of beach, dotted today with sunbathers. I notice for the first time how sunny and warm the day is, and I ask for a seat on the deck, figuring Sandra would like to sit outside as well.

I've got the deck mostly to myself, except for two diners at the other end and a seagull that has perched on the railing and is eyeing what remains in a breadbasket on a table yet to be cleared. It looks insolent, hostile even, and when it catches my eye, it lifts its wings in what seems like an aggressive gesture.

My wait turns out to be a mercifully short one since Sandra arrives early herself. She's dressed down today, but still impeccably—skintight designer jeans and a teal, light cashmere tee that looks great with her shiny dark hair. She makes a striking figure as she crosses the deck.

"I'm so glad you picked a spot outdoors," she exclaims as she reaches the table. She brushes my cheek with her lips. "It's so nice to see you again, Bryn."

"Same here."

"I hope you didn't have any trouble finding the place. It's

a bit removed, but I thought it would be a perfect spot for a Saturday lunch."

"It *is* perfect, yes."

"Please thank your husband for me, will you?"

"My husband?" I say, startled by her remark.

"For letting me spend Saturday afternoon with you. I'm sure he'd love to have you to himself."

"Oh, he's got a ton of work to do, so it's not a problem." I force a smile, trying to look upbeat, sensing I'm failing miserably. Sandra's deep brown eyes study me quizzically.

"Is everything okay? You're not still feeling badly, are you?

"No, no, I'm fine now. Tell me about your event. How's it shaping up?"

"If it was in two weeks, I'd say we were in fabulous shape. Unfortunately, it's this coming Friday."

"I'm sure you'll pull it off beautifully. Who's it for, anyway?" I've never bothered to ask.

"It's a fund-raiser for an area women's organization. The money goes to a good cause—plus, it's a chance for local businesswomen to network their butts off."

"And you're doing the PR?"

"Yes, and much to my chagrin I offered to help put the whole thing on. By the way, I've been scouring around trying to find a seat for you, but the damn thing's sold out and nobody wants to cough up a ticket."

Oh, wouldn't that be fun, I think, me networking this week with local women. If someone asked what I was up to these days, I could smile and say I was a suspect in the Eve Blazer homicide.

"That's so nice of you, Sandra, but don't worry about it. I've got a crazy week ahead."

"Well, I hope you'll at least let me show you the venue. It's worth taking a look at."

"Let me see how the week goes, okay?"

The waitress interrupts and we order. Sandra asks about the kind of PR that's considered most effective for authors these days, and I throw out a few scattered comments about Twitter, Instagram, and newsletters. Thankfully the food comes quickly. With the drone of motorboats behind me, I do my best to keep up my end of the conversation. We segue into small talk about the arts scene in Saratoga. At moments I feel ready to jump out of my skin and want nothing more than to bolt from the table and race home. But I remind myself that stewing alone in the house would be far worse than sitting here with Sandra.

As the waitress arrives to remove our plates, I sense Sandra poised to say something, but she waits until the table's cleared before speaking.

"Bryn, are you sure you're okay?"

"I'm just a little tired, that's all."

She leans closer, clearly so her voice won't carry. "It's not the police, is it? I hope they've stopped hounding you and your husband about your dinner party."

Is my anxiety about this morning *that* transparent?

"No, no, nothing like that," I say, and I can tell my words sound forced. For a brief moment I consider sharing what's going on with the cops. Because of her job, Sandra probably has excellent resources and contacts in town, and knows the lay of the land. She may even be able to confirm whether

Maycock is the right lawyer for me. But I don't dare. Based on what I know so far of her, she seems a bit indiscreet.

"I'm so glad to hear that. The police here can be such bullies."

I shrug, as if I haven't got a concern in the world. "I'm sure they're just doing their job."

She shakes her head in dismay, and her shiny black hair catches the sunlight. "Of course it now looks as if I had my locks changed for nothing."

I tense, confused.

"What do you mean?" I ask.

"We don't have to worry about a serial killer on the prowl. They're saying she was killed by someone she knew, someone with—if you'll excuse the expression—an ax to grind."

I flinch at the words. Am I supposed to be the person with the ax to grind?

"*They?* Who are *they?*"

"People in town, so maybe it doesn't amount to much. But there's been all this buzz about the fact that Eve Blazer had a lover, and that's probably what led to her murder."

"You mean a boyfriend?"

"No, *lover*—as in a married man. She'd apparently confided to a few friends about him. She claimed he was in a marriage he was dying to escape from, that his wife was extremely fragile and had sucked all the joy from his life. Who knows? Maybe *she's* the one who did it.

Chapter 19

IS THE MARRIED MAN *Guy*? AM I THE SO-CALLED "FRAG-ile" wife? Did my husband tell Eve I'd sucked all the joy from his life?

"Don't people here have anything better to do than gossip about a dead woman?" I snap. The words spit from my mouth before I can catch them, but part of me doesn't care. I can't stand to hear any more of this.

Sandra appears taken aback by my response. She flips a hand over in a gesture that says she doesn't have an easy explanation. "It's hard to blame them. I'm sure everyone in town is feeling anxious about having a murderer at large. It's cast a terrible pall."

"Let's table the topic, can we? I'm sick to death of it."

"Of course."

Speaking of casting a pall, I've done exactly that with lunch. Sandra averts her gaze and glances down at the table. She picks up the saltshaker and studies it, as if she can't think of anything else to do. I'm sure she's wondering what nerve she just hit, and I can't let her start to speculate.

"Excuse me for sounding grouchy, Sandra. I guess I've

been worrying about the murderer, too, and really want to put the whole business out of my mind."

"Understood." She offers a pleasant smile, but I sense I haven't mitigated the situation. At that moment the waitress sidles over to the table, preventing what's bound to have been an awkward silence.

"Can I get you ladies any coffee?" she asks.

"I'd love that," I say, hopeful Sandra will agree and I can smooth things over. "Do you have time, Sandra? I'd love to talk a little longer."

She checks her watch. "Yes, I've got time," she says fortunately.

We order, and before the waitress heads off, I ask that she please bring the check to me.

"Why don't we split it," Sandra insists.

"No, please, it's my treat. And I loved discovering this restaurant."

"It's a cute place, isn't it?" She nods toward the window into the restaurant. "I like to come here in winter, too, and eat inside."

"I'll have to try it then." Though right now that seems like the most improbable idea in the world.

Sandra taps her fingers absentmindedly on the table and I see her eyes flicker. She checks her watch again.

"Oh dear," she exclaims, her hand flying to her mouth. "I read my watch wrong a minute ago. I'm afraid I'm not going to be able to do coffee after all. Will you forgive me? I need to get back to the venue."

"Don't worry about it," I say, though I'm finding it hard to buy her explanation. "Why don't you dash? I'll sit for a while and have my coffee."

"You're a sweetheart. And next time's on me. I'll call you when I'm postevent."

Okay, I think, as she crosses the deck and descends the wooden steps to the parking lot. I've just managed to offend a potential ally. But if Sandra's as gossipy as she seems, she might not be the best ally to have anyway.

My mind careens back to the ugly tidbit she shared. It could be confirmation of my fears, that Guy was sleeping with Eve. *No,* I tell myself. The rumor has to be about someone else. Whatever frustrations Guy might have because of my accident, I can't believe he's felt like I've sucked the joy from his life.

The coffee arrives, and after a minute I realize my stomach is roiling, so much that I have no desire for it anymore. I extract a credit card from my purse and glance through the window, searching for the waitress. As my gaze sweeps over the dining room, I'm met with a surprise. Guy's assistant, Miranda, is sitting at one of the tables, her red hair lifted slightly by the breeze from an overhead fan. She's with two other women her age, probably enjoying a Saturday girls' lunch with her friends.

I raise my arm about to wave, but then catch myself. She's listening intently to one of the other women and hasn't even noticed me. It's just as well. If she saw me she might feel compelled to say hello, and that's the last thing I need today. I'm sure Guy hasn't divulged that he's been living back at his apartment, but knowing Miranda, she'd detect from talking to me that all isn't right with my world.

I pay the bill and make my way to the parking lot. Right

as I'm about to start the car, my phone rings, and I catch my breath when I spot "Dallas, TX" on the screen. Gavin Bloom is calling me.

"Are you somewhere you can talk?" he asks as soon as I answer. "Privately?"

So I was right yesterday. Bloom *wasn't* being honest with me, and he's clearly calling back to come clean.

"Yes, I can talk now."

"You caught me off guard yesterday. I wasn't expecting to hear from you."

"I'm sorry I phoned out of the blue—there didn't seem to be a way around it." *Keep it slow and easy*, I tell myself. *Don't rush him.* "I appreciate hearing from you."

"There's actually some information I'd like to pass on to you, information I wasn't prepared to divulge before. I needed to discuss the matter with my wife first."

This sounds significant. Maybe Paul *was* suffering from depression and Bloom was privy to that.

"Okay." Every muscle in my body seems to vibrate in anticipation. I may finally have a clue to what happened to me on that dreary stretch of highway out of Boston.

"No offense, Ms. Harper, but Paul didn't have any romantic interest in you. He was crazy about Stephanie—and by the way, I've called and reassured her since the two of us spoke yesterday. But there *was* something he felt he needed to share with you."

"I've wondered if that was the case." Maybe it was a career crisis after all.

"I doubt he concocted the Boston trip in order to tell you. Rather, I suspect that he decided to take advantage of the fact that you were both there on business, away from the fray of New York. From what you've said, it doesn't sound like he had the chance to bring it up the night of your speech. My guess is that he was going to discuss it with you during the car trip home."

"Was it about his work?"

"His *work*?" he says, obviously surprised by the question.

"I've wondered if he was at a crossroads professionally and wanted to bat ideas around with me." But clearly not. *So just tell me*, I think. I realize I've started to perspire in the hot car, and I crack open the door a few inches to catch the fresh air.

"No, everything was good in that department. Look, Ms. Harper, I need you to know that I'm going out on a limb here. It's . . . it's awkward. But my wife and I feel Paul would want me to pass this along. Because that's what he'd intended to do."

"What *is* it?" I exclaim. I don't have the patience anymore to go slow.

"It's about your husband."

Everything that had started to race a few moments ago—my heart, my breathing—now freezes. It takes me a moment to even make my lips move.

"What do you mean, my husband?"

"Like I said, this is very awkward. Are you aware that your husband lived in Dallas once?"

"*Dallas?* No, he never lived in Dallas."

"Your husband worked in Dallas for about two years as the president of a charity that employed my wife as well—a community foundation called Dallas Gives. He left about seven years ago. Paul didn't think you were aware of it, and he felt he had to let you know."

My exasperation intensifies.

"You clearly have him mixed up with someone else."

"Look, I feel terrible telling you this, but I'm sure I'm right."

"But what are you *basing* this on? How would you even know who I was married to?"

"That picture Stephanie found, the one you told me about? Paul happened to show it to me when I was visiting him in Hastings that day. He was really impressed by you, and he loved your book. Said it had actually clarified a few points for him professionally, and he was going to have the photo enlarged and hang it on the brag wall in his home office. But when I saw it, I recognized the man standing at the edge of the photo. Richard Carrington. Paul told me you'd married him last year."

I exhale. Okay, it's all a simple misunderstanding. "My husband's first name isn't Richard, it's Guy. Richard's his middle name. Like I said, you've mixed him up with someone else."

"I'm aware that he doesn't go by Richard now, but he did in Dallas. Paul let me borrow the photo so I could show my wife and make sure it was him. Paul wrote something on the back of the picture about it being the only photo he had with your husband in it. When I showed the photo to my wife, she confirmed that the man in the picture was the same person she'd worked with. At the time he went by the name Rich Carrington."

I realize I'm shaking my head back and forth, though of course Bloom can't see me.

"The man your wife worked with may look like my husband and have the same last name, but it's not him," I say. "My husband lived in Chicago, not Texas. And then he moved to Miami."

"I know he lived in Florida eventually. Allison heard he moved there, and was going by Guy."

"And you're saying that the reason Paul came to see me in Boston was because he was under the impression—mistaken impression, I should say—that my husband once lived in Texas, and he wanted to tell me that?" I'm trying to sound controlled, but I hear the mix of frustration and fear leaking through my words.

"Ms. Harper, look, I know this must be upsetting. And that's why I was reluctant to say anything when you phoned yesterday. But based on details you told Paul about your husband, he suspected that he hadn't been straight with you about his past."

"Why would my husband be afraid to admit he lived in Dallas?"

"Because . . . because there was a situation here."

He pauses, gathering his words or his nerve or both.

"He embezzled funds from the charity," he says finally. "Close to a hundred and fifty thousand dollars. He'd worked out a whole system—accepting checks directly from several donors and then depositing them into a checking account he'd established with the initials DG. My wife discovered the deception and reported it to the board. Once Rich was caught and fired, he paid the money back and after much agonizing, the board chose not to prosecute. They wanted to avoid the damage bad publicity would cause."

I feel like I'm suffocating, as if I've been wrapped tight in a blanket and heaved into the trunk of a car. I want to protest, to tell him he's wrong, but I can't get the words out.

"Ms. Harper— May I please call you Bryn? Is there a—?"

"There's got to be a mistake," I say, ignoring his question.

"I don't think so, unfortunately."

I'm shaking my head again, but thoughts are ricocheting in my mind, demanding I pay attention to them. There are Guy's omissions over the past days—about the drink with Eve, about going to the police. There's the flirty text. None of it seeming like the man I thought I knew.

And then a memory rams me from out of nowhere.

It was last April, a few months before our wedding, and I was midway through the book tour for *Twenty Choices*. Guy and I were missing each other intensely, and during a phone call we'd discussed the possibility of him flying out to be with me during the San Francisco leg of the tour. He'd been totally game, it seemed. But when I called the next morning to inform him that joining me in Dallas would probably be a better option, the situation changed.

Damn. I don't think I'm going to be able to get away after all.

Why? What's happened?

Brent happened. He's got a huge project he's demanding I take on.

"Bryn, are you still there?" Bloom asks.

"Yes."

"Is there someone you can be with right now? A friend?"

"I don't need a friend. I need proof of what you're saying. You don't expect me to simply accept your word that my husband is a liar and an embezzler, do you?"

"Of course not. I can send you a link, to an item in the *Dallas Business Journal* that I shared with Paul. It'll prove your husband was in Dallas. As for the embezzlement, I've only my word to offer on that."

I mutter okay and spit out my email address. There are too many questions I want to ask, but my need for answers is overridden by my desperation to jump off the phone and try to think this through, make sense of it. He assures me that I'm free to call him back.

"But please," he adds, "this is an extremely delicate situation for my wife, so you can't tell anyone where this information originated from."

The call over, I toss the phone on the seat, shove the door open, and swing my legs out of the car. I feel light-headed. I lean my head into my lap, sucking in air.

This *has* to be a mistake, I think again. Some totally freaky coincidence. Those things *happen*. A bizarre coincidence drove one of the people I wrote about in my last book toward the choice he made—he'd seen it as a sign from the gods. *Wait for the link*, I tell myself. Maybe Bloom's got it all wrong. And why should I take the word of a total stranger?

The almond scent of suntan lotion wafts into the car along with the cackle of people talking and laughing on the little beach. It's a perfect June day, the sun high in the bright blue sky, and yet I feel totally detached from it all, like I'm watching the world on a screen.

Within a minute or two there's an email from Bloom along with the promised link. I resituate myself in the car, grab a breath, and tap the link. I'm taken to a section of the *Dallas*

Business Journal website headlined "People on the Move," and almost instantly the bottom falls out of my stomach. Because I'm now staring at the photo of a man who can only be Guy. Or should I say Guy about nine years younger. Or a doppelganger so uncannily like him it could make you believe that alien body snatchers really do exist.

The section appears to cover new hires and promotions at regional companies, and there's a short paragraph of copy along with each photo. The one I'm studying says that G. Richard Carrington has recently been named president of Dallas Gives. It lists his education below: MS from the University of California, Santa Barbara; MBA from UCLA.

The schooling matches up perfectly with what I know of Guy's education.

There can't be any mistake that this is my husband, that he lived and worked in Dallas like Bloom said. I'm married to a liar and a fraud and, if I'm to believe Bloom further, a *criminal*. A wave of nausea sweeps through me, and I grip the steering wheel, trying to fight it off.

This is what Paul wanted to tell me. Why he'd searched me out in Boston and, after I'd declined dinner, offered me the ride home the next day. During one of last year's lunches together, we'd exchanged info regarding our spouses, and I'd shared certain aspects about Guy's background—the jobs in Chicago and then his own small business in Miami—and after talking to Bloom, Paul would have suspected I was clueless. According to Bloom, Paul respected me. He must have convinced himself he had an obligation to tell me so I wouldn't be duped any more than I already had been.

Did he have the chance, I wonder, in the minutes before the car went off the road? Have the nightmares been my unconscious's way of reminding me of what Paul shared?

Before my thoughts unspool any further, I catch myself. Bloom hasn't offered a shred of evidence that Guy stole the money, and it's foolish to accept a secondhand report from a stranger.

Then I realize the absurdity of my thinking process. Regardless of whether Guy embezzled the money, he's deceived me about a big chunk of his past—living in Dallas, the work he did, even the name he went by.

Others must be in the dark as well. The few friends of his I've met are fairly new in his life—like his pal who knew the couple I was staying with in Rhode Island the summer we met—so they probably wouldn't be privy to much about his past.

What else has he lied about? I wonder in panic. It's not much of a leap now to believe that he *was* screwing Eve. There may have been other women. Other cities he's inhabited. Maybe his whole past is a lie. Was he *always* Richard until Miami?

But wait, I remind myself, I met his mother and she called him Guy, and she was hardly party to a hoax. Nor were the cousins and family acquaintances I met at her small memorial service in San Diego.

There's one detail that makes no sense, and for a few seconds it sends a flood of relief coursing through me. Surely the opera company would have done a background check on him and discovered any discrepancies on his résumé.

Yet if they searched only under the name Guy provided, the Dallas job might not have surfaced, even in this glorious age of the Internet. And, of course, the embezzlement itself has been kept under wraps.

A chill runs down my spine. I wonder if Guy has stolen from *me*. I've been careful overall about money, but my mind has been elsewhere since the accident. We have a prenup, at least. Casey had urged me to go there, claiming it was advice she'd offer to any client on a roll financially and about to marry.

Shouts pierce my thoughts. I look up to see that it's two kids waving lightsabers at the edge of the parking lot. I become aware of how long I've been sitting in the car. Miranda may be departing soon, and I certainly don't want to run into her and risk triggering her nosiness.

Bryn, are you okay? You look shell-shocked.

No, I'm not okay, Miranda. Did you know your boss is not at all who you think he is?

I start the car and maneuver out of the parking lot, too stricken to take the gas gauge over forty once I'm on the road. I manage for a few minutes, keeping much of my concentration focused on what's on the other side of my windshield, and then, while I'm still on the lake road, I start to shake, my hands doing freaky little bounces off the steering wheel. I quickly pull over and park on the shoulder. I take long breaths and try to calm myself.

Suddenly, as if touched in the dark by a ghost, I feel it. A hand reaching across to tap my arm. Someone speaks to me in a gentle voice: *Bryn, there's something I need to tell you, and I'm afraid it's going to be upsetting.*

It's Paul. On the car ride from Boston. The memory is faint but unmistakable. I squeeze my head with my hands, hoping for more, but it escapes from me, like a piece of melody carried on the wind.

Is that why the car went off the road? Had Paul reached over to comfort me and become distracted? The thought is unbearable.

I take more breaths, in and out. Finally, I feel well enough to drive. I start the car again and slowly wend my way back around the lake.

Arriving at the junction of Route 9, I make a right toward town. As I reach the outskirts, I pass sights that have now become familiar—Saratoga Park; the Lincoln Baths, one of the old bathhouses, now closed, I believe; the Museum of Dance. At the sight of the museum, a thought strikes me and I slow the car.

If Guy is a master liar, if he's deceived both the police and me about the extent of his relationship with Eve, it stands to reason that he might have lied to me about where he was at the time of Eve's murder. What if he *killed* her? I can't believe I'm asking myself this question, though in light of what I now know, I'd be a fool not to.

I pull over the car, and twist around in my seat, staring back at the dance museum. I have to go in there, I realize. Nick told me at dinner that while he had been there purely for glad-handing, Guy had taken in the performances, which suggests they may have separated during the evening. I have to confirm Guy's alibi and make sure there's no possible way he could have murdered Eve.

I pull back onto the road, make a crazy, jerky U-turn and direct the car into the mostly empty parking lot of the dance museum. While I know there can't be anyone watching me, as I step out of the car, I glance around just to be sure.

I pay the museum admission fee at the entrance window and, from there, step into a huge white room that has a row of floor-to-ceiling windows facing a courtyard in the back. Though there are a few women milling around, the space is devoid of furnishings or displays. This is probably where the reception was held, I realize. I need to figure out where the performances took place, where Guy would have been.

Two separate hallways lead off from the right and left sides of the room, each functioning as exhibition space. I start to the right. The walls are lined with multicolored posters featuring photographs of famous ballet stars and notes about their backgrounds. There are also glass display cases stocked with headpieces and slippers, video screens flashing dance performances, and mannequin torsos decked out in costumes.

The hallway eventually leads to an actual exhibit room, windowless and without doors. Maybe one of the dance performances was in here. It would have been easy enough to set up rows of folding chairs and still give dancers a place to perform.

My attention is tugged to the left. There's yet *another* room unfolding from this one. In some ways, moving through these endless rooms feels familiar. They're like all the revelations about Guy, one after the other, that have spun out over the past week—the drinks with Eve, the flirtation with her, the secret life in Dallas—each adding to my shock and suspicion.

I step inside. This room is filled with a visually cacophonous tribute to tango stars. A performance could have easily been held in this space, too, on the night of the party. I picture Guy standing here, separated from Nick by an endless stream of people and displays.

And then I see it: an exit door, leading out to the courtyard and another parking lot beyond it. I flinch at the sight.

It would have been easy enough, I think. Guy could have snuck out of the museum by this exit, or a similar one on the other wing of the building.

He could have driven to Eve's, murdered her, and then returned without anyone being the wiser.

Chapter 20

No, no, it can't be true. It's impossible to picture my husband raising an ax and plunging it into Eve Blazer's skull. Besides, he would have been spattered with blood if he had.

And yet what I've learned today is that I don't *know* Guy, and so I have no clue what he's really capable of. He could have killed Eve and somehow managed to wash up before returning to the event. An image thrusts itself into my mind: the spare, clean shirt he always keeps on the backseat of the BMW in case he's going to a business dinner directly from work and wants to look fresh.

I need to get out of here, away from all this visual chaos, so I can think straight. I hurry to the front of the museum, past a cluster of women moseying through the exhibits like a small herd of sheep.

"Is everything okay?" the man at the front desk asks as I pass. He's the one who sold me a ticket only minutes ago.

"Yes, lovely," I blurt out over my shoulder.

"Would you like a reentry pass?"

"Not today, thank you."

Crossing the parking lot, I wrestle my phone from my purse. I promised Guy I'd have dinner with him tonight, but I don't want to see him, not until I think through how to handle the situation.

"Can't meet tonight," I text him.

"Bryn?" a male voice calls. I nearly jump, thinking at first that it's Guy. But as I spin around, I see it's Nick Emerling standing several parking spaces away, his car key in hand.

"Oh, hi."

"You look startled. You didn't think I was a crazed fan, did you?"

"No, just surprised to see you."

"I'm not sure if Guy told you, but I'm on the board here. Great that you could stop by."

He presses the button that locks his car, triggering a chirping sound, and, to my dismay, he struts over in my direction. No golf getup today. He's in crisp tan pants and a blue dress shirt, open at the collar. Reaching me, he leans over and kisses my cheek. And it's not an air-kiss. He smushes his chubby lips into my face and simultaneously gives my arm a squeeze. Pulling back, he leaves an almost overpowering trail of spicy cologne. I fight the urge to gag.

"Is this your first trip to the museum?"

"Yes, it is."

"I've got to drop an envelope off at the office, but then I'll treat you to your own private tour."

"Oh, sorry, I'm actually just leaving." I hesitate, my mind racing. If I engage a little with Nick, I might be able to figure out if Guy had the opportunity to slip out of the event that night and return later. "Have you enjoyed working with the museum?"

He grins. "You bet. I may not look like a ballet guy, but I'm pretty informed on the subject."

He pulls a wallet from his pants pocket, snaps out a business card, and thrusts it toward me. "I'm in town a fair amount. Give me a call when you've got the time."

I accept the card and, ignoring his lingering eyes, nod toward the museum. "Guy keeps talking about how much he enjoyed the dance pieces he saw here. Were they performed in some of the small exhibit rooms?"

"Yeah. Though, as I might have mentioned the other evening, I was too busy working the reception to see any of them. What makes you ask?"

"I was trying to imagine it." I fashion a lie in my mind, hoping to flush out the truth. "Guy said he got really immersed. He . . . he lost track of the time once and was afraid you had no idea where he was."

Nick squints an eye, clearly curious about where I'm going with this. "Yeah, but he's a big boy. I knew he could find his way home."

So they were definitely apart. *And clearly didn't even leave together.*

I decide not to press it any harder. It could set off alarm bells, and he might even mention my curiosity to Guy.

"Next time," he adds, "you'll have to come, too. In fact, I'm sorry I didn't include you."

"Don't worry about it. You treated us to that great dinner the other night."

He studies me, his olive-green eyes intense. "Speaking of that, do you mind if I ask you a question?"

As far as I can tell, he hasn't budged an inch since we began talking, but he seems closer now, invading my space. I ease my torso back. He doesn't wait for me to respond to his query.

"Did something happen with Kim the other night—when we were on our way out from dinner?"

I feel blindsided by the question, unsure how to answer. I don't want to stir up more trouble with Kim, but I need to determine if she's the one who left the matches.

"What gave you that impression?"

"It suddenly got awkward. I couldn't help but wonder if there'd been an issue."

"Um, things did feel a little awkward," I say, testing him. "I worried I may have said the wrong thing to Kim."

He folds his arms across his chest.

"Look, I love my wife. She's a great mother, and she's in terrific shape. But it can be tough for her to be around really successful women. I don't mean someone like Barb, for God's sake. Kim's not gonna be threatened by a person who spends her time selling garden gnomes. But a woman like you can be intimidating."

Is that what it all comes down to? Kim doesn't like the fact that I have a career and she doesn't, so she played a nasty trick to put me in my place? As much as I want clear answers, there are more serious matters to consider right now. I reach for the door handle, signaling I'm set to take off.

"It's too bad she feels that way," I say.

"Not your fault." He shrugs. "I don't help things, of course. She knows I'm totally impressed by women like you."

Oh, great, he's coming *on* to me.

"That's nice of you to say, Nick. And nice to see you. I'm afraid I have to dash."

He squeezes my arm again.

"I'm counting on you taking that rain check. I give a wicked tour."

The ride home is a blur. I try to focus on the traffic, but at moments my thoughts overwhelm me. My husband is a liar and possibly an embezzler. A colleague may have died because he wanted me to know the truth. It's easy to assume that Guy is also a cheater, too, and, though the chances are remote, maybe even a murderer. And oh, the icing on the cake: the cops are wondering if *I'm* the one who axed Eve to death.

Once home, I unlock the kitchen door and enter the house, listening intently. Guy has a key, of course, and nothing prevents him from letting himself in. I toss my bag on the kitchen table and search the downstairs rooms, looking for any indication that he's been here today. Next, I check the master bedroom and his office. There's no sign of him.

As I start to retreat from the office, I turn and let my gaze sweep the room. I take in Guy's desk and the stack of books he's left on the side table. They might as well belong to a stranger.

I can't help it. I feel like such a fool for reading Guy all wrong, for being the kind of woman who allows love to blind her. I'd been so ridiculously thrilled for myself as our relationship accelerated in warp speed from flirtation to fling to full-blown love affair. Despite my age at the time, I didn't initially see marriage as a possibility for me. Then, almost out of the blue, I *did* want it. I asked myself if the desire had been hiding in me all along, or had been born simply out of the intensity of my passion for Guy. I had no clue. I just knew he would be a fabulous partner for life.

I feel an urgent need to talk to someone, to try to gain another perspective. Dr. G has already indicated that she won't be available again this weekend. I do the math in my head with regard to my brother. It's 3:00 a.m. right now in Jakarta, so he's out, at least for now. There are friends in New York I could phone, but I feel so out of touch with them.

There's something else I need: a lawyer besides Maycock to represent me. In light of what I've learned today, he can't be both Guy's lawyer and my own.

I change into jeans, and as I trudge back downstairs, I hear my phone ring from the kitchen. Reaching the table, I see that it's Guy. The phone feels hot in my hands, as if it will burn through my skin. I don't want to talk to him until I get my hands on more information and decide how to proceed, but it will seem odd if I avoid him. I accept the call and say hello.

"Bryn, what's going on?" he demands as soon as I answer. His voice exudes concern with a trace of exasperation. "Why are you blowing off our dinner?"

"I'm not feeling well. I . . . I think it's best if I lay low today."

"Can I help?"

"No, that's not necessary."

"At least let me come over, Bryn. I can bring food. We can talk. Maycock—"

"No, Guy, please. My head is killing me. I just want to rest."

"But what about this news from Maycock? That the cops are asking for your alibi? We should discuss this."

"We'll talk about it later, okay?" I say, praying he doesn't suspect I'm on to him. "I'll call you to reschedule."

I head to my office. After forwarding the key emails to Maycock, I turn my attention to Guy. I've had to undertake a significant amount of research for each of my books, but mainly it's involved coaxing people to share their stories, which they often yearn to do. I don't have investigative-reporter chops, though, and that means I lack the know-how to do a deep dive on someone, finding data that a person is trying hard to conceal. At best, all I'm going to turn up on Guy today is stuff bobbing on the surface.

Since I've been to his hometown and met people who knew him at his mother's memorial service, it's clear any serious fabrications must have occurred after he left for college. I decide to start there. I remember hearing his mother mention something about his time at UC Santa Barbara, and I assume, at least for now, that's where he actually did his undergraduate work. I bring up the college's website and click on "Alumni" in the navigation bar, which takes me to an alumni page. There's no way I'm going to be allowed access to the directory without a password, but I try to log in anyway. No such luck. As I'm about to leave the page, I notice a search bar up at the top. I type in Guy's name just for the hell of it.

To my surprise, stuff pops up. Not his profile, but rather a page of links to articles in the alumni magazine featuring anyone with the last name of Carrington. And there's one that features a Guy Carrington from the class he always said he graduated in.

I click on the link. It takes me to a piece that ran in the alumni magazine when Guy was twenty-six or so, about grads who were born and raised in California and were now living and working elsewhere. There are a couple of photos of graduates, though none of Guy, but halfway down the article, there's a quote from him about living in Chicago and working in the fund-raising office of the Illinois Medical Center. "The first winter was tough, with a ton of snow," he reports, "but Chicago is a great city, so all is forgiven."

It sounds just like him—all smiles and ready to see the upside. The article mentions that he will be headed to UCLA in the fall for a master's in business administration.

All of this squares with what he's told me about that period of his life. And he was clearly going by Guy then.

I try the UCLA site next, to no avail. I press a hand to my head, trying to recall the sequence of employment after that, or at least the sequence that was fed to me. After business school, Guy supposedly returned to Chicago and rejoined the medical center's development office at a higher level. Following that was a stint at a small start-up in Chicago whose name I don't recall. Nothing to do with fund-raising, but he was ready for a change. Then, just over nine years ago, it was on to Miami and back to fund-raising, launching a firm with a B-school pal who grew up in Florida. They helped raise money for organizations too small to have their own fund-raising department. The friend had the contacts, and Guy was the strategist. It was after they sold the company two and a half years ago that Guy moved to Saratoga—eager, he claimed, to be back with a well-regarded organization and to move up from there.

I steel myself for more. I Google "Guy Carrington, Miami," as well as "Carrington-Wolfe," the name of the firm. More than a handful of references actually turn up. The firm is referenced in back issues of online regional trade magazines, and Guy is even quoted in a couple of them.

So far nothing seems off about the Miami stint of his career, but it occurs to me that none of the links are more than seven years old. So maybe part of the time he claimed to be in Miami was covering for the stint in Dallas.

I lean my head back against the top rim of the desk chair and smile grimly to myself. My mother used to say that a key to decorating on a budget was to mix a few quality antiques in with cheaper stuff, and people would assume it was all expensive. That's kind of been Guy's MO with me, I realize—to mix truth in with the lies. What he told me about college seems to be legit, and so probably was the info he shared about his first job in Chicago. But I'm left in doubt about everything that followed from there. That's when he was in Dallas, according to Bloom.

I understand now that my husband is a liar but there's one detail in particular that confuses me. Guy went back to using his first name when he moved to Miami, but why did he decide to go by Rich when he moved to Dallas? Maybe there'd been trouble in Chicago as well, trouble that he was trying to distance himself from. I wonder if he'd cooked the books other places, like at the medical center.

Cooking the books. I jerk forward in the chair, remembering the night Guy fretted because he said the numbers weren't coming out the right way. Has he embezzled from the opera company, too?

I glance around my tiny office. The windowsill is lined with a row of basil plants, a touch I added to make the space homier. Sitting here now, I feel like someone who has woken up in another woman's house and has no clue how she got there. The lovely, perfect life I've created for myself is all a sham. Regardless of whether Guy's a crook, he's deceived me about his life, and there's no way I can stay married to him.

Thank God, I think, my parents aren't here to see the mess I've made of things. Yet at the same time, I long for the comfort of their presence. As my eyes well with tears, I brush them away. It's not going to do any good to wallow in my misery. I've done enough of that during the past three months.

As I reach to turn off my laptop, I notice an email from Maycock. He's reviewed the emails, he said, and will share the news with Corcoran, and promises to be back in touch. It's too vague to be comforting.

What I need to do, I realize, is escape this house. While there's no way I can leave town now—the cops wouldn't stand for it—I can at least find someplace else to stay. I'll use tonight to pack up and move out first thing tomorrow.

A sound pierces the silence, making me jerk in the chair. It's the doorbell at the front of the house. I wonder if Guy's come by despite my protests and decided to ring the bell.

I spring from my seat and hurry to the front of the house. But it's not Guy. Peering through one of the side windows along the door, I spot Barb Donaldson standing on the porch, bearing a huge bouquet of white flowers. In a crazy way, she's a sight for sore eyes. I compose my face and swing open the door.

She's in another Palm Beach–style dress today, this one in bright pink and green stripes. Her pink lipstick has smeared a little, probably from the flowers having brushed against her face.

"I hope I'm not interrupting anything," she says brightly.

"No, not at all. Come on in. Would you like an iced tea?"

She steps into the front hall and thrusts the bouquet toward me.

"I can't actually stay. I just wanted to drop these off for you."

"That's so sweet of you, Barb. Let me find a vase."

"I thought you might like them. There's nothing like calla lilies to cheer you up when you're not feeling well."

I spin around so fast the movement seems to startle her. What's Guy been saying? I wonder.

"Who told you I wasn't well?"

"Oops, I hope I'm not blabbing something I shouldn't. Kim Emerling mentioned it when I ran into her at an event yesterday. She said she'd had dinner with you and Guy, and that you've been under the weather."

I can't believe it. That woman definitely has it out for me.

"Well, I hope this doesn't mean I have to give the flowers back, but I've actually been fine. I'm not sure how Kim ended up with that idea."

Barb throws up her hands in mock bafflement.

"Who knows? It's probably no picnic living with that bad-boy husband of hers. Oops, I shouldn't have said that either."

I let that one go.

"Are you sure I can't offer you something?"

"Nope, I gotta skedaddle, but we'll get together another time—and I still have to send you dates for the book club." She lets her gaze roam the hall. "Where's that handsome hubby of yours? He's not working today, is he?"

"Just running errands," I say too quickly.

"Well, tell him I sent my regards."

As she straightens her bag's strap on her shoulder, I reach into the pocket of my jeans, where I know there's a clean tissue.

"Barb, the flowers smeared your lipstick. Let me fix it before you go."

As I lean in closer, I pick up the scent of wine from her lips. She's been drinking. Maybe more than a glass. I think of the wine she served at the shop and wonder if it might be a daily routine.

"I so appreciate women who look out for each other," she says when I'm done. "Have a nice evening, okay? I bet a couple of newlyweds like you two always end up doing something fun on a Saturday night."

I manage a smile. I don't have the urge to manufacture a fake comment in reply.

After she's gone, I consider again what she's revealed about Kim. While she may not be my priority right now, it's key to watch out for her.

Back in my office, I research hotels in town. There's a small inn on Broadway called the Saratoga Arms that miraculously has a room free from tomorrow until Friday. I book it. Before

I complete the information, I look to see if I could actually check in tonight, but the inn is full.

As dusk settles over the house, the dread I've felt each night returns, like a predatory creature slinking through the weeds. I go from room to room, flipping on lights, and then I start to pack, hoping it will be a distraction.

I manage to stuff the clothes I've brought into two small roller bags and my office supplies into three boxes I locate in the garage. I told myself when I moved here that, based on how low in energy I was, I probably wouldn't require many clothes. Now I can't help but wonder if on some deep level I intuited how short my stay in this house would be. I haul everything to the area by the kitchen door so I can quickly load it into my car come morning.

Finally, at eleven, I head upstairs. I envision another night of endless, wide-eyed flopping in bed, but as I slip in between the sheets, I realize that not only has the packing made my bones ache with fatigue but also the idea of decamping from the house tomorrow has calmed me. I find myself quickly drifting off to sleep.

And then I'm awake again, staring into pitch-darkness. Something has stirred me into consciousness. For a moment, I wonder if I've had another nightmare, and I lie there quietly, trying to summon it. But nothing comes.

I consider then if a noise has woken me. I struggle up on my elbows and switch on the bedside lamp, creating a small pool of light in the room. *It's probably just the* house, I tell myself.

And then I hear it. Not the house creaking. It's a rhythmic, metallic sound that's coming from downstairs. My heart hurls itself against my rib cage, and I bolt all the way up this time.

It stops. And comes back a couple of seconds later. A clicking, something moving back and forth. And then nothing again.

Fear practically immobilizes me, but I force myself out of bed and grab my phone off the table. I tiptoe from the bedroom into the hallway, to the top of the stairs.

I freeze in position there. Seconds pass. It's now utterly silent. Could I have heard a branch scraping against a window? Holding my breath, I descend the stairs. I have to figure out what it was.

I reach the downstairs hall, where the wall sconces are burning brightly, and stand perfectly still again. The sounds, I realize, must have come from here or the living room, or else I wouldn't have heard them. I peer out one of the windows alongside the door. The porch light is on and there's nothing there.

Cautiously I step into the living room. It's all lit up, just as I left it, but it seems odd to find it this way in the middle of the night, as if an emergency has roused the entire household. I swing my head back and forth, checking every corner. Nothing seems amiss. I move to the windows next, looking for branches. But I can't see anything that could have produced the noise.

As I turn to leave, my heart still thrumming, my eye falls on the door to the screened porch. I step forward and reach for the metal handle. I jiggle it several times, and at the sound my body goes limp. This is what I heard from upstairs. Someone moving the handle up and down, trying to get in.

Chapter 21

INSTINCTIVELY MY GAZE SHOOTS OUT ONTO THE screened porch. I left a small table lamp burning, and it illuminates most of the interior space. Nobody's there. But the outside door to the porch has been flung open.

I jerk my body around so I'm facing back into the living room, wondering if the prowler has managed to penetrate the house. The room's empty, untouched. I turn back toward the door. The bolt's still on—I can see the gunmetal-gray sliver of it between the door frame and the door. No one could have entered this way.

I tear from the room and check the bolt on the front door. It's in place. As, thankfully, is the one on the kitchen door. I glance toward the double window above the sink. Though the room is as bright as a movie set, it's pitch-black outside and I can't see a thing.

Who tried to get in tonight? Was it *Guy*? Was it the murderer, intent on hurting Guy or me or both of us?

I need to call 9–1–1. As I lift my finger to tap the number, the phone rings, startling me so much that it almost flies from my hand. The caller is unknown. With a trembling finger, I press accept.

"*Yes?*" I say.

A few moment of silence follow and then, strangely, the sound of rain. I pull the phone from my ear and listen. There's no rain falling outside the house.

"Who *is* this?" I demand.

No one speaks. There's only that sound, rain splattering on the ground. And then I realize the noise is too fast for rain. It's . . . it's the sound of *fire*, the brisk, rhythmic crackling of something burning. And then, far off, a siren wailing.

My knees go weak and I let out a cry, almost a howl. For a few moments I am in hard-packed snow at the bottom of the ravine, watching the flames from the car fire above, feeling, the heat even from below.

I punch desperately at the screen with my finger until the call disconnects. I take several deep breaths, trying to tamp down my panic.

9–1–1. I have to call. But if patrol cops are dispatched here tonight, Corcoran will learn about it soon enough, and she may lump this in the same category as the mystery caller I described days ago. She may assume that I'm fabricating this, too, that I'm up to something again. I can't have her fixated on me any more than she already is.

My gaze falls on the kitchen table. I picture Derek, sitting there the other evening, stressing that he wanted to help me. I scroll through my contacts, searching for his number, and finally tap it, my fingers still shaking. The clock on my phone says 12:34.

Three rings. Finally he answers, his voice groggy.

"Derek, did I wake you?" I blurt out. "It's Bryn."

"No, um . . ." I sense him looking at a clock or trying to get his bearings. "I was just listening to music. Is everything okay?"

"I think someone was trying to break into my house."

"Christ, are you okay? Have you called the police?"

"I'm fine, but I'm scared the person's still out there. And . . . and there's a reason I can't call the cops."

"What about Guy? He's not with you?"

"No. I'm alone."

"Okay, I'm on my way. Give me ten minutes. I'll come to the front."

Ten minutes, I reassure myself as I head back to the hall. The wait seems interminable. Finally I hear a car screech to a halt on the street outside. Peering through the window, I spot Derek bolt from the car and race up the path to the house. As his feet touch the top step of the porch, I fling open the door.

"Thank you. I didn't know who else to call."

"Tell me what happened." He's wearing jeans and a T-shirt that looks like it might have been lying rumpled on his floor a few minutes ago.

"Here, let me show you." I lead him through the living room until we reach the windowed door to the screened porch. "I woke up hearing the handle being rattled." I point out toward the screened door. "And I'm positive the outside door was locked when I went to bed."

He stares through the glass, and I see his eyes reach the door to the side yard. He unbolts the door we're standing at and grabs for the handle.

"Be careful," I urge.

"Whoever was out there is probably gone by now, especially after seeing my car pull up."

He swings open the door to the porch. The night is completely silent.

"Stay here, okay?" he says. He steps onto the brick floor and crosses the porch to the open doorway. I watch him examine the frame, and though I can see only half his face, I can tell he's squinting. Reaching into the darkness, he grabs the screened door and pulls it closed. A sigh escapes his lips.

"What is it?" Ignoring his earlier directive, I hurry toward his side.

"I wondered if the door blew open from the wind, but it looks like someone's punched out both the hook and the eye. Come on, we'd better go back inside." He takes my arm and ushers me into the house, where he bolts the door again.

My heart is back to racing. "Why don't we go into the den," I say, and Derek follows me in. As we both drop onto the couch, I realize that I'm still in my T-shirt and pajama bottoms.

"Is Guy away on business?" Derek asks.

I gnaw at my lip for a moment, trying to decide how much to reveal. It seems wrong to appeal for his help in the dead of night and then not be straight with him.

"Guy's not living here at the moment. I . . . I'm not sure what's going to happen to us."

"Bryn, I'm so sorry," he says. He touches my shoulder gently. The rustling that his hand makes when he pushes against the fabric of my T-shirt is the only sound in the room. "That's tough in light of everything else going on."

"It does feel pretty piled on at the moment."

He glances away, as if distracted by a thought, and then back to me.

"Could it have been *Guy* out there tonight?" he asks. "Is that why you didn't want to call the police?"

Oh God, he's wondering if I've lured him into a riptide of marital stife.

"No, I'm pretty sure it's not Guy. I think someone is trying to mess with my head." I describe the call and the crackling-fire sound, clearly meant to conjure up memories of the car accident.

His face wrinkles in confusion. "But who would do something like that?"

"One of the people at the dinner party that night." I take him up to speed on the missing money and the burnt matches left in my drawer.

"Did you even *know* the other guests that night?"

"It was the first time I'd met any of them. Initially, I thought one of the waiters was responsible, or even Eve, though I had no clue why they'd do it. Lately, I've suspected Kim was the guilty one. She seems to be nursing this weird, irrational dislike of me."

"Bryn, you've got to alert the police. I can understand that your privacy is important, but you need to figure out who's behind this."

"It's not about privacy, Derek. It's more complicated—I'm a person of interest in Eve Blazer's murder."

His jaw drops in complete surprise.

"That's absurd," he says. "What motive are they suggesting? That you hate the taste of mango in your crème brûlée?"

"They think I suspected Guy was shacking up with her."

He stares at me, clearly stunned again.

"*Was* he?" he says finally.

"Maybe. I just don't know."

"If that's the case, why don't the cops think *he* killed her?"

"They like his alibi. I've got a decent enough one, too, so in the long run I should be okay. Right now everything's still a mess, and it doesn't seem smart to have the cops trooping through my house."

"What are you going to do then? It may be dangerous for you to keep living here alone."

"I've already packed up. I'm moving into the Saratoga Arms first thing in the morning."

He nods as he briefly weighs the idea. "Good . . . And you know what? I'm crashing on the couch here tonight."

On one level it's absurd that he's here, that this man I didn't even know two weeks ago has come to my rescue and is offering to camp here for the night, and yet right now my whole life seems like nothing but an endless string of absurdities. His presence happens to be one I'm grateful for.

"It's a lot to ask of you, Derek. I could try to find a motel instead."

"A Saturday night during the summer? Fat chance." He smiles for the first time tonight. "Tell me this—is breakfast included?"

"For sure. And the spare room has a great mattress."

Derek insists, however, on bunking down in the den because that way he'll be more likely to hear if anyone is skulking about.

I go back upstairs and pull down bedding from the hall linen closet. When I return to the den, Derek is by the window, peering searchingly into the night. I catch my breath.

"Did you see something?"

"No, just keeping an eye out." He turns toward me. "You say you're positive you put the cash in your desk drawer the day of the party. So the thief—and the person who left the matches—*has* to be someone who came to your house that night."

"Yes."

"Of course, Guy was there, too. Did you ever consider whether *he* was the one who left the matches?"

The thought had never entered my mind, but now I realize it's worth consideration. If Guy thought nothing of embezzling from at least one company, he might have been helping himself to some of the money I've made. Were the matches part of a plan to keep me off balance so I wouldn't be paying attention to money matters? I shrug, at a loss.

"It's hard to imagine, but in some ways I don't know him at all."

I've told Derek so much already and I'm tempted to share the rest, the details I've uncovered about Guy's background. I ultimately decide to hold back. I can't bring myself to smear Guy. Maybe, just maybe, there's an explanation.

Derek touches my shoulder again.

"You'll figure it out, Bryn," he says. "Why don't you try to sleep now. If there's another call, wake me immediately, okay?"

"Thank you, Derek. I'd better charm the hell out of your class to make up for all of this."

It's not until I'm back in bed that I realize how much my arms and legs are throbbing from stress and fatigue. But sleep doesn't come as easily as it did earlier. I keep recalling the sounds from the phone call, the crackling flames and the distant wail of a siren.

At some point I finally drift off, though when I wake a little after seven, I can tell that it's been a troubled sleep. I dress quickly and hurry downstairs. The door to the den is open, but when I peek in, I see that the couch is empty and the bedding folded neatly at the end. A minute later, I find Derek sitting at the kitchen table, drinking an espresso and staring out into day. The sight of him is totally comforting.

"Hey, good morning," he says. "I hope you don't mind I helped myself."

"Well, I *did* promise breakfast. Were you able to catch any sleep last night?"

"I clocked a few hours, though this house creaks more than my dad's knees. How about you? Those look like some pretty big circles under your eyes."

I smile at his candor. "I didn't do super well. But I felt safe at least. I can't thank you enough for coming over, Derek."

"The more I think about this whole business, the more concerned I am for you, Bryn. I checked the door in the daylight and it looks like someone definitely hacked out the lock, probably with a tool."

I tense at this news. A tool suggests premeditation and a definite attempt to gain entry. And then why the call, too? Just to make sure I was scared out of my mind?

"What if . . . ?" I'm forming the thought even as I speak

the words. "What if the two incidents happening last night were purely coincidental?"

"How do you mean?"

"Though the two things happened around the same time, they're different in some ways. Someone trying to break in, someone trying to freak me out. Maybe the call was from the person who wants to mess with my head—Kim, for instance. And someone else entirely tried to get into the house."

"A burglar, you mean?"

"No, the person who killed Eve."

He straightens in the chair, jolted by my words. I share the theory I've been toying with: that if a jealous lover murdered Eve, he might be in a rage, rightly or wrongly, about Guy as well.

"All the more reason for you to leave here," Derek says.

We discuss a plan over scrambled eggs and toast and decide that after Derek helps me lug my stuff out to the car, we'll drop by the Saratoga Arms. According to the website, check-in is two o'clock, but perhaps I can finagle something earlier. I just don't want to force Derek into playing bodyguard for a huge chunk of my day.

I grab a quick shower while Derek has another espresso, and then it's time to go. I take a last look around the house, making certain I've left nothing important behind. Part of me should probably feel stricken about leaving, but I don't. This place never really felt like a home to me.

"Wait," Derek says as I start to unbolt the kitchen door. "Let me check outside first." He steps out into the driveway, searches the area, and then nods for me to follow. It's overcast out, and the air is raw, like on an April day rather than a June one—fitting weather, it seems, for the state my life is in. Though Derek has given the all clear, I can't help but look around anxiously, wondering if someone has eyes on us.

Once my car is loaded, Derek suggests I pull out first and he'll follow close behind until we reach Broadway. At this hour on a Sunday morning, the streets are nearly empty.

We both park in the designated side street lot and enter the building from the front, up the steps of a long white porch. The lobby is a small, oak-paneled space with a desk, a staircase rising behind it, and a stand stuffed with brochures for local attractions. Off to the right is an inviting parlor. There's not a soul in sight at the moment, and it's only after ringing a bell on the desk that a buxom blond woman, around fifty, hurries into the lobby and greets us warmly. When I say I'm hoping a room will open up before two, she announces, to my surprise, that there's one ready and she's more than happy to let me check in.

"We had a cancellation late yesterday, and there's no point in making you wander around downtown at this hour. You won't find a darn thing to do on a Sunday morning other than eat too many blueberry muffins."

I thank her profusely, and after I handle the paperwork, Derek and I retrieve one of the roller bags from my car. As we mount the steps of the porch again, I notice that Derek looks perturbed.

"Something's on your mind," I say.

"I don't like the fact that the front desk isn't always manned. It doesn't seem like the best place to be."

"I'll have to be cautious. At this point I don't have a choice."

His soft green eyes meet mine. "You could stay at my place—in my spare room. No one would ever suspect you're there."

His comment almost knocks me over. I'm not sure exactly how to read it.

"That's really generous of you, Derek, but this is probably the best spot for me for right now."

"Do you promise to hang in your room and keep a low profile?"

"Definitely. I've got about ten books stored on my iPad, to say nothing of a book proposal I'm supposed to be finishing."

I'm not being straight with Derek, though. I don't have any intention of hanging at the inn, at least for the morning. After we've said good-bye and promised to talk later, after I've unpacked a few items in my room, I text Guy, informing him that I'd like to meet. It's finally time for me to face him. What I'm going to do, I've decided, is confront him with what I've learned and watch how he responds. I know Guy's deceived me, and yet I'm not sure of anything beyond that. Embezzling money—and risking the chance of prison—sets you apart from the mere liars of the world. It means you've dared to cross a dangerous line, and that there might be other dangerous lines you aren't afraid of stepping over. Like murdering someone. I have to find my way closer to the truth.

Within seconds he's texted back: "Of course. Why don't I swing by the house in fifteen?"

"I'm taking a walk," I write back. "Let's meet in Congress Park. Near the main entrance."

For at least a minute there's no response. I'm sure my suggestion has aroused suspicion. Then just, "Sure."

I grab my umbrella in case there's a downpour and start out. Congress Park is seven or eight blocks away, at the other end of downtown, and it should take me less than fifteen minutes to reach there. Despite the hour and the weather, there are now clusters of tourists meandering down the street, window-shopping and sipping coffee from cardboard cups.

With each block I cover, my unease intensifies. In only a matter of minutes, I may know the truth about Guy. And about my life as well. *Please*, I pray, *let him be nothing more than a dirty rotten liar.*

I'm the first one to arrive at the nearly empty park. I stand a step inside the entrance, not far from one of the many fountains that dot the grass. At the far end of the park, a few kids are already riding the carousel, with their parents keeping step and holding them by their waists.

Only a minute passes before Guy appears at the entrance. He's in jeans and a navy barn jacket, and his hair is still damp from his shower. In some ways it's like the moment we met, Guy stepping onto the deck of the beach house in Rhode Island and me looking up, drawn by his forceful presence. And yet everything has changed between us.

Spotting me, Guy heads in my direction. As he moves closer, I see that the muscles in his face are tight, as if he's fighting to contain his true emotions.

He murmurs hello and kisses me on the cheek. As his lips touch my face, they feel strangely unfamiliar, like someone pressing a raw chicken cutlet against my skin. It unsettles me even more.

"Why don't we go someplace and grab coffee?" he says. "I've got a client lunch at one o'clock, but there's plenty of time to talk before then."

"I'd rather skip the coffee and talk here."

"Bryn, what's going on, for God's sake? It's barely sixty degrees out."

"I just feel like being outside." I nod toward a nearby bench, and he shrugs in resignation.

"Fine. You seem to be calling all the shots these days."

"Is that what you think?"

"No, I misspoke." His tone softens. "It's only that I've been trying to see you and talk to you, and all I get are road-blocks."

"Let's talk now then."

Guy takes a seat and stretches his arm across the back of the bench, and though I don't sit close to him, the gesture still feels possessive, as if he wants me within his grasp. I can't believe that the idea of his touch makes me nearly cringe now.

"Maycock filled me in on your interview with the cops," he says. "It scared the hell out of me, but he told me you have tons of emails proving that you were at home on your laptop that night."

"Hopefully, that will be enough." I'm not here, though, to talk about Maycock. It's Dallas, Texas, I'm interested in.

"I want to come home, Bryn. We need to put this whole ugly mess behind us."

He reaches out and touches the hair by my temple ever

so lightly with his hand. It's something he's always liked to do, particularly in the early months of our relationship. His fingers barely graze my skin, light as feathers, in a way that has always seemed both loving and erotic to me. For the first time, though, I see it as something else. *Slick.* It seems like the gesture of a man who wants to play me.

"I know about Dallas, Guy," I say.

His hand freezes momentarily, and then he lowers it to his lap.

"What do you mean?" he asks, his voice totally neutral.

"You know exactly what I mean. The years you lived and worked there."

He shifts his body ever so slightly. I try to read his eyes, but it's tough. On such an overcast day, the slate blue has gone even darker, like the color of the sky right before dusk turns to night.

"And do you mind my asking who's been telling you this?"

"What does it matter, Guy?"

His next move takes me aback. He sighs heavily and lets his body sink into the bench.

"I can't tell you what a relief this is, Bryn. I've wanted you to know from the beginning about the time I lived there. It's been this horrible cloud hanging over my head, eating away at me."

Of all the scenarios I imagined, this was never one of them. That he'd cop to the truth immediately and try to evoke my sympathy.

"Why *didn't* you tell me?"

"Because something happened when I was there. Something I'm gravely ashamed of, and I kept struggling to find the right words to convey it to you."

"You embezzled money."

He rears back, as if stung by the comment.

"For God's sake, no. But I was *accused* of it. By this woman in the organization who'd been passed over earlier for the president's job and had it out for me from the moment I arrived. I *started* to tell you once. Remember that weekend you came up here early last summer, right before the wedding? We drove up to Lake George and were wandering around the park, the one where they found remains of the old settlement. I said I had something I wanted to share, but before I had a chance, you had a call from your agent about an issue that needed to be addressed right away."

I vaguely remember. There'd been a snafu with my UK publisher and I ended up stuck on a ten-minute call as we returned to the car. Later, when I asked Guy what he'd wanted to tell me, he said it had been about the settlement, nothing important.

"If you weren't guilty, why flee the state?"

"It was a total nightmare, with me in this horrible catch-22. At first, I wasn't overly concerned because I was sure an investigation would prove I was innocent, but she—this woman—had planted things to implicate me. I hired a lawyer after they let me go, but it was evident that if I sued, it would cost a fortune. Plus, everything would become public that way. In the end, the only viable option, if I wanted to salvage one ounce of my reputation, was to get the hell out of Texas."

Is it possible that he's telling the truth? That this woman—he must be talking about Gavin Bloom's wife—actually conspired against him? Should I believe a stranger more than my husband?

"So you weren't in Miami all the time you said you were?"

"No. I wasn't straight with you about the time line. I was in Dallas part of that time and moved to Miami from there, not Chicago."

My eyes drift away as I try to weigh the veracity of his words.

"Bryn," he says when I don't reply. "I have no clue who's feeding you all this information, but you have to believe me. And you have to try to see it from my perspective. I was always terrified that if I told you, you'd reject me, which is exactly what's happening *now*."

I pull my lightweight anorak tighter against the chill of the day.

My thoughts are in a total jumble. Should I believe him? Should I try to see the Dallas omission from his vantage point, a part of the past he didn't know how to share? Should I ask for proof, demand to speak to the lawyer? My doubts about Guy wrestle with my need to right my world again, to have my life return to normal.

"What else have you left out, Guy?"

"Nothing, I swear." He reaches out and lays one of his hands over mine. "Please try to understand. I can't let this come between us."

There's another question still, one I've almost forgotten to ask.

"You moved to Texas directly from Chicago?" I say.

"Yes, that's right."

"Why suddenly start using your middle name? You'd never gone by Richard before."

His eyes widen almost imperceptibly, and his lips part. I sense his mind racing, and I realize he's searching for an answer. An answer that will work better than the truth.

Chapter 22

So there *was* trouble before Dallas, a reason for a name change. I wonder if he was caught embezzling in Chicago, too, and that's why he hightailed it to Dallas. I can't let myself hope any longer that Bloom is wrong, that Guy's simply a liar. He's a thief. And maybe more.

"There's an explanation for that," Guy says after a moment.

Of course there is. He's got an explanation for everything.

I stare at him, baffled, wondering how only weeks ago the same eyes and hair and navy barn jacket—it's the one he wore last fall on a weekend trip we took to the Adirondacks, where we lay naked in each other's arms at night while listening to the eerie, wolflike call of a loon on the lake outside our window—once added up to be someone entirely different.

He mistakes the intensity in my expression for eagerness to hear his explanation.

"After I was hired for the Dallas position, the board chairmen mentioned that someone in the organization had a name similar to mine—Guy *Carris*—and that there might be a bit of confusion at first. The last thing I needed was having someone on my staff getting emails and memos meant for me, that sort of thing—so I decided I'd go by my middle name instead at work."

I nearly scoff at the ridiculousness of his explanation, though maybe he should be awarded a few points for manufacturing it out of thin air, and in record time.

"You're saying if I were to call Dallas Gives, announce I was thinking of hiring Guy Carris and ask them to confirm that he'd worked for the organization, they'd know who I was talking about?"

He opens his mouth and I sense he's about to tell me, *Of course, go ahead and make the call*, but he pauses, and in his eyes I spot the first flicker of indignation.

"Why are you doing this to me, Bryn?" he demands instead.

"Why am I doing it to *you*?"

"I explained why I wasn't forthcoming about Dallas. I thought you'd be more sympathetic."

"Sympathetic to the fact that you've deceived me about a huge chunk of your life?"

"I've been nothing but a great partner to you. I helped you through the god-awful mess you've been in since March, as well as this god-awful mess you initiated by going down to Eve Blazer's and demanding your twenties back."

I can't miss the disdain in his tone. And I can't believe he's claiming I'm responsible for the nightmare with the cops. Even if I'd never confronted Eve, the cops would have stumbled upon Guy's texts to her and we'd be in the exact same boat. Though part of me wants to press him about Eve, I don't dare. I don't want him to suspect my fears about the night she died.

"I should go," I say. The light wind that's been blowing

picks up, sending an empty water bottle spiraling down the path in front of us.

"*Go?* Bryn, we have to hash this out. And I need to come home. I'm done being banished to that two-by-four apartment."

"There's nothing to hash out, Guy. Or Richard, or whoever you are. As for the house, it's all yours now."

"You're planning to leave?"

I rise from the bench and pull my anorak tighter. "I already have."

He's on his feet now, too.

"Who've you been talking to Bryn? Did you hire a *detective* to hunt down information on me? Is that what this is all about?"

"I didn't hire anyone, Guy. Your lies are finally catching up with you. I'm surprised people at the opera company aren't wise to you by now. What would they think if they knew you'd embezzled money? Miranda certainly wouldn't be so adoring of you."

He grabs my arm, not hard, but it's unexpected, and I flinch at his touch.

"Miranda? Have you said something to her?

"Let go of me, Guy."

"What did you say to her?" He doesn't loosen his grip, and his voice is low now, almost a growl.

He scares me. The words form in my head and I can't believe I'm thinking them. But it's true. I don't know him and I don't trust him and I'm afraid of what he might do. I yank my arm away.

"I don't need to wreck things for you, Guy. You've wrecked them enough for yourself."

I take off then, walking fast and hard toward the park exit. I'm afraid he's going to follow me, but the only sound behind me comes from the empty plastic bottle being dragged again by the wind.

I walk even faster once I'm back on Broadway. One block. Two blocks. Three. I wonder if Guy's on the sidewalk now, watching me from a distance or even trailing behind me. I don't want to look back and risk meeting his eyes.

There's a café open up ahead, and I decide to duck inside. That way there'll be no chance of him following me to the inn. Entering, I twist my head a little to the side so I can observe the street in the direction I've come from. I don't see any sign of Guy.

Inside I find a table at the back. The place is only a quarter full right now, people in small groups murmuring over their coffee or eating alone, reading newspapers or their tablets. A woman checks me out, as if she may know me, but quickly looks away. I keep my eye on the plate glass window in the front, making sure Guy isn't lurking out there.

I order an espresso. It's the last thing I should be drinking with my heart still racing, but I need the caffeine to help my mind sort this out.

Now what? I can still feel the crunch of Guy's fingers through the sleeve of my jacket and wonder how alarmed I should be. I've assured him I won't make trouble for him at work, but he has no guarantee of that. He knows that if Brent finds out how much he misrepresented parts of his background, he'll be fired in disgrace immediately. And the organization will waste no time taking a closer look at the books.

I think again of that day Guy went into work—anxious, he said, that he'd miscalculated the numbers. It was the same day I found Eve's body, and I'd hurried to his office after being questioned by Corcoran. I'd been surprised to find Miranda in the office, too, supposedly catching up on paperwork. I wonder now if there was another reason for her presence that Saturday, that maybe, just maybe, she and Guy are in cahoots on an embezzlement scheme and have been ripping off the opera company. That could explain her protectiveness of him.

But it's not shady financial dealings that worry me most; it's the stuff about Eve. Snippets of evidence suggest that Guy was involved with her, and I can now see that any assurances from him to the contrary are utterly worthless.

Did he *kill* her, though? Perhaps she tried to break off the relationship, and he couldn't stand it. Maybe he discovered she was shacking up with another guy—Derek said she dated around—and he couldn't stand *that*. Or maybe Eve figured out he was embezzling money and threatened to blow the lid off. I think back again to Eve's comment to me in her office: *Ask your husband.* The underlying message could have actually been, *Your husband's a thief, so maybe* he *took the cash.*

I set down my cup and rest my face in my hand. How did I get here? I wonder. Sitting in a café hours from my real home in New York, wondering whether my husband is not just a thief but a murderer, too.

Perhaps there were always signs, and I simply chose to ignore them as I carved out this shiny new life with Guy. I think of my friends and their surprised reactions when I announced my engagement after a six-month courtship. *Wow, it's moving so fast*, one of them had said. Maybe that had been code, an attempt at warning me to slow down and get a better read on Guy.

I finish the espresso and dig out my wallet. The place has started to fill up with new customers, mostly younger people in yoga pants or cargo shorts, looking like they've recently rolled out of bed. As I flag down the waitress, the woman who checked me out when I arrived catches the movement of my arm and glances over again, studying me intently. I realize finally what's going on. She's recognized me from my book-jacket photo or a TV appearance.

For the first time, I consider how much damage I'd sustain to my career as an author if Guy were exposed. I've never pretended to be an expert on making choices, only someone fascinated by the decisions people make and how those decisions shape their lives, and yet I have been presented at times *as* an expert, an interpreter. What an idiot I'd look like now. An expert on choices who'd made the stupidest one imaginable.

I can't let that distract me, though. There are steps to take right now, and they include finding a lawyer who can convince the cops to allow me to return to New York—and also help me decide whether I should alert the cops to Guy's past. When the waitress presents the bill, I hand her cash and tug my anorak back on, ready to bolt.

And then a surprise. Conrad, the older of the two waiters who worked the dinner party has emerged from a back room and is tying a short white apron around his waist as he moves.

"Take tables five and two," I overhear my waitress tell him. "They both just got here."

I'm pretty sure he hasn't spotted me. I rise from the table, snake quickly through the tables, and exit the café.

Outside I survey the street again, checking not only for Guy on foot but also for Guy in a car, possibly parked along the curb so he can keep tabs on me. Luckily there's no sign of the BMW. Maybe he's driven to the house to confirm that I've really moved out.

I start off, walking as fast as I can. I've gone less than a block when I hear footsteps coming up fast behind me. I spin around with fists clenched in my pockets.

It's not Guy, as I suspected. It's Conrad.

"Hey," he calls out. "I need to talk to you."

"What do you want?" As he advances, I see the tattoo on his neck dart out from under his shirt collar. I step back.

"Don't worry, I'm not gettin' into some big, heavy discussion with you," he says, clearly reading the discomfort on my face. "But you need to get your facts straight, lady."

I study him—his face and his manner. He looks agitated, distressed, but there's nothing hostile or threatening about him.

"Fine, go ahead."

"I didn't take your money. I know you told Eve you thought I lifted it from your office, but I never went near there."

"Well, someone took it that night. What about the other waiter?"

"Scooter? No way. We were working in tandem, and I would have noticed if he went in there."

"What about Eve? You think Eve could have taken it?"

He reels his head back, as if astonished by the suggestion.

"Why would she screw with a customer? If I were you, I'd be focusing on one of those guests of yours. Maybe one's a klepto." He looks back over his shoulder toward the coffee shop. "I need to get back. I don't want you spreadin' it all over town that I'm a thief."

"Which guest? Do you have one in mind?"

"I dunno. I saw one of the women go into the head. It could have been her."

"The one with the short blond hair?"

"No, the real talky one. Who was flapping her lips all night."

He means Barb. I already know she used the powder room. And Nick, too. What I need to find out is whether *Kim* had access to my office.

"Was she the only one who went in there? Besides the male guest?"

"I wasn't exactly on potty patrol that night. As for the guy, I'm not sure if he went to the head. He was in the back hallway—talking to Eve."

"He spoke to *Eve*?" The revelation flabbergasts me. "What about?"

"Scooter was closer, so he may have overheard, but I didn't. What I do know is that it seemed kind of private."

So not only was Nick aware that Eve had been in our home that night, he might actually have known her personally.

"Did either of you tell the cops?"

"All the cops were interested in was where we were the night Eve got whacked, and what we could tell them about her social life."

"Did she ever discuss her social life with you?" I know there's desperation in my voice, but if Guy was involved with Eve, Conrad may have had a clue to it.

"She kept that stuff under wraps." He flips the lock of hair out of his eyes. "Look, I gotta go. I can't afford to lose this gig, too."

"Please, just one more question. Is there a woman who worked for Eve with a baby-doll voice?"

"The cops asked me that, too. No, nobody like that."

He takes off, sprinting, and seconds later disappears back into the café.

I start off again, hurrying. The encounter has thrown me, especially the part about Nick. Not only does it mean that he probably knew Eve, but there's the curious fact that, after the murder, he never commented on her having catered the dinner. Guy was so determined that his blessed donors never learn they'd been served chicken tagine by a woman who was later axed to death, and yet it turns out that Nick knew all along.

I wonder if Nick was one of Eve's many suitors.

As for Conrad himself, my instincts whisper that he's telling the truth. I don't think he would have chased me down the street to defend himself otherwise.

The rain finally starts, with drops that are fat and icy. I start to reach for the umbrella I've stuffed in the pocket of my anorak but decide to run instead. Twice I look back over my shoulder, to be sure I'm not being followed. By Guy or anyone else. I've been so preoccupied with Guy's deceptions, I've pushed the events of last night out of my mind. I have to stay focused on those, too. Someone is trying to fuck with me, maybe even hurt me.

I'm relieved when I reach the inn to find that the woman who checked me in is standing at the front desk. Maybe earlier, when Derek and I found the desk unmanned, was merely a fluke.

I go straight to my room, taking the old staircase to the second floor. Though I had to cover only two blocks in the rain, my anorak is damp and I quickly shrug it off. My body feels chilled, and it's hard to know if it's from the rain or what the morning has served up.

I cross the room to the bed and flop across it sideways on my back, with my feet dangling over the edge. The room is papered in green-and-white toile, with curtains and bedspread to match, the kind of charming mix that under other circumstances I'd love to relax in. I stare at the ceiling as tears start to well in my eyes. I feel alone, at loss.

I think suddenly of a note card I found on my mother's desk just after she died. Typed on the card was a quote she'd read somewhere: "What lies behind us and what lies ahead of us are tiny matters to what lies within us." I knew my mother had placed it there as inspiration, a mantra to repeat during the fight for her life. What she'd be telling me now, I'm sure, is to summon the strength inside of *me*.

I propel myself off the bed and take a seat at the small antique desk by the window. I do a Google search on my laptop for locksmiths in Tribeca and jot down the number for the one closest to my apartment. Next I text my assistant the info, explaining that I want her to arrange for the locks on my apartment door to be changed and to overnight me a set of the keys. This will guarantee Guy can't gain access. I bought the place a year before I met him, with spoils from my second book, and the prenup protects it.

I take a breath and start composing my next email. It's to a friend of mine from college, Susan Bruno, who's now a highly regarded defense lawyer in Manhattan. Because of her jam-packed schedule, we rarely get together more than twice a year, but she's always happy to answer the occasional legal question by email or phone. I ask if she has the name of a top-notch criminal defense attorney in the Albany, New York, area, promising that I'll explain later. I pause, wondering how to frame the next question. I know I can trust Susan—she's the master of discretion—but I momentarily recoil from putting the words out into the universe. I don't have a choice, though, and I take the plunge: "And a divorce lawyer. Unfortunately I need one of those, too."

A moment later, my phone rings from inside my purse. To my surprise, it's Sandra. Considering the way she took off yesterday, nearly leaving skid marks, I wasn't sure I'd ever hear from her again.

"Sorry to rush off from lunch like that," she says.

"Don't worry about it. I know you've got this big event coming up."

Though I no longer consider her a potential ally, I'm glad that she at least doesn't seem miffed.

"And were you okay with the bill? I realized later that they might only take cash or a check, and I'd left you high and dry."

"No, they accept credit cards—I was fine."

"Good. I'll give you a call later this week. I still want you to see the venue where we're holding the event."

"Okay, thanks," I say, though I have no intention of following up on her offer.

Something starts to nudge at my brain as soon as I disconnect, and I sense it relates to a comment Sandra made. It's an hour later before I realize that it was her comment on the restaurant only taking cash or checks. *My checkbook.* I tossed it one day in the drawer of my desk, and I don't think I retrieved it when I packed. I tear through my messenger bag, and roller bags, but there's no sign of it.

I check the time. Almost two thirty. Guy could very well be back from the client lunch—if there even *was* one—and I don't dare return to the house today. I'll have to go tomorrow when he's safely at work. I dread the idea, but I don't want to leave the checkbook for him to find.

For the rest of the afternoon, I stay put in the room, munching on free bags of chips from the kitchenette off the lobby and trying to hold my panic at bay. Derek texts to see how I'm doing and promises to phone in a while. Later there's a call from Susan.

"Hey, what's going on?" she asks.

I explain the situation in broad strokes. It feels at moments as if I'm talking about someone else, someone I knew years ago and have heard these crazy rumors about. Susan tells me to stay calm, that she'll help me sort this out, and she assures me that before the day is over, she'll have names for me,

At a little after six, I realize that the bags of chips have done nothing to assuage my hunger, only intensified it. There's no restaurant at the inn, and the only room service options are small cheese-and-fruit plates. I decide to make a run for food.

After retrieving my car from the parking lot, I end up driving southwest. There's a small village in that direction called Ballston Spa, which Guy and I passed through once, and I figure I can probably grab a meal there with slim chance of running into Guy or anyone else I know. The trip takes longer than I remember, but once I'm there, I find a place to eat easily enough. It's a small, wood-paneled restaurant on Front Street, in the center of the village. I settle at the counter and order a burger.

It's after eight by the time I finish, and I'm surprised not to have heard from Derek by now. I realize how much I've relied on him in the past twenty-four hours, and not simply for his willingness to show up at my door after midnight.

So I call him. Five rings and then voicemail. Hearing his voice and the easygoing message he's left, I admit to myself that I also find Derek attractive, both physically and personally. I've got no business thinking about that right now. I leave a brief message and point the car toward Saratoga.

Maddeningly, the return trip takes even longer than the initial one. I lose my way while dusk fades. The GPS lady becomes hopelessly confused, and I find myself for a second time on an empty back road that seems to go absolutely nowhere. Finally I override one of the GPS commands and eventually spot a sign for Saratoga Springs.

Once I reach the inn parking lot, I let my eyes roam the area before exiting the car, just making sure Guy hasn't tracked me down. There's no one in sight, though as I cross the lot a minute later, I hear boisterous laughter coming from the street behind me.

Back in my room, I put on the TV and find a movie. I might as well be watching a tank of water. I turn to my computer, checking email for what seems like the millionth time. Gratefully, I see that Susan has sent the names of two firms in Albany, specializing in criminal law, the first of which she particularly recommends, along with a specific name. She's left messages at both firms, saying I might be in touch. More on divorce lawyers later.

Still no word from Derek.

I finally dress for bed and crawl under the covers. Despite how raw my emotions are, I find my muscles relaxing into the mattress, as if eager and ready to surrender to sleep. It's because I feel safe here, I realize, away from that big old house and from whomever's eyes were on me.

I'm not even aware of drifting off to sleep, but the next thing I know, I'm being roused from it, conscious of my phone ringing again. Squinting, I make out Derek's name on the screen.

"Did I wake you?" he asks before I manage a hello.

"Yeah, that's all right. How are you?"

"I'm okay, but I've got weird news."

My breath catches. "Tell me."

"Remember me mentioning that buddy of mine who's a reporter for the paper here? He called to say that there may have been another murder, and it's apparently someone who works at the opera company."

"*Guy?*" My heart has frozen in my chest.

"No, no—it doesn't sound that way. The body was discovered at 53 Kintner Road, out in an area called Knoll Spring Park. Does that ring a bell?"

The name of the area is vaguely familiar, though I can't quite place it. I tear through my memory, only half listening as Derek makes a comment about his reporter friend hightailing it there now, and something about the neighborhood. That it's upscale.

And then my brain has it. Brent Hess, Guy's boss. When Guy and I were first engaged, we ended up going to a stiff, dreary cocktail party at Brent's million-dollar home in what I'm almost positive was Knoll Spring Park.

"No bells, no." I'm uncertain why I'm not being straight with Derek. Maybe because I don't want anything leaked to the press until I know what's going on. "That's all this guy knows?"

"For now, yes. He's going to call me once he gets out there, and then I'll fill you in. You doing okay otherwise?"

"Yeah, though this is distressing. I won't go back to bed. I'll wait for your call."

After I hang up, I lie back against the pillows, feeling my alarm balloon. If Guy's boss has been murdered, there's no way in hell this is a big coincidence. This has to have something to do with Guy. Perhaps he really *has* embezzled from the opera company and wasn't able to keep a lid on it any longer. Brent might have figured it out and confronted Guy tonight. And Guy killed him.

Or what if it was Guy who was killed during a confrontation?

I can't lie here endlessly speculating and waiting for third-hand information—I've done enough lying around these past months. I have to see for myself what's going on. Though showing up at another crime scene is surely a dumbass idea, I need to make sure that the victim isn't Guy or someone he knows.

After throwing my clothes back on, I descend to the ground floor, this time using a back staircase I've noticed, which takes me closer to the parking lot. I input the address that Derek has given me, hoping that this time the GPS will cooperate.

It's clearly rained again since I've been back from dinner. The streets are wet, and they glisten eerily wherever the street lamps cast their light. Ten minutes later, I reach Knoll Spring Park, a fancy-pants development of winding drives, big houses, and perfectly groomed lawns. All the homes are expensive, though some are more posh than others, their driveways protected by automatic iron gates.

I'm closing in on the address when I see the glow. The whole sky to the west is lit, as if there's a traveling carnival or circus around the bend.

Finally turning unto Kintner Road, I discover that there practically *is* a carnival. Three or four houses down the street is an array of white TV news vans, each emblazoned with station call letters. Beyond that, from what I can see, is at least one ambulance and several police cars. There are people, too, a throng of them milling around.

I've made it as far as I can go by car, so I park along the side of the road, careful not to block a driveway. I step out of the car. The night is filled with the hum of the TV vans.

I take off on foot, moving closer to the action. There are probably forty people congregated on either side of all the vehicles—mostly neighbors, I assume, based on the worry etched on their faces and the fact that at least one woman is still in a nightgown with a light coat tossed over it. Farther ahead are TV reporters, mics in hand. It seems as if an invisible barrier is keeping everyone from surging forward toward the house, but as I reach the outside of the crowd, I see that the yard has been ringed with yellow plastic caution tape, just like at Eve's. Please, I think. Don't let it be like that. And don't let it have anything to do with me.

Finally I see the house, visible from the street but situated at the far edge of a huge front lawn and illuminated courtesy of the TV lights. It's made of clapboard, painted gray, with arched doors and windows, and a white chimney running up the front.

It's not Brent's house. His was much bigger, and made of stone.

I step even closer to the crowd and try to eavesdrop, but people are either whispering or standing in stunned silence, sometimes straining their necks in order to see better.

"Excuse me," I say to a woman near me, keeping my voice hushed. "What's going on?"

She turns to me, her eyes wide. She's about fifty, dressed in sweats, but her hair is coifed, as if she'd changed into something casual after an evening out.

"A neighbor of ours was attacked tonight. It's just horrible."

"Is he still alive?"

"No. She's dead. The body's up there."

She cocks her chin toward the front of the crowd, and I follow with my eyes, letting my gaze weave among the heads of rubberneckers. At last I see what she's talking about. There's a form in the driveway, covered with a white sheet. My stomach clutches. For a few seconds I'm back in Eve Blazer's office again.

"*She?*" I whisper.

"It's Miranda. Miranda Kane."

Chapter 23

ER WORDS ARE LIKE A PUNCH IN THE FACE. No, please, it can't be true. It can't be Miranda under there.

"Oh dear, is she a friend?" the woman asks. She reaches out and touches my arm as the man next to her turns to observe our exchange.

"Uh, yes. I mean, I know her . . . That's her house?" I'd always assumed that Miranda might be struggling financially as a single mom with kids in college.

"Yes. She was bludgeoned right in her driveway. Someone said the person must have been waiting for her."

Unbidden, my mind plays back the encounter with Guy in the park this morning. Me taunting him, asking what people at the opera company would think if they knew of his crime, and whether Miranda would still adore him. He'd grabbed my arm and demanded to know if I'd talked to Miranda.

Did Guy do this? Was he afraid I'd blabbed to Miranda about Dallas and that she'd make a beeline to Brent with it on Monday?

At the very least, this can't be a coincidence—Eve dead, and now Miranda. It defies the laws of probability that two single women were violently murdered by different people within a week of each other in such a small city. They must have been killed by someone who knew them both—or else I'm supposed to believe that a serial killer has blown into town and begun a bloody spree.

I can't stay here, I think. I have to get back to the inn, where it's safe. Before I can turn, I hear the sound of a car approaching from behind me, undeterred by the crowd. I glance over. It's a dark four-door with a pulsing red light on the edge of the roof, directly above the driver's door. The man behind the wheel noses the vehicle ahead, forcing people to shift to the left. With a jolt I note that Corcoran is riding shotgun.

I avert my gaze, hoping she won't notice me. As soon as the vehicle has disappeared beyond the TV vans, I retreat to my car. The only way to escape the area is to return the way I came, which means putting the car in reverse, backing into a nearby driveway, and then pulling out so that I'm pointed in the opposite direction. As I maneuver the car, I notice several clumps of people on the fringe of the crowd turning to watch me.

I'm barely conscious of the drive to the inn. All my thoughts are on Miranda, lying lifeless under that sheet with her bright red hair and creamy skin. *Bludgeoned* to death. I need to talk to Derek and find out if his reporter friend has spilled more details.

And where the hell is Guy right now? I feel sick thinking that he might have done this and that a single remark from me might have compelled him. If he wanted to keep Miranda from talking, he might have the same plan in mind for me, to shut me up.

As I near the center of town, I check the rearview mirror. There are headlights several car lengths back, and I have a sense, without being sure why, that they've been there for a little while. Fortunately, by the time I reach the inn, they've vanished. The town, in fact, seems deserted.

After parking, I make a mad dash through the night to the front of the inn and up the steep steps of the porch. I reach for the door handle. It's locked. Damn. I squint, searching for a buzzer to ring. I see the panel then, and realize I need to use my key card. I fumble in my purse for the card and jab it into the slot. It's like my freaking nightmare, again, the door I can't make open.

Finally the lock clicks and I shove the door, nearly stumbling into the small foyer as it opens. There's no one at the front desk. To the right, the parlor is empty, with only a small lamp burning on a side table, and the breakfast room, just beyond the parlor, is totally dark, though there's enough light cast in that direction for me to see that the tables have been set for breakfast.

I hurry toward the staircase. As I take the first step, I hear a noise from far off, possibly from the back of the inn. I freeze and listen. The sound comes again. It's a faint clanging, as if someone has banged a pot against a counter or pushed a metal object out of the way. There must be a kitchen back there, I realize. Maybe a helper is prepping food for breakfast tomorrow morning.

I take the stairs, two at time. The second-floor corridor turns out to be utterly quiet, with not even the drone of a TV escaping from under a door. Flying down the hall toward my room, it feels as if I'm slicing through the silence like a fish through water.

Inside my room I take a minute to catch my breath before calling Derek.

"Did you end up falling back asleep?" he asks.

"What?" But then I see from the screen that he phoned fifteen minutes ago. I probably missed the call because I left my purse on the front seat of the car when I joined the crowd of rubberneckers. "Oh, sorry, I didn't hear it."

"Okay, the woman who died is Miranda Kane. She was apparently beaten with a heavy object—they're not sure what yet. Do you recognize the name?"

"Yes. She's Guy's assistant."

"My God. You knew her then?"

"Yes. And I went there, Derek—after talking to you. I had to see it for myself."

"To the crime scene?"

"Yup, I just got back. Whatever she was beaten with, the crime's not so different from what happened to Eve."

"True, though the two murders may not be related. According to my buddy, Miranda Kane is divorced and the house is in the ex-husband's name. This might have involved bad blood from the split. Are there kids, do you know?"

"Yes, but they're in college, so there's no custody issue. And she's been divorced for years, as far as I know."

"So maybe *not* the ex-husband."

Neither of us speaks for a few moments, and I can practically see the question forming in Derek's mind.

"I have to ask you," he says finally. "I know you said Guy

had an alibi for Eve Blazer's murder, but is there any chance he could have killed both of these women? He's a big common denominator."

I sigh, not wanting to utter out loud that I've considered the same idea. Though I've relied on Derek for support, I don't know him well. There's no way I dare mention the exchange Guy and I had about Miranda or my doubts about Guy's alibi. "It's hard to imagine he's capable of that."

"You have to be very careful, Bryn. You told me you were going to keep a low profile."

"I know, and I don't like exposing myself, but going out is the only way to gather information."

I tell him then about running into Conrad earlier in the day and the case he made in defense of himself, the other waiter, and Eve as well.

"So if the kitchen crew didn't leave the matches, who did? Like I said, it had to be someone who was there that Thursday."

"Yes, and . . ." A thought forms, one that feels like it's been slowly knitting together in my mind for days. "And part of me wonders if the missing money and the matches are connected to everything else. There's this weird overlap."

"How do you mean?"

"I'm not sure exactly. It just seems strange that everything unfolded at the same time—me being harassed *plus* the murders. Could it really be a coincidence? Here's something else interesting. Conrad said one of the male guests had spoken to Eve by the kitchen that night. A quick, private conversation."

"Really? Which guest?"

"I didn't have to ask him. I saw Kim's husband come from

that direction at one point, though I assumed he'd gone to the bathroom.

"You're not thinking *he* killed Eve, are you?"

"No, not necessarily, it's just odd. He was there that night, he clearly knew Eve, and yet after the murder, he never *mentioned* he knew her."

Silence again. Is he trying to make sense of it as well?

"Derek, please don't share any of what I've told you with the reporter. It's just between the two of us right now, okay?"

"Absolutely. And promise me you'll be careful, Bryn. Is there any chance I can convince you to stay in?"

"I don't have plans to go anyplace else," I tell him. Though at some point I'm going to have to return to the house and collect my stupid checkbook.

"Call me in the morning. I'll be around."

After hanging up, I double-check that the security bolt is in position on the door. Earlier I felt safe here, but I don't right now—even with that steel door between me and the hall.

I peel off everything but my T-shirt, and slide between the sheets. All I can think about is Miranda. Her poor kids. They've surely been told by now and must be on their way home from their colleges, shocked and grief-stricken and forever changed.

Though I'd never compare my loss to theirs, I'm grief-stricken, too. There's an ache in me, resulting not only from the death of my marriage but also from the loss of my life as I knew it to be. I've been conned by Guy. I might even be in danger from him.

Detective Corcoran, I realize, is going to grill me hard

about Miranda's murder. She'll want to know about Guy's relationship with his attractive assistant, whether it was amicable, whether it could have been more than a work relationship. After I began to lose trust in Guy, I wondered briefly whether he'd ever slept with Miranda, and yet I can't imagine tossing that kind of conjecture out to the cops without any proof.

But then what *should* I tell them? They'd surely be interested in Guy's secret years in Dallas and the way he demanded to know if I'd shared the news about his past with Miranda. And yet I don't think I can bring myself to throw him under the bus when I don't know for sure how culpable he is.

My eyes pop open, and I jerk straight up in bed, staring into the darkness. Derek's comment has wiggled its way back into my brain, the one about Guy being a common denominator. I realize *I'm* a common denominator, too. If Corcoran thinks I hated Eve for possibly having an affair with Guy, she may assume I also suspected Miranda and fixated on her as well. That I'm a jealous, murderous maniac.

Something else: I was out tonight, without a solid alibi for every moment.

No, it's all too far-fetched for Corcoran to actually believe. With the first murder, she let herself become snarled in the idea that I was hounding or stalking Eve. She could hardly think the same in regards to Miranda. I've seen her only twice since I'd been living full-time in Saratoga, the two times I dropped by the office.

But wait, those aren't the only times. Through the sheet I feel goose bumps pop on my arms. I saw Miranda yesterday at the restaurant, eating with her friends as I finished my coffee alone. It was all pure coincidence, both of us ending up at the same lakeside spot on a Saturday.

If in tracing Miranda's last steps, the police check the credit card receipts at Dock Brown's, they'll know I was there at the same time and may conclude that I'd stalked her, too, obsessed with the notion that she was involved with Guy. I'd have to count on Sandra telling the cops that the restaurant pick was all her idea.

I use the words on my mom's note card to calm me. Tomorrow is Monday, and I'll be able to reach out to the law firm that Susan recommended. I just have to stay strong until then.

As soon as I wake in the morning, I splash water on my face and take a seat at the small desk where I've set up my laptop. I search the *Saratogian* website for any news about Miranda. There's a short item saying that her body was discovered last night by a friend dropping off a package. No weapon mentioned. No suspect at this time. Police are trying to determine if there is any connection to the murder of another local woman, Eve Blazer.

Surely it won't be long before I hear from Corcoran. She'll want to meet with me in person, demanding to know where I was last night and when I saw Miranda last. I need to line up a lawyer before that call comes in.

And maybe, I think, it would actually be smart to forewarn Sandra. That might be a better tactic than simply giving her name to Corcoran and counting on Sandra to confirm that Miranda and I were both at the restaurant by pure chance.

With still an hour to go before I can reach the law firm Susan recommended, I venture down to breakfast. The room is nearly full, and disconcertingly noisy, with a chatty couple at one table humble-bragging to the people next to them about trips they've taken all over the planet.

By the time I'm on my second cup of coffee, the room has mostly emptied. I've been waiting for quiet to help me think, but now that it's arrived, I still can't make sense of why Eve and Miranda have been killed a week apart. Guy *is* a common denominator. But because both women worked with the opera company, there must be other people they both interacted with. They may have even been connected somehow outside of work.

My mind snakes its way back to the idea I floated by Derek last night—that the murders and the scary things that have happened to me over the past few weeks may be related. I don't have any rational reason for thinking this, but they *do* seem weirdly mushed together. From the moment I tugged open my desk drawer and found the burnt matches, everything began to unravel.

The key may be to finally figure out who left the matches. The answer will be a thread I can begin to follow, and even if it leads away from the murder, I'll at least finally know who was trying to shake me up.

I toy with an idea. Maybe Kim *was* the one who stole the money, but not because she felt resentful of my success. Rather it could be because Nick was sleeping with Eve and Kim found out. Maybe she caught her husband talking to Eve in the kitchen and knew from their body language that something was up. And . . . and she took the money so it would reflect badly on Eve. She would know I'd suspect Eve or one of the waiters and likely never use the catering company again.

As for the matches, perhaps Kim spotted them someplace and stuffed them in the drawer, so that I'd be even more upset with Eve and her crew. And later she killed Eve in a jealous rage.

Or *Nick* killed her in a rage, after sneaking off from the party. If he did, that doesn't explain why he'd try to break into my house or call me on the phone with the crackling sound of fire playing.

And it doesn't explain Miranda. Nick must have spoken to her on the phone intermittently, as he set up activities and appointments with Guy. He may have even met her on occasion. But I can't envision a reason that he'd have for killing her—or that Kim would have, for that matter, even if she's the one who murdered Eve. It might be that the two murders have absolutely nothing to do with each other.

Or they do, and Guy is the killer, after all.

My head hurts from thinking so hard. Coffee cup in hand, I ascend to the second floor and finally, at exactly nine, I call the law firm Susan recommended the highest. An assistant picks up the line for the partner I'm supposed to talk to, Kyle Landry. She informs me that Mr. Landry has been expecting my call but won't be able to speak with me until one o'clock. I tell her I'll be waiting.

Next I phone Sandra. Voicemail picks up, and I leave a message for her to please call me. It's an hour before I hear back from her.

"I'm sorry to bother you when you've got your event coming up, but I could use your help on a matter."

"Of course, Bryn. What can I do for you?"

"Is it possible for us to meet briefly? I'd rather tell you in person."

She hesitates, probably perplexed. An in-person meeting suggests that it's serious, perhaps sensitive. After the awkwardness of our conversation yesterday, I don't want to spit out my request over the phone.

"Um, all right. And since I'm working at the venue today, it will give you a chance to see it. Are you familiar with the Washington Baths?"

"Yes, they're in Saratoga Park, right?" I've driven by the large brick building she's referring to. It's one of the legendary old bathhouses still in operation. "What time?"

"How about eleven thirty? We'll have the place to ourselves today, so we can talk. Park around the back and use the door there."

The time works perfectly. Guy will be at work then, giving me the chance to swing by the house right before for my checkbook, and I'll be back at the inn in time to speak to the lawyer at one.

After I've thanked her and disconnected, I spot a text from Derek, asking if I'd like him to stop by in a while with sandwiches for lunch.

I don't want to mislead Derek again. I type that I have to run out this morning and I'm not sure when I'll be back.

"Thought you were going to lie low," he writes in response.

"Mostly, but this is important."

"Where you headed?

"Washington Baths to meet friend. Won't be long. CUL."

I bide my time for the next couple of hours, sometimes trying to read, sometimes pacing the floor. I keep returning to the idea that, first and foremost, I need to solve the mystery of the matches and money. Without giving myself much time to think it through, I track down the phone number for the café I was at yesterday, call it, and ask to speak to Conrad.

"Hold on," a woman says, the air behind her filled with clattering dishes and blurred conversation. A moment later Conrad barks hello.

"Hi, it's Bryn Harper. When we spoke on the street, you mentioned Scooter. Can I please get a number for him?"

"You must be kidding me. Why would I do that?"

"Please, I need to talk to him. I have to figure out what Eve and Nick Emerling were discussing."

"Emerling? You mean the real estate dude?"

"Yes, exactly.

"He wasn't the guy talking to Eve. It was the other one, the guy with the epic nose. Seated by you at the table.

"*What?*" He obviously means Derek.

"You heard me . . . I've got to go. And leave Scooter out of this."

He disconnects the call, and I'm left standing there in complete bewilderment. Derek and I talked about Eve that night—and after the murder, too—and he's never once mentioned seeking her out and speaking to her at the party. And when I told him that the waiter had seen Eve with a male guest, he didn't admit it was him . . .

How weirdly *sneaky*, I think. What reason would he have to keep that from me? I've trusted Derek to help me these past few days, but I've been stupid to do that if I can't believe everything he says. Maybe the only one I can trust is myself.

I'm in my car by eleven, providing enough time to retrieve my checkbook before I stop by to meet with Sandra. I keep reassuring myself that there's next to zero chance of running into Guy. There was that day I came back from my walk and unexpectedly discovered him in the bedroom, but that was out of the ordinary for him.

I approach the house the back way and park my car in front of the next-door neighbor's, under a large, full maple where it will be less obvious to anyone around. I survey the area, nudge open the door.

Keys in hand, I cross the lawn, planning to scurry up the driveway on the far side of the house and enter by the kitchen door. This will take three minutes tops, I tell myself. All I need to do is unlock the door, scoot to my office, grab the checkbook, and go. I reach the edge of the lawn and turn right into the driveway.

I freeze as my breath catches in my throat. Guy's BMW is parked in the driveway. I turn, sprint back across the lawn, and fling myself into the car. The engine doesn't start the first time I turn the key, and as I try again, I look back at the house, worried that Guy has seen me. There's no sign of him. I try again and again, and finally the car starts up.

I gun the engine and take off, checking the rearview mirror every few seconds to make sure Guy isn't tailing me. What is he doing home at this hour? With Miranda dead, it would seem as if he should be at work, comforting staffers and dealing with the fallout. Unless the situation is unraveling for him, and the cops have told him to stay put until they can speak to him again.

Approaching Broadway, I consider bagging the conversation with Sandra and then tell myself that's stupid. I need the meeting to ensure that she'll set the cops straight about my lunch with her at the lake, that it was all her idea. So I take a right at the light and head toward the Washington Baths. I'm going to be early but can wait for her in the parking lot.

Now that I'm in a busier part of town, there's plenty of traffic, and as I drive toward the outskirts of the city, I'm conscious of the cars behind me. I make the turn into Saratoga Park and notice that one sedan is still behind me. It's not a black BMW, but I don't like the way it practically hugs my bumper. When I reach the building, I shoot right past it. I do a loop through the park and then maneuver onto the main road again, driving until I see the car turn off in another direction. Only then do I circle back to the baths.

The building looks a little like an old temple, constructed of yellow marble with four double-story columns standing proudly along the front. In the thirties, thousands of people apparently visited Saratoga bathhouses each week to soak in the local mineral waters, believing that they provided all sorts of medicinal benefits. Visiting one of the few still open had been on my to-do list for the summer. I can't help but scoff at the memory of that list.

As I pull around to the back, I see the parking lot is empty except for a black Lexus that must belong to Sandra. She'd indicated that we'd have the place to ourselves today. I assume it's closed on Mondays.

I sling my messenger bag over my head and slide out of the car. There's no one in sight, though through the trees to my right I hear shouts and a burst of laugher from what sounds like a group of young boys.

I approach the back door as Sandra advised and tug. It's ancient-looking, and the black paint is peeled and chipped. I step inside and find myself in a square, dim room. The only light comes from a rusted fixture in the ceiling, with a bulb that can't be more than sixty watts. There's one piece of furniture—a rusted metal table.

"Hello?" I call out. My voice echoes eerily down the long narrow passage in front of me, at the very end of which there's a faint glow of light. When no one responds, I start walking in that direction, passing a number of closed doorways. Though the hall is also poorly illuminated, there's enough light emanating from the end for me to see that the floor tiles are chipped and worn. I reach for my phone to call Sandra, but before I can dial, I hear her voice call out.

"Bryn, is that you?"

"Yes. Where are you?"

"Down here. Just keep walking."

A moment later I emerge into a huge, double-storied hall. Sandra is standing beside a card table—the only furniture in the room—strewn with several binders, a water bottle, some tools, and a half dozen or so of what I assume are swag bags. She dressed in dark jeans today, a short-sleeved black turtleneck, and ballet flats, and her cell phone is in hand, as if she finished a call only moments ago or is about to make one.

"Welcome to the historical Washington Baths," she says, smiling.

I glance around, taking in the space with my eyes. It's not unlike the Museum of Dance, with a large reception hall and two wings shooting off from the left and right sides. Running along the upper level is a row of windows that are so grimy, it would make it difficult for the light to pour in even on a morning that wasn't overcast. It finally hits me: the spa is permanently closed for business.

"When you said we'd have the place to ourselves, I assumed it was just closed on Mondays. It's not a day spa then, like the Roosevelt Baths?"

"No, unfortunately, they were forced to shut down a couple of years ago. Thankfully, they preserved the building. It's been a great place to hold events."

That's a little hard to fathom. There's such a weird institutional feel to the space, and a faint medicinal smell seeps from the walls.

"I know, at first glance it leaves a lot to be desired," she says, as if reading my thoughts. "But the event company we've hired works miracles."

"They've got their work cut out for them."

"Would you like a swag bag?" she asks, nodding toward a table. "I have a few extras."

"Sure, thanks," I say, plucking one up from the table. I want to keep the mood light so I don't spook her with my request.

"So tell me, how can I help?"

As I open my mouth to answer, her phone rings. She glances at the screen. "Sorry, I'm going to have to take this."

"No problem." All I want right now is to spit out my request, but I have no choice but to cool my heels.

"I'm already on site," she says into the phone. "I was just telling someone that they're miracle workers, and trust me, this one is in the loaves and fish category. . . . Yes, I can wait."

She lowers the phone from her ear and glances in my direction. "I should only be a minute," she says quietly. "Why don't you take a look around? Down to the right are some of the old baths."

I feel too antsy to wander, but suspecting Sandra requires privacy for the call, I head down the wing she's indicated. It's a mirror image of the one I came down earlier on the opposite side of the building. There are dozens of doors along here, too, some open, some closed.

I take a peek into one of the rooms, squinting to see. The walls are lined in black and white subway tiles. There's a bathtub against the far wall, and even in the faint light, I can detect that it's ringed with deep brown stains.

I keep going. Toward the very end of hall, between two of the tub rooms, there's a rusted metal door in the wall with a handle, which must open onto a laundry chute once used for towels and robes. Directly in front of me is a square empty room, identical to the one I entered through earlier. It might have once been a lounge or even a storage space. Light struggles to find its way in through a set of small, smudged windows. There's a door to the outside here, too, but this one is padlocked shut.

I can't for the life of me figure out who would want to hold an event in this building. It's less like an old bathhouse and more like a haunted sanatorium.

From far off, I hear the dull drone of Sandra's voice as she converses on the phone. I set the swag bag down on the windowsill, and pluck out the yellow tissue paper. Inside I discover a few gift certificates, a miniature bottle of white wine, a lip gloss, and one of the candles Sandra was buying the day I bumped into her in town.

I pull it out from the bag. "Sandalwood," a sticker on the glass holder says. I'm not sure why, but I bring it to my nose and smell. It's exotic and woodsy . . . and somehow familiar.

And then I realize. It's the same scent I noticed that day in Guy's bedroom.

Chapter 24

INSTINCTIVELY MY HAND FLIES TO MY MOUTH AND I press it there, my thoughts in a tangle. It can't mean anything, I decide. Tons of people must like sandalwood. Just because Sandra has picked this candle for the swag bag doesn't mean she once brought one like it to Guy's bedroom. It doesn't prove she was sleeping with my husband.

Still, it scares me. I've felt uneasy, I realize, from the moment I walked in the door of this hellhole. I drop the candle back into the bag and quickly stuff the tissue paper over it. I don't care anymore about guaranteeing that Sandra says the right thing to Corcoran. All I want is to get out of here as fast as I can.

I step from the room and hurry back toward the lobby. Halfway there, I hear Sandra speak again, her voice drifting down the long, dim corridor. I freeze and listen.

"Yes, yes," she says, clearly still on the phone. "But I really need to hop off. Someone's stopped by to see me."

Her words trigger a memory—Sandra dropping by the house that day to welcome me to the neighborhood. I was on the screened-in porch when she knocked at the door, napping and not looking forward to the dinner party we were hosting later. She presented me with the bag of brochures . . . and I gave her a copy of *Twenty Choices*, one I retrieved from the box in the spare room upstairs.

And then Derek's words echo in my head, the comment he made earlier when we were discussing who might have taken the money: *It had to be someone who was there on that Thursday.*

All this time I've focused on the people who were there that *night*. Eve and the waiters. The dinner guests. Even *Guy*. But the money had been sitting in the desk since midday. It was there when Sandra stopped by the house and I trudged upstairs to grab the book for her. She was alone downstairs on Thursday for at least five minutes. I didn't look in the drawer until after the dinner.

Is she the one? The one who took the cash and left the matches behind? Because she was screwing my husband and wanted to do her best to make me come unhinged?

Is she the one who played the fire sound into my phone and tore the lock off the door to the screened porch?

My heart's racing now. I really need to get out of here. I force myself forward, my breath stuck in my chest. As I reach the lobby, Sandra is dropping her cell phone into her purse.

"There you are," she says, smiling. "I was worried you'd fallen into one of those old tubs back there and couldn't get out."

"No, just browsing." I'm so rattled, I can't get the right words to come out of my mouth.

"*Browsing?*" She chuckles lightly, as if amused by the odd phrasing I've chosen.

"I mean, just looking. Looking at the rooms."

"What do you think?"

"Interesting." I flick my gaze briefly off her face toward the front entrance. For the first time, I see that there are at least six feet of link chain coiled around the handles of the two doors. The only way out that I know of is down the corridor I came along earlier. But Sandra's stationed in the direct path to that corridor, and I'm going to have to maneuver around her to escape. I have to appear calm, I tell myself. I can't let on that I'm freaked.

"So many people passed through here years ago," she says, throwing her arm out in gesture. "They thought taking the waters would cure what ailed them."

"Did it do any good?"

"The water?" She's standing very still, her dark eyes fixed on me. "It probably soothed sore muscles, but that's about it . . . Are you okay, Bryn? You look pale suddenly."

"Actually, I started to feel kind of claustrophobic when I was wandering around all those little rooms. I need to get a breath of fresh air." I shift my body to the left a little, readying myself to edge around her. *Please*, I pray, *don't let me spook her.*

"I doubt that's going to help on a day like this one," she says, cocking her head to the side. "It's too muggy out. Here, have a sip of water."

My dread mushrooms. I can tell she senses that something's up. She takes a step toward the table and reaches for an unopened bottle of water.

"Thanks, but I really should go."

"I thought you wanted my help on a matter."

"It wasn't that important."

"Well, it sounded important on the phone. What's going on, Bryn? I can tell you're fretting."

"It can wait, really. There's no urgency."

"Something's come up, hasn't it? Since you first arrived. Did you get a call when I was on the phone? Did the person tell you something?"

"No, it's nothing. I just need air. I can always come back."

She snickers. "Please, Bryn. What do you take me for? I'm a better reader of people than that."

She takes a small step to the left so that once again she's squarely in front of me. She smiles, but this time it's malevolent, the grin of a fairy-tale witch. I realize she's got no intention of letting me leave. Her plan was always to lure me here.

"You know, I like you, Bryn," she says, "though I must admit, I wasn't expecting to. We've actually got a lot in common."

"You mean professionally?" I need to humor her, force her guard down and then, at the right moment, tear around her.

"*Please*," she scoffs. "That's a given. I'm talking about *Guy*."

So it's true. She knows Guy. Has she really slept with him? "My husband?"

"Yes. He's been a cad to both of us, hasn't he?"

"I don't know what you mean."

"Guy seems so fucking solicitous, so eager to please, but at the end of the day he's looking out only for number one, isn't he, Bryn?"

"You . . . you had an affair with him?"

"You make it sound like such a cliché. It wasn't *just* an

affair. You need to know that Guy and I had something *very, very* special."

"Sandra, you can be with Guy if you want. I've already moved out."

She smiles again. I let my gaze sneak over her shoulder, calculating the distance to the corridor. I have to pick the right moment to flee, when she least expects it.

"I know that, Bryn. I've been keeping an eye on you. But you were never the problem, *really*. Guy was going to leave eventually; he needed to take it slow, though, especially after your mental meltdown."

As much as I need to escape, I feel desperate as well to know the truth.

"Did you leave the matches in my drawer?"

"Oh, don't seem so stern about it, Bryn. I was simply having a little fun, messing with your head. I planned to leave the matches in your mailbox, but when you hobbled upstairs, you gave me the perfect opportunity—and the cash was just a nice bonus for my efforts."

"How did you know about the accident?"

"Guy told me, of course. About how you went all Miss Mopey on him. Guy's a *doer*, and no offense, it's hard for him to relate to someone whose go-to stance after a trauma is the fetal position. You really shouldn't take these things so personally, Bryn."

Even through my fear I feel a stab of deep sadness. Guy not only betrayed me, but he shared private details about me with this horror show of a woman.

"And you tried to get into the house one night?"

She shrugs. "I realized Guy had moved out and was back in the apartment. Again, I was just having a little fun. Like I said, you were never the real problem, Bryn. That bitch Eve was. She was the one who needed to be dealt with."

My breath catches. She did it. She killed Eve. Panic floods me, and the bones in my arms and legs seem to dissolve. Sandra rears her head back and looks at me dismissively, as if I'm just not getting it.

"He was *sooo* fucking obsessed with her," she says. "I could see it at the events she catered for him—he was practically *drooling* over her. When he told me we had to cool it for a while, he said it was because you were coming up here, that you'd absolutely *insisted* on living here this summer, but I could tell the real reason. He wanted to be with *Eve*. She was toying with him, working him into a lather, and it was only a matter of time before he got his way. Guy *always* gets his way, doesn't he?"

She's becoming more agitated. I can't fathom how I'm going to dodge around a woman who is strong enough to kill another person with an ax, but I'm going to have to do it—and bolt for the door.

"I don't care, Sandra," I say. "It's between you and Guy."

"You don't *care*, Bryn? You found the body that day, how could you *not* care?"

Something snags in my mind.

"You were the one who called me that morning? I'd told you how the money was missing after our dinner."

Sandra flashes an impish smile. "I figured that bitch was catering the dinner when you said it was a firm your husband used for work. When I called, I actually planned to say Eve had something to tell you. Something about *Guy*. I figured your alarms bells would have already gone off when you set eyes on her in your house. She oozed temptress, didn't she? But on the phone, I realized you were mostly worried about the money."

"But why lure me down there? To make the cops think I'd done it?"

"*Fun*, Bryn. A little more fun for me. Plus, a way to remind you of your fragile state. I never planned to hurt you, though. You were too weak to be a threat to me. I had other fish to fry."

A thought slams into my brain, hard as a fist.

"Miranda," I exclaim before I can catch myself.

Again, an impish smile, as if we're merely gossiping about the latest town scandal.

"That couldn't be avoided unfortunately."

"Was she sleeping with Guy?"

"Lord, no," Sandra says, her eyes wide in mock horror. "Though I'm sure she would have liked that. Miranda spotted you and me that day at the lake. That's why I had to bust my ass to get out of there. Guy included me in every function he could, and I was pretty sure she was wise to us. I knew that as soon as she saw Guy at the office on Monday, she'd blab to him that I was with you. She really didn't leave me a choice."

And I'm next, I realize. After everything she's confessed, she's going to try to murder me, too.

"Sandra, let me help you. We can fix this, I'm sure."

"Oh, please, Bryn. You're supposed to be the expert on choices, so face facts. There's only one way to fix this. And by the way, my name isn't Sandra, so stop fucking calling me that."

For a brief second her gaze shifts to the table. I can't help but follow it. Among the scattered tools, there's a hammer. A hammer with a claw at the end. Sandra looks back at me and grins the witchy grin again. I know now what the hammer is there for. She's going to use it to bash in my head.

With only a second to think, I glance over her shoulder, draw my hands to my face, and scream, "Who's *that*?" Dumb, but it works.

The second she spins around to see, I take off across the lobby. But in no time, she's caught up to me. She yanks me by the back of my shirt, jerks me to the right, and punches me hard in the back of my head. It feels as if part of my brain has shifted in my skull. I stagger to the side and reach up with my hand, trying to block the next blow.

But it doesn't come. I hear Sandra behind me, moving fast. My head is throbbing, but I manage to turn around. She's back at the table, I see, reaching for the hammer. My heart collides against the inside of my chest. I'll never be able to outrun her.

I stagger a few steps backward. I realize that I'm still holding the swag bag. Desperately, I tighten my grip on the handle. It's all I've got to defend myself with.

Sandra steps forward, the hammer raised. Her eyes are as dark and blank as a shark's. As she aims the hammer at me, I swing the bag in her direction. She dodges to the left, losing her balance a little. I back up again, not daring to take my eyes off her. Sandra rights herself and lunges forward, her arm raised again.

I reach into the bag for the candle and grab it tight in my hand. In one swift motion, I heave it at Sandra's head.

She howls in pain as the candle makes contact with her face before splintering apart on the floor. I take off again. I haven't run in months, but I sprint as fast as I can. There's no time to unearth my phone. I just have to make it to the end of hall, to the door, to my car. I reach the corridor and keep running. Behind me is only silence.

I'm halfway down it, and then, finally, all the way.

It's only when I'm in the room at the end that I see my mistake: I've gone down the wrong corridor, the one with the padlocked door. I cry out in despair. There's no way to get out.

I grab the padlock anyway, hoping it might not be in place, but it is. Frantically I search the room with my eyes, looking for a key, but there's nothing.

I spin around and start back down the corridor. Maybe I can barricade myself into one of the tub rooms and call 9–1–1. Before I can check, I spot Sandra. She's at the start of the cor- ridor, headed in my direction. Even from here, I can see that she's got the hammer ready.

I press my hands to my head, trying to think. How to escape? There's no way she can easily be overpowered. As I pull my hands away, my gaze falls to the metal door in the wall, the door to the laundry chute.

It seems crazy, ludicrous, but it's my only choice if I want to live. I take one step closer, yank open the metal door by the handle, and climb inside feetfirst.

As soon as I've wedged myself in there, I press my arms and

legs hard against the sides. The trick will be to try and shimmy down the chute, but when the door clangs shuts, leaving me in total darkness, I lose my bearings. A second later I'm hurtling down the chute, my body ricocheting hard against each side. I brace for the landing, knowing I could break my neck.

It's over in seconds. I land hard, feetfirst, but it's onto something dense and soft rather than cement. The ankle of my right foot takes the brunt of the fall. I moan in pain and collapse in a heap.

For a moment or two, I just lie there, trying to catch a breath. It smells and feels as if I've landed in a big pile of moldy bath towels. All the wind's been knocked out of me, but I'm fully conscious. I bend each limb, testing them. My ankle hurts like hell, but beyond that I don't seem to have sustained any major damage.

I squint my eyes and peer out into the basement. The space around me is huge and much of it in darkness, but the area closest to me is lit dimly by a series of small, grubby windows set high on the wall. Across the way from me, I can pick out a row of ancient-looking washers and dryers. And above them, running horizontally along on the walls, are lengths of metal pipes.

I feel in the dark for my messenger bag, still in place across my chest. I rifle through it, frantically, until my fingers find my phone and I grab it. I steady my hand enough to tap 9–1–1.

"Someone's trying to kill me," I tell the operator, keeping my voice low. "I'm hiding in the basement of the Washington Baths. You have to send the police, right away. *Please.*"

"Can you repeat your location?"

"The Washington Baths in . . . in Saratoga Park. It's closed, but I'm here, in the basement."

"Are you in imminent danger, ma'am?"

"Yes, yes. I mean, I'm pretty sure she's still in the building. She killed two women and she tried to attack me with a hammer."

And then there's a noise. Fifteen feet above me the metal door to the chute cranks open again. I don't think Sandra can see me from above, but just to be sure, I roll over as fast as I can manage, holding my phone tight in my hand.

"Ma'am, are you still on the line?" the operator asks.

"Yes," I say, my voice a hoarse whisper now. "But she's still here. She's still here in the building."

I hear the chute's metal door shut with a creak. She's not done, though. She's surely going to come looking for me.

"Please hurry," I beg the operator. I glance frantically around the basement. Though the faint light from the windows allows me to see within a few yards, the far reaches of the space are dark as night. Somewhere there's got to be a stairway to the first floor. Yet if I go up it, the likelihood is high that I'll bump smack into Sandra. And I could never outrun her now.

"The police have been dispatched," the operator says. And then, as if reading my thoughts, "Is there someplace you can barricade yourself into?"

"I don't know. I . . . I'll try to find one."

I roll over two more times toward the end of the towel pile and sit up. I fumble on my phone to activate the flashlight app and direct it out in front of me. At first, all I see is an endless cement wall. But off to my right, there's what appears to be a passageway.

I slide off the pile of towels and force myself up, careful not to put too much weight on my right foot. It's shooting with pain now. Dragging my right leg behind me, I hobble across the floor.

But it's not really a passageway. It's more of a primitive-looking tunnel, with walls made of crumbling cement and reeking of dirt and decay. Except for the few feet I can see with the flashlight, it's pitch-black in front of me. I feel like I'm standing at the mouth of Hades. I don't dare go down there.

And then I hear it. The sound of footsteps far off to my left. They're descending a set of stairs, slow and deliberate as a jungle cat.

"Are you still there, ma'am?"

"Shh," I say, "she'll hear us." I tap the disconnect button and then try to kill the flashlight. My fingers are so wet with sweat, nothing happens. I press again and again, desperately. Finally the beam goes off.

Some of the light from the windows still filters toward me. Hugging the wall, I struggle along the tunnel until I'm in total darkness. For a few moments the only sound is the blood rushing in my head, but then there's something else. The sound of a door swinging open, followed by the distant tap of ballet flats. I move deeper into the tunnel, using the wall to guide me. The footsteps seem closer. I freeze, pressing myself as hard as I can against the wall.

And then, mercifully, there's the muffled sound of a vehicle approaching the building and jerking to a stop. It's got to be the police. They wouldn't use their sirens for fear of alerting the attacker.

I hear Sandra curse, probably not far from the mouth of the tunnel. Soon she's on the move again, but this time her footsteps recede and moments later a door slams again.

Still, I wait in the dark. Finally it's utterly silent again. With my hand grazing the wall for support, I reverse my route along the tunnel, wincing in pain. When I reach the end, I search the basement with my eyes, but there's no sign of Sandra. A motion from on the other side of the window makes me jerk in surprise. I look up to see legs in dark pants.

"I'm down here," I yell.

A moment later, a man, lowering himself, peers in through the window. I can barely make out his face because of the grime.

"Who are you?" he asks.

"Bryn Harper. A woman attacked me."

"We're on our way."

"Be careful," I call out. "She may still be in the building."

"Just stay where you are."

I do, as tears of relief start to trail down my face.

Chapter 25

THE FOOTSTEPS RECEDE FROM THE WINDOW, AND I wait in the dull light, counting the seconds as my heart hammers in my chest. A moment later, somewhere above me, there's a brief rumbling sound, perhaps heavy footsteps. It might be Sandra running, trying to escape.

Minutes pass, at least ten, and each one interminable. At last, I hear a door swing open again, from somewhere off to my right, but I can't see that far away. Beams from flashlights suddenly bounce across the basement floor. Two men in uniform emerge from the darkness, each with a flashlight in one hand and a firearm in the other.

"I'm here," I call out.

"State your name," a voice demands.

"I'm Bryn Harper. I'm the one who called 9–1–1."

"Is there anyone else here?"

"No, the woman who tried to hurt me followed me down here, but she went up the stairs when she heard your car."

They step closer, and I can make out their faces now. One's older, at least fifty, and the other can't be more than twenty-five.

"Okay," the older guy says, holstering his gun. "Let's get you out of here."

They usher me across the basement and up a dark, musty-smelling stairwell. My ankle is practically yelping in protest, and the older cop notices that I'm dragging my right leg behind me. I explain that I injured myself trying to escape.

We emerge from the stairwell into a short corridor, and moments later we're in the huge lobby, where only a short time ago, Sandra was determined to drive a hammer through my skull. Just being back in the space jump-starts my panic. At least the swag bags are still here, and a few of the random tools. They'll add credence to my story.

Slowly the cops lead me down the long hallway I traveled when I first arrived, and out to the parking lot in back. The younger cop lags a little behind us, conveying info into a walkie-talkie.

There is a black police patrol car parked not far from mine, but Sandra's car is gone. I realize in dismay that the only description I'll be able to give of her car is that it's a black luxury vehicle. For that matter, I don't even know her real name.

"What about the woman who tried to kill me?" I ask the older cop. "Has she gotten away?"

"We have officers in pursuit," he says. "Now why don't you tell us what happened. And let's find you a spot to sit down."

He motions me toward an old cement bench near the door, and I lower myself gingerly, with my right leg stretched out in front of me. I glance down at my ankle. It's so swollen and lumpy, it looks as if there's something lodged under the skin.

The older cop—his badge reads "Garcia"—tells the younger

one to call an ambulance. Then he nods, pulls a leather-bound notepad from his belt, and turns his attention back to me.

Before he can even ask a question, I start hurrying through what happened today. That a woman obsessed with my husband lured me here and tried to kill me, that she admitted in so many words that she murdered Eve Blazer and Miranda Kane, that she fled when she heard cars pull up. Garcia manages to disguise any surprise he's experiencing, but the younger guy, who's already called for the ambulance, looks like I've just announced that there are rows of alien eggs ready to hatch in the basement. I ignore him and focus all my attention on Garcia.

"You can't let her get away," I say, nearly pleading. "I don't know what her real name is, but my husband will." I provide him with Guy's cell phone and work numbers.

As he jots down the info, I see his mind forming a question, but at that moment an unmarked car pulls into the parking lot. Mazzola is driving, and Corcoran's in the passenger seat. As soon as the car lurches to a stop, she throws open her door and strides in my direction, with Mazzola right behind her. There's no surprise in her eyes at the sight of me, and I realize that certain facts have already been relayed to her, probably by the cop who's been on the walkie-talkie.

"Talk to me," she says before she's even reached the spot where I'm sitting.

I repeat what I've told the uniformed cop but flesh out as many details as possible this time. As I'm spilling the story, I realize that what I'm trying desperately to do is measure my words as I go, making sure that I don't sound crazy or guilty or anything in between on the spectrum. It's going to be my word against that of Sandra's—or whoever the hell she is—at least until they can link her, through evidence, to the murders.

I expect Corcoran to pepper me with questions, but mainly she listens, her expression neutral. Until I reach the part where I hurled myself into the basement. She pulls her head back, startled.

"You're telling me you jumped into the laundry chute and risked breaking your neck."

I can't help it. I feel a rush of indignation at her comment.

"Yes. A woman who admitted bludgeoning two other people to death was coming at me with a hammer, and I took whatever risk necessary to get out of her path."

Corcoran pumps her head up and down a couple of times, as if she's buying what I'm saying, but I can't be sure. From the tug of Mazzola's mouth, I sense he's actually impressed.

"Okay, we need to take you downtown to make a full statement," Corcoran announces.

What if she thinks *I'm* the crazy one?

"Detective," the older cop interrupts, "we've got an ambulance coming for her. She's banged up her ankle pretty badly."

For Corcoran's sake—because I know my credibility factor may still be lousy with her—I reach down and pull the end of my jeans up. By now my ankle has ballooned to the size of an orange.

She lets out a frustrated sigh. This is going to throw a big fat wrench in her plans. And right on cue, we hear the wail of an ambulance siren. Corcoran glances back toward the ununi-formed cop.

"Meet the ambulance at the ER," she orders. "And tell them this is a priority. We need her at the station as soon as they've had a look."

Part of me wishes I could bag the hospital and go directly to the police station—not only to get my statement over with but also to suss out what I can about Sandra. The one cop said other officers were in pursuit, but I've no idea whether they caught up with her. Going to the hospital will at least buy me needed time. Time to call the lawyer's office and explain that I require more than a phone consultation right now. And time to think.

I stand up, ready to make my way to the ambulance, when a form rushes around the corner of the building. I tense, scared it's Sandra, and one of the cops touches the gun in his holster. To my utter shock, I see that the person who's darted into view is Derek.

"Sir, step back," one of the cops demands.

"I know him," I call out. "He's a friend."

Is he? I flash on the omission he made about Eve.

"He still can't be here," the cop says. "It's a crime scene."

"Bryn, just tell me you're okay," Derek yells.

"Yes, only a little banged up. But . . . why are you here?"

"I kept thinking about what you said—about the baths. I realized they were closed."

"Stay where you are." This time it's Corcoran calling out. She turns to Mazzola and tells him to detain Derek and question him. And then, before I can say anything else, I'm escorted into the ambulance.

We're no sooner pulling out of the parking lot than one of

paramedics is ripping open the right leg of my jeans. He takes a look at my ankle and explains that I'm probably dealing with a sprain, not a break, but an X-ray will have to confirm that. The hospital, he says, is minutes away. As he activates an ice pack and applies it to my ankle, I dig my phone from my bag and call the law firm that I was expecting to hear from at one. I explain to the assistant that I've been attacked and will need a lawyer in Saratoga as quickly as possible.

Five minutes later we're in the ER and I'm given a kind of VIP treatment, quickly ushered by an attendant onto a bed at the far side of the large open area. The patrol cop Corcoran has ordered to meet me here arrives almost simultaneously. He pulls a chair from against the wall and drags it over to the area near my bed. Two minutes later, a woman with "PA" on her badge arrives, yanks the curtain closed, and takes the first look at my ankle. Like the paramedic said, she thinks we're looking at a sprain, not a break. She promises to get me down to X-ray as quickly as possible.

She closes the curtain behind her, and it feels like I'm ensconced in a thin cocoon. On the other side is a big soup of ER sounds—quick bursts of conversation, footsteps, beeping, clanging, clicking, announcements heard over a loudspeaker. It must be similar to the kind of sound track playing when I was brought in March to the ER in Massachusetts, though I recall none of that one. My initial memory is of waking up in the ICU.

For the first time I'm conscious of my body beyond the throbbing in my ankle. My head is pounding lightly, my right elbow aches, probably from being banged during my trip down the chute, and there's this weird jittery sensation in my arms and legs,

Out of nowhere a thought streaks through my mind: *I've got to call Guy.* But it's an old instinct, one I'm going to have to eradicate. I'm on my own again. At least, I think grimly, Guy isn't a murderer. He's just the person who set everything horrible in motion.

I take a few deep breaths, trying to calm myself, and lie back with my head on the pillow. After a couple of minutes, I feel some of the tension seep away and my body soften a little. And then, improbably, I find myself smiling. Because the bottom line, despite whatever nightmare unfolds from here and how it must be faced alone, is that I'm *alive*. I saved myself. Maybe some of my recent decisions have been stupid ones, but back in that dilapidated bathhouse, as I stood in terror before the laundry chute, the lizard part of my brain, fueled by adrenaline, weighed the odds and made a choice that saved my ass.

It's a full two hours before I'm on the way to police headquarters, sitting in the back of a cruiser. My ankle sprain has been designated as the grade 1 variety, meaning it will fortunately heal within a couple of weeks. It's been taped up, and I've been issued a set of crutches.

I know from email and phone communication that a lawyer is waiting for me at the station. It's not the original one recommended by Susan—he's now tied up on another matter—but one of his partners, Tina Oliver.

When I enter the station, Oliver is sitting in the small vestibule, dressed in a navy gabardine suit and looking ready for action. She's about fifty, African American, with hair cropped close to her scalp, and a round face. She shakes my hand, and conveys that there's a small room available for us inside. I can tell from her brisk manner that she doesn't want me uttering a word until we're safely in that room.

The uniformed cop must have let Corcoran know we'd arrived because she comes striding out less than a minute later. She eyes the crutches I've been issued but doesn't comment on them, though she at least dishes out some respect to Tina Oliver. She directs Tina and me through the door into the center part of the precinct.

There are only two words to describe what it seems like back there: *overturned beehive.* There are about a dozen cops huddled around the open seating area, either talking to one another or speaking into phones. Based on their uniforms, a few belong to the sheriff's department. Almost all of them glance in in our direction as we pass through the space and start down a short corridor.

"We'd like to get Ms. Harper's statement as soon as possible," Corcoran tells Oliver as she shows us into a small cramped room with a table and couple of chairs.

"Understood," she replies. "But I do need to speak to my client privately. We'll let you know when we're ready."

The first question she asks me as soon as Corcoran has shut the door behind her is whether I'm up to giving a statement at all today.

"You've been through a lot, Bryn—may I call you that? I can easily have this postponed until you feel up to it."

"No, I want to get it over with," I say. "Particularly while it's all fresh in my mind. First, though, I have to know. Have they caught her? The woman who attacked me?"

"From what I've picked up, they've apprehended a woman named Lisa Wallins who has a small PR firm. I'm assuming it's the same person."

"Is she *here*?"

"No, don't worry. They apparently took her to the county correctional facility. That suggests they've got reason to hold her. The private detective our firm uses did a background check, and the woman has two different stalking charges against her, several years apart. Neither involved jail time."

"Oh, wow, so she has history as a nut job. Thank God she's not here. I couldn't stand seeing her again."

"I should warn you, though. Your husband is apparently in the building."

My body tenses at the revelation. After Sandra, he's the last person on the planet I want to set eyes on.

"How do you know?"

"I've been in communication with Mr. Maycock, explaining that I'm taking over, and he said he was headed down here, too. I saw him come in an hour ago with a man I can only assume is Guy Carrington. He looked very shaken."

"He *should* be shaken," I say, not hiding my anger.

Tina withdraws a legal pad from her soft leather briefcase, drops it on the table, and motions for us to sit.

"I know you shared a lot on the phone, but let's go through it once more. Then, we'll work on springing you from here."

By the time I'm finished with my story, I'm sick to death from hearing myself talk. But I'm impressed with Tina. Her questions are smart and intuitive. She manages to seem both buttoned-up but also empathetic to my plight and invested in me.

"I know this isn't a pretty situation, Bryn," she tells me when I can't think of anything more to add. "But we'll get you through this."

The interview with Corcoran and Mazzola goes decently, better than I anticipated. They want to know everything they can about Lisa Wallins—when she first surfaced, the times we were together, every comment she uttered on those occasions, as well as the exact statements she made in the bathhouse. There's nothing about Corcoran's attitude this time that suggests she thinks I'm culpable of a crime or I'm withholding essential information.

Unsurprisingly, Corcoran's annoyed when I finally divulge the detail about the matches, but I explain that the information didn't seem in any way relevant to Eve Blazer's murder. She shoots me a "let me be the judge of that" look before moving on.

They want to know about Guy, too, whether I have any evidence of his relationship with Lisa Wallins.

Are they thinking I might have been keeping Sandra/Lisa close because I was suspicious of her?

"I never had a clue," I say. "The first I learned about their relationship was today."

"What did your husband say when you told him a woman had dropped by the house and given you the brochures?"

"I don't think it ever occurred to him it was her."

Corcoran taps her pen on the table a few times, clearly forming the next question in her mind.

"You said you're staying at the Saratoga Arms. Are you and your husband not living together now?"

No, we're not. I began to think he'd been involved with Eve Blazer. I didn't feel I could trust him anymore."

I leave it at that. Based on what's occurred, what Guy set in motion with his infidelity, he's not going to have a job with the opera company much longer, and I don't have the stomach to tar him any more than necessary.

Later, when we're alone in the vestibule, Tina whispers that she thinks I did very well.

"They can't just be taking my word, right?" I say. "They've got to have another reason to suspect this Lisa Wallins."

"That's my bet, too. They may have found evidence that implicates her. Maybe the burner phone she used to call you the day of the murder. Or something even more incriminating. But it's time for you to rest. Let me drop you at the inn."

I realize suddenly that my car is still back at the Washington Baths—though I wouldn't be able to drive it anyway. I nod, wondering how I'm going to cope over the next few days.

As soon as I step onto the sidewalk I see him: Derek.

"Bryn, what's happening?" he says, rushing toward me. "I tried to find you at the hospital, and they wouldn't tell me if you were there. I finally realized I should come here."

Part of me is comforted to see him and appreciative of his efforts to track me down, but I'm still discomforted about what I learned—that he spoke to Eve privately in the kitchen that night.

"It's a very long story. Why don't I call you later? I'm headed back to the inn now."

"Can I at least drop you there?" he says.

Tina has her eyebrows raised, as if to ask, *Are you cool with this?* I think for a sec, and then consent. After thanking Tina for everything, she squeezes my arm and promises to speak to me later.

"I was so worried about you," Derek says as soon as Tina's departed.

I look at him, unsmiling.

"Why didn't you ever admit to me that you'd spoken to Eve?"

"What?"

"That night, at our dinner party. I know you spoke to her. When we talked about the murder over lunch, you didn't say anything about that. And when I mentioned to you earlier today that the waiter saw Eve talking privately to a man by the kitchen, you never volunteered it was you. That seems like a pretty odd omission."

"Okay, I see your point. Remember how I told you that she catered for a friend of mine? They dated for a while and he was completely smitten with her. That night she came up to me in the hallway and asked about him, acting all flirty. She had an agenda, but I had no idea what it was."

"Why not tell me?"

"My only excuse is that I was being protective of my friend. If I brought up his obsession, you might feel obligated to tell the cops and they'd want to talk to him. I knew he could never have killed her, but he's the type of guy the cops would have loved to have hounded."

I look into his eyes, trying to gauge the veracity of his

words. Over these past weeks, I've been forced to deal with a nearly endless stream of secrets and lies, and I can't be sure that this isn't just one more. For the moment, at least, I decide to believe him.

"Okay."

He says he needs to retrieve his car and sprints down the sidewalk, yelling over his shoulder that he'll be back in two minutes. I stand there alone, letting my weight fall on my crutches. The Tylenol they gave me in the ER has started to wear off, and my ankle is throbbing again, a nasty reminder of the morning.

A shadow crosses the sidewalk, and when I look up I discover, to my shock, that Guy is standing there. He's got his suit jacket off and his shirtsleeves rolled. His face is haggard and pale, as if it's been drained of blood. Not a look I've ever seen on him, not even at his mother's funeral.

"Bryn," he says, and stops three feet away from me. "Please tell me you're okay.

"Just go away, Guy."

"I know a little about what went on today. I'm so sorry and ashamed. If anything had ever happened to you . . ."

"Oh, please. You didn't think your actions would have consequences?"

"I never meant to hurt you, Bryn. I felt at a loss this spring. I didn't seem to be able to help you."

He's so *slick*, I think once more about him. No wonder he was so good at seducing donors.

"I said go away, Guy. I don't want anything to do with you anymore."

"But . . ."

"If you say another word, I'm going to yell for the cops."

He sets his mouth, turns, and walks up Lake Avenue, his shoulders sagging. I sense a worm of bitterness eager to work its way into my heart, but I refuse to let it.

I'm alive, after all. I took a crazy, absurd dive down a laundry chute and survived.

Chapter 26

ALMOST FOUR WEEKS LATER, ON A BRIGHT JULY DAY, Derek meets me, as planned, in the parking lot of the Saratoga National Historical Park, the site of the Revolutionary War battlefield and about twenty minutes from the city of Saratoga Springs. I've come in a new rental car, one I picked up for my trip north. I'm living back in Manhattan now, and my plan is to be in this area for forty-eight hours tops.

As much as I tried to tamp down my anxiety, I ended up with a pit in my stomach from the moment I pulled onto the New York State Thruway yesterday afternoon. Shortly before I left Saratoga, Lisa Wallins, a.k.a. Sandra Dowd, was charged with the murders of both Eve Blazer and Miranda Kane. Though in the case of Miranda, the cops have, in addition to my statement, only circumstantial evidence against Lisa, DNA evidence has fortunately tied her to the ax that killed Eve. The district attorney and I have spoken several times on the phone during the past weeks, but she was eager for an in-depth, face-to-face meeting. That's where I was this morning, with Tina next to me.

There's another reason I wanted to make the trip north,

and that's to spend time with Derek. We grabbed dinner one night before I left Saratoga—after I was able to confirm his reason for speaking to Eve in the kitchen—but I was still so crazed from everything that had happened, I'd barely been able to focus on him. Despite all the upheaval still in my life, I feel far less fatigued now and I've been looking forward to this afternoon. Derek was the one who suggested a picnic at the battlefield.

Derek is already in the parking lot when I arrive, dressed in jeans and a heather-green T-shirt and leaning against his car in the sunshine. The sight of him fills me with even more pleasure than I anticipated.

"You still up for this?" he asks after we've hugged hello. I can smell the almond-scented soap he's showered with.

"Absolutely."

"And your ankle can handle it?"

"Yup, all better," I say, smiling. "I'll be fine as long as your plan calls for more picnic than tour."

"You got it."

He grabs a tote bag from his car and we set out, meandering across the wildflower-studded grounds, bordered by lush farmland and, in the far distance, blue-green mountains. It's an exquisite day. Though the sun's high in the sky, the humidity is low, and there's a light, lovely breeze.

Derek shares some of what he knows about the clash of armies here, which was actually two battles a couple of days apart. The scrappy colonial militia managed to outsmart the brilliant British army, profoundly altering the world. I feel more than a twinge of sadness as I think of the lives lost in this place, and the loneliness the British soldiers must have endured from being so many thousands of miles from their homes, knowing they might never see their families again.

After about twenty minutes, we reach a secluded spot with a view of the gleaming Hudson River, so much smaller here than in New York City, and Derek suggests we park ourselves for the picnic. From the tote bag he pulls out a small chenille blanket for us to sit on, a couple of sandwiches wrapped in butcher's paper, and two bottles of sparking water. Saratoga Spring Water, actually. And then some Saratoga potato chips.

"I couldn't resist," he says, grinning. "I want you to have a *couple* of positive memories of the town."

"Oh, I love the town *itself.* Just not what happened here. It's kind of a battlefield for me, too."

I help him spread out the blanket and we settle onto it. After the meeting with the DA, I used the ladies' room of the county municipal center to change from a skirt and heels into shorts and sandals, and it feels nice to have the sun on my arms and legs. While Derek props the water bottles against the tote bag, I unwrap the sandwiches. They turn out to be baguettes with tomatoes, basil, and mozzarella, and I tell him how much I love that combo.

"I figured you for a caprese kind of girl."

"Someday I intend to make a pilgrimage to Capri just to taste that dish in its natural habitat."

"It sounds good to hear you talk that way—I mean, concentrating on the future and not all the crap that happened."

"Yeah, I'm trying to think ahead as much as possible. About trips I'd like to take . . . My next book. It's about reinvention, and I may end up including what happened to me here"—I offer a rueful smile—"because I've got a bit of reinventing to do myself."

I'm not sure why the words began to flow again this past month. Maybe because I was finally in a truthful place.

"How did your meeting go today?

"Good. The district attorney seems really smart, and she treated me with a lot more respect than I ever got from Corcoran. It's possible that Lisa—God, I'm still not used to calling her that—will plead insanity and will take some kind of deal, but there could also be a trial, and I'll have to steel myself for it."

Derek shakes his head in dismay. "To think that Miranda Kane died basically for nothing, for simply being in Dock Brown's that day and catching Lisa's eye."

"Well, Eve died for nothing, too. Guy told the police that they hadn't been involved. When I had lunch with Lisa, she claimed she'd heard Eve had been having a fling with a married man, but I think she did that just to taunt me. My guess is that Eve was going to be Guy's *next* conquest. He just hadn't closed the deal yet."

As Dr. G suggested, Guy is a man who hates to be boxed in, and I now know that nothing I did in our marriage was ever going to stop him from feeling that way.

"I heard some news about Lisa from my reporter pal," Derek says after taking a bite from his sandwich. "He interviewed people who knew her, mostly clients from her PR business because it doesn't look like she had many friends. The one word that kept popping up was *intense*. Like *too* intense. Not when people first met her, but as they got to know her. It's as if, sooner or later, her craziness would rear its head."

"I bet the same thing happened with Guy. That day at the baths she told me he had cooled it with her for a while because I was moving up here. I'm thinking it was actually because he began to sense that she was a very troubled woman."

Derek reaches out, touches my hand, and smiles wanly. "I know this may sound crass, but I'm so glad she chose to fixate on Eve initially, and not you," he says. "You probably wouldn't be alive otherwise."

I smile back, taking him in with my eyes—the easygoing way he's stretched out on the blanket, plus the wild way all his features come together to create an improbable appeal.

"In the beginning she clearly saw Eve as the real threat," I say. "I was an albatross around Guy's neck, but she figured he'd dump me when the moment was right. All she had to do was nurse things along by making me even *more* of an albatross. The burnt matches, luring me to the murder scene, that call with the fire crackling—they were all meant to wig me out as much as possible."

"Why do you think she switched plans and decided to kill you?"

"She'd been keeping an eye on me, at first out of curiosity and then probably making sure I wasn't figuring stuff out, suggesting I might want to see the event venue in case I gave her any reason to be worried. When I called and told her I wanted to speak to her privately, her alarm bells clearly went off. She lured me to the baths—she'd tricked a former client into giving her access—and then five minutes after I arrived, she could tell that somehow the truth had all come together in my mind."

I take a swig of water and tear open the bag of potato chips, offering them first to Derek and then indulging in a handful myself.

"I may have to take a few bags of these back with me."

"Has it been good to be back in the city?"

Derek fixes his gaze on me, and I spot what I think is a trace of wistfulness in his green eyes. I know that he's been eager for me to be back here.

"It was good to just be *home*, to have my friends rally around me. And though I begged him not to, my brother insisted on coming from Jakarta. Fortunately he was able to combine it with business here."

"It's a shame he lives on the other side of the world."

"Yes, but it won't be for much longer. He's moving to the city for good in November. I feel guilty because I know I played a huge role in his decision, but selfishly I feel so grateful that he'll be back in my life. I sometimes think that if he'd spent any time with Guy, he would have tried to talk me out of marrying him. Of course, I have no idea if I would I have listened."

"Guy's an *awfully* charming guy. Hell, after I met him, I gave a donation of a hundred bucks to the opera company, and I don't really *like* opera."

"But I'm the girl who wrote the book about choices, and I ended up making the world's dumbest choice. I think *one* mistake on my part was never actually viewing marrying Guy as a decision that had to be made."

"Why didn't you?"

It's a fairly blunt question, not one most people would go for in the situation, but I'm glad he did. It reflects a straightforwardness in Derek that I like. And it's certainly a question I've been struggling to answer.

"For years after my parents' deaths, I wasn't open to any kind of deep romantic commitment. I told myself it was all about me throwing myself into my writing, but I think I was really afraid of being attached to someone, and at times I started to assume I'd never be with a man long-term. When I met Guy and fell in love with him so quickly, it felt almost magical, as if the gods had finally decided to release me from my grief. I saw it as a gift, not as something I needed to evaluate as right or wrong for me."

"They say Guy got canned from the opera company."

"Yeah, but from what I heard, that was based on his bad behavior in town. I'm not sure if they know about any of his past sins yet."

"I wonder if anyone will ever know all that he was trying to hide."

"I actually have a better idea on that. The divorce lawyer arranged for a private investigator to look into his past since it was essential for me to know as much as possible. He confirmed the issue in Dallas. And apparently the reason Guy arrived in Texas using his middle name was that he'd been let go from a start-up in Chicago for charging a bunch of personal expenses on his business credit card. That seems to be the extent of it. Unlike Sandra, Guy's not a sociopath. He's just your average-bear not-so-good guy, someone who likes to play close to the edge and take what he wants, even if he has no right to it. He clearly saw me as a nice meal ticket, but I still think part of him really loved me."

What I don't bring up, because what's the point, are all the emails and calls from Guy in the past weeks, trying to convince me to take him back. Though I never responded, I read the notes and listened to the voicemails, and the phrase that popped in my mind was the same one that had first occurred to me that day in Congress Park: he's *slick*. I finally had the divorce lawyer order him to stop.

Derek bobs the bottle cap a few times in his hand, his expression pensive.

"You know what I've never asked you? How did you find your way to the man in Dallas who ended up sharing everything?"

I tell him then about the hotel-room dreams, and how they always seemed to be sending me a message. Derek shakes his head, not in disbelief, it seems, but simply because the whole thing is so hard to fathom.

"That's pretty amazing," he says. "When I started teaching, I had those classic dreams about standing up in the front of the class and realizing I'd forgotten to prepare a single thing, but never anything like yours."

"I know, it's incredible what the subconscious is capable of. When the dreams first started and it was obvious they were related to the accident, I couldn't understand why they only began after I was living in Saratoga. Dr. Greene thinks that moving here put me in regular proximity to Guy, and in a way I didn't even recognize, I probably felt threatened. My subconscious became insistent on making me recall what Paul Dunham had said in the car that day."

"That's a pretty dazzling example of how the brain works."

I nod in agreement. Of course, there's still one detail I'm aching to know, something that seems forever out of reach. Why did the car go off the road? If only my dreams could tell me *that*.

I take another sip of water. The sunlight is intoxicating, and part of me doesn't want this picnic to end, but when I glance at my watch, I see that it's close to three. I need to be heading back to the hotel I'm staying at in Albany, near Tina's office. Derek reads my mind.

"Is there any way I can entice you to stay around for dinner? We could eat north of here—or even at my place—so there'd be no chance of running into Guy."

"Thanks, but I better not. I want to get an early start home in the morning. By the way, I'm so sorry I never had a chance to speak to your class."

"I had my reporter buddy do a guest appearance. It wasn't the same, but it was a break from me at least."

We stuff everything back into the tote bag, shake out the blanket, and retrace our steps to the parking lot. Derek is quiet on the walk, and I can't tell if he's feeling talked out, or if there's something on his mind.

"Hey, I forgot to ask," he says as we near the edge of the lot. "What about that nasty woman Kim? At one point, didn't you think *she* might be behind some of the stuff that had happened?"

"In hindsight I think she felt weirdly competitive with me.

The matches she handed me at the restaurant were pure coincidence. She'd thrown a little stink bomb my way as the two of us were talking together, but once we caught up with Guy and her husband, she tried to make it look like she was sweet as pie."

Derek arches a brow. "What was the stink bomb?" he asks.

I think for a minute, letting my memory snake back to that night.

"It was actually about *you*," I say, smiling. "She commented on how nice and cozy we looked at the dinner party. As if there was something between us."

He doesn't respond right away, and I realize that I've opened a door of sorts. Though, of course, it's already been opened. We wouldn't have been lounging on a blanket in the summer sunshine if it hadn't been.

"I guess I shouldn't be so hard on the wicked Kim then," he says. "It seems she had me figured out that night."

We've reached my rental car by now and stop by the driver's door. I sense something else is coming, that he's finally going to acknowledge what's been in the air for weeks. And he does.

"From the moment I sat next to you that night," he says, "it's been hard to stop thinking about you."

I meet his gaze.

"I felt a connection with you, too, Derek. Of course, at the time, I saw it only as a friendship. I wouldn't have allowed myself to go anywhere else with it."

And I wouldn't have. I was fiercely loyal to Guy.

"But how about *now*?" Derek asks. "I know your life is

nuts, that the timing may seem all wrong, but I want to see you again. And not as friends. This can't be good-bye, Bryn."

I've had Derek on my mind a lot over the past weeks, and I've admitted to myself that my interest isn't purely platonic, but I've never gone any further in my thinking, never projected to the idea of us being together. There's just too much else I need to contend with.

"There's an attraction on my part, too, Derek—I'd be lying if I said otherwise. But it just doesn't seem possible."

"I know you're only a few weeks out of your marriage. We could take it at any pace you're comfortable with." He smiles. "Slow-boat-to-China pace if that's what you want."

There's a crazy part of me that wants to say yes, to plunge in and allow myself moments of pure pleasure right now, but I've vowed to be smarter about the choices I make.

"It just feels too soon for me," I say. "I still have a lot of thinking to do—about decisions I made and so much more. Plus, you're here and I'm in New York, and I just don't ever want to do the commuter thing again. It's not that I have anything against that kind of arrangement, per se, but it probably hindered me from seeing what I needed to see with Guy."

He smiles again, this time with just one side of his mouth tugged up.

"Would January be too soon?"

"What?"

"I've promised myself that, come hell or high water, I'll be in New York after the fall term ends. Teaching, writing, whatever."

Nice, I think instinctively. Something to look forward to, something that may be good. I can't help but laugh.

"That sounds very enticing. Maybe you can take the train to New York at the end of the summer and we can discuss it over a long lunch."

He hugs me and kisses me tenderly on the cheek. I feel myself flush a little, and I'm grateful for whatever this crazy thing I have with him is.

I tell him that he should leave first because I'm going to make a call from the car. We hug again, and a moment later, as he pulls out of his parking space, we wave good-bye to each other. I don't really have a call to make. I simply want a few minutes to decompress and gather my thoughts. A lot can happen between now and January, but who knows. The idea of it fills me with hope.

Finally I ease out of the parking lot and pull out onto the rural road that will take me to the Adirondack North-way. The chance of running into Guy on this leg of my journey is slim, but still I regularly check the rearview mirror for a dark blue BMW, and tense each time a car heads in my direction.

For a stretch, I'm the only car on the road. It's going to be okay, I reassure myself. I'll be in Albany in less than thirty minutes and back in New York by noon tomorrow. Except at a mediation table and possibly in a courtroom, I won't ever have to face Guy again.

Just as I feel my body relax, a dark red shape darts from the woods to the right and streaks in front of the car. I hit the break. It's a squirrel and I've missed it by inches. I sigh, grateful not to have crushed it.

And then, without warning, I'm shaking, shaking so much

that my hands bounce off the steering wheel. And I'm crying, too. I have no idea in hell what's going on.

I ease the car over to the shoulder of the road and jerk the gear into park. Every inch of me is still trembling.

Then the memories unfurl. Snippets one after the other.

Paul and I on the road. I'm raking my hand through my hair, which was long then and to my shoulders. He's just told me the news—about Guy and Dallas.

"There's got to be a mistake, Paul," I say. "It has to be someone else.

"That's possible, of course. But I saw the photo of him. Why don't I let you talk to my friend?"

I shake my head, not so much against the idea but because I can't take it all in. What if it's true? No, it can't be.

"We'll sort this out, Bryn," Paul says. "And maybe it's all a terrible mistake. I just wouldn't have been able to live with myself if I hadn't told you."

He directs his full attention back to the highway. I can even see the road in my mind. For some reason the traffic is light on this stretch, and we have the road briefly to ourselves. I sit there, brooding in silence, wondering what to do.

And then, out of nowhere, a dog, golden brown, sprints across the highway. Paul swerves to avoid it, and we go careening off the road.

My shaking subsides, but tears keep rushing down my face. I make a feeble attempt to brush them away with the side of my arm.

Finally I know. I know why Paul lost control of the car that day. He didn't do it intentionally. And I didn't distract him in some terrible way with my concerns. It was nobody's fault, just a horrible accident that cost a wonderful man his life.

I take a deep breath and close my eyes. At last, I think. No more secrets.

Acknowledgments

I really enjoyed researching this book, in part because it meant spending time in the charming city of Saratoga Springs in upstate New York. I also interviewed a bunch of people on other subjects I touched on in the book, and I'm so appreciative of all the time they gave me.

I'd love to specifically thank Nathanial White, attorney; Barbara Butcher, consultant for forensic and medicolegal investigation; Cheryl Brown, fundraising guru; Maureen Rossley, my wonderful guide of Saratoga Springs; Caleb White, police officer; Dr. Dale Atkins, psychologist; and Dr. Karen Rosenbaum, psychiatrist.

Thank you as well to my awesome agent, Sandy Dijkstra; to Mary Sasso of HarperCollins for all her creativity on the marketing front; and to my absolutely wonderful editor, Laura Brown, who has been a huge joy to work with every step of the way.

About the Author

Kate White, the former editor in chief of *Cosmopolitan* magazine, is the *New York Times* bestselling author of four additional psychological thrillers (*The Wrong Man, Eyes on You, The Sixes, Hush*), as well as six Bailey Weggins mysteries. White is also the author of popular career books for women, including *I Shouldn't Be Telling You This: How to Ask for the Money, Snag the Promotion, and Create the Career You Deserve,* and editor of the Anthony and Agatha Award-nominated *The Mystery Writers of America Cookbook: Wickedly Good Meals and Desserts to Die For.* She lives in New York City. Read more about her at www.katewhite.com.

BOOKS BY KATE WHITE